FLIRTING WITH THE SOCIETY DOCTOR

BY
JANICE LYNN

WHEN ONE NIGHT ISN'T ENOUGH

BY
WENDY S. MARCUS

MILLS & BOON

Janice Lynn has a Masters in Nursing from Vanderbilt University, and works as a nurse practitioner in a family practice. She lives in the southern United States with her husband, their four children, their Jack Russell—appropriately named Trouble—and a lot of unnamed dust bunnies that have moved in since she started her writing career. To find out more about Janice and her writing visit www.janicelynn.com

Janice Lynn won
THE NATIONAL READERS' CHOICE AWARD
for her first book
THE DOCTOR'S PREGNANCY BOMBSHELL

Wendy S. Marcus is not a lifelong reader. As a child, she never burrowed under her covers with a flashlight and a good book. In senior English, she skimmed the classics, reading the bare minimum required to pass the class. Wendy found her love of reading later in life, in a box of old paperbacks at a school fundraiser where she was introduced to the romance genre in the form of a Harlequin Superromance. Since that first book, she's been a voracious reader of romance often times staying up way too late to reach the happy ending before letting herself go to sleep.

Wendy lives in the beautiful Hudson Valley region of New York with her husband, two of their three children, and their beloved dog, Buddy. A nurse by trade, Wendy has a master's degree in health care administration. After years of working in the medical profession, she's taken a radical turn to writing hot contemporary romances with strong heroes, feisty heroines, and lots of laughs. Wendy loves hearing from readers. Please visit her at www.WendySMarcus.com.

This is Wendy S. Marcus's debut book!

FLIRTING WITH THE SOCIETY DOCTOR

BY
JANICE LYNN

First published in Great Britain 2011
by Mills & Boon, an imprint of Harlequin (UK) Limited,
Eton House, 18-24 Paradise Road, Richmond, Surrey TW9 1SR

© Janice Lynn 2011

ISBN: 978 0 263 88592 7

Harlequin (UK) policy is to use papers that are natural, renewable and recyclable products and made from wood grown in sustainable forests. The logging and manufacturing process conform to the legal environmental regulations of the country of origin.

Printed and bound in Spain
by Blackprint CPI, Barcelona

Dear Reader

Lighthouses fascinate me. Everything about them— the way they look, their purpose, their history—all of it. However, I'd never actually seen one until I was researching for this story.

During a visit with a dear friend, we and our two full-of-personality daughters drove to the Cape May lighthouse. I remember feeling giddy at my first glimpse, and was just wowed when I was actually standing at the top, leaning against the railing, looking out over the horizon.

Like me, geeky Dr Faith Fogarty has never seen a lighthouse— not until she spends a high society weekend away from reality with hunky Dr Vale Wakefield. Faith has been enamoured of her brilliant playboy boss since before they even met in person. But while in Cape May she discovers a whole new side to herself—one she embraces. And, like the lighthouse they visit, she lets her inner light shine in the hope that Vale will find his way to her and to her miniature poodle Yoda.

Vale and Faith pass two women and their giggly daughters in the stairwell. Well, I won't say who they are, but I'm betting you can guess. I hope you enjoy Vale and Faith's Cape May adventure as much as I did my visit there and writing their story.

Happy reading!

Janice

To my dear writing pal, Kathleen Long.
Thank you for your unfailing friendship
and belief in me, all the late-night hotel room giggles
at writer conferences, and for giving me
my first glimpse of a lighthouse. Love you!

And to Abby Lynn and Annie Long,
since Abby says this book has to be dedicated to them,
too, since they helped with the Cape May research. ☺

CHAPTER ONE

"No WAY am I going to a wedding with you." Faith Fogarty shook her head, knowing this time her boss had pushed her too far. "Uh-uh, no way. I won't be lumped into the category as one of your girls."

Glad no one seemed to be paying them the slightest attention, probably because their co-workers were all trying to look busy so as not to attract the boss's attention, Faith retreated into the privacy of Dr. Vale Wakefield's office, him hot on her heels.

"I'm not asking you to be one of my girls," he pointed out, unnecessarily.

Of course he wasn't asking her to be one of his girls. She wasn't his type. She had a brain.

"I'm asking you to accompany me to a family gathering where I will be tortured mercilessly by my family if I don't bring a date. They'll try and hook me up with every single female there." He made a gagging sound.

Having no sympathy whatsoever for one of New York City's most sought-after eligible bachelors and top-notch neurosurgeons, Faith shrugged. "So take Lulu."

Lulu was the willowy blonde who'd accompanied Vale to a big charity ball the previous Saturday night. Faith had read about the event, seen a photo of the model plastered to Vale's side in the society section of the Sunday paper.

An entire column had been dedicated to whether or not the exotic model would be able to get the Wakefield heir to the altar. Faith had wadded up the paper and tossed it in the trash, where such gossip belonged. Of course Vale wouldn't marry that woman.

"To quote you, 'Uh-uh, no way.'" Vale emphasized each word. "Do you have any idea what type of problems I'd create if I brought Lulu or any woman with me to a family gathering, much less to a wedding?" He shuddered with all the drama of a person who'd just bit into the bitterest dish. "She'd be hearing wedding bells long before we got to the ceremony. There is absolutely no way I'd take a *real* date to my cousin's wedding." His intense blue eyes narrowed with the steely purpose that put most in a tizzy. "I'm taking you."

And that was where Faith fit into Vale's life.

Not a real date. Not someone he would consider dating or bringing to a New York City charity ball. Not someone he would consider loving or having a real relationship with. Not that any of Vale's relationships were real, not unless no-strings-attached sex counted.

He'd pretty much just admitted that he didn't even see her as a woman. Great. She was a sexless brain.

Sucking in a deep breath, she shook her head. "No, thanks. Accompanying you to family functions is not in my job description."

He grinned the devilish smile that had her heart thumping overtime whenever he flashed his pearly whites. "I could have my attorney add an addendum to your contract."

"Forget it." She narrowed her gaze in as menacing a glare as she could pull off when he grinned at her that way. Why couldn't she be immune to him? After all, he was a bra-size before brain-size typical male. "I'm not going to a wedding with you."

"I'd pay you."

As if that made one iota of difference. As a neurologist specializing in Parkinson's disease, she earned a good salary from her job. A job that didn't require her fending Vale off from wannabe bridezillas and well-intentioned family members.

He named a figure that made her head spin.

"No." Fighting to keep her composure, she picked up a stack of consult requests from the long mahogany table that occupied one side of the expansive room that served as his office. One by one, she flipped through them, sorting out the more urgent cases that she wanted to discuss as possible surgical candidates with Vale.

He crossed the room, standing so close that if she'd turned toward him she'd likely bump him. She wouldn't look, wouldn't turn, but would he please quit staring at her?

"You might as well concede, Faith." He put his hand on her shoulder, eliciting a thousand tiny shivers that caused tremors all the way to her very core. "In the long run I always get what I want."

He was right. He did always get what he wanted. With women. In life. Vale Wakefield led a gilded life. One where he'd been blessed with money, looks, intelligence, gifted surgical hands, and that something more that just made him impossible not to like. Women wanted him. Men wanted to be him. Little old ladies made him cookies and cakes, for heaven's sake.

At work she could maintain distance, keep her unwanted attraction to him safely tucked away, but at a wedding? Would he take one look at her and realize she dreamed of being the one he danced with at ballroom charities? The one warming his bed?

A *wedding*.

Not even for Vale would she face another wedding.

She was not going to give in. He did not have to get his way with her every time he crooked his finger. This time he'd passed the limits of her endurance.

"What I want is for you to come with me to my mother's this weekend and accompany me to Sharon's wedding."

Faith dropped the consults onto the table, turned to face him, anger sparking deep in her chest. Why did he just assume that she was at his beck and call 24/7? "Did it ever occur to you that I might already have plans for this weekend? That I might have a life outside work?"

Rarely was Vale caught off guard. Even more rarely did he show shock when someone actually did surprise him. But the darkening of his pupils gave clue to the fact that he truly had never given any thought that she might not live every moment in hopes of him deigning to ask her to work late, to come in over the weekend to review an important surgery case, to drop everything and go to his cousin's wedding with only four days' notice.

Of course, he hadn't given any thought to her potential plans. Why would he? He didn't find her attractive and apparently couldn't imagine anyone else doing so. Why wouldn't she be available at his every whim?

Which hit a bit too close to home.

Faith's teeth ground together. Sure, she wasn't glamorous like the women he dated. She couldn't be even if she tried. Not with her stick-straight dishwater blond hair, plain green eyes, and too big mouth. Still, his split-second shock at the possibility that someone might want to spend time with her for non-work purposes hurt. Hurt so deeply that had she put her hand to her chest to find her life blood seeping out, it wouldn't have surprised her.

Because whether she'd wanted to or not, she'd fallen head over heels in lust with Vale the day she'd come to work for him eighteen months ago.

Eighteen months of the sweetest mix of pleasure and pain at working so closely with him and him never seeing her as anything more than a neurologist who shared his passion for finding a cure for Parkinson's disease. Which was for the best, really, since a one-night stand, which was all he ever seemed to do, would only destroy her career with Wakefield and Fishe Neurology, Inc.

"This isn't up for debate. I'm not going to your cousin's wedding." She really wished he wasn't standing so close. So close she could make out the darker blue rim surrounding his vivid eyes, so close she could smell the musky scent of his aftershave, so close she could press her body to his with only a step forward.

Gee, if she stripped naked, would he even notice she was a woman? Or would he just frown, tell her to get dressed, they had more brain mapping to do? That her attraction to him was simply her olfactory mucosa sensing the overly abundant androgens he emitted, causing her cortisol levels to skyrocket, and that was why she wanted to lean in and press her lips to his throat?

"You already have plans this weekend?" he pushed. Just as she should have known he would. The spoiled little rich boy in him couldn't stand to lose, not get his way. Her fate had been sealed before the conversation had started.

"Somewhere you are supposed to be that you can't attend with me?" His eyes pierced her, seeming to know the truth without her having to answer.

She wanted to lie, wanted to say that some gorgeous man was anxiously awaiting Friday evening so he could whisk her off her feet, wine her, dine her, *make her cortisol level go through the roof*, and show her the time of her life.

"I don't have specific plans—" unless cleaning her apartment and walking Yoda, her miniature poodle, counted "—but that isn't the point."

His expression brightened. "Of course it's the point. You don't have specific plans. I need you to accompany me to Cape May. We'll review the latest data from Brainiac Codex while we're there and make the weekend a working one so it won't be an entire lost cause. It'll be perfect."

"No, it won't be perfect. I do not want to go with you to a wedding in Southern New Jersey." Neither did she want to spend her weekend reviewing the computerized brain-mapping research they were conducting. Yes, she loved her job, but she'd actually thought that with him out of town for the weekend she'd have some time to herself for once.

Why was she bothering to argue with him? Why did she think she could dissuade him when he'd set his mind to something? No one could, least of all her.

Still, she stubbornly held on to her pride. "No. No. No."

"Don't you like weddings?" Creases marred his forehead. "What am I saying?" He shook his head as if to clear his thoughts. "All women like weddings."

Maybe in his world, but not hers.

"Not this woman."

His brow lifted and she knew she'd said the wrong thing, revealed too much. Stubborn was one thing, stupid quite another.

"Why not?" he asked, as if she'd tell him about just how many weddings she'd been to as her mother's maid of honor. Obviously one too many as just the thought of going to another made her histamine concentration double. Any moment she'd break out in hives. She scratched an already itchy spot on her neck.

"I just don't." No matter how much he pried, she wasn't going to tell him more.

He studied her a moment, then dismissed her comment as too inconsequential to be taken seriously when in opposition to his wishes.

"You'll like this one," he assured her. "My cousin Sharon never does anything halfway, and she's marrying the Philadelphia Eagles' quarterback. You'll have fun."

"Sure, I will. That's why you're so excited about going. Because of how much fun you'll have." Faith sighed. He wasn't going to be dissuaded. Wasn't going to let her off the hook. Whether she wanted to or not, she was going to be spending the weekend at Vale's family's beach house in Cape May, a couple hours' drive south of the city. As his date to his media darling cousin's wedding. The paparazzi loved Sharon Wakefield and the former beauty queen was never far from the press's spotlight.

"Okay, you're right." He grinned at his admission. "Weddings aren't my thing, but Sharon is my favorite cousin and I'm in the wedding party. It isn't as if I can send an exorbitant gift and beg out of this one."

"Like you usually do with family and friends' get-togethers?" He was in the wedding party? Although the media knew of the upcoming nuptials, the exact details were very hush-hush. Faith hadn't realized when she'd heard Vale mention his cousin's wedding to the famous football player that he'd be wearing a tuxedo and standing near the alter. Experiencing Vale in a tuxedo was quite possibly worth whatever heartache she'd suffer at attending yet another wedding that would only serve to remind her that nothing was for ever despite promises made.

He waggled his dark brows. "You'd better believe it."

"Fine, I'll go." It wasn't as if he'd give her a choice when all was said and done. He'd be like a dog with a bone and gnaw away at her protective covering until he sank his teeth into her vulnerable center.

His perfect mouth curved into a devilish smile. "I knew you would."

He could have at least sounded surprised, not quite so cocksure. Then again, that was Vale. Always confident. Always sure. Always a winner.

"Let's start going through these." She motioned to the latest data on their brain-mapping research that would hopefully lead the way to new treatment modalities for neurological disorders. "I've got to be in clinic at nine."

Twenty minutes later, Vale leaned back in his chair, staring across the table at the godsend he'd hired based solely on gut instinct a year and a half ago. There hadn't been an actual opening for another neurologist at Wakefield and Fishe Neurology, but quite frankly the young woman who'd finagled an appointment with him had impressed the hell out of him.

He'd learned long ago after a few eye-opening experiences to trust his gut and his gut had said not to let this one go. He'd hired her on the spot.

Even now he could hear her stunned "Don't you want to check my references first?"

He'd stared straight into her big sparkly eyes that made him think of the green apple hard candy he'd loved as a boy. Her dull framed glasses couldn't hide their appeal or their honesty. The ugly frames still didn't.

He'd never regretted his decision that day.

Faith was more like his right-hand man…er…woman. When he'd been awarded a grant to do research on

Parkinson's, which involved the surgical implantation of an innovative two-lead device that emitted electrical impulses at the brain stem, he'd immediately convinced Faith to come on board. In the office and with his research they were a team. Working as many hours as he did, she never disappointed him, often pointing out fresh angles to cases, looking at the facts with intelligence and with an out-of-the-box canniness that almost matched his own. More and more he relied on her insight, on her thoughts as to the best way to approach each patient.

Now he was relying on her to bail him out of an uncomfortable situation with his family. During last night's call from his mother, letting him know just how many single females were going to be in attendance and were looking forward to meeting him, he'd immediately put a stop to her matchmaking by announcing Faith would be coming to the wedding with him.

He probably should have asked her first, but she'd never balked at any request to work late or over the weekend. True, spending the weekend at his mother's beach house wasn't exactly the same thing as working late.

Still, her comment about possibly having plans intrigued him in ways he couldn't explain. Just what did Faith do in her free time?

"Do you have a boyfriend?"

She glanced up, staring wide-eyed at him with an open mouth. "What does me having a boyfriend have to do with anything?"

"If there's someone special in your life, he might take exception to us spending the weekend together. I'd be happy to reassure him your virtue is safe with me."

Faith chewed on her lower lip, staring at him as if trying to decide on the right answer.

A flutter started in Vale's chest, one similar to that

he felt in surgery when encountering something imaging scans hadn't picked up on. Was there someone warming his employee's bed? Someone she went home to night after night complaining about her slave driver of a boss? Why did the thought of anyone touching her bother him?

Her eyes sparked green fire and her chin lifted, as if his question had offended her. "Whether or not there is someone special in my life, I am quite capable of keeping my personal life in order, Dr. Wakefield, and of assuring any man of mine that he has nothing to fear where *you* are concerned."

Vale bit back a grin. His ever-efficient neurologist had just put him in his place. "I didn't mean to upset you, Faith. Sometimes I forget not everyone is as dedicated to their career as I am."

Her lips pursed. "You've never had cause to question my dedication to my job."

"True. Which is why you're coming with me this weekend. I'll have Kay send you the itinerary for the weekend so you'll know how to pack."

How had Thursday evening arrived and Faith still hadn't found time to go shopping for a new outfit? Of course, she knew how. For exactly the same reason she currently wasn't shopping.

Because she was working. Vale had seemed intent on occupying every second of her time this week. Worse than normal. To keep her from having time to come up with an excuse not to accompany him this weekend?

She, Vale, two neurosurgeons, two neurophysiologists, and a couple of research assistants working on the Parkinson project were spread out around the twenty-seat cherry table at one end of Vale's office. Despite the long hours they'd put in every night that week, they'd barely made a dent in the pile of work to be done before they tested the hypothesis in the operating room. Although deep-brain stimulation therapies had been in use for years, with the new data from the Brainiac Codex, the hope was that the new device would relieve the tremor associated with Parkinson's. If successful, great strides in the treatment of the debilitating disease would be made.

She wiped her hand across her face.

"Something wrong?" Vale leaned in and whispered next to her ear, his warm breath making the tiny hairs on her nape stand at attention.

She glanced his way, wondering where he drew his boundless energy from, wondering how nothing ever fazed him or made him lose his infamous control. He'd work all day, most of the night, and still have photos of himself and some beauty queen appear in the papers when he'd hit a late-night club or fancy restaurant.

"Nothing a good night's sleep won't solve." True. She hadn't slept well since he'd told her she was going to Cape May. Plus, no way was she going to tell him that her mind was wandering from the data they were poring over to thinking about what she was going to wear at his cousin's wedding. No way would she risk losing the respect she'd fought so hard to gain.

Unfortunately, he didn't look convinced by her answer, studying her with eyes too intelligent for his own good. "You're sure?"

"Yes, I'm sure." She glanced at her watch. A little after seven. If they finished up within the next hour, maybe she could swing by a dress shop and pick up something new to lift her confidence at spending the weekend with Vale's glitzy family. She looked around at the room full of researchers who were settled in for the long haul and bit back a sigh.

"Got a hot date?"

"What?"

He'd spoken low, for her ears only, but her response came out as a squeak that had several pairs of eyes glancing their way and just as quickly going back to their work.

"That's the third time in the past fifteen minutes you've looked at your watch," he pointed out. "We must be keeping you from something important."

Again Vale spoke low, but Faith's ears burned. Was everyone trying to look as if they were ignoring them or were they truly so absorbed in their work? Marcus Fishe was the only one whose gaze lingered on them. Faith quickly looked away from Vale's partner's curious eyes. Although Marcus's focus within the clinic was geared more toward issues with multiple sclerosis, he'd jumped on board with the Parkinson's project in the hope that the brain-mapping data would lend itself to other treatments.

"My work is important." Determined to keep her mind absorbed on her work and not on the fact she'd be spending her weekend with Vale, Faith highlighted an abnormal signal recording from the basal ganglia to the motor cortex on the patient profile. "I've still got to pack for this weekend, and I'd hoped to... Never mind."

There was no reason to tell him she'd hoped to go shopping, to spend time with Yoda, to have a break from Vale to recharge herself prior to attending the wedding.

Setting his ink pen down, he continued to study her in a way that made her feel as if she'd grown an extra nose on her face. "You did get the itinerary from Kay?"

"Yes, your head nurse slash assistant is as efficient as ever." She liked Kay, thought her brighter than many of the clinic's more educated personnel, including a few of the neurologists and surgeons. "The itinerary seems standard. Rehearsal tomorrow night followed by dinner, Saturday pre-wedding activities, the wedding ceremony, and then the reception with champagne, dancing, and a romantic sunset at the beach."

He snorted. "I'll warn you not to be fooled. There's nothing standard about my family."

"I wouldn't expect otherwise."

Vale rarely spoke of his family but it was impossible not to know about them as they were constantly in the press. His cousin Sharon had won Miss Pennsylvania a few years back, had gained notoriety when she'd posed topless for an exorbitant amount of money that she had then handed over to the New York City Widows and Orphans of Firefighters Fund, and had then been promptly de-crowned. Another cousin was a congressman. Another a senator. Vale's mother headed so many charities it was impossible for Faith to recall them all. His father had built a real estate empire prior to his death in Vale's teens. Apparently all Wakefields were over-achievers, the one grinning at her no exception.

"Oh?" His eyes glittered with amusement. "What do you expect?"

Her and her big mouth.

"I just meant that you're a highly successful man with good genes," she whispered, casting a leery glance around the quiet group at the table. Yet again, Marcus was watching them. Great. She glared at Vale. "Surely that trait must run in the family?"

"I'll let you decide for yourself tomorrow night." Leaning close, he flashed a wickedly dangerous smile. "I have good genes?"

She rolled her eyes. "You don't need me to answer that. You know you do."

"Right." His grin widened.

Face burning, ears roaring, Faith resumed an intent

study of the brain wave data she held, resisting the urge to glance at her watch again or to sneak a peek at the man sitting next to her. She could feel his gaze searing into her with the power of hot metal slicing into butter.

Two hours and several cups of coffee later, Faith rotated her neck, trying to work out the crick that had developed while studying the last patient profile for some missed detail, as they narrowed their choices on who met their study criteria for surgical implantation of the device.

So much for her shopping trip before heading home. And poor Yoda. Another late night with Mrs. Beasley. Before long her baby was going to think he lived at the elderly neighbor's apartment rather than with Faith. Especially as the cream-colored poodle would be spending the weekend in Mrs. Beasley's care, too.

Much later, Vale pushed the stack of patient brain-mapping profiles away from him, surprising her since they'd not made it through the rest of the stack. Although all of the others had left a little after nine, she'd already surmised she and Vale wouldn't leave before midnight.

"I've had enough." He stretched his arms above his head, drawing her gaze to how his shirt pulled taut over his chest.

She quickly glanced away, looked down at her watch. Maybe she'd have time to shop yet.

She sighed.

Maybe not.

The nicer dress boutiques would all be closed. Great.

She'd just wear the black cocktail dress she'd bought for last year's Christmas party. She wasn't crazy about the idea of wearing black to a wedding, but with its skirt flared at the hem the dress would do in a pinch and was the closest thing she had to appropriate wear for media darling Sharon Wakefield's glamorous wedding. As far as the reception, she'd make do with whatever she could find in her rather boring closet.

"Will he still be waiting?"

She blinked at Vale. "Who?"

His blue eyes darkened. "Whoever I've kept you from."

He almost sounded as if he'd intentionally kept her at the office. Actually, when the others had left and she'd started to stand, he had asked her opinion on a patient report he'd just read, ensuring she'd stay on to read the profile.

Had he intentionally kept her there? What possible reason would he have for doing so?

She took a deep breath, telling herself she was tired, imagining things, but for once gave her boss a flippant answer. "Regardless of how late you keep me, he's always glad to see me."

She wasn't lying. Not really. But, seriously, she expected Yoda not to know who she was if she didn't start spending more time with him. Thank goodness for their nightly snuggles and early morning walks.

"Maybe you should go ahead," he suggested, his dark eyes unreadable. "I'll finish these."

He was staying? Telling her to go on? Was he testing her? Seeing how dedicated she was to her career?

"When you said we should call it a night, I thought you meant both of us. I don't like the thought of leaving you here alone."

Leaning back in his chair, he laughed. "Do you think I can't take care of myself?"

No matter how she tried she couldn't keep her gaze from lowering, from tracing over the strong lines of his neck, over the tanned V of skin exposed where he'd removed his tie and unbuttoned the top couple of buttons, down his broad shoulders that his tailored shirt accented, down his forearms bared where he'd rolled up his sleeves. And his hands.

Lord, how she loved his talented hands.

Tanned, strong, long-fingered, ring-free. She particularly liked that last part, although eventually he'd marry one of the beauties he bedded. Then what? Would she be able to continue working with him, knowing how she dreamt about him, knowing he belonged to someone else?

That question was one that crept into her mind from time to time, filling her with panic, filling her with the dreaded knowledge that some day she might leave Wakefield and Fishe.

She lifted her gaze back to his, was startled to look into smoky blue eyes filled with awareness.

Awareness that she'd looked at him not as his employee, not as a fellow physician, but as a woman with real needs.

What was wrong with her?

She swallowed, trying to clear her throat, trying to buy herself time while she racked her brain for something to say that would defuse the situation.

Only, she didn't know what to say.

Regardless of how much his awareness scared her professionally, as a woman, the flicker of interest in his eyes set light to a hope that threatened to consume her very soul.

CHAPTER TWO

VALE finished his cellphone conversation with his cousin Sharon and turned toward Faith. They'd just left the hospital following a globus pallidus DBS implantation, and were walking back to Wakefield Tower, where Wakefield and Fishe occupied the entire fifty-sixth floor.

Vale was enjoying the late spring air, enjoying the hustle and bustle of the busy New York sidewalk, people from all walks of life rushing past him and Faith. Numerous vendors lined the streets, selling everything from designer sunglasses to cheap "I Love New York" T-shirts. A hot-dog street vendor called out to someone and Vale's stomach growled in response.

"Let's grab an early lunch before heading back," he suggested. Quite often they'd pop into a restaurant or grab take-out so they could review a case while dining. Working with Faith made lunch more enjoyable. "Subs or Chinese?"

"Neither." Not a single hair out of place on her tightly pulled-back hairstyle, Faith shook her head. "I can't do lunch today."

Mentally, he ran through her schedule. They were leaving the office early to head to Cape May so she only had a few afternoon appointments. "You aren't scheduled for anything until one, are you?"

She didn't meet his eyes. "No, but I have other lunch plans. Sorry."

Vale's gut tightened. Had she made plans to meet the mysterious man in her life? The one who'd been glad to see her the night before even though Vale had managed to keep her out past eleven? Had she lain in his arms recounting the day's events?

How had he not known she was seeing someone? Why did the fact that she was make his stomach knot?

Not because when she'd looked at him last night, he'd grown hard in response to her visual undressing. She'd liked what she'd seen and hell if he hadn't wanted to preen under the intensity of her green gaze.

Which was all wrong. He never, ever got involved with a colleague, and particularly not one who worked for him.

Besides, she wasn't his type.

Sex with Faith would be complicated, would come with all kinds of expectations on her part. He only had sex with uncomplicated women who knew better than to expect more from him. He'd learned long ago not to want or expect more either.

Sex?

He did not want to sleep with Faith—which was the truth. Sleep had nothing to do with what he'd found himself thinking of last night, this morning when he'd awakened.

He didn't like being aware of her. Of waking with the scent of her perfume and sound of her laughter fresh in his mind.

"I'm allowed to take a non-working lunch break." Shoving her glasses up the straight slant of her pert little nose, she looked as exasperated as she sounded.

"You should have told me. I'd planned to review the

information we compiled last night prior to making a final decision on the initial patients to receive the procedure." Why was she being so evasive? Who was she having lunch with? The mystery man? Perhaps they weren't having lunch at all? "Cancel your plans."

Annoyance flashed in her eyes, surprising him. Faith never argued with him, never went against his wishes, never made lunch plans. She ate lunch with *him*. The only time they didn't share a working lunch was if *he* made other plans.

Glancing at her watch with a disgusted look, her shoulders fell a notch, slamming him with unaccustomed guilt rather than the satisfaction that should have come with knowing he was about to get his way. And what was with her and looking at her watch the past two days? Faith wasn't a clock-watcher.

"Fine." She exhaled deeply, "I was fooling myself that I had time to get my hair done and find a dress for the wedding in an hour anyway."

Vale stopped walking, standing perfectly still on the sidewalk as throngs of people continued to bustle around them without missing a beat. He stared at Faith, and decided that, yes, like he was often told, he really was a selfish jerk. Here Faith was going to his cousin's wedding, spending the weekend working and protecting him from his family's matchmaking, and he hadn't given one thought to the fact that she might want to have her hair done or buy a new outfit. He hadn't given one thought that Faith was a woman with normal female urges, like desiring new outfits for social events.

Then again, during the entire time he'd known Faith, she hadn't acted like other women. Why should he have thought this weekend would be any different? If he'd thought about what she'd wear, he would have said scrubs or maybe a hyper-masculine gray suit and a hairstyle any librarian would be proud of.

"What time is your appointment?"

She didn't glance up. "It doesn't matter. I'll cancel."

But beneath the clear lenses of her glasses, her eyes had grown shiny and his sense of guilt gnawed at his belly, threatening to give him an ulcer if he didn't make amends. What was the aura about her that made him want to make her happy?

"Why did you leave your appointment until so late? Surely you could have shopped for a dress earlier in the week?"

Her mouth dropped and if glares were bullets he'd be six feet under. "Did you really just ask me that when you've had me at the office every night this week until after ten?" Realizing what she'd said, her jaw dropped even lower. "Not that I mind," she recanted. "I like my job. It's just… well…" She fumbled, taking a deep breath. "I don't have anything appropriate to wear to the wedding and I've been thinking about getting my hair cut anyway. I thought prior to the wedding would be as good a time as any."

His gaze immediately went to her hair. She always kept her hair pulled tightly into the professional bun. He couldn't recall ever having seen her hair down. Odd, considering how long they'd known each other.

What did she look like with her hair down?

He was struck with the need to know, the need to see her dark blond locks loose. Would the strands barely brush her shoulders or would they cascade down her back?

"Get your hair done." He ran his gaze over the sleeked-back strands nestled at her nape. "But not short, okay?"

He wasn't sure why he added the last. The length of her hair was none of his business. If she wanted to go bald, other than their patients' reactions, he had no right to say a word.

"I probably wouldn't have had time anyway, Vale. Thinking I did was wishful thinking."

He'd give her time. He owed her that much. She was saving him from his family's matchmaking.

"I'll see your patients."

Her face flushing, she shook her head, eyeing him as if he must be running a fever. "That won't be necessary."

But it was necessary.

"Look, Faith, I'm a slave driver. There's no question of that." He raked his fingers through his hair, wondering why the spring air that had felt so good moment's earlier now cut into him. "But you're right. Your lunches are your own, even if I do monopolize them. Go. Get your hair done however you want. Buy yourself a new dress."

"But—"

"Actually," he withdrew his wallet from his back pocket. "Take the rest of the afternoon off and buy yourself a dress for tonight, too. On me."

Her face pale, she stared at the cash in his hand. "I can't take your money."

"Sure you can," he teased. "You do every pay period."

"That's different." Her lips pursed. "I've earned my paycheck. This is different."

"Look, it's my fault you need new clothes and to have your hair done. It's only fair I pay." He shoved the cash into her palm, closed her hand around the money. How his fingers lingered, how he wanted to hold her hand for real, surprised him. He forced his smile to stay in place despite his unhappiness with his wayward fingers, despite his confusion over what the hell was going on with his reactions to Faith.

"Go," he ordered. "Have fun, and I'll pick you up from your place."

"Yep, Yoda," Faith agreed with the yapping dog bouncing around at her feet while she studied her new image in the mirror, "I barely recognize myself, too."

She couldn't believe the difference a decent hair cut, highlighting, and facial could make. A fairy godmother waving a magic wand and singing "Bippity-boppity-boo" couldn't have conjured a more drastic transformation.

Faith hadn't had time over the past few years to worry about her appearance. Instead she'd focused on studying for boards and becoming the best neurologist she could be. Then she'd landed a dream job with Wakefield and Fishe straight out of school, an opportunity of a lifetime she wouldn't screw up.

So, no, her appearance hadn't been a priority in eons, if ever, but, wow, an afternoon of pampering could sure make a huge difference in the way a girl looked and felt about herself.

Or maybe it was the contacts burning her eyes that only made her think she was seeing such a difference.

She'd worn disposable lenses during high school and as an undergraduate, but during medical school she'd gone almost exclusively to her glasses. She'd bought the contacts at her check-up a couple of weeks ago during lunch when Vale had been in a meeting with Marcus. But she hadn't taken time to even pull them out of her handbag. When the make-up artist at the salon had complained about Faith's glasses, she'd surprised him by producing the sealed vials containing the lenses.

Then there were the clothes.

Clothes as in plural.

She hadn't wanted to spend Vale's money, had felt guilty taking the cash. She could have found a way to slip the money back to him over the weekend. Perhaps she still would as she still wasn't comfortable with the thought of him paying for her shopping trip even if, in a way, he was right. It was his fault she'd needed a new dress. She certainly wouldn't have gone shopping if he hadn't pressed her into accompanying him.

She hadn't just bought a new dress. She'd bought three. And new underwear that made her feel delectably feminine and a bit of a siren at heart. Really, would she like the black thigh highs and garter belt quite so much otherwise?

Then there was the daring bikini she'd let the sales clerk talk her into, even though she'd never have the nerve to wear the deep red triangles in public.

She'd also bought a few semi-casual outfits. She wasn't really sure what Saturday's schedule would require, but she felt prepared for whatever came up. Of course, she'd had to drag out the largest of her suitcases to fit in all her purchases, but that was a small price to pay for being prepared.

Then again, maybe she'd gone overboard and Vale would read her make-over as a desperate plea for him to notice her as he had the night before.

Was her make-over a desperate plea for him to notice her?

She winced. No, if he hadn't noticed her for the woman she was on the inside, she certainly didn't want him to notice her for changes to her outer appearance. Not that the changes were that glamorous, anyway. Not in comparison to the supermodels usually draped across Vale's arms.

Regardless, Vale wasn't interested in investing time with a woman. He got what he wanted and moved on. Next.

What he wanted from her was a working weekend where she played decoy to his mother's matchmaking.

Still, she'd be lying if she said she wasn't eager to see his reaction when she opened her apartment door. Quite simply she didn't look like the same woman he'd walked to the salon. And had it been her imagination or had he touched her hand a half dozen times spreading wildfires up her arm?

She bent and picked up Yoda. "Hey, boy, are you going to miss me? Hmm, are you?" She rubbed her nose to the dog's, laughing when he licked her. "Now quit that before you mess up my make-up." At the dog's head quirk, she laughed again. "I know, I know, I've never cared before, but tonight's special and I suspect this make-up isn't doggy-kisses proof."

Yoda licked her again, obviously not caring if her make-up was doggy-kiss proof or not. Scratching the miniature poodle behind his ears, she praised him, telling him how much she was going to miss him over and over, and re-minding him how much he loved visiting Mrs. Beasley.

"Come on. I guess I should go drop you there before His Highness arrives." Cradling the dog in one arm, she gathered the diaper bag of dog goodies she'd packed him. "Let's get you next door."

Saying goodbye was difficult, but once inside Mrs. Beasley's, Yoda didn't seem to mind at all that Faith would be gone all weekend.

"No worries. He's Miss Cupcake's favorite guest," the older woman promised as they walked to the door. "She and I will take good care of Yoda, and you know I can use the extra money from dog-sitting."

Standing in the doorway, Faith leaned in and kissed Mrs. Beasley's weathered cheek. "I know. Bye, love you."

Closing the door, she turned to go back to her apartment and caught Vale in the hallway admiring her backside.

Vale blinked, attempting to clear his eyes.

That stunning derrière and killer legs he'd been admiring were Faith's?

He'd known she had a decent body, he wasn't blind, but her scrubs did nothing to accent her curves and apparently everything to hide them. Where had all that tantalizing flesh come from?

And her eyes.

He'd always liked Faith's eyes. But without her glasses they were huge, luminous, *tempting*.

No, he wasn't tempted by Faith.

Only he was.

Tempted to push her up against the apartment hallway wall, push up that nipped-at-the-waist tease of a skirt, and thrust between those long, long legs.

Where had she gotten those legs and why hadn't he noticed before?

Okay, so he had noticed a time or two when she'd had on one of those ugly gray suits she sometimes wore that she had great calves. The kind that plumped out when she reached for a book on a high shelf. But Lord help him at the expanse of thigh on display beneath the hem of the dress she wore now.

And her shoulders.

His fingers itched to rub over her bare skin. He'd never seen her shoulders bare before. There should be laws against covering shoulders like hers. He liked what he saw beneath the stringy dress straps. He liked it a lot. Her hair was up but, unlike her work style, long, highlighted tendrils hung low, daring him to set free the caught-up strands. The style revealed the tantalizing curve of her exposed neck. He wanted to kiss her there, taste her, work his way down, sensitize every neuron in her body.

Oh, hell. He was in trouble. He couldn't bring her to his parents' house like this, with him on the verge of busting through his pants just from looking at her, with him practically licking his lips in anticipation of her feminine delights.

"My money bought that?"

Her lower lip disappeared between her teeth. Uncertainty marred her expression. She glanced down at the blue dress she wore, exposing those long legs that had his brain working overtime—or, more like, not working at all.

"You don't like my dress?"

"What's not to like? You're gorgeous, Faith." The insecurity in her eyes had him scampering to put the glow back on her face. "Absolutely stunning."

Her gaze lifted to his and a smile played at her lips. "Really?"

He laughed at her obvious fishing for a compliment.

"Best return I've ever gotten off a few hundred bucks." Immediately, he could see he'd said the wrong thing. Again. And again the overwhelming need to repair the damage filled him. "Why do you hide yourself away when you were obviously meant to be admired by the world?"

But this time she didn't light back up, just moved past him and unlocked her apartment door.

Knowing he'd unintentionally hurt her, but not sure how, he followed her into the apartment and grabbed her wrist, turning her to face him.

"I didn't mean that the way you obviously took it. You're a beautiful woman, Faith, always. If what I said made you think I was implying otherwise, then you're wrong. Nothing could be further from the truth."

Without looking his way, she shrugged. "Okay."

Placing his finger beneath her chin, he forced her to look at him and felt his heart kick up at the swirling emotion in her green-apple-candy eyes. Had he ever seen bigger, more expressive eyes? "No, it's not okay. I've hurt you."

"I'm not some fragile ninny who needs coddling, Vale." Her gaze lowered, settling near his throat. "We're business colleagues going away for a working weekend at your cousin's wedding. There's no reason for you to explain your comment. I know I made a big change."

Like a beautiful butterfly emerging from its cocoon. The same on the inside, yet so utterly different on the outside.

He felt humbled to have played a role in the transformation, even such a tiny role. Yet he wanted her to see what he saw—a stunning young woman.

His thumb stroked along her jaw line, caressing the soft skin, noting the pink flush spreading across her cheeks, the parting of her pouty pink lips, the way his heart beat faster in his chest when her stunned gaze met his.

Vale did something totally out of character.

He lowered his lips to hers.

Faith's knees wobbled. Firecrackers detonated in her chest, pounding her heart against her ribcage, demanding freedom to burst into a million projectile pieces.

No way was Vale kissing her!

If a trip to the salon and an upscale dress boutique was all it had taken to get his lips on hers, why hadn't she gone shopping months ago? Had her hair streaked with strands of gold and a trained professional paint her face?

What was she thinking? This was Vale. Her boss. She should not be letting him kiss her.

He cupped her cheeks, drawing her closer, tasting her lips with a softness that belied the tough man she knew him to be.

She stood stock still, hands at her side, sure if she moved or even breathed, the fantasy would disappear, a pleasurable vapor she'd grasped at but failed to hold on to.

For eighteen months she'd wondered what this man tasted like, what his lips would feel like against hers, and now he was kissing her. So she gave in to the desire erupting within her, kissed him back, tasted his lips, opened her mouth to let him inside and hoped he'd never let her go, that he'd never stop kissing her.

Tiny explosions ripped through her one after another in the wake of his tongue thrusting into her mouth.

He was no longer cupping her face but her bottom, pulling her fully against his hard body.

He was hard. Amazingly, eye-wideningly... *Oh, my!*

As much as Faith wanted to spread her arms wide and welcome him, to take whatever he would offer her, she had to stop him before she completely lost her mind and became one of the many women to move in and out of his life.

Before he realized just how much she wanted him. Because Vale only wanted one thing from women. She had to think of her career.

She pushed against his chest. "Stop."

He lifted his head, his lids half covering his desire-laden eyes. He wanted her. He had kissed her, wanted her, might have carried her to her sofa and made heart-pounding, thigh-slapping love to her if she hadn't told him to stop.

Her head spun. Her eyes blurred. Her equilibrium shifted.

Regret that she'd stopped him filled her, making her wish she'd dragged him into her bedroom rather than push him away. But make-over or not, she wasn't one of his playthings. She was his employee, a physician with plans to have a phenomenal career within his neuro clinic, and not by sleeping her way to the top.

Although with her lack of experience, sleeping with Vale might get her sacked instead of promoted.

"Why did you do that?" Wiping the back of her hand across her mouth, she stepped back, wishing she wasn't shaking, wishing she didn't want to beg him to kiss her again. She had to take control of the situation prior to him figuring out just how much she wanted to jump back into his arms.

"You needed to be kissed."

If he thought his hot kisses had left her any less in need of being kissed, he was wrong.

All he'd managed to do was to show her what she'd been missing, what she now knew she desperately wanted. His kisses.

Determined to salvage her pride, she frowned, wishing he wasn't still touching her. "Says who?"

He rubbed his thumb across her lower lip. "Says me."

A shiver whipped through her body, prickling her flesh. "Even if I did need to be kissed, that's not your place. I told you on the day I agreed to this trip with you—I won't be lumped into the category of one of your girls."

He seemed to consider her comment a moment. "You're wrong, Faith. Kissing you is exactly my place. This weekend, you are my girl."

CHAPTER THREE

OF ALL the arrogant comments Faith had ever heard!

She was not Vale's girl. Just because she'd agreed to a working weekend to save him from his family's matchmaking, that did not make her his property and certainly not one of the arm decorations he paraded around New York's social scene.

She snuck a glance at his powerful profile. Staring straight ahead, watching traffic as he drove to Cape May, he looked exactly the same as he always had. Same sun-kissed light brown hair, same sparkling blue eyes that could pierce a person's soul with their intensity, same handsome face. Same calm presence, completely untouched by the kiss they'd shared.

He was whistling, for goodness' sake. An upbeat melody that was slowly driving her insane.

Urgh. He frustrated her. Infuriated her. He'd kissed her. Taken notice of the fact that she was of the opposite sex and kissed her. A toe-curling, thigh-melting, neuron synapse-searing, honest-to-goodness kiss.

Yes, she'd been the one to stop him, because she'd had to. But she'd wanted him to take her into his arms, tell her he'd been a fool not to see what was right beneath his nose, and could she ever forgive him?

Okay, so that was pure fantasy and not the kind of thing

that happened in reality. But men like Vale kissing her didn't happen in her reality either.

At least, nothing like that had ever happened before.

"You're staring a hole through my head."

How did he know that when he hadn't glanced away from the traffic on the New Jersey Parkway?

"Impossible."

As if she hadn't just taken a shot at him, he grinned. "I meant figuratively, not literally."

"I knew that," she pointed out, determined not to let him get the upper hand. "I was referring to your hard-headedness making staring a hole through your head impossible in any shape, form, or fashion. Figuratively or literally."

He laughed, a husky male sound that warmed her insides. "Point taken."

Eyes narrowed, she twisted in her seat to more easily look at him. "Are you mocking me?"

She'd swear his lips twitched with amusement. What was so funny? He'd kissed her and turned her world upside down and now he was laughing at her? If he hadn't been driving, she'd…she'd…well, she'd have come up with some horrendous punishment, if her life wasn't literally in his hands.

"Relax, Faith." He glanced away from the road long enough to meet her gaze. "Maybe we shouldn't have brought the patient profiles with us."

"Why not?"

"This isn't going to be a working weekend after all."

She wouldn't gulp. Not even if she really, really needed to gulp.

"Why?" She gulped.

"Because I've been working you too hard, and you need to relax, have a little fun."

"I have fun." She didn't want him thinking she was a

dull Jane. Even if she was a dull Jane who worked most of the time and spent too much of her precious little spare time working even more so as to impress him when next they met.

"With whomever you were kissing goodbye in apartment 907?"

Mrs. Beasley? She started to laugh, but then realized he was serious, had made note of her neighbor's apartment number, and, most surprising, sounded a tad bit jealous.

Was it possible? Could a make-over and one kiss have him feeling possessive? Oh, what was she thinking? He was probably just worried that if she had a life she wouldn't be at his beck and call for work. Just look at how he'd reacted to her making lunch plans that didn't involve work.

"Apartment 907 is my neighbor."

"And you tell this neighbor you love him?"

He'd heard that? And why was he using his annoyed voice on her? She glared at him in silence. Even with only being able to see his profile, she could see his expression harden.

"It's a simple question, Faith. No harm in answering."

Oh, enough was enough.

"My neighbor is a seventy-year-old sweetheart who dog-sits for me while I'm at work. I was dropping off Yoda, not telling a man I loved him. Not that it's any of your business if I was."

His brow rose. "Yoda?"

"My dog."

"You have a dog?"

"Yes, a miniature poodle."

"A miniature poodle?" His nose curled with unpleasantness. "Not much in the way of protection."

"You'd be surprised. Yoda might be small but he has the heart of a lion."

He smirked. "You're not one of those women who puts clothes and bows and such on her pet, are you?"

Faith didn't answer.

He burst out laughing. "You are, aren't you? My little miss organized neurologist plays dress-up with her dog."

She took a deep breath. "Yoda happens to like his Darth Poodle pajamas."

Vale snorted. "May the force be with him, because he's going to need all the help he can get when the other dogs who still have theirs get through with him."

"Yeah, well, other than Miss Cupcakes, Mrs. Beasley's female Chihuahua, Yoda doesn't spend a lot of time around other dogs. He'd like to, but I'm always at work and Mrs. Beasley's idea of a walk is to the end of the block and back for potty breaks."

He glanced toward her. "I'm sensing some latent resentment. Are you telling me you're working too many hours?"

"I am working too many hours." What was wrong with her? Why was she telling him this? Eighteen months she'd busted her butt without a single word of complaint. Eighteen months she'd gone above and beyond whatever needed to be done just to impress him.

What had they highlighted her hair with? Truth serum?

Or was his kiss what had loosened her tongue?

"Which is why we should forget the Parkinson project for the weekend and just enjoy ourselves. The rest will be good for both of us, will have our minds refreshed when we return on Sunday," he mused, not looking at her. "Too bad we didn't bring Yoda with us. He might have gotten a chance to show off his fancy duds on the beach."

Faith's gaze narrowed in his direction, not that he noticed as he was watching traffic and not her. "Quit making fun of my dog."

"If you put clothes on your dog, you have to expect him to be made fun of. By real men and real dogs."

"I expect no such thing and Yoda is a real dog. The best dog. The sweaters are to keep him warm."

"And here I thought that's what fur was for." He shot a horrified look her way. "You didn't shave him, did you?"

"No." Taking an exasperated breath, she shook her head, pursed her lips at him. "I know what you're doing, and it isn't going to work."

He had the audacity to glance at her, all innocence and good looks. "What isn't going to work?"

As if he didn't know exactly what he was doing.

"What you're doing."

"Which is?"

"Trying to get me flustered about the dog so that I will forget to make my case regarding this not being a working weekend." She fixed him with a determined glare. "This is a working weekend, Vale."

Changing lanes on the parkway, he passed a slower car. "What's wrong with us just having some fun?"

Was he kidding? "The only reason I'm here is because this is a working weekend."

"That's not true. I asked you to accompany me this weekend because my mother was determined to parade every single female at the wedding in front of me in the hope I'll not be able to resist making a walk down a long aisle to a short-noosed rope." He pulled off the parkway, zipped through the EZ Pass lane at the toll booth, and headed toward downtown Cape May. "With you by my side, she'll leave me alone. I can spend time with my family without having to call out the National Guard."

The National Guard? Did he expect such a rush of

female would-be suitors? Casting another quick look at him, she decided that, yes, he probably did and rightly so. Forget his money, power and prestige, Dr. Vale Wakefield was still the finest catch in New York.

For the weekend she was to defend his bachelorhood? Where was the 1-800 hotline to the National Guard? She'd be the one needing reinforcements.

"She won't buy that I'm anything more than a colleague."

Vale shot her a quick look. "Why wouldn't she?"

Should she list the reasons? Write him a thesis perhaps? "I'm not your type."

"Obviously, you are." And obviously he found her comment amusing since he chuckled.

"What's that supposed to mean? You like tall, willowy women with IQs lower than their bust sizes," she reminded him.

"I kissed you," he parried.

As if those three little words explained everything.

She bit her lower lip. "Why did you?"

"I wanted to."

He'd wanted to. Pleasure bubbled inside her like just uncorked champagne, overflowing with rich, foamy giddiness, intoxicating her senses.

She was drugged. Drugged by the insanity being around a man as potent as Vale caused. She didn't want this, didn't want to feel this way. Not about him or any man.

"What about what I wanted?"

"Are you saying you didn't want me to kiss you? Because I don't believe you." His expression said, Yeah, right. Tell me another one.

"I stopped you," she reminded him, chin high.

"Not until after a good bit of tongue thrusting and spit

swapping had taken place. Face it, Faith, you wanted me to kiss you as much as I wanted to kiss you."

"Eww." Ignoring his second sentence, she wrinkled her nose at his coarse words. "Don't be gross, Vale."

"I was making a point."

"Grossing me out is more like it."

They came to a stop at a traffic light and he turned to face her, his eyes boring into her soul. "Kissing me grossed you out?"

With his gaze fixed on her, she couldn't lie to him. Not even when that was what she really wanted to do. Instead she blurted out the embarrassing facts in the most revealing of ways.

"Kissing you didn't gross me out." Except at the abandoned way she'd kissed him back when she knew better.

"What did kissing me do?" His voice was husky, confident, as if he knew exactly what his kisses did to women.

Of course he knew what his kisses did to women.

Just as she knew.

Kissing Vale made women crazy, fanatical, addicted. She knew that. She'd watched his effect on women, knew the dangers of being near him in any capacity not business-related.

Vale didn't mix business and pleasure. He just didn't. Not ever.

Only he had by kissing her.

"Kissing you made me think I'm crazy for agreeing to this when I had the opportunity to spend a weekend relaxing at home because you'd have been otherwise occupied, not calling me to meet you at the office for yet more work."

His eyes narrowed into deep blue slits. "You don't like working with me?"

"I love my job, but someday I do hope to have a life outside work."

"What kind of life?"

Why on earth had she started this conversation? Or had he started it? Either way, she wanted out.

"The usual," she said dryly, grateful they'd moved beyond what his kisses did to her, but hoping he'd let their new subject drop.

"What usual?"

Of course he wouldn't. Not the great Dr. Vale Wakefield, New York's most eligible bachelor.

"You know," she admitted reluctantly. "A house in some smarmy little suburb that I can call my own. A yard for Yoda to dig holes in. A neighborhood where I can take him for long walks."

His brows drew together in a deep furrow, his lips tight with displeasure. "That's your idea of the usual? What about marriage? Children? That usual?"

Maybe that was usual for some women. To Faith there was nothing usual about marriage or having children. Not in the marriages she'd witnessed. And, although she was mightily attracted to Vale, she didn't kid herself that it was anything more than that. Men didn't stick around. Even men who promised to, and Vale wasn't the type to make such promises to begin with.

"Women who want to make it in a high-powered career shouldn't reveal to the boss that they also want to have a family," she answered in the hope of steering him in a direction other than the truth. "Not if they want to be taken seriously."

"You think I'd penalize you if you said you wanted a family?"

"I think you're more likely to advance someone who didn't have to take time off for maternity leave and pediatric visits." Dear Lord, someone really had slipped her some truth serum. She couldn't shut up. "My career is important to me. I told you that from the beginning."

"Yes, you were quite vocal that day."

Why did the way he spoke make her think he was mocking her?

"Laugh if you want to, but I'm serious." She shrugged. "After I've achieved my career goals I'll think about marriage."

Not that she'd want marriage ever. She was more than happy with Yoda. Her dog would never leave her for another woman—except perhaps Mrs. Beasley and her cutie pie Miss Cupcake.

He seemed to digest her comment. "After you've achieved your career goals you plan to marry and have kids?"

"After I achieve my career goals…" tired of the picking apart of her life goals, she gestured toward the green light that had changed at some point during their conversation, but neither had noticed "…I'll make plans for the rest of my life."

Faith had already decided she wasn't going to allow herself to be intimidated by the Wakefield family fortune. She just wasn't.

Yes, she knew the family was as iconic as the Vanderbilts, the Kennedys, and the Fords, but Wakefields were human beings, too, just like her. No better. No worse.

Telling herself this and actually being able to keep her jaw from dropping when Vale whipped his low-slung red road devourer into the circle drive of a house that looked more like a hotel were two different things. Holy medulla oblongata! This was really just a house?

"This is your family's beach home?"

He glanced at the lumbering three-story beige house with balconies jutting out on every level. "The East Coast one, yes. My mother had the old house torn down, and this one built a few years ago. Personally, I preferred the former one."

They had a beach house for each coast? Had torn down their previous beach house to rebuild another? Somehow, she doubted the East Coast home had been torn down due to being rundown. Faith let that digest. Sure, Vale had money, lots of money, but the side she generally saw of him could have been just another hard-working physician, not the son of a family worth billions.

Except for the society-page photos with women hanging all over him. Those she could do without.

Vale switched off the ignition, but made no move to get out of the car. Stretching forward, his arms wrapped around the steering-wheel, he took a deep breath. "Remind me why I'm doing this wedding again."

Wondering exactly the same thing, Faith tore her gaze away from the monstrosity where they'd be staying and unbuckled her seat belt with shaky fingers. "Because your cousin Sharon expects you to be here."

"And Sharon must get her way."

Did she? Faith had never met any of Vale's family, but could only imagine that they must be used to the world bowing at their privileged Italian leather–covered feet. Just looking at the enormous house before her made her knees want to buckle. She was so out of her league.

"Must run in the family," she mused.

"Must." He grinned, opening the door of his car that probably cost more than triple her annual salary. "Let's go in. I'll grab our luggage later."

First checking her appearance to make sure she wasn't committing some faux pas such as lipstick on her teeth,

Faith reached for her doorhandle and was surprised when the door opened before she could.

"What are you doing?" She blinked up at Vale. Lord, the man was fast. In so many ways, a total speed demon.

"Opening your door."

"Why?"

"I already told you why," he said with exaggerated patience. "This weekend, you're my girl. A gentleman opens the door for his girl."

A thousand birds took flight in her belly at once.

"No, Vale." She spoke just as slowly as he had so there would be no misunderstanding between them. "For the record, I'm not your girl and you are not a gentleman."

Reaching for her hand to help her out, he gave her a mock sympathetic look. "You're wasting your breath. We've already established that we Wakefields always get our way."

True, but being here as his colleague for a working weekend was one thing, pretending to be his girl or whatever it was he wanted from her was something completely different. Not when part of her wanted to be his girl. For real.

"And to set the record straight—" his grin was lethal "—I'm always a gentleman when it comes to the ladies."

Stepping from the low-slung sports car, she turned to face him, determined to make him understand. "Vale, I won't—"

Tugging on her hand, he pulled her flush to him and she forgot how to breathe. The respiratory centers of her brain literally shut down and left her woozy.

"Sure you will, and you'll have fun. I promise."

Looking into his twinkling eyes, Faith believed him. Being his girl, even for a weekend, would be fun. Only then she'd have to pay the piper the price for that fun. And, dear Lord, could she please have some oxygen in her lungs please?

"Don't look now, but we're being watched."

She started turning toward the house, but Vale's forehead lowered to rest against hers, and, grinning, he said, "My mother and aunt are standing at the window and I told you not to look."

"Yes, but if this isn't a working weekend, you're not my boss, are you?" she bit out, trying not to gasp for air.

He started to speak, but she rushed on.

"I'm not doing anything I don't want to do and you can't make me because I don't have to do as you say. Not away from work. And when I don't do as Your Highness commands, you're not going to say a word to this lady who has her own mind and isn't afraid to use it." She pulled away from him, shut her car door herself, then smiled as pretty as you please, only feeling slightly dizzy in the process, especially when he immediately recaptured her in his arms. "Because you're a gentlemen when it comes to the ladies, remember?"

CHAPTER FOUR

VALE conceded that Faith had made a great point, wondering why he was suddenly as nervous as he'd been during his first stint in the operating room, wondering why he cared so much what Faith thought of his family, why it felt so right to have her in his arms when nothing could be further than the truth.

His gaze lowered to her all-too-kissable lips. "I'm always the boss, Faith. Always."

Eyes wide, she swallowed. "Your family is originally from Philadelphia, aren't they?"

So she wanted to change the subject? He'd let her, but he wasn't letting her go, even if she was squirming against him, trying to free herself. Actually, he should let her go because she was squirming against him and he was rapidly getting turned on. Talking about his family should cure that.

"Yes, Philadelphia is their home base, but we spend more time together here." With his arms still wrapped around her waist, he glanced toward the house his mother had thought they'd needed a few years back. He missed the more traditional beach house she'd had torn down to make room for its too-modern, too-big replacement. She hadn't been able to bear the original beach house after his father had died, though, and Vale had never contradicted her claims that they'd needed more room.

"These days," he continued, "it's rare for the entire family to be together, though. Holidays and special occasions. That's about it."

"You worked through last Christmas," she reminded him, no longer struggling to free herself and staring at him with her amazing eyes. He'd swear he could look into her eyes for hours on end without getting bored. Not with the ever-changing gold flecks and the deep rings around her green irises.

"I flew to Philly for Christmas morning and spent the day with my family." He pressed his palms into her low back, relishing how she molded to him, how his gut tightened with the desire to feel her naked beneath him.

"You were back home that night, working," she gulped, staring at him as if she could read his mind and wasn't sure what to think of this change in him. Hell, he didn't know what to think of these new reactions to her either.

"How do you know I came back that night?"

She rolled her eyes. "Because, no thought whatsoever to my holiday, you called, wanting me to assist on the Parkinson's article you were writing."

Ah, now he remembered. He'd been alone, digging through medical records, compiling data for his article, wishing Faith was there. Before he'd thought twice about the day being Christmas, he'd dialed her cell number. "You came."

"Yes," she agreed, her eyes taking on a far-away look. "You called, and I came running. Even on Christmas Day. My career is important to me, remember? Having my name next to yours in a prestigious medical journal looks good on my résumé."

Had she been with her someone special? Unwrapping

presents and sitting on the sofa, watching multicolored lights flicker on the tree?

"Did I interrupt a Christmas dinner?"

Her face pinched. "Nothing that I minded having interrupted."

"You weren't with lover-boy?"

"Who?"

"Whoever you spend your time with when you're not with me?"

"I spent Christmas Day with my mother and stepfather. Your call was a mixed blessing."

He'd met Faith's mother once. A vivacious woman with lots of spirit who'd stopped by the clinic unexpectedly. He'd liked her instantly, but a flustered Faith had rushed her mother and her stepfather out the door within minutes of their arrival. "What's your stepfather's name? Curtis?"

Nose curling, Faith sighed. "Curtis was her previous husband. This one's name is John."

"That's right. She remarried earlier this year. John Debellis, the stockbroker you don't like."

"It's not that I don't like him. John's okay." Her lips thinned to white lines and her eyes stayed on her freshly manicured hands.

He'd never seen her nails painted, missed their usual natural gleam.

"I can tell you're jumping for joy over how okay he is."

"He's my stepfather. One of many I've had." She shrugged. "There's no point in liking him. Within another year or two he'll have found someone new and my mother will become involved with someone else that she'll likely go on to marry, and he'll do the same. It's the way life is."

Just how many times had Faith's mother been married?

He would have asked, but the front door flung open and his cousin bounded down the steps, flinging herself at him full force, practically knocking Faith out of his arms.

"Vale!"

Faith squared her shoulders, stood her ground, as if bracing herself for an unpleasant experience. Immediately that unwanted protectiveness came forth in Vale. Did she think his family wouldn't accept her?

"Meet my cousin Sharon." He set his cousin on the ground next to him, placed his hand low on Faith's back. "Don't mind her antics. She's been throwing herself at men since she was three."

Sharon slapped his arm. "Behave. You'll give your friend the impression I'm wild."

"You are wild," he replied, smiling indulgently at the blonde beauty he'd spent most of his youth exploring with, despite being two years older than her. In addition to their Wakefield blue eye color, they'd shared an adventurous spirit.

"Not any more." She flashed her ring finger in front of his face. A large, multi-faceted diamond twinkled in the sunshine.

"If Steve thinks a rock is going to make you settle down, he's in for it."

She grinned. "What makes you think Steve wants me to settle down?"

Vale threw his head back and laughed. "Brave man."

"Smart, scrumptious man." Sharon turned to Faith and hugged her as enthusiastically as she'd leapt into Vale's arms.

He should have known his cousin would make Faith feel

welcome. Sharon might be renowned for her outer beauty, but her real beauty came from within.

"It's so good to meet the woman Vale deems worthy of attending my wedding as his date." Sharon plopped a kiss on Faith's pale cheek. "You must be special."

"I'm more of a friend than date," she immediately corrected, her posture so perfect the sternest school matron would have applauded.

He stepped forward. "What Faith is trying to say is that we're co-workers and she doesn't want anyone to think she's trying to sleep her way to the top. Particularly me."

Red splotched her cheeks. Her gaze snapped to his and she outright glared.

Sharon burst out laughing, pulling a stiff Faith into another hug. "Oh, I like her, Vale. She's not a doormat like most of the women you hang out with. Keep her around, okay?"

Grinning, Vale followed the two women into the house.

He had every intention of keeping Faith around.

Vale's mother looked more like an older sister than a woman of more than fifty years. Actually, she looked like grown-up Barbie come to life, buzzing in and out of the main living area of the biggest house Faith had ever set foot in.

The Wakefields' beach home. Their second home. Or would it be their third home as they had a west coast home, too? Hadn't she read something about an estate on the coast of Italy, too? The whole idea of having multiple homes of this magnitude made Faith's head spin.

She'd never had a single-unit home, had always lived in an apartment building or college dorm, had always lived in New York. How boring Vale must find her compared to the well-traveled women he usually spent his non-working time with.

But she wasn't going to let him push her around, or push her into a physical relationship just because she was convenient. Not when her career was at stake. Otherwise she'd be leaping into his arms with just as much exuberance as his cousin had—only Faith's motives would have been much less pure.

His mother had rushed them inside, thrust drinks into their hands, and directed them to the living room that was double the size of Faith's entire apartment. Long rectangular windows along every wall boasted panoramic views of the sun going down over the Atlantic. Absolutely breathtaking. Absolutely terrifying. She was so out of her league.

"We're so glad Vale brought you this weekend, Faith." His mother leaned in to give her a quick air kiss. Diamonds the size of Texas sparkled on Virginia Wakefield's manicured fingers. "Be sure to let me know if you need another drink. Or if you forgot anything from home. I always keep extra bare essentials."

Guilt swam through her at the warm reception Vale's family greeted her with since she was there under what she considered false pretenses. She'd been so leery of their wealth and figured her lack thereof would be an insurmountable barrier, but they'd been nothing but kind to her from the moment Vale's exuberant cousin had jumped him.

"I had your luggage put in your room. Faith's, too."

"Yes, Mom," Vale intoned as his mother flitted toward Sharon's younger sister, Angela.

Faith turned to him. Her luggage was in his room? She supposed that asking for a separate room would raise a few eyebrows. Obviously the women he brought home slept in his room. But she was not one of his women and had no intention of losing her brain this weekend.

Her heart, well, she planned to keep that closely guarded as well because falling for him would be way too easy when he already occupied so much of her thoughts.

Her suitcase was in his room.

She wanted to say something, but bit her tongue. She'd put him on the floor, because if he thought they were sleeping in the same bed, he had another think coming.

Since arriving, he'd been unusually quiet. Unusually attentive. Probably in an effort to convince his family they were truly involved so they wouldn't start up with the matchmaking.

"Seeing you with your family almost makes you seem like an ordinary man." Right, because ordinary men drank Cristal from real crystal while walking on gleaming marble floors with million-dollar paintings hanging on the walls. It was enough to make a girl's neuron synapses fuse.

"I don't want you to think I'm ordinary."

She almost snorted. As if.

"No one would ever think you're ordinary, Vale," she assured in a purposely condescending tone.

His lips twitched in amusement. "You have a sharp tongue, Faith Fogarty."

"That's why you hired me," she reminded him. "My sharp tongue and sharper wit."

Vale threw his head back and laughed. Reaching out, he took her hand into his and lifted it to his mouth. "You might just be right about that."

What was he doing?

Why wasn't she stopping him?

Why were her knees trembling?

Why was every cell in her body going berserk, wanting to get closer and closer to him?

"Come on. Let's head outdoors," Sharon called, rushing everyone out the elaborate glass French doors that led onto a patio boasting a sparkling blue pool and hot tub, along with privacy created by the sand dunes behind the back yard.

A large white marquee had been set up along the back side of the property where the wedding reception would take place. On the opposite side, white chairs had been lined up in neat rows facing a gazebo where the bride and groom would stand, their attendants on the sides.

Still reeling from Vale's attention, Faith sat in one of the chairs near the middle and watched as Sharon ordered everyone around like a five-star general.

Thirty minutes later, Faith watched Vale take his place yet again two spots down from the groom, watched as they ran through the events one last time. He was bored but humoring his family and as much as she wanted him to be enough of a distraction to fully occupy her mind, for once he wasn't.

Sitting was pure torture. Being there was pure torture in so many ways. Each time the wedding march started, bile sloshed in her stomach, burning her throat, making her clench and unclench her fingers.

She detested weddings.

Had from the very first one she'd attended.

That had been the moment she'd had to admit to herself that her father wouldn't be coming home ever again. That she'd never have her happy family back.

That her father had truly abandoned her and her mother.

That her mother had moved on and so should she. And although her mother moved on, time and again, Faith never had.

Next to Faith, Virginia clapped her hands and sighed,

apparently not suffering from a similar distaste for weddings.

"Oh," she sighed. "Everything is just perfect."

Perfect, because that's what weddings were.

Gag. Gag. Gag. Faith resisted the urge to put her finger in her mouth and stimulate her glossophayngeal and vagus nerves. Instead, she glanced back toward Vale.

He'd been looking at her, an odd expression on his face. Not a bad expression, more a quizzical one. Then he smiled, dimples digging into his cheeks, tiny crinkles forming at the corners of his brilliant eyes.

Faith no longer wanted to gag. Instead she fought drooling. Vale Wakefield was one gorgeous man.

He winked and for the first time since they'd come outside she felt a smile tugging at her lips. How could he do that? Take her from misery to better with a mere wink?

"He really likes you."

Reality kicked in as she turned to Vale's mother and was once again slammed with guilt, her stomach roiling at the tumultuous ups and downs her emotions were taking. Deceiving this gracious woman just felt wrong. "We work well together."

"Of course, you do, dear." Virginia patted her arm and smiled graciously. "You must or he never would have invited you here. I'm so pleased that he did."

A man setting up the dance floor beneath the pulled-back sides of the tent caught Vale's mother's eyes and, with another quick pat and smile, she went off to direct the worker.

"Enjoying yourself?" Vale asked, coming up behind her, pulling her from the chair and wrapping his arms around her waist.

"Vale, don't," she bit out. Why was he being so touchy-feely? She wasn't sure how much more touchy-feely she could handle.

"Don't?" He didn't take the hint, didn't let her go. "I have to keep you close. You're here to protect me from my family."

"Sure," she snorted. "Because now that I've met them I see how scary they are."

"They scare you, too? Now you understand why I need you to intervene." His smile was contagious, and melted away the worry gnawing in her belly, melted her insides to silly feminine goop.

"They just want you to be happy." She stepped back, unable to deal with what being in his arms did to her. "If you don't want them matchmaking, just tell them."

"I'm so glad you suggested that, because I've never thought about just telling my mother that I'm not interested in meeting a nice girl and settling down."

She narrowed her gaze. "In case you're wondering, sarcasm does not become you."

"Haven't you heard? Everything becomes me." His movie-star white teeth flashed. Rather than saying anything, he took her hand and led her away from the wedding festivities and out toward the high gate that opened to the sand dunes behind the mansion. A private boardwalk led out to the billowing Atlantic.

Faith's breath caught at the beauty of the white-capped waves rolling in, at how the almost set sun painted the sky with pinks, purples, and blues.

For just a moment she wanted to believe this was real, that Vale had invited her to his parents' this weekend because he wanted to be with her, that he missed her as much as she missed him when they were apart. She wanted to believe that they were going for a walk on the beach, holding hands, sharing the moment when the sun dipped from the sky. Not for show, not as friends or colleagues, but as lovers.

And that when it was all over she wouldn't have a broken heart. She definitely wanted to believe that because otherwise how could she allow herself to even indulge in the fantasy?

"Why haven't you?" She slipped off her heels and wiggled her toes in the warm sand.

He glanced up from where he pulled off his shoes and socks, dropping them onto the sand, and rolled up the cuffs of his dark slacks. "Why haven't I what?"

He was so gorgeous. More breathtaking than the sunset. More beautiful. More what she wanted, but shouldn't.

She dropped her heels next to his shoes. "Met a nice girl and settled down."

"Don't start, Faith." He grabbed her hand and headed toward the surf.

"What?" She stumbled, trying to keep up with his pace as he dragged her behind him, sand flying up at her ankles.

"Matchmaking," he spat the word out. "I don't need you fixing me up with friends any more than I need my family doing so."

As if she'd fix Vale up with one of her friends. Besides, thanks to the long hours she worked, few of her friends would even claim her these days.

"I can assure you I'd never do that to any of my friends. I like them too much to introduce them to you."

"Good, because if I ever marry, I'll find the woman all by myself."

Which meant he hadn't already found her.

Not that Faith thought he had. Just that part of her had hoped someday he'd realize how good it might be between them. Then again, she imagined Vale was the kind of man who it was always good between.

Between the sheets, between the car seats, between the sand and the waves.

Where had that thought come from? She wasn't prone to lust. Was used to dealing with how he made her feel and usually did a great job of suppressing her baser instincts. So why hadn't she then?

She gulped, tearing her gaze from him to stare out at the ocean. Coming here with him had been a horrible mistake. One she'd likely live to regret.

"What about you?"

"Me?" She knew his gaze was on her, but she didn't dare look at him. He'd see too much in her eyes, would instantly realize that she'd met the man she wanted for all time during a job interview eighteen months ago.

No! She hadn't met the man she wanted for all time. Vale was not that man. There was no *that man*. All she felt for Vale was physical attraction and professional admiration. That was it. Nothing more.

"Why haven't you married?" he clarified, his words nipping at her soul as surely as the tide tugged at her feet.

"I imagine someday I'll meet someone who'll sweep me off my feet." Someone who'd make her forget how Vale's lips had felt against hers, how even now thoughts of him pushing her back onto the sand and kissing her danced through her mind. Not that she thought things would last with that man either. She didn't.

Men left. It was what they did best.

"And give you babies to take to soccer practice?"

She tried not to let images of blue-eyed imps dribbling the ball toward the goal take over her mind. She did not want to have Vale's babies. She didn't want babies period.

Sure, the making them might be fun, but then she'd be like her mother, alone, raising a child.

Only her mother hadn't been able to stand being alone and had flitted from one loveless marriage to another, from one man who'd eventually leave her to another.

"I'm in no hurry at this point in my life to meet someone or even think about marriage and babies. My career is what's most important."

"Until you achieve your career goals?" he teased, but his eyes held a steely quality.

"It's not as if I'm going to reach a certain point, mark my career off my life to-do list, then move on to marriage and children, Vale." She glanced out at the horizon, spotting the silhouette of a ferry off in the distance. "Just that at some point down the line I'd like to believe I can have all the things I want."

She wouldn't remind him that what she wanted was a real house with a real yard for her dog to play in. No man required.

"You're a special woman, Faith. If anyone can ever have it all, I'm sure it's you."

She glanced at him, saw the sincerity on his face, and smiled. "Thank you, Vale. That quite simply might be the nicest thing you've ever said to me."

"You jest." His forehead wrinkled. "I've complimented you before."

"About my work, yes. Me? No."

He stopped walking, turned to face her. His hand squeezed hers reassuringly. "Just tonight I told you what a beautiful woman you are."

"Tthat's d-different," she stammered, wondering at the light in his eyes. Was it the reflection of the last golden rays dancing across the sky? Or was Vale looking at her as if she really was beautiful?

His brow lifted. "Because you don't believe me when I say that you are beautiful?"

"I've seen the women you date. I'm not even in the same league." Models, actresses, heiresses, he went through them all.

"True," he agreed, twisting the knife in her gut. He could at least have been polite and not said anything.

She'd never have him, knew she never would, and was foolish to have these momentary lapses where she dreamed she might.

"None of the women I've known hold a candle to you, Faith. Not a single one."

She wanted to look away, wanted to shield her eyes from his, but she couldn't. Not when he looked at her as if he believed what he said, as if he really did believe she was more beautiful than the women he escorted to New York's finest venues. What else had they put in her hair color other than truth serum? A dose of *hear what you want to hear*?

"Thank you," she said for lack of knowing what else to say but knowing the situation called for something. She was imagining the softening of his gaze, the pressure of his hand holding hers. "That's a kind thing to say."

"You don't make me feel kind, Faith."

She stared up at him. "No?"

"No." Had his mouth moved closer to hers?

She licked her lips, nervously, yet even as she did so, she'd instinctively known his gaze would follow her movements. She wasn't a fool, wasn't imagining this chemistry between them. Truth serum, gullibility, whatever, the sparks arcing between them would light up lower Manhattan. "What do I make you feel, Vale?"

* * *

Great question and one Vale wasn't sure of the answer to.

He wanted her. Which surprised him. Usually he was either instantly attracted to a woman or he wasn't attracted at all.

With all women, he got what he wanted with little effort. Faith was different. He'd spent more time with her than with any other woman, knew her better, had let her know him better, yet what did he really know? Not even the name of her mysterious boyfriend.

Vale immediately lowered his mouth to cover hers, telling himself the surge of emotion in his chest was not jealousy of a man he'd never met. Whatever, Faith's lips were sweet beneath his and pleasure soon replaced the unwanted emotional surge.

Soft, full, yielding, yet demanding, she returned his kiss. If there was another man in her life, their relationship couldn't be too serious. Otherwise Faith wouldn't kiss him back. Yet she didn't do so whole-heartedly, which gave him pause. He could read her every thought, feel the conflicting sensations swirling inside that brilliant mind of hers. She wanted him, yet she didn't.

He understood perfectly because he felt exactly the same.

"I want to make love to you, Faith, but I'm not willing to ruin our professional relationship."

Her eyes widened at his admission, greener than the most precious emerald.

"You're more important to me than a quick rumble between the sheets." His words said one thing, but he asked her a question with his eyes. A question he knew the answer to, but asked all the same in the hope he was wrong about Faith.

"Professional relationship at stake or not, I'm not willing

to be just a rumble between any man's sheets, Vale. I'm not you. I don't do casual sex."

He'd known, but still disappointment filled him at her response.

"Understood." He ran his fingers along her cheek, thinking her more beautiful than the sunset, more tempting than any siren of the sea, more precious than any gem in a treasure trove, loving how his name sounded on her lips. "But another kiss wouldn't hurt anything."

"No." Her lips hovered centimeters from his mouth, her breath warm, inviting, making him want more than she was willing to give. "One more kiss wouldn't hurt, Vale. But just one more because I won't be one of your girls. We aren't having a weekend fling or rumble between your sheets or whatever you want to call it."

"Okay," he agreed, breathing in her warm, vanilla scent, so clean and refreshing, like her. "Just one more kiss because you aren't one of my girls and don't want to be a rumble between my sheets this weekend."

He continued to tell himself once more while he kissed Faith reverently, his hands cupping her face, his fingers partially threaded into her pulled-up hair, his gaze locked with hers.

The kiss was gentle, searching, desperate and yet lingering as if they had all the time in the world to explore each other's lips. It was a kiss unlike any Vale had ever experienced.

A kiss that made him wonder what else with Faith would be like nothing he'd ever experienced.

That wonder both thrilled him and scared the living hell out of him.

Feeling like a plucked chicken in a room full of swans, Faith sat in the upstairs media room with the women staying at the Wakefields' Cape May mansion. Sharon, Angela, two of Sharon's college friends, Vale's other cousin Monica, and Steve's younger sister, Francis Woodard. Vale's mother and Sharon's parents had retired to bed around ten, claiming they were too tired to sit up with the younger women and reminding Sharon to be sure to get her beauty sleep so she wouldn't have bags under her eyes.

The men had gone out for drinks and Steve's bachelor party, Vale included. Each second that ticked by brought his return closer. And when he returned they'd be expected to share a bedroom. Did Vale sleep in pajamas? Or would he slide between the sheets in nothing more than he'd brought into the world?

"Tell us," Francis cried after downing a shot of something bright red and grabbing Faith's hand, pulling her from her meanderings. "What's it like, dating Very Scrumptious Vale?"

She didn't want to lie, but what could she say? "Mostly, we just work together."

"Honey, we all saw that kiss down on the beach." Francis fanned her face with exaggeration. "If you were on the clock, sign me up for medical school."

Faith's face burned. Okay, so the groom's little sister had a point. But how did she explain what she didn't understand herself?

"It's complicated."

"Love always is," Sharon sighed.

"We're not in love," Faith quickly denied, unwilling to perpetuate the misconception.

"I saw the way Vale looks at you." At Faith's raised eyebrow, Sharon went on. "He looked at you as if you're the only woman in the world, as if he would have liked to push you down in the sand and made love to you right there, the world be damned." She smiled, taking on a dreamy look. "I know love. It's exactly the same way Steve looks at me."

"You're mistaken." Vale had looked at her with lust because she was convenient, because they were at a wedding and people did stupid things at weddings. Like get married and believe in happily ever after.

"I know Vale," Sharon boasted. "He wants you."

Yes, he'd told her that. And, truth was, just having Vale desire her was so much more than she'd ever dreamed possible. So why had she said no?

He hadn't said the words out loud, but essentially he'd been asking her to have an affair with him. A fling that would last the weekend and be done when they left the magic of the beach.

But she couldn't say yes, not when she'd be expected to work side by side with him as if nothing had happened.

Lord, how was she going to work with him night after late night now that she knew his kisses tasted of ambrosia?

"Oh," Sharon cooed, "you're in love with him, aren't you?"

Faith opened her mouth, ready to deny his cousin's claim, but nothing came out. Nothing at all, because she didn't know how she felt about Vale. Not any more. From before they'd met, she'd admired him professionally, had known she wanted to work with him, had used every resource within her repertoire to arrange an interview. When they'd met, she'd been thunderstruck by emotion so potent the magnitude had almost blinded her.

She admired Vale, professionally and personally, although she'd hesitate to admit the latter to anyone other than herself. Physically she wanted him, but what heterosexual woman wouldn't?

This weekend she had the opportunity to be with him

and was too scared to accept the risk that chance would change everything between them. Bok. Bok.

Only sometimes change was inevitable, and inevitably her relationship with Vale had undergone a change she couldn't undo even if she wanted to.

Taking that chance would strip her soul bare, would let him see into her heart, and therein lay the problem.

She didn't want to give Vale that power over her future. Didn't want to become her mother, settling for whoever came along because she'd tasted love and couldn't hold on to it, forever searching to feed a hunger that couldn't be satisfied.

No, she didn't love Vale and would never, ever allow herself to be that foolish.

CHAPTER FIVE

FAITH tossed and turned in the enormous bed in the giant bedroom their suitcases had been placed in. How could she sleep when eventually Vale would return? Would be sleeping in the same room? Possibly crawl between the sheets beside her if she didn't stay awake and order him to the sofa?

Although his family had been nothing but kind to her, she'd had a difficult time relaxing. How could she fit in when their conversation ran from spending the month in Europe at their favorite French resort to having their thighs liposuctioned in Beverly Hills?

Which should only serve as yet another reminder of why she shouldn't become involved with Vale this weekend. Despite how dedicated he was to his career, to finding a treatment or, better yet, a cure for Parkinson's, the reality was he moved in a different world from that she did.

A jiggle of the doorhandle had her breath catching. Vale.

Peeking through barely open eyes, she took in the outline of his sleek body in the doorframe. So beautiful. So tempting.

Softly, he closed the door, walked over to the sofa and sank down onto the leather. She could feel his gaze on her, could feel his presence so overwhelmingly that she swore the room pulsed with him. His scent. His aura. His heartbeat.

Forcing her breathing to remain even, she closed her eyes completely, feigning sleep. She couldn't deal with him. Not tonight. Not if she didn't want to do something she might regret.

Might, because she wasn't sure.

Perhaps not doing something would be more regrettable than taking action?

She just didn't know, didn't have the experience to know, and for that reason she'd pretend to be asleep to avoid having to act.

"Faith?" he whispered, almost as if he knew she was faking.

She didn't answer and after a few moments he sighed, but didn't call her bluff.

Instead, he disappeared into the en suite bathroom, returned, and slid between the sheets. Next to her.

Would it give away that she was awake if she piled pillows between them? Or if she peeked under the covers to see what he was wearing? *Or not wearing?*

She swallowed, fighting to breathe, fighting to keep her eyes closed in case he was looking at her and could see her through the sliver of moonlight breaking the darkness, fighting to keep from scooting next to him, spooning her body to his.

Because, really, if she did that while still feigning sleep, what would it hurt? She could always plead that she'd gotten cold. Which didn't explain the droplets of sweat forming between her breasts.

She bit the inside of her lower lip, forced herself to count sheep, to count the soft sounds of Vale's even breathing. That he'd crawled into bed and fallen immediately to sleep didn't say much about her effect on him, did it? He was in bed with her for the first time ever and had immediately dozed off.

The last time she recalled taking a peek at him soft streaks of sunrise had started filtering into the room. His dark head lay against the pillow, his lashes fanned out across his cheeks, his face relaxed in sleep.

Unable to resist, she reached out, brushed her fingertip across his cheek, marveling at the smooth perfection of his skin, at how her heart raced at the contact.

Without his expression changing in the slightest to indicate he'd awakened, his hand caught hers, clasped it to him. Faith watched his face for some sign she'd woken him, but none was forthcoming. Neither was escaping his death grip, so she relaxed, cherishing the contact of their skin.

Her hand cradled in his, she finally drifted off into dream-filled sleep.

With the sun streaming into the room through the magnificent windows, Faith woke very aware that she was in Vale's king-size bed that smelled of his spicy aftershave.

She opened her eyes, startled to find the bed empty.

Only the imprint on the pillow next to hers told the tale that he'd shared the bed, that she wasn't imagining his musky scent. Unable to resist, she reached out, touched where his head had lain, calling herself every kind of stupid.

She'd touched him during the night. Had he woken up and known of her foolishness? God, she hoped not.

Slowly, she became more aware of her surroundings. She'd been too restless the night before to fully appreciate the bedroom suite.

Double glass doors led out onto a balcony that ran the length of the room. Pale blue walls with clean lines were broken only by the huge windows and a gorgeous seaside painting. Wow. A panoramic view of the ocean took her breath, easily visible even while lying in the bed. A two-sided glass fireplace divided the room, separating a living area with a sofa and television from the bed area. A couple of medical magazines cluttered the solid mahogany end table. To the far end of the living area a desk with a state-of-the-art computer was set up. A yellow legal pad had notes scribbled on the top page in Vale's distinctive penmanship. Had he worked this morning before leaving the room?

This wasn't a guest suite. This was Vale's room. If she walked to the closet, his clothes would be hanging there. Those had been his personal items in the en suite bathroom, which was bigger than her entire apartment, and not because he'd brought them from home. No wonder he hadn't carried more than his small overnight bag, so sharply contrasting with her large suitcase. He hadn't had to.

But what she didn't see in the room was Vale. Where was he? Had he wakened, taken one look at her, and been frightened away? Probably, she mused. As much as she'd tossed and turned prior to his arrival in the bed, she imagined her hair was every which way.

Stretching, Faith decided she'd get up, shower, and go in search of her host. Only before she'd so much as lowered her arms the door opened and Vale entered, carrying a tray full of breakfast goodies that had her stomach growling in appreciation.

"Good morning, sunshine," he greeted her, fully dressed in khaki slacks that hugged his narrow hips, a white button-down with the sleeves rolled up on his tanned forearms and a sexy V exposing where the top two buttons were undone at his neck.

He'd been the one out partying all night so it was totally

unfair that he looked marvelous, and she suddenly recalled the fact she'd just woken up, looked horrendous with not a speck of her new make-up, and her hair wild as Friday evening rush-hour traffic.

She winced, fighting the urge to try to tame the messy strands about her head. No doubt she looked like Medusa with hair snaking about her head in every direction.

"Good morning, yourself." She scooted up in the bed, only to become conscious of her pajamas. During her shopping spree she hadn't considered sleepwear, had never dreamed she and Vale would be thrown into the same room by his mother. She didn't expect her fuzzy *Star Wars* pajama bottoms and T-shirt top to start any fires.

Hold up. Did she want to start fires? Hadn't she told herself time and again while lying in his bed last night that she needed to keep distance between them this weekend if she didn't want to destroy her career? If she made love with Vale, no way could she continue to work with him when he moved on to another woman. To do so would be torture of the cruelest kind.

She considered herself a modern woman, but she didn't do casual sex. She didn't do sex at all.

She flopped back on her pillow with a sleepy sigh.

"Not a morning person?" he teased, placing the tray on the bed. "I brought you breakfast."

She glanced down at the tray. Fresh fruit, yogurt, bagels with peanut butter, juice, milk, a pot of coffee, and…she lifted a metal lid off a plate…eggs, bacon, sausage links, and toast with butter and jelly.

"You don't really expect me to eat all this?"

His gaze raked down her bare arms, instantly covering her with goose-bumps of awareness. *She was in his bed.* Could he see how her nipples strained toward him? She hoped not.

"Wouldn't hurt you if you did," he assured her, "but I thought you might share."

Not waiting for her to respond, he climbed into the bed beside her. Faith grabbed for the tray, certain the contents would topple, but it didn't budge. What kind of mattress was this anyway? A very expensive one, she decided, trying to ignore Vale's long frame stretched out beside her, fluffing pillows behind his back. Trying to ignore that now every cell in her body strained toward him as if she were metal and he the most powerful of magnets.

Mr. Magnetism pulled back a plastic wrap and spread cream cheese on a bagel, offering the pastry to her. "Have fun with the girls last night?"

Reaching for the bagel, she nodded. "You have a lovely family, Vale."

"Lovely?" He curled his nose, preparing a plate of food for himself. "They've snookered you."

"And you?" she asked, popping a bite of the bagel into her mouth. "Did you have fun with the boys, doing all those wild bachelor party things men do?"

She'd meant her question to be teasing, casual, but when he turned to her there was nothing teasing in his eyes, nothing casual in the way her heart mimicked a space-shuttle launch.

"I'd rather have been with you."

Vale watched Faith's eyes darken to a deep green at his admission. He wasn't accustomed to things spouting out of his mouth that he hadn't planned to say. But his words were true.

He would much rather have been here with Faith than at Steve's bachelor party.

Several of the groom's football buddies had apparently thrown him a huge bachelor party in Philadelphia the weekend before so last night's had been more about tradition than one last yahoo on the town.

The entire time Vale had wondered what Faith was doing, how she was getting on with his family.

He wondered that a lot these days. He'd be sitting at home and would glance at his watch and wonder if she'd still be awake and, if so, what she was doing. Sometimes he wondered if Faith wasn't why he worked so many hours, just so he'd have an excuse to see her.

Which was crazy. If he wanted to see her outside work, all he had to do was ask her out.

But something in the way her green eyes darkened and her bagel stopped halfway to her mouth told him maybe that wasn't all he had to do.

Which was perhaps why he'd never asked her out.

That and the fact she had a bright career ahead of her at the clinic and didn't need personal issues muddying the waters. He didn't need personal issues muddying the waters. Other women were disposable in his life, but he enjoyed working with Faith. Enjoyed the constant she provided.

"Was Steve's party not a success?" Her gaze didn't quite meet his.

"Bachelor parties aren't my thing." Did she have any idea how beautiful she was this morning? He'd wondered about her hair—now he knew. The long tousled-from-sleep golden strands looked like extensions of the sunbeams streaming in through the windows, casting a halo around her angelic face.

Her eyes were huge, her lips full, her face naturally classic. He'd never wanted to brush his fingers over a woman's skin more. Never wanted to tangle his fingers in a woman's hair more. Never wanted to kiss a woman more.

Never wanted to be inside a woman more.

Which was why he should climb out of the bed just as he'd done after lying next to her for a couple of hours, unable to sleep for the temptation of her sweet vanilla fragrance and warm body. He'd not slept a wink and had known he wasn't going to with her lying next to him. Still, he'd lain next to her, knowing she was feigning sleep and wondering why she bothered, wondered why he himself bothered. Had she thought he'd force her into something she didn't want? That he'd seduce his way beneath those awful fuzzy pajamas she wore?

When she'd touched his face, he'd thought he imagined the light touch and had instinctively clasped her hand. Lying in his bed, holding Faith's hand, had felt right, but had left him throbbing with need. After she'd gone to sleep properly, he'd risen, logged into his computer, and gotten some work done, all the while distracted by Faith in his bed and by how much he wanted to wake her with his mouth, his hands, his body over hers, moving in hers.

"Is there anything about weddings you like?" she asked, apparently oblivious to where his thoughts had gone. Or purposely ignoring that he was likely looking at her as if he'd like to have her for breakfast.

"Open bar?"

"Besides the free booze?" She popped the torn-off piece of bagel into her mouth and he envied the food.

"The cake?" Why was he imagining that pink tongue of hers licking frosting from her lips? His tongue cleaning a spot she missed?

Her gaze met his. "Be serious."

"I am." He seriously wanted to push her back on his bed and settle between her thighs and *seriously* make her orgasm over and over.

"No, you're not."

She thought not? He shrugged. "I imagine the honeymoons aren't bad."

She rolled her eyes. "You would think that."

"You asked." He picked up a strawberry and placed the fruit on her plump lips.

Her pupils dilated as she stared at him with a "What are you doing?" expression, but she took a bite of the berry, wiping at the juice that covered her lips. "Thank you."

"You're welcome." His pants shrunk around him, restraining him. What would she do if he really did push her back on the bed, stripped those hideous pajamas off her, and ran his tongue over her, tracing a path to her core and dipping inside?

"What are you doing, Vale?"

His gaze shot to hers, saw the uncertainty shining in her eyes. "What do you mean?"

"This." She spread her arm toward the tray. "I'm your colleague, not your girlfriend. You shouldn't be serving me breakfast in bed or feeding me strawberries. This is crazy."

"This weekend, for all intents and purposes, you are my girl."

"Vale…" She took a deep breath, swallowed. "I won't be used just because I'm convenient."

Convenient? "You think I want to make love to you because you're convenient?"

"Let's be real here, Vale. We've known each other for months and you've not exactly had to hold yourself back to keep from ripping my clothes off."

He couldn't deny her claim. Yet… "You're different from the other women in my life, Faith. You have been from the beginning."

"Because I'm one of the few women under forty you

haven't jumped into bed with," she pointed out with a snort that didn't come across as being quite natural.

"Actually…" he gestured to where they were "…I have jumped into bed with you, but that isn't the point."

She regarded him with obvious frustration and confusion. "Just how many women have you jumped into bed with that you haven't had sex with?"

"None," he answered immediately.

"One," she corrected, picking up a strawberry and biting into the juicy flesh.

"Yet." Because he was damned sure he was going to make love to her soon. Today. Never had he wanted a woman so much. But he shouldn't make love to her. Deep in the recesses of his brain, he knew he should keep his hands off Faith.

"I thought we decided to end this madness last night with the kiss on the beach? That our having sex would ruin our professional relationship?"

"Tell me, Faith, when you closed your eyes last night, did memories of that kiss fill your head as you drifted to sleep? Did you dream about me waking you with my hands on your body, my mouth on yours?"

"No."

But she was lying. That was why she'd touched his face, his lips. She'd been wondering what them making love would be like.

"When I came in here last night, found you in my bed, I wanted to strip you naked and make love to you. Good thing you were asleep or I might have."

With a guilty wince, she averted her gaze. "You were drunk."

"If I'd been drunk, we'd be having a morning after." Stone-cold sober, it had taken all his willpower not to pull her to him and kiss away any objection she made.

"A morning after where you reminded me that sex with you means nothing?" Her brow lifted accusingly. "That I'm nothing more than a quick rumble between your sheets which I've already told you I refuse to be?"

Was that what he'd be telling Faith if they'd had sex? It was what he'd be reminding any other woman of, what he'd have stressed long before they'd got to the bedroom. Yet the thought of telling Faith that she meant nothing to him other than mutual physical satisfaction didn't sit well with his conscience.

Yet he didn't want more than mutual physical satisfaction with any woman. Not even Faith. Just look at how his few relationship attempts had ended when he'd involved more than his body. Not good and not something he'd repeat.

"I don't know the answers to your question, Faith," he answered honestly, struggling with his conflicting desires where Faith was concerned. "Like I said, you aren't like other women."

"Because I work for you?"

"Maybe." He enjoyed working with her, enjoyed the sharp way her mind tackled problems, came up with innovative solutions, the way her eyes lit up when they operated successfully, when they discovered a new abnormal neuronal pathway trend on the brain maps Brainiac Codex generated on their Parkinson patients.

"I like my job, Vale. A weekend romp with you isn't worth destroying my career or placing myself in a position where I'd be forced to relocate."

That said it all. A weekend romp wasn't worth losing his relationship with her either. Was that why he'd let her feign sleep when he'd wanted nothing more than to spread her legs and lose himself? They'd said as much the night before but, having spent the night tormented with being so close to her yet so far away, he'd lost sight of that. Something he couldn't allow himself to do. Otherwise he'd seduce Faith before the weekend ended, and then where would they be?

Other than blissfully sexually satisfied, that was?

Faith could easily have felt like a fifth wheel with all the wedding activities. Between Vale's constant attention and his family including her as if she'd been a part of the family for eons, only the occasional doubt plagued her. Sharon Wakefield had been a doll, more genuine and kind than Faith would have believed possible of someone so physically flawless.

Most of the day had been planned to a T, but not long after lunch Faith had time on her hands and a heart longing to walk on the beach. She wore white Capris, a silky green top the sales clerk had said perfectly matched her eyes, and sandals she could easily kick off for a beach walk.

First telling Virginia that she was going to take a walk, Faith weaved her way through the flowers, chairs, and wedding regalia, to head down the path toward the water.

Once barefoot on the sand, she opted to head in the opposite direction from the one she and Vale had taken the night before. She'd had enough problems keeping her mind off him today without reminders of that kiss. A long walk on the beach would do her good, would help clear her mind so she could think straight.

"Hey, wait up."

On hearing Vale's voice, she bit back both a sigh of appreciation and a wince at not having the much-needed break from his overwhelming appeal.

"I thought Sharon needed you?" She waited while he rolled up his pants to mid-calf, exposing the sprinkling of dark hair covering his legs. Faith gulped back another sigh, staring down at his bent head. Sunshine glistened off the natural lights in his thick locks, off the flexed muscles in his neck.

He glanced up, caught her watching him, and grinned. "Sharon can get by without me for a few minutes. She has everyone else jumping to her tune."

"It's her wedding day. Everyone should be jumping to her tune. Besides, you don't have to entertain me 24/7," she responded, resuming her walk along the edge of the water. "I'm a big girl and can take a walk on the beach by myself."

"I know you can, but humor me. I've had about all the wedding I can stand and the ceremony hasn't even begun yet."

That, Faith understood. For a few brief moments every now and again she got caught up in Sharon's excitement, forgot how much she detested weddings, but most of the time that same old pain gnawed in her belly.

"I'm no more a fan of weddings than you are."

"Because of your mother?" He fell into step beside her.

"I suppose." She didn't want to talk about her mother and her many weddings. Not on the beach with Vale on the day of his cousin's wedding. The only wedding Faith had agreed to attend other than her mother's. She'd refused every single invitation from friends, had pleaded out of the weddings of two med-school friends who'd asked her to be a bridesmaid. Yet Vale had convinced her to come this weekend without too much cajoling. Why was that?

"How many husbands has she had?"

Why did he always push when she wanted him to leave a subject alone?

"John's her sixth." She stepped into the oncoming wave nipping at her feet.

"Ouch."

"Yes, ouch." And not the cold Atlantic water rushing around her ankles, although that had definitely bitten. "It's difficult to watch her make the same mistakes over and over."

Having stopped beside her, he considered her answer. "They're her mistakes to make."

"True, but you'd think she'd eventually learn."

"Maybe she's just lonely."

"A person doesn't have to get married to abate loneliness. She could have gotten a dog, you know."

His expression became thoughtful and he asked a bit too casually, "Like Yoda?"

She spun toward him. "Yoda is my best friend and not because I'm lonely. Far from it."

Had she sounded defensive? What was she saying? She *was* defensive.

"A dog is your best friend?"

"Obviously you've never had a dog or you wouldn't ask that question." She glared at him. Of course he wouldn't understand. How could he? He'd probably never been lonely a day in his life and if he ever was, all he had to do was crook his sexy little finger and women would come running to do his bidding.

Not that she was lonely. She so wasn't.

"You're right," he admitted, meeting her glare head on. "I've never had a dog. I always wanted one while I was growing up, but Mom's allergic to pet dander."

"Poor little rich kid."

One side of his mouth lifted in a half-smile. "I'm not going to get any sympathy from you, am I?"

"No." She turned back, gestured to the mansion still easily visible in the distance. "That's your house, Vale. Not even your main house, but your East Coast beach house. It looks more like a modern-day castle."

"That's my mother's house. Not mine. I live in a Manhattan condominium."

"In a building your family owns." She took a deep breath, gave him her pretty-as-you-please smile. "Besides, the room where we slept, that's your room."

"How do you know?"

As if she could not know. "You're stamped all over the place."

He chuckled. "I'm what?"

"The medical magazines, the toiletries in the bathroom." She resumed walking away from the house. "I don't know specifically what it is, just that the room looks like you."

"I look like a bedroom?"

Oh, yeah, she looked at him and saw a big bed. With their naked bodies twined together. He looked like sex. Sex she couldn't have. Not with him, and she'd never wanted sex with anyone else. Why did he have to be the one to make her body come alive? Why him? A rich playboy who was her boss and frustrated her so much?

"Let's change the subject," she ground out, wanting to hit him for the mess he'd made of her emotions. She'd been able to keep her attraction to him neatly tucked away until this weekend.

Why had he had to push her into coming when she'd known she shouldn't?

Faith hadn't thought it possible that she'd doze off when Vale had ordered her to lie down for a nap—a nap!—while he showered. But her lack of sleep from the night before and the beach air must have been working on her because when she opened her eyes after what she'd thought had only been a few minutes, he had finished showering and was gone.

He'd left a note on the bedside table, saying he'd see her at the wedding but wouldn't likely come back to the room prior to the ceremony.

She glanced at her watch. Wow. She'd slept for almost two hours. She'd better get started or she'd be late.

Donning the dress she'd instantly known was "the one" when she'd seen it in the shop, she zipped the side zipper, loving the body-hugging shape of the emerald-colored dress with its flounced hemline.

Usually she dressed to blend in with her surroundings. As a woman competing in what many still considered a man's world, she'd always felt the need to tamp down her sexuality. Not today.

Today, she wanted to feel all woman.

Today, she did feel all woman.

Because of Vale and the way he kept looking at her.

She still wanted to pinch herself that he wanted her, that she was the one holding back on them having a weekend fling.

She had no doubt he was telling the truth when he said he wanted to have sex with her. Part of her thrilled that even that was possible after a year and a half of him seeing her as a sexless colleague.

But she knew his attraction was circumstantial. That he'd want to sleep with any halfway attractive woman he'd brought with him this weekend. It wasn't her specifically he wanted. Just that he was a highly sexual man and she was a young, healthy woman. Of course his hormones would be kicking in. She didn't fool herself that him wanting her could possibly mean more.

If she even slightly let herself believe him wanting her meant more, she'd be a goner.

Imitating the style the hairdresser had done the day before, Faith loosely piled her hair on top of her head, securing the strands with a rhinestone comb. She brushed make-up across her cheekbones, accented her eyes, painted and glossed her lips until she looked like a perpetual pouter.

When she'd finished, she stood back, surveying her handiwork. Not bad. Not enough to erase the first scary image of her that morning that was probably forever imprinted on Vale's brain, but not bad.

She made her way down one of the matching curved staircases, careful not to disturb the white silk ribbon and flowers tied to the handrail.

People were everywhere. Caterers, wedding guests, more family members and friends she only recognized from having seen their photos in magazines. What was she, Faith Fogarty, doing here in this paparazzi orgy?

Following the trail of people, she made her way to the back of the house, reminding herself with each step that she was a successful neurologist and she was here because Vale wanted her here. The patio area had been decorated with hundreds of white flowers and miles of white silk ribbon. Beyond the gated pool, a pristine white carpet ran the length of the rows of chairs to where the gazebo had been laced with white gardenias, vivid green leaves, and ribbon. The sun slowly beginning its descent toward the ocean provided the perfect backdrop.

If she wasn't so anti-weddings, she might think Sharon's wedding beautiful. Oh, who was she kidding? This was a beautiful wedding. Just as her mother's weddings had all been beautiful.

Just that, like the beauty of the sunset, none of the marriages lasted.

Where was the beauty of putting all your hopes and

dreams in another person only to have those hopes and dreams trampled on?

Would Sharon's wedding last? With her mega-wealth and role as former Miss Pennsylvania, she was a celebrity, just as her professional footballer husband was. The odds were against them even before they made their vows.

"You look absolutely stunning but, then, my son has superb taste," Vale's mother interrupted her thoughts, meeting Faith at the back of the chairs. "Come with me. The family is sitting up front."

Faith blinked at the woman wearing a designer dress that probably cost more than she made in a year. "I'm not family."

"Nonsense." Virginia smiled at her. "You're here with Vale. That makes you family."

Touched by the woman's continued unexpected generosity, Faith followed her to one of the front aisles and sat down. "Do you treat all Vale's guests so warmly?"

His mother's blue gaze, so similar to his, met Faith's. "If you're referring to the women in his life, he's never brought a *guest* to a family function. You're the first and only."

A warning went off in Faith's head, leaving her feeling dizzy and unsure of what she'd thought she'd known about him. "Vale's never… But…"

His mother laughed at her astounded expression. "I know my son is no saint. I see the pictures of him with all those women. But family functions aren't a place for him to bring some woman he's passing time with. He knows that. That's why we were all so excited when he said he was bringing you."

And Vale thought bringing her was going to protect him from his family? Hello, he'd created a whole new range of problems by bringing her.

"B-but we work t-together," she stammered, still digesting the news that Vale didn't bring women home. None of the beauties he wined or dined had ever slept in the big bed occupying his suite in the beach house. Just her.

"Which explains why my son works so much." Her eyes twinkling with delight, Virginia patted Faith's hand. "You don't have to explain your relationship with Vale to me. Just know that I'm happy you're here. We all are because it's been so long since Vale's let down those shields of his."

Faith wanted to crawl under the seat at the hopeful anticipation in his mother's eyes. Besides, what was she referring to? Vale's shields? That made it sound as if Vale had once had his heart broken. Had he? It seemed a strange thought. Faith couldn't imagine any woman not falling under Vale's spell. The man was a hypnotist, a wizard of wondrous proportions when it came to wielding power over the opposite sex.

"Vale and I really are more friends."

His mother's penciled on brows rose in perfect arches. "Are you saying I'm wrong? That you're not in love with my son?"

She studied her so intently Faith closed her eyes, took a deep breath. "You're not wrong."

Faith swallowed. Hard. Had she really just said she loved Vale? She didn't. *Did she?* Sure, she was fascinated by him, admired him, wanted him. What sane woman didn't? But love? Did such a fanciful emotion even exist?

Dear Lord. He was a hypnotist and she'd fallen completely under his spell this weekend.

"Good." Virginia squeezed her hand. "Now, let's sit back and enjoy this wedding we've been planning for years. I can't believe our little Sharon is all grown up and getting married."

Faith couldn't figure out how to politely remove her

hand from Vale's mother's so she left it. Seconds later the groom and his men came to stand at the gazebo and Faith could only stare at Vale, in awe at how handsome he looked in his tuxedo, how tall and confident, how he completely outshone the groom and every other man who'd ever lived.

He took her breath away in his black and white tuxedo. Somewhere in the time since she'd last seen him he'd had a haircut and fresh shave. He came to a stop in his designated place, his hands clasped in front of him, his eyes immediately searching out hers.

When he spotted her, his gaze lingered on hers a moment, then raked over her, taking in her appearance, appreciation glimmering in his eyes when they returned to hers.

"You're beautiful," he mouthed, obviously not caring who saw.

Faith blushed, feeling as if she'd just won the lottery.

"So are you," she whispered back, wondering if he'd be able to read her lips, if he'd see how much she wanted him at that moment, how no one existed for her except him.

One corner of his mouth lifted in a pleased grin and he winked.

Faith's brain went fuzzy and she couldn't breathe.

A tight squeeze of her hand had her breaking away from Vale's gaze to stare half-unseeing at his mother.

"Looks as if we'll be planning another wedding by Christmas," she said excitedly, smiling at Faith.

Another wedding?

"Not my wedding. Uh-uh. No way." She shook her head, knowing that, regardless of how Vale made her feel, she didn't want to marry him. Never, ever would she set herself up for that kind of failure, that kind of disappointment. Having watched her mother's heart break time and again,

Faith would never go through that. Never. "I don't want to get married to Vale, or any other man."

Virginia frowned, but didn't have a chance to comment as the small orchestra set up along the back of the yard began to play. Bridesmaid after bridesmaid walked up the rose-petal-strewn carpet until the wedding march sounded.

Everyone in the crowd stood, turned to see the bride in all her spectacular glory.

Faith was sure Sharon made a beautiful bride, but her vision had clouded over and she saw another wedding, another bride. Although she tried to choke them back, tears streamed down her cheeks now as they had then. Tears of pain and sorrow. Tears of loss. Tears of knowing her heart would never be complete again.

Her mother's wedding.

The first of several that had followed over the years.

She never wanted to be like her mother. Yet wasn't she?

Tears flowed at the realization she wasn't so dissimilar after all, despite years of walking a straight and narrow path, putting her education, her career before all else. Still, she'd foolishly done as her mother had, doomed herself to wanting a man she'd never really have. Vale.

"Here's a tissue, dear." Virginia pushed a clean but wadded tissue paper into her hand. "I came prepared as I always cry at weddings too."

Embarrassed that she was weeping at a virtual stranger's wedding, Faith took the tissue, knowing nothing would dry the tears that would flow when Vale broke her heart, as he inevitably would.

Because if he really wanted her he'd have her before the weekend ended and there was nothing she could do to stop him unless she left right this very moment.

CHAPTER SIX

How many photos did one need at a wedding? Too many, Vale decided a half-hour after the ceremony had ended and the photographer was still imitating a general on the battlefield. Forcing yet another smile, he held his pose.

He'd had enough and just wanted to go find Faith to see if she was okay.

When the rest of the guests had been looking at Sharon walking down the aisle toward her groom, Vale had been watching Faith, noticed she'd only half turned, had seen the tears in her eyes.

Not tears of joy over the bride-to-be's happiness, but tears of sorrow and pain. Tears that alluded to past hurts.

Instinctively he knew Faith's hang-up with weddings had to do with her mother, probably to do with her numerous weddings. Faith had admitted as much without telling him any real details. He'd wanted to ditch his role in the wedding and go to her, comfort her, take her in his arms and kiss her until she never cried again.

Had his mother not turned, handed Faith the tissue, not patted her hand in comfort, not reminded him with a quick meeting of the eyes that he had a duty to Sharon not to ruin her special day, maybe he would have. He certainly hadn't been thinking of his cousin when he'd spotted Faith's tears.

All he'd been thinking about had been the woman he couldn't stop thinking about, the woman he'd watched sleep, wondering what it was about her that fascinated him so. He'd known she was hurting and he'd wanted to go to her.

How had his mother known to turn, to catch him watching Faith, to see his inner turmoil over her tears?

Maybe a mother just knew. His certainly always had.

"I've had enough," he announced to no one in particular. "Any other photos requiring my presence will have to be taken later."

The photographer must have been finished with him anyway because no one seemed to mind when he left the wedding party to find Faith.

The guests had been served a sit-down meal and Faith had to be at one of the long white tables dotted across the lawn or inside the tent. But he didn't spot her. Not even with his mother, which is where he expected to find Faith.

His mother's gaze shifted purposefully toward the house and he sent her a silent "Thank you".

She wasn't downstairs, so he headed up to his suite.

"Faith?" he called when he entered his room, not seeing her in the sitting area. When he turned toward the bathroom she was coming out, another tissue in her hand. Some of her hair had worked loose from its upswept style. Her nose was red and her eyes puffy. Her make-up was slightly smudged.

"What are you doing in here?" she asked, looking at him in confusion. "Aren't you needed for photos?"

He couldn't move, could only stare at her and wonder at the pangs in his chest. "You've been crying."

She winced, wiping at her eyes as if that would somehow

disguise the truth from him. "It's nothing. Weddings make me cry, that's all."

She was a horrible liar and unaccustomed guilt hit him.

"I shouldn't have made you come with me this weekend. You told me you didn't like weddings and I didn't listen."

She forced a small smile. "It's okay, Vale. I need to get over my phobia about weddings. Besides, you needed me to protect you from your mother's matchmaking."

Rubbish, he thought. He could handle his mother. Sure, she'd been hinting more and more for him to find someone to share his life with, telling him he worked too much, needed to enjoy life, and had paraded female after female in his path the last time he'd visited. Having Faith at his side had ensured she wouldn't do that, making his weekend less complicated. Only perhaps having Faith at his side had complicated things in ways he wouldn't be able to easily undo. Regardless, at the moment all he wanted was to protect her, to take away her pain and promise her everything would be okay.

Whatever the everything that had upset her was.

Was he right and it had to do with her mother or was her phobia something more personal? Had Faith been engaged in the past? Married even?

His chest pang grew stronger.

"I wanted you with me, Faith." He pulled her into his arms and she willingly went, laying her head against his tuxedo and wrapping her arms around his waist. The pang clawed at his throat, threatening to give him heartburn. "But it was unfair of me to force you to come to something that obviously distresses you so much. I'm sorry."

* * *

In all the time Faith had known Vale she'd never heard him say he was sorry. Not that he was the type of man who thought he was too good to do so, just that he was rarely wrong. Maybe never.

"It really is okay, Vale," she breathed against his chest, loving the strength she found in his arms, loving how tightly he held her, as if he planned to hold her for ever. "I wanted to be with you this weekend, too."

Now, that was really stupid. Why was she telling him that? The next thing she'd be blurting out that she was in love with him. She wasn't in love with him. This wasn't love.

"I mean…" Oh, what did she mean? With him holding her, she couldn't think and her mind had already been cloudy from her cry-fest. Silly that weddings made her sad, made her miss her father, made her wonder if she'd been responsible for him leaving, and if she was doomed to repeat her mother's mistakes.

"I don't know what I mean, Vale. I'm so confused about everything this weekend. Weddings confuse me. You confuse me. The way I want you, yet I know I shouldn't." There she went, saying stupid things again. "I can't seem to think about anything but you, Vale. Make it go away."

He tilted her chin, stared into her eyes, then did what she wanted more than anything, what she'd been waiting for nearly a lifetime. He kissed her with all the passion of a man who wanted a woman intensely. With all the gentleness of someone who cared about her and didn't want her to hurt, who really did want her pain to go away. He kissed her with all the fierceness of a man who wouldn't be denied, a man used to conquering the world.

Faith kissed him back with matching passion, gentleness, and fierceness, but also with everything in her heart, knowing that he alone could take away the ache in her chest, that only he could make her feel whole.

Was that love? Was that what she was feeling for him?

She couldn't think of that now. Not while he was touching her.

He trailed kisses over her exposed neck, onto her bare shoulders. Cupping her bottom, he held her to his groin, pressing her into where he'd grown hard for her.

For her.

Because he wanted her.

And she wanted him.

For once she wasn't going to deny herself a guilty pleasure, wasn't going to deny herself what she'd likely spend every day of the rest of her life regretting.

She'd regret not making love to Vale more. Lots more.

She kissed his throat, tugging on his bow-tie to loosen the material so she'd have better access to his body. She kissed the open V of his tanned chest when he tossed the tie to the floor, undoing the top couple of buttons. She continued to kiss him while her fingers worked the remainder of his buttons loose and pushed his shirt open, exposing the ripped planes of his abdomen.

"You have a beautiful body," she praised. A gorgeous body that looked more like it belonged on a pin-up poster than a physician.

"Isn't that my line?" A half laugh, half groan sounded from deep in his chest, changing to a full-blown moan when she bent and kissed his flat belly.

"Faith," he growled from beneath clenched teeth, "you'd better know what you're doing because my willpower is almost gone. Has been almost gone from the moment I spotted you at the wedding. I wanted to ditch the ceremony and carry you up here, spend the night making love to you."

He'd thought all that when he'd looked at her? When he'd told her she was beautiful?

She rubbed her cheek across the sculpted planes of his lower abdomen, loving his indrawn breath, how he pulled her to his mouth, pressing a kiss to her lips.

"Much more of that and I'm going to push you back against my bed and make you mine," he breathed against her mouth. His fingers bit into her bottom, grinding her against him. His gaze held hers, branding her with his hot desire. "All mine. Be sure this is what you want or stop me now because I want you."

Did he intend his words to deter her? Because if he was almost gone, she was all the way. Gone out of her mind with need and longing and the desire to feel wanted, loved, to be enough for someone. To be Vale's whole world, even if for just a few moments in time.

Rather than heed caution, she slid her hands beneath the open flaps of his shirt and pushed the material off his shoulders, letting her fingers trace over the taut muscles. "I don't want your reason, Vale. I want you to make love to me."

"Faith." His eyes deep blue seas, he shrugged out of his shirt and claimed her lips again. He feasted on her mouth, drawing out every morsel of pleasure within her, making her tingle from head to toe in sheer awareness of her very being.

She wound her arms around his neck, ran her fingers through the short hair at his nape, held him to her.

Not that she needed to hang on to him.

Vale wasn't going anywhere. He wanted, needed, as much as she did. His fingers had worked up her skirt, bunching the clingy material at her waist, revealing the garter and thigh-highs she'd bought to go beneath her dress.

"Faith," he hissed against her mouth, leaning from her long enough to take in her new sexy undergarments. "You're killing me."

She might have felt embarrassed except for the raw desire shining in his eyes. No way could she want to do anything except stand in the glow of his gaze when he looked at her as if he'd just awakened on Christmas morning and found exactly what he wanted beneath his tree. Her.

Thank God she'd listened to the saleslady and bought new underwear to go with her weekend wardrobe. The scraps of silk and lace had been worth every high-priced penny.

"Faith," he repeated, tugging her back to him, his groin thrusting hard against her belly, his hands everywhere on her body. "I want you so much."

She'd have told him to take her, but he was kissing her again, so she told him with her mouth, her hands, her body, with every fiber of her being.

She lowered his zipper, sliding his pants down his thighs and marveling at his body, at his reaction to her every touch, marveling at her boldness with his body.

She freed him, encircling him with her hands, stroking over the silky smooth skin. He was big, hard, jutting out proudly toward her, magnificently male, but she wouldn't have expected anything less. Not from Vale.

When his fingers pushed aside her lacy panties, rubbed across where her every single nerve ending culminated into one tiny nub, she cried out his name.

"You like that?" he asked, although surely he knew the answer as her body moved in rhythm to his touch, moved as if she were a puppet he controlled.

"Please," she whimpered.

Please don't stop.

Sliding one finger then another inside her, he stroked until she could stand no more, until she was on the verge of shattering, until her legs turned to jelly. She was thankful he held her, otherwise she'd be a puddle of hot liquid on the floor.

"You're so tight."

"Vale, I need you inside me." Please. Please. "*Oh, please*," she pleaded against his neck, amazed by the warm waves washing through her, amazed that he was holding her, touching her, wanting her, amazed at the foreign sensations swamping her body. Her head dropped forward, resting in the crook of his neck as each cell in her body performed acrobatics, pulsating toward him in sweet, gratifying throbs of pleasure. "Vale!"

First donning a condom, he gave a satisfied growl, looped his hands beneath her bottom, lifted her legs to wrap around his waist, to press against where he'd created the most fabulous magic inside her. He backed her against the bedroom wall, using the sheetrock to help support her, to help keep her in position. She didn't stop him. Not when the full length of him glided against her, testing her moist readiness. Not when the thick head of him pushed inside, making her breath catch in her throat, stretching her beyond belief.

"Vale!" she gasped at the same moment his eyes widened with horrified realization, at the same moment every muscle in his body tensed.

"Faith…" He sounded tortured, seemed to hate that his hips moved in automatic response to her tight pelvic muscles, even when he was hurting her. She could feel his restraint oozing from every pore of his body, could feel that he barely held on to his control as he gently stroked within her. Yet hold on to his control he did in slow, methodical flexing of his hips that tormented as much as pleased her.

She didn't want his control. She wanted him filling her, making her a woman, his woman. She wanted him thrusting against her, hard, wild, as out of control as her heart.

She squeezed him between her thighs, gyrating her pelvis, wanting him to re-create the magic his fingers had spread through her earlier, wanting him to forget his control, to forget everything except the coming together of their bodies in unfettered passion.

"Faith," he groaned, sweat beading on his forehead. He stared into her eyes, his breaths coming hard. "You have to stop. I can't— I don't want to hurt you."

"Then love me," she urged, opening her body to him, opening her heart to him. She gripped his shoulders, stared into his eyes, letting him see everything she felt for him, hugged him tightly with her inner thighs, drawing him as deeply into her body as she could. "Love me now because I need you, Vale. I need you so badly. Please."

His pupils darkened, his eyes growing feral at her plea. His lips covered hers, smashing her mouth, thrusting his tongue into the deepest recesses as he lost the battle he'd been waging and slammed his body into hers with primal need beyond his control.

A battle Faith was glad he lost, because in him doing so she won.

Won the most glorious of colors bursting through her.

Won the hottest heat, the moistest heat, a heat that burned her the whole way through, scorching her skin, searing her insides.

Just when she thought she'd reached the pinnacle of sensation overload, she fell.

Into mindless oblivion.

Mindless orgasmic pleasure.

Further emotionally tangled with the man she clung to in hope of not floating off into another dimension.

Vale wondered whether anyone would notice if he failed to show back up at the reception. Because what he wanted was to carry Faith over to the bed and make love to her properly.

Not with her dress bunched at her waist, not with his pants sagging to his ankles. Not with him so out of control that he'd taken her like a savage beast when she'd been a virgin.

A virgin.

He'd just taken Faith's *virginity*.

She'd been right there with him, wanting him as much as he'd wanted her. But he felt a heel all the same. He'd known she was upset, that she'd been crying, that she was vulnerable. He shouldn't have taken advantage of the situation. Not with Faith.

"I shouldn't have done that."

The smile that had been on her lips faded and he felt an even bigger heel.

Her eyes became guarded and she twitched at his waist, reminding him of all the reasons they shouldn't have done what they'd just done.

What had he done to her? To them? And how the hell was he going to fix it without losing the relationship he'd enjoyed with Faith before the wedding weekend?

CHAPTER SEVEN

"PUT me down." Faith pushed against Vale's chest, wanting to stand on her own two feet, wanting to pull her dress down, wanting to be able to think and knowing she couldn't when their bodies were still joined.

Thank heavens he'd used a condom.

Not once had she thought of protection. Stupid and immature and something a teenager might do, but she truly hadn't thought of anything except needing Vale.

So much for being a modern woman.

How much more stupid could she have been?

He stepped back, gently disconnecting their bodies and lowering her to the floor. He held her shoulders a moment until he was certain she was steady on her feet. "Dear God, Faith, why didn't you tell me you were a virgin?"

His voice held a strangled mix of what sounded like anger and frustration. *Great.*

She tugged her dress over her hips. "What does that matter?"

"It mattered." He ran his fingers through his hair. "I've never done that before."

Wasn't that her line? She glanced at him, grimaced at the regret on his handsome face. "What?"

"Been with a virgin."

"Really?"

He nodded, wiping his hand over his face, before meeting her eyes. "Oh, yeah."

Was it wrong that she liked being the only virgin he'd ever been with? His *first* first?

"I shouldn't have taken your virginity, Faith. Not me. Not like this."

"In case you didn't notice, I wasn't complaining." As much as she'd like to let him shoulder the blame for what she'd likely later classify as a moment of insanity, she couldn't. She'd wanted him, had begged him to make love to her.

"Faith, why were you still a virgin?"

She bit her lower lip and sat down on the end of the bed, all her happiness gone. This wasn't the conversation a woman wanted following her first sexual experience.

She forced a smile, hoping to recapture the closeness she'd felt to him only minutes before. "Seriously, Vale, it's not that big a deal."

"Apparently it is." He lifted her chin, stared straight into her eyes, and asked a question she didn't want to answer. "Why haven't you had sex with any of your past boyfriends?"

Past boyfriends? Yeah she'd had a few, but she'd never let any get close, never wanted to risk having her heart broken when they packed up and left, as they'd inevitably do.

With Vale she'd only acted on instinct, followed her heart. Which was cause for grave concern. "The timing was always wrong."

"You're almost thirty. You're not going to convince me that 'timing' is why you were still a virgin." His gaze pinned her, not allowing her to look anywhere but into his eyes. "Maybe you'd like to explain what your real reasons are."

Actually, she wouldn't like explaining her reasons at all.

Because then she'd have to admit to him something she hated to admit even to herself. Whereas her mother welcomed men into her life, believed their lies, Faith did the opposite. She'd pushed away the few who'd tried to get close.

Because she was beating them to the punch.

She squeezed her eyes shut, unable to take his probing blue gaze a moment longer.

"Faith?" His voice was gentle, his thumb stroking along her jaw in a tender caress. "Did someone hurt you?"

She kept her eyes closed. "Let it go, Vale."

"Not until you tell me why a woman as beautiful as you opted not to have sex until me."

He wasn't going to drop this. She knew he wasn't. This was Vale. He would keep at her until she told him.

Taking a deep breath, she opened her eyes, glared at him. "Why would I want to have sex with someone who was just going to leave?"

His expression darkened, but his touch remained gentle. "You mean me?"

"I mean men period. All men leave."

"Not all men," he denied, his fingers soft against her cheek.

"Yes, all men." She pulled away, walked across the room to stare out at the ocean. "My own father didn't even stick around. Why would I expect any other man to stay when I wasn't good enough for my own flesh and blood?"

"If your father left, it was because he wasn't good enough for you, Faith. Not the other way around."

Spinning to face him, she rolled her eyes. "Right."

"I'm serious."

"Fine, but you know it's not even just me. It's men and women in general. Men leave. It's what they do best."

His brows knotted together in a V. "How is it that I never knew you were so jaded about the opposite sex?"

"Being logical is not being jaded," she pointed out, moving her head enough to free herself from his hold, but she stuck her ground. "I'm just realistic."

"Right," he mimicked her earlier sarcasm.

"Fine." She shot him a challenging look. "Give me one example of a man who stuck around."

He shrugged. "Easy. My father stuck around, Faith. Until the day he died he loved my mother, was faithful to her. They had a loving and happy relationship."

"Oh? Why don't I see you leaping down the path of love and happy relationships then?"

"That's different."

"How?" This time it was her eyes pinning him into place, his gaze averting. "You have a wonderful family, Vale, and you just said that your parents had a wonderful relationship. Why wouldn't you want the same for yourself?"

His lips compressed into a tight line. "I'm not my parents."

"Meaning?"

"Meaning what they had was rare."

She gave him a "duh" look. "My point exactly."

"Point taken." He grinned wryly. "But times are different from when my parents fell in love. Now women are more concerned with the Wakefield name, the fame and fortune, than they are with the man."

"Shall I say it?" Her brow arched and she gave a snide *"Right"*. Surely he didn't believe it was money and notoriety that made women flock to him? No way. "I've seen how women chase you, cling to you, want to be with you," she reminded him. "Don't fool yourself that it's because of anything other than *you*."

"You might be surprised," he said so sincerely that Faith blinked, took a step back.

"A woman used you for your name in the past? Someone you cared about?" Did she sound as shocked as she was?

"Let's just say that some life lessons are learned the hard way and that's a mistake I won't be repeating." He took a deep breath, glanced around his suite. "Let's straighten up and go back down to the reception."

His admission kept echoing through Faith's mind while she cleaned up in his bathroom, making herself presentable. His words were still echoing through her mind when, hand in hand, they returned downstairs to the reception, which was in full swing and without their absence having been noticed.

Seeing so many happy wedding-goers seemed a slap in the face following the conversation she and Vale had just had.

They stepped into the giant reception tent. The bride and groom had been toasted, had cut the cake and were now sharing their first dance as man and wife. A few other couples had joined them on the parquet dance floor that had been set up beneath the tent.

A photographer immediately snapped a candid picture of Vale and Faith and then requested they pose, which they did. Faith glanced at Vale, wondering if he was upset at them having their photo taken together, but he seemed oblivious. Then again, he was used to having his photo taken.

She, on the other hand, wasn't and felt highly self-conscious of her every move, of every camera flash. Could everyone tell what she and Vale had been doing?

Was it stamped across her forehead that she'd just lost her virginity?

Oh, my. She'd just had sex. With Vale. Amazing, glorious sex. With Vale. Vale. Vale. Vale, who some crazy woman had once used and obviously hurt.

She snuck another glance at him.

"Let's dance," he suggested, tugging her toward the dance floor and into his arms as if nothing out of the ordinary had happened between them. As if her mind wasn't racing in a hundred different directions.

She didn't argue, could barely find words to speak at all.

Her first sexual experience hadn't exactly been a romantic coupling but, wow, she and Vale had lit fires.

Fires that still burned low in the pit of her stomach.

Relishing being back in his arms, she let him guide her onto the dance floor, memories assailing her. They'd danced before, at the office's New Year's party. That had been the first time Faith had been in his arms. She'd floated home that night, positive the year was going to be her best ever.

The second time had been after she'd helped perform her first DBS two-lead implantation as Vale's second. He'd been so proud he'd popped a bottle of champagne that evening, poured her a glass, and he'd toasted her. Just he and she over a working dinner where they discussed the surgery and ways they could improve technique and efficiency.

Always she'd been aware of wanting him, of how desirable he was, of how he made her so aware he was a man and she was a woman. Looking back, she had to wonder about Vale.

Had the chemistry between them been building from the moment they'd met? Had he felt it all along too? Or had it truly just been that they had been thrown together by circumstances this weekend and otherwise what they'd shared would never have happened? That he never would have seen her as anything more than a surgeon in his employ?

"Faith?" he whispered next to her ear, startling her back to reality.

"Hmm?"

"Let's forget about what happened."

Any hope that what they'd shared had been special to him died.

"Okay." What else could she say? No, I don't want to forget what we just shared because it was amazing and I want to experience it again? True, but not appropriate when he was obviously not feeling the same and trying to back out of the corner he'd landed in. "We'll forget what happened."

But she knew she would never forget Vale making love to her. Not ever. Not even when she'd pray to forget in the hope of finding inner peace.

"What I mean…" his hands moved over her back, settling on her shoulders "…is that I want us to have fun tonight, to enjoy each other's company and not focus on what we did."

"Fun. Right."

He tilted her chin. "Are you saying I'm no fun?"

She stared into his blue eyes. Maybe he was right. Maybe they did need to forget about what they'd done, even if only for a short while.

"Who, you? The original Mr. Workaholic?" she attempted to tease, but knew her eyes were filled with longing, confusion.

"Hey." He pulled her close, and instantly she was taken back to what they were supposed to be forgetting, "I've barely cracked a patient profile all weekend."

"True, but you've been busy."

"Spending time with you this weekend has been immensely enjoyable."

His body pressed so tightly against hers was immensely enjoyable, too. She couldn't help but smile. "Okay, I concede your point."

The music changed to another slow song and Vale kissed the top of her head, weakening her knees. "Before the night is over, you'll be conceding much more, Faith, because I'm going to make love to you again."

Hadn't they just said they were going to forget what they'd done? Knees knocking, she met his gaze, saw the desire that still burned there, and understood fully what he'd meant. He didn't want the fear of what they'd done and how it would color the future affecting the rest of their weekend together. Their wonderful, magical weekend where they would have fun and enjoy each moment as a man and woman who wanted each other and were free to explore that desire.

And although it went against logic, against what was deeply ingrained in her psyche, Faith's smile widened and she relaxed in his arms with the knowledge that somehow everything really would be okay. She leaned her head against his shoulder, joyful at the feel of his lips at her temple, and let her imagination run wild with thoughts of acceding to Vale's every sexual whim.

Senator Evans's son couldn't be more than seven or eight, but the kid had more energy than a power plant. Unfortunately that worked to his disadvantage when he raced around the reception tent and knocked over a large vase filled with flowers, causing him to let out a blood-curdling scream as the arrangement tumbled down on him.

At the commotion, Vale stopped in mid-sentence in his

conversation with the lead singer of an up-and-coming rock band he'd been talking to and rushed to where the boy cried.

Faith beat him to it, though, and was gently examining the little boy she'd knelt next to. "Hi, sweetie, my name is Faith. I'm a doctor and saw that vase attack your head."

The boy just kept his hands over a spot on his head and continued to cry.

"Can I see where the vase hit?" she asked, gently pulling his hands away so she could see.

Vale knelt next to her, ordered a waiter to bring them some ice and to find Senator Evans and his wife.

"Amazingly, there isn't a cut," Faith voiced Vale's thoughts and held her fingers up in front of the boy's face. "Can you tell me how many fingers I'm holding up?"

The boy, whose sobs had begun to abate to just streams of tears running down his smudged face, stared at Faith's fingers and said pitifully, "Two."

"Very good," she praised, giving him a gentle hug. "Can you follow my fingers with your eyes without moving your head?"

The boy nodded and did as she asked as she checked his visual tracking. Vale pulled out his keychain, which had a tiny flashlight on it, and handed it to her so she could check the boy's pupil reflexes.

She did so, smiling and continuing to praise him in a voice that Vale found mesmerizing.

Watching Faith interact with the boy, give him praise and a quick hug, made him want to praise her, hug her. Made him think she'd be a good mother.

She would. Faith put her whole heart into anything she did. The thought of her body round with child, of her giving birth, of seeing her holding a baby, hit him.

He blinked, wondering what was wrong with him,

wondering where his crazy thoughts had come from. He didn't want Faith pregnant. *She'd leave him*.

Not him.

She'd leave the clinic, at least for a while, would devote herself to her child, to her child's father.

Which had his throat tightening.

Was it because he knew he was her one and only lover that he felt so possessive? That he didn't like the thought of another man touching her? Impregnating her? That he thought of her as *his*?

She'd been a virgin. A *virgin*. Because she believed no man would stick around for her. And she'd let him be her first, him, a man who never stuck around and had no intention of ever doing so. She deserved better.

Which made the grip on his throat tighten even more.

What was wrong with him? He didn't have thoughts like this. Ever. He shook his head to clear his mind.

"Vale?"

His vision cleared, focused on where Faith stared strangely at him, the young boy now hugged up against her.

"You okay?"

"Fine," he assured, although he wasn't sure of any such thing.

"Here's your light. Thanks." She held the keychain out to him, her fingers brushing his, and desire shot through him again. "Billy doesn't appear to have a concussion. Thank goodness."

Vale looked into her beautiful face, into her eyes, and another wave of possessiveness hit him. A wave of protectiveness.

A wave of something he couldn't recall ever having felt before and honestly couldn't say he liked feeling now.

Panic clawed at him, made him want to high-tail it back

to New York, back to his comfortable relationship with Faith. But memories of her saying that leaving was what men did, of the hurt in her eyes when she'd commented on her father, had him standing his ground. So he smiled at the vulnerable woman responsible for the odd feelings in his chest and reached for her hand, lifted it to his lips.

"You're an amazing woman. I'm glad you're here with me."

Her brows drew together in confusion, but then a smile spread across her lovely face and he was glad he'd resisted the urge to run, because for the rest of the weekend he was going to indulge in heaven.

"Me, too."

Had Sharon's bouquet toss been rigged? When Vale's cousin had turned, winked at Faith, she'd suspected, had tried to step back, not wanting to catch the flowers. But the throng of women had pushed her forward, preventing her escape. The bouquet practically jumped into her hands, making her wonder if Steve had been teaching Sharon passing secrets. Instinctively Faith had closed her fingers around the flowers.

If for the right reasons, none of which involved marriage, though, she could be very happy with Vale. At least tucked away in this magical world of Cape May where he only had eyes for her, she believed she could. In the real world, he'd eventually move on to greener pastures and break her heart. But during their fantasy weekend she could forget the real world existed and pretend she could have a happily-ever-after of her own.

"What are you thinking?" he asked, leaning in to where she sat at one of the decorated tables, sipping a glass of water. She'd had all the champagne she could handle earlier—a mere two sips. Three and she might be dragging Vale beneath a table.

"That I didn't want to catch this." She gestured to the flowers on the table. "Sharon purposely tossed me the bouquet."

"You think?" He was grinning still, which eased the tension ebbing through her. He didn't believe she was trying to push him into anything. Good, because she wasn't.

"Okay, so the wink gave her away," Faith admitted.

He took her hand in his and studied their clasped fingers. "My family likes you."

"What's not to like?" She mimicked words she'd heard him say on numerous occasions.

His gaze lifting to hers, Vale laughed. "Have phenomenal sex with a woman and it goes to her head each and every time."

"Really?" she asked, searching his eyes for a hint at how he felt. How he really felt about what had happened beyond the *phenomenal sex*. "You've had this happen before?"

His expression grew serious. "Nothing like you has ever happened to me."

"Because you'd never been with a virgin before?" Why was she pushing? Did she really even want to know the answer?

"I don't know."

What else would there be different about her compared to every other woman he'd known? Other than a brain? Vale was brilliant, gorgeous, successful, and as rich as sin. He had his pick of women and, despite whatever had happened in his past, he was never in short supply.

Except as wedding dates. For that he'd chosen someone who knew him well enough to know he had no desire to settle down, someone he himself had said wasn't a real date.

"If not that, then what?" she asked, unable not to push, unable not to try to glean better insight as to how he felt about what she'd classify as the most earth-shattering experience of her life.

"The not being able to stop even when my brain told me to," he clarified. "I only hope I didn't hurt you too badly."

"You didn't." At his raised eyebrow, she relented. "Okay, you hurt at first, but only for a few seconds, Vale. Then it was wonderful. Perfect."

He shook his head. "Not perfect. You're first time shouldn't have been against a wall with our clothes still on."

Puh-leeze. She couldn't imagine a more perfect experience. He'd been consumed with wanting her.

"I'm not complaining."

His gaze swept over her, caressing each feature. "You should be."

She drank in the warmth of his expression, the desire in his eyes, and realized she wielded a feminine power previously unrecognized. "If I was complaining?"

His gaze darkened and he lifted her hand to his lips, pressing a kiss to her fingers. "I'd have to do my best to make amends for my lack of finesse as your first lover."

"Do your best?" Excited shivers shot through her body, congregating at the juncture of her thighs. "As in?"

"Take you to my bed and show you just how good sex can be."

"It gets better than this afternoon?" She found that difficult to believe. He'd been amazing. More than amazing.

His gaze not leaving hers, he nodded. "Much better."

"Vale," she began in her most serious voice.

"Hmm?" he played along, his fingers tracing over

her bare arm, leaving a path of goose-bumps dotting her skin.

"About this afternoon…" She brushed her foot against his calf, dipping her toes under his pants cuff. "I have a complaint…"

His eyes not leaving hers, he stood, lifting her to her feet along with him as if she weighed nothing. "Let's go."

She glanced around at the reception still in full swing, despite the bride and groom having left earlier for a surprise destination. "Don't we need to say good night or something?"

"Good night or something," Vale mocked, clasping her hand tighter. He walked up the steps that led to the patio and pool, not stopping until they were in the house, up the stairs, and in his room.

CHAPTER EIGHT

"Now, tell me about that complaint." Vale shut his bedroom door, locked it, and turned to the woman who was driving him crazy.

Crazy with lust.

He wanted her again.

As much as he had this evening.

As if he hadn't already had her rough and ready against his bedroom wall. Just the memory had him groaning with desire, groaning with need to plunge inside her again, over and over as deep as he'd go until he spilt himself deep in her belly.

That thought had him pulling his wallet from his tuxedo jacket, removing a foil packet and tossing it onto the nightstand. There was a box in his shaving kit but that would require a trip into the bathroom. A trip he'd make later because once more wasn't going to be enough.

He hadn't stopped wanting Faith. Another first for him. Never had he not been satiated with sex. Never had he been left wanting round two before they'd even made it out of the bedroom after round one. If not for his love for his cousin, he'd never have left his suite. Not for the rest of the weekend.

He wanted round two with Faith *now*.

If he wasn't careful, he'd lose control again. No, he

wouldn't. He refused to hurt her again. He'd make love to her, gently, relishing her body and teasing her senses to highs so grand she'd think she'd left earth.

"Vale?" She took a step backward, but her eyes danced with mischief, danced with excitement at their flirtatious play. "You're making me nervous."

He took a menacing step toward her. "You'll like it better."

"Promise?" A smile curved her full lips, lit her eyes, sucker-punched him in the gut.

How was it possible to want her so much?

"Oh, yes." He advanced on her, closing the gap she'd created between them. "I promise you'll like what I'm going to do to you. You're going to like it a lot and beg for more."

Vale set about making his point, proving that he was a man of his word.

By her whimpers of pleasure he would say he was right. Faith enjoyed every single touch, kiss, lick, suck, thrust.

She moaned her delight, matched his passion, tested his willpower beyond what he thought he could endure. Somehow he managed not to lose his control, not like he had that first time, never like that again, not until she'd thrown back her head, arched off the bed, and screamed his name.

Then he allowed himself to let go, to lose himself inside the sweet escape she so generously offered.

Faith was in no rush to leave Cape May. Maybe she wanted to stay for ever, just stay wrapped in the exquisite cocoon of Vale's undivided attention.

Unfortunately Sunday morning arrived all too quickly. She and Vale were sitting on his private balcony, having breakfast that had appeared while she had been in the shower, letting the hot water ease the subtle aches in her muscles. She stared out at the ocean waves.

Cape May was a place of magic. No, the amazing man sitting across from her was the real magic.

"Could we walk on the beach before leaving?" she asked, wanting to prolong the fantasy as long as she could. She didn't need him to spell it out for her to know that everything would change once they were back in New York.

Vale would be back in his zone, would have the world at his fingertips. She'd go back to being his neurologist in the operating room, jumping to his every command.

Only she hadn't quite figured out how she was going to convince her body that she was no longer allowed to ignite from just looking at him. It had been bad enough prior to the having made love.

Now that she had experienced the wealth of his knowledge, she wasn't sure she had the strength to deny how her body danced to the music of his touch. She didn't fool herself otherwise, that somehow she was different from every other woman Vale had cast his spell over.

His gaze went out to the ocean.

"Most of my family is still here," he mused, taking a sip of his juice. "Now that the wedding is over, they'll be anxious to start plotting their next big event." His face wrinkled with displeasure. "I'd rather not be around for that."

His meaning dawned on her. "You think they'll be plotting about us?"

He finished off his glass of juice. "You caught Sharon's bouquet. Of course they'll be plotting. To no avail, but they'll be plotting."

To no avail. There it was. A reminder that they weren't a couple and nothing had really changed between them. He was her boss. She was his employee. When they returned to the office, they'd pretend they hadn't kissed every inch of each other's bodies. At least, she'd try.

Vale no doubt had enough experience with weekend-afters that going back to the norm would be no problem.

He leaned across the table, brushed his finger at the corner of her mouth. Ack! Had she had a crumb on her face? He just smiled. "But if you're not in a rush to return to the city, we could drive to the lighthouse."

His unexpected offer caught her off guard, had her gaze shooting to his. "The lighthouse?"

Faith had barely set foot outside Manhattan and had never had the time or money for tourist stops. "I've never seen a lighthouse in real life."

"Never?" His brow rose. "That settles our plans for the day, then. We'll drive to the state park where the Cape May lighthouse is located, and go up."

Delight filled her. "We can go up it?"

"All the way to the top," he said in a teasing tone. "A hundred and ninety-nine steps."

She gave him a quizzical look. "A hundred and ninety-nine steps? You know that how?"

"I'm a brain surgeon. I know everything," he teased.

With an eye roll, she smiled. "Of course you do."

He just grinned. "When I was a little boy I climbed to the top of those steps and had the T-shirt to prove it."

"I bet you were a cute little boy."

He waggled his brows. "I'm a cute big boy, too."

"That you are," she agreed, loving that he was smiling at her, whatever had been weighing on his mind apparently pushed aside. For the time being, at any rate. "That you are."

Virginia Wakefield hugged them both goodbye, promising to call for lunch the next time she was in Manhattan.

Faith just hugged the woman back, accepting a kiss to her cheek, wondering why she wanted to burst into tears at the kindness Vale's family had extended toward her. She followed him to the car where he stowed her suitcase.

Lost in thoughts of the weekend's events, she truly hadn't been prepared for her first sighting of the lighthouse above the tall grass blowing back and forth along the roadside.

"Wow." She strained her neck, trying to keep the red top in her line of vision.

"We're almost there," he promised, turning the car down a winding, tree-lined road.

"We can really go to the top?" she asked again, not quite believing that she was looking at a real-life lighthouse. "Is that something anyone can do or just a Wakefield?"

"You think I get special privileges?"

"I know you do."

He chuckled. "For a few bucks anyone can go to the top, but it is a good hike up the stairs. You up to it?" He shot her a quick glance, his gaze dancing over her with obvious intent. "After last night you might be too sore to climb stairs." His grin was lazy, wicked, full of hot, steamy seduction. "I seem to recall you swearing you weren't going to get out of bed today."

Yeah, she had sworn that. She'd slept very little, instead reveling in the fact she lay cradled in Vale's arms, her cheek against his strong chest, listening to his heartbeat.

"Good thing I'm a girl who likes a challenge."

He'd definitely challenged her. Time and again. Over and over. Guiding her through wave after sweet wave of pleasure. Just the memory of him maneuvering her onto him, his hands cupping her hip bones, guiding her, her back arched just so, angling her against him until she'd shattered. Completely and thoroughly *shattered*. She'd collapsed onto his chest, smiling, gasping for breath, amazed at how he'd played her body like a master musician, making her sing his praises, cry out his name. Just remembering had her squirming against the soft leather of the passenger seat, wanting him yet again.

Knowing if she didn't get her thoughts under control she was going to forget the lighthouse and climb into his lap instead of up the steps, she shifted her gaze out the car window. "The lighthouse is magnificent, isn't it?"

Vale parked the car in the lot between the lighthouse and the bird sanctuary also located in the park. A wooden boardwalk led down to the beach. Beyond that, she could hear the Atlantic crash into the shore.

"Yes." Vale's voice was low, husky.

Her gaze shot to his. She swallowed hard at what she saw glimmering in his azure eyes. Lust. Hot, sweaty, climb-into-my-lap-right-now-and-use-me-for-your-pleasure lust. Oh, my!

An elderly couple with binoculars walked past the car, bursting their sensual cocoon, reminding them both they sat in a public parking area. Faith sucked in a deep breath, wondering if she had the strength to climb the stairs after all. Her legs had turned to jelly.

"Let's go." Vale raked his fingers through his hair, cleared his throat. He opened her car door and extended his hand. He didn't let go as they crossed the parking lot. "Cape May's a functional lighthouse, a means of saving ships from crashing against the shore. The coastguard maintains the lights."

They walked to the base, entered the building just inside the gate of the fencing around the lighthouse, and bought two tickets. The usual touristy type gifts were also on sale. T-shirts, postcards, snow globes, and keychains. Faith picked up an inexpensive snow globe with the lighthouse inside, fluffy specs of white drifting around when she turned it upside down.

When she set the globe back on the shelf, Vale pulled out his wallet. He handed the trinket back to her. "I want to give you a keepsake of today."

Swallowing the emotion clogging her throat, she nodded, knowing she'd treasure the globe for ever. While she waited at the base of the lighthouse, chatting with the lady inside, Vale returned to the car and stowed her snow globe.

Step by step they climbed to the top of the tower. They paused at each of the five small landings, reading the history of the lighthouse. Their privacy was only broken by two young women and their giggling daughters' descent. Faith smiled at the girls' delight in counting each spiraling step in a sing-song manner. She didn't want kids, but those two were cute and the women's smiles made her just a touch envious. Which was ridiculous. She was there with Vale. They should be the envious ones. With the way the blonde's gaze flickered over Vale, perhaps they were.

No wonder. The man was multiple orgasms just waiting to happen. Faith sucked in a breath, clenched her thighs, and willed her body to quit throbbing.

Vale greeted the worker who sat at the top by name, shook his hand, and bent to say something to him. The leathery-faced senior glanced her way, nodded, and left. Truly alone, they went out to the barred railing hand in hand.

"I can't believe I'm here. With you," she admitted when she stepped out onto the roost.

The wind whipped at her hair and a fear of heights she hadn't known she possessed tugged at her belly, leaving her a little dizzy. Or maybe the fact all her blood pulsed down south was why her head spun. With her free hand, she grasped the handrail running against the exterior of the lighthouse. They walked to the far side, looked out over the ocean, having a bird's-eye view of the sanctuary and surrounding property.

"Beautiful," she gasped. "Absolutely beautiful."

"Yes, you are. Come on." He tugged on her hand. "Let's make our way around and check out the views from up here."

"Wish I had a camera," she mused minutes later, staring out over the ocean, "but experiencing picture-worthy moments is really what life's about."

Something she'd not done up to this point in her life.

She'd been living inside a cage of her own making. A huge city-size cage, but a cage all the same. A cage she hadn't realized until experiencing a weekend with Vale.

"You have a way of seeing things in a unique light, Faith."

If he only knew.

She leaned against the red bars protecting her from falling, gazing at the ground below, reeled at the beauty of the coastline.

Vale's hands clasped her waist, pulling her against him.

"What?" She turned, pressed her hands flat against his chest, confused by his sudden motion, wanting him more than she should.

He kissed her. Right there at the top of the lighthouse. Any dizziness that might have been from heights was replaced by the mind-numbing dizziness his kisses carried.

"I've always wanted to do that," he admitted in a low tone, holding her close.

"Kiss a girl at the top of a lighthouse? Is that why you got rid of that man?"

"Kiss a beautiful woman at the top of this lighthouse and, yes, I asked Ray to give us some privacy."

Wrapping her arms around his neck, she threaded her fingers through the hair at his nape, wondering what he'd say if she told him she wanted him.

"I want you," he told her against her lips, molding her body to him.

Yep, she couldn't miss that. Not with his body fitted so tightly to hers. He kissed her again, his hands cupping her bottom, keeping her pelvis ground against him. Not that Faith needed any encouragement. Most likely this was the last time she'd get to experience Vale like this, to taste his lips.

Definitely the last time because anything more and she might fall into some fantasy world where she believed she and Vale had a chance, might end up like her mother down the road. No, she'd take this moment, make the most of it, and then she'd go on with her life. It was what she wanted. What Vale wanted. Everything would be okay.

Desperation flowed through her veins, making her crazed, making her crave him with an addict's fervency. Maybe he felt crazed as well. His hands caressed her everywhere, his mouth marauded hers with demanding kisses, his body moved against hers.

When he tugged on her skirt, lifting the material, sliding his fingers beneath the lace of her panties, Faith moaned.

"Vale," she breathed, vaguely recalling that they stood at the top of a lighthouse

"Shh, no one can see us," he assured her. "And even if they can, they can't tell what we're doing. We're too high up."

Which didn't really reassure her, but his flinger flicked across where she throbbed, and all sane thought disappeared in the pleasurable fog that followed. His gaze locked with hers, he brought her to orgasm, smiled with satisfaction when she melted against him.

"You first. Now it's my turn." With that, he spun her and was inside her in the space of a breath. Hard, fast, deep, he thrust, stopping only long enough to swear and don a condom, before plunging back into her in a climactic finish.

Trying to catch the breath he'd stolen, Faith let go of the railing, turned and placed her hand on his cheek. His skin was warm beneath her palm, smooth and spicy from where he'd shaved that morning, moist from where he'd just made love to her.

She stared into his eyes, the intense blue shaming the sky around them. Her chest threatened to explode with the emotions she felt for this man. She could only imagine the outpouring of her love beaming out the top, lighting up the world with a kaleidoscope of colors. Vale's world. The brightness of her love a guide to lead him safely home, to her. For ever.

Oh, Lord. What was wrong with her? She'd gone all sappy. For ever? For ever didn't exist. Not outside fairy-tales and romance novels.

"Faith." Her name came out a breathy sigh and he closed the gap between their mouths, brushing his lips across hers in a soft, reverent kiss, then pulled back to stare into her eyes.

Could he see the truth? Could he tell how much she wished this day would never end? That they could go on inside this magical beach bubble for ever? A bubble where just the two of them existed in this magnificent world?

Lord, her thoughts had gone corny. She wasn't some silly schoolgirl prone to fantasies. She was a highly skilled neurologist, logical, realistic.

"We should go," she insisted, pulling away from him. Their weekend was almost over. It was time for her to get back on track with life, with what was important. Her career. "I need to get back to the city."

Back to reality.

His pupils dilated, and he watched her as he straightened his clothes. "If that's what you want."

She nodded, but felt a sharp jab when he turned without another word, without meeting her eyes. In that moment she knew that to Vale she was merely another woman he'd spent an enjoyable weekend with.

They'd had a weekend together. No strings attached. And that was all she wanted. Really.

CHAPTER NINE

VALE stared at the heavy traffic impeding him from putting his pedal to the metal the way he longed to do. Anything to abate this sense of unease weaving its way through him.

Faith was shutting him out.

The drive back to the city had grown more and more tense as blue skies had transformed into Northern New Jersey gray smog. Silently, they'd crossed over the Hudson and back to reality.

She'd not said a word to him. If he asked a question, she gave a short, almost snippy response. Had he hurt her at the lighthouse?

No, he knew he hadn't. Not physically.

Emotionally? God, he hoped not. He'd made her no promises, had only been acting on the intense attraction between them. He never made promises to women. Hadn't he learned better than that years ago?

Plus, there was the added complication of he and Faith working together. An affair between them would jeopardize the easygoing relationship they'd always shared.

But the reality was he'd be willing to continue his relationship with Faith. Willing? More like he didn't know how he was going to be near her without touching her. Without wanting to hear his name on her lips.

Had she seen that in his eyes? Was that why she'd pulled away from him? Why she'd begun to shut him out?

Because she was afraid that if they continued it would have an impact on her career?

He pulled up outside her building.

"Just let me out so you don't have to park."

"Parking isn't a problem," he assured her as he turned into the parking garage. "Besides, I'll get your suitcase."

Turning to stare out the passenger window as if she was looking at the most amazing sights rather than the boring concrete of the parking garage, she went back to ignoring him.

Vale had had enough. "Talk to me, Faith."

She didn't look at him. Only the stiffening of her spine gave a hint that she'd even heard him.

"Faith?"

She sighed. "What do you want me to say?"

"Tell me what you're thinking. What you're feeling."

"That going with you this weekend was a big mistake."

"We don't have to end with the weekend, Faith." Had he really just offered to have a relationship with Faith? A real relationship where emotions were on the line? Where they would exclusively see each other? Where they would share much more than their bodies? Hell, they already did share much more than their bodies.

She spun in her seat to face him. "That would be an even bigger mistake."

He parked the car, turned off the ignition. "Why?" Not that he couldn't name a hundred different reasons. Not that he could believe he was trying to convince a woman to have a relationship with him. Women chased him, not the other way around.

"Why?" she scoffed. "Because I'm not the kind of woman you date."

She had a point. He'd never dated anyone like Faith. Had never even met anyone like her.

"Maybe you should be."

"I'm not changing into one of those arm-candy girls." Her retort bordered on snide.

"That's not what I meant, Faith." He raked his fingers through his hair, searched for the right words, words that wouldn't leave his lips easily as they lowered the shields he'd painstakingly erected so long ago. "I meant maybe I should be dating women like you. Specifically, I should be dating *you*."

"Why?"

Why? Was she kidding? He frowned. "After this weekend you have to ask why I want to date you?"

She waved her hand dismissively. "That was just sex."

"Really? Just sex?" He'd had sex before. Whatever had happened between Faith and himself had never happened before, though. He'd never felt that protectiveness, never lost reason. Just the memory of being inside her was enough to make his brain cloudy. "I thought it was more."

Her green eyes narrowed, her jaw dropped a bit, and she regarded him quizzically, before laughing a bit hysterically. "Oh, I get it. You're worried that because I was a virgin I'm going to have all these great expectations of you. Don't worry, Vale. The only expectation I have is for us to continue our working relationship as if this weekend never happened."

A strange pain shot across his chest. "You don't want to see where whatever this is between us could go?"

"I know where it would go. Nowhere. And I'm not willing to mess up my career to go nowhere."

Her words stung, yet he recognized the validity of what she said. Still, he played devil's advocate. "How can you be sure we wouldn't end up making my family very happy by making an announcement of our own?"

She snorted. "Because that's one announcement I'll never be making. Never."

He wrapped both hands around his steering-wheel, squeezed the leather. "You wouldn't marry me?"

"I wouldn't marry any man."

"Because of your mother?"

"Because I don't want to be married."

"Fine, I have no intention of marrying anyway, so we're on the same wavelength." So why did her blatant rejection bite so deeply? Why did it make him want to wrap her in his arms and love away the pain she associated with weddings because of her father's abandonment? "Invite me to stay the night."

Her answer was immediate and confident. "No."

"You want me as much as I want you." Was he saying the words for her benefit or his ego's? "I know you do."

She shook her head. "That's just my autonomic neurophysical response to you. I imagine now that I've had sex I'll respond that way to any attractive male."

What a load of garbage. "Because of your hang-up about your father leaving you, you won't have sex with me again?"

Her face paled and he regretted his sharp question, wondered why he didn't just get her bag out and drive away, never looking back.

"What would be the point?" she finally asked.

"Other than a whole lot of pleasure?"

"There are other women who can give you pleasure. Lots of them. This weekend shouldn't have happened. Let's

forget it did and go back to just being work colleagues."
Her lips compressed into a fine, stubborn line.

He stared straight into her big green eyes, held her gaze,
and fought all the warring emotions within him. "That's
what you want, Faith? What you really want? For us to
forget about what happened and go back to just working
together?"

She hesitated only the briefest of seconds, then
nodded.

"Fine." His pride kicked in, reminding him that he was
Vale Wakefield and had never begged any woman for her
attention, for her affections. He sure as hell wouldn't start
now. "You're right. There would be no point to pursuing
a relationship between us. No point at all."

Monday morning arrived bright and early, just as it always
had. Faith had slept little the night before, despite how tired
she'd felt when she'd crawled into her bed. Alone.

No, not alone. Yoda had snuggled next to her, grateful
his mistress was home.

But Faith had felt more alone than she had in a long
time. Perhaps since her father had walked out on her and
her mother.

She knew why.

She'd missed Vale. Two nights in bed with a man should
not leave her feeling so lonely. Yet she'd curled into a fetal
position and cried. Cried. She'd been the one to tell him to
leave, so why had she cried?

Because somewhere during the weekend, when she'd
been telling herself over and over that she was no different
from any of the other women who'd fallen for him, she'd
started to believe that maybe he could someday love her.

And when he'd looked at her at the lighthouse, she'd seen such sweet emotion in his eyes. And that had scared her.

Vale wanted a relationship for however long those sweet emotions lasted, but how could she do that? Because ultimately he would leave her and then where would she be? Just look at how two nights in bed with the man had messed with her head.

She'd had to face facts that she and Vale had to end things before she forgot to protect her heart, before she got so tangled up in the magic that was him that she lost herself, before she ended up like her mother, chasing an elusive dream of happily-ever-after that simply didn't exist.

Now she had to go and face Vale.

How would he act? Would he acknowledge the hot sex they'd shared or would he go about business as usual?

After her shower, she donned a gray suit that felt shapeless after her Friday shopping spree, scraped back her hair. Unfortunately, with her recent trim, strands kept working loose and she couldn't capture her usual no-nonsense look. Finally, she gave up and twisted her hair in a looser style, securing it with the comb she'd used over the weekend.

Staring at her clean face, she considered slathering on a protective coating of make-up. But if she did, Vale might read too much into it. Much better to go as usual than to have him think she regretted not continuing their weekend. She even made a point to wear her glasses instead of her contact lenses.

Although she need not have worried.

Vale wasn't at the office when she arrived.

"He called to say he had a meeting at the hospital and would see you in the operating room," Kay informed her, handing Faith a stack of papers. "He also asked for you to handle any of these phone calls that you can, to save him time this afternoon. He's got a full day ahead."

Didn't they always? Faith sighed. "Of course."

Kay gestured to Faith's hair. "I like your hair like that. Did you have it highlighted at your appointment on Friday?"

So much had happened between this morning and last Friday Faith had forgotten her co-workers hadn't seen the changes she'd made. "Cut and highlighted. I couldn't get it pulled back right this morning."

"If right is how you usually wear your hair, then good. I like you better this way," Kay said in her usual blunt manner. "How was the grandiose Steve Woodard and Sharon Wakefield wedding?"

"Grandiose," Faith said, not wanting to be reminded of how she'd spent her weekend. In bed, naked, with her boss.

And he'd wanted to continue... If she'd said yes, would she have woken in his arms? Shared breakfast with him? Walked to work with him hand in hand?

No, she'd been right to end things now. Why wait for the inevitable? Why give Vale the chance to break her heart? A relationship between them would never have worked.

"I saw photos in *The Post*. There's a really nice one of you and Vale. You looked gorgeous, by the way, and happy."

There had been photos of her and Vale in *The Post*? What had the caption read? *Wakefield heir goes slumming? Wakefield heir dumps top model for smart chick, what was he thinking? Wakefield heir...* Faith winced, hoping Kay didn't read too much into the reaction.

Of course there had been photos of the wedding. No

doubt gossip rags and papers alike would have a whole section on the famous heiress's wedding to a sporting legend.

"Did you get to meet many stars?"

"A few," she answered honestly. Almost every guest in attendance had had a recognizable face. "Vale kept me pretty busy."

And how. Faith fought to keep heat from her face.

"The man is a workaholic!" Kay accused, but with admiration in her voice. "Well, I hope you got a chance to sightsee. Cape May is a gorgeous historic town. I love all those old Victorian houses. Was the Wakefield home close enough to the park for you to see the lighthouse? I visited there once when I was a kid."

Faith didn't wince again, barely. She even managed a half-smile. "I did get to visit the lighthouse. Thanks for asking." She held up the stack of papers Kay had handed her. "Guess I'd better get started clearing these before meeting His Highness in the O.R. to implant Mr. Anderson's two-lead DBS device. Keep your fingers crossed we cure his dyskinesia and tremors today without any negative side effects."

When Faith arrived, Vale was already scrubbed and preparing to enter the surgical suite. She hadn't intentionally dawdled, but time had slipped away from her while fielding his phone calls and catching up on her own workload.

"Did Kay give you my message?" he asked, glancing briefly at her when she'd finished scrubbing.

"She gave me all of your messages. I was able to take care of most of them." Did she sound bitter? Ridiculous. She'd been helping Vale from the moment she'd started at the clinic. Why would doing so bother her now? But, then, screening his messages wasn't what caused the bitterness in her throat.

"Good." He stepped into the sterile gown, allowed the nurse to do up the back, then gloved up. Except for the rare comment regarding their patient, he ignored Faith throughout the remainder of the surgery.

Never had he ignored her. Never. Today, he was making a statement. One she was getting loud and clear.

There was no going back to the way things had been before their weekend together.

Unlike her, he looked as if he'd slept well. His appearance was impeccable, as always. No dark circles beneath his brilliant blue eyes, ever. No glances of longing at the woman he'd made passionate love to all weekend.

How dared he make her want him so badly!

Only, really, what had he done? Had sex with her and told her he wanted to continue their relationship beyond the weekend? How could she hold that against him?

But naive as it might be, she hadn't expected such a drastic change in their professional relationship.

He turned, caught her watching him, met her gaze for the briefest of seconds. He never missed a beat in how he guided the DBS lead under the neuro-physicist's guidance, never looked the slightest moved by the questions she knew she hadn't kept from her face.

Then again, the man was performing brain surgery. One wrong move and their patient could have lasting effects. She should be grateful his concentration was on the patient because for once her mind kept veering off track. Not good. Her career was everything to her.

Her guarantee to never fall into the same pitfalls as her mother, to never need a man.

Her gaze shifted to Vale yet again. She didn't need him. Want him, yes. Of course she wanted him. He was gorgeous, successful, brilliant Vale Wakefield. But want and need were two very different things.

Thank goodness she didn't need him, or any man.

No doubt that would hurt even more than the sharp twinges she kept experiencing in her chest just looking at him caused.

Knowing she had to get her feelings safely tucked away, Faith took a deep breath and focused on what she'd focused on her entire life, the one thing she had control over.

Her career.

"Well done, Vale," Faith congratulated him when they stepped outside the surgical suite. "The DBS implantation went superbly."

Hearing her say his name brought back memories of the weekend when she'd called out his name in sexual release.

Memories he didn't want because what had happened between them had ended with the weekend. What happened in Cape May stayed in Cape May.

Unfortunately.

"We won't really know how successful the implantation was for a few days." Did he sound embittered? Fine. Let her deal with his moodiness.

He hadn't been ready to call quits to their affair. It had been years since a woman had ended a relationship with him. He'd forgotten how much it stung to want someone he couldn't have.

Oh, he could have her. He'd seen how she looked at him this morning. She wanted him whether she wanted to admit it or not. But if he pursued their personal relationship any further, Faith would end up leaving the clinic.

She'd stressed how important her career was to her. What right did he have to screw that up just because he wasn't ready to let go of her delectable body? Just because, even now, looking at her in her hideous glasses and unflattering scrubs, all he could think about was how she'd come alive tangled with his body, how she'd stared at him in wonder at her orgasms, at how she'd looked while sleeping in his arms?

God, he'd missed her last night. Had lain in his big bed alone and wondered why he'd never noticed how quiet and lonely his penthouse was.

Sure, he'd thought of sex from time to time when sleeping alone, but to want to hold a woman, to breathe in her vanilla scent, to sleep knowing she was next to him, would be there when he woke up? *Never.*

Not looking at her, he peeled off his protective gear.

When he turned to go, she touched his shoulder. "Vale?"

Not wanting to, he faced her, but didn't look into her eyes. He couldn't. Not when he wanted to slide her glasses off her face, lose himself in her gorgeous eyes, and tell her he wasn't willing to let her toss him aside when she so obviously wanted him, too.

"Yes?" He sounded a jerk, but it couldn't be helped. Her gentle touch had electrified his body, had made him acutely aware of how close she stood, of how much he wanted her.

He'd told her he wanted her, that he wanted to continue what they'd started, to see where it took them. She'd been the one to say no. Yet here she was, looking uncertain, hurt. He wasn't going to play games. Did she want him to chase her? To beg her to admit she wanted him? Hell, no.

"I…" She paused, uncertainty darkening her eyes. "Are we going to lunch today?"

Lips held tightly together, he shook his head. "You made your point last week, Faith. Your lunchtime is your own.

Unless it's unavoidable, you won't be scheduled for meetings during lunch."

"But—" she began, but he interrupted.

"Don't look a gift horse in the mouth, Faith. Go, have lunch, and enjoy your free time. I have other plans." He turned to walk away, paused, turned and flashed a grin that was difficult to pull off, but by the paleness of her skin he knew he had, knew he had to drive the point home that either she admitted she wanted him, that she wanted to continue what they'd started, or he would move on. "With Lulu."

He left Faith to stare a hole in his back.

Fortunately, she couldn't see the hole in his chest that hurting her ripped open.

But he wouldn't beg any woman for her affections. Not even one he wanted as much as the one he'd just walked away from.

Three weeks passed. Three weeks in which Faith had barely seen Vale. He hadn't asked her to lunch, hadn't asked her to work late to review the latest data, hadn't asked her input on the Parkinson project. She'd gone from essentially being with him almost constantly to seeing him during roundtable discussions regarding surgical consults and in the surgery suite.

Because he acted as if they were no more than colleagues. She hadn't expected him to continue to pursue her, but she hadn't expected such a drastic change from their pre-wedding weekend either.

Thank goodness she'd gotten her period, that an unplanned pregnancy hadn't resulted from her weekend of foolish fantasy.

Despite the additional time she had at home with Yoda,

time she'd desperately wanted, she wasn't happy, was actually quite miserable.

Was actually quite lonely.

She missed Vale.

All the extra hours she'd put in had never seemed like work because she'd been with him.

Now work was a drudgery. She had to force herself to go in each morning. To know that if she saw Vale, it would only be a glimpse, would only be from a distance, because he avoided her, acted as if she had the plague.

Even Kay commented on the change in the relationship between and Vale, asking Faith if she was okay. Everyone else in the office had either not noticed or failed to comment, probably the latter.

"Faith?" Kay beeped Faith's office. "Sharon Wakefield Woodard is on the phone for you. She called in on Vale's private line. Do you want to take the call or shall I take a message?"

"Faith Fogarty," she said into the phone, confused why Vale's cousin would be calling her. Surely she'd only just returned from her honeymoon?

Sharon didn't bother with pleasantries, actually sounded a bit perturbed. "We need to do lunch."

Do lunch? Faith glanced over her schedule for the day, saw that she was booked full with patients, including a follow-up with Mr. Anderson. Except for lunch, of course. Ha. "I'm not sure I can get away today," she hedged, not sure how Vale would feel about her having lunch with his cousin.

"Nonsense. Of course you can meet me for lunch." Sharon dismissed her objections in pure Wakefield expectation of the world bending to their will. "You're a brain doctor, so that means you're smart, right?"

"Uh, right," Faith said slowly, wondering where Sharon was going with her question.

"Steve had an affair," Sharon confessed, her tone going up several octaves. "Vale says I should just forget it, that the affair happened in the past, but I can't forget something like that, can I? Steve cheated on me. What's to say he wouldn't again? How can I ever trust him?"

Unbelievable. And yet another example of a marriage gone wrong. Another reason Faith should stay far away from men. Eventually they all ended up proving they were...well, men.

"I need someone really smart to talk to and Vale's who I usually go to, but he's all man on this subject. Plus, he's family. Please, Faith."

Feeling herself weaken, Faith took a deep breath. "Perhaps we could meet somewhere close to the office around noon?"

"Where have you been?" Vale demanded, shutting the door behind him with a loud thud as he entered Faith's office.

Wearing a boring gray suit and her glasses, she glanced up from the computer screen she was studying, eyed him as if he had no right to be in her personal space. As if she'd been on the computer for hours rather than only a few minutes. He knew that because he'd been listening for her return.

Should he remind her he owned the office? The whole building, for that matter?

"At lunch. Remember, that thing you insisted I take?" she pointed out with a sarcasm that didn't become her.

Fighting the wave of frustration he'd felt at Kay's news that Faith had called to say she was taking a long lunch, he placed his hands on his hips. "Insisting you take lunch did not entail your patients having to be rescheduled due to you deciding to take longer than the allotted time."

Caught off guard at his announcement, she blinked. Her mouth opened, then closed. "Since when did I start punching a time clock?" Her voice sounded as irritated as his.

"Who were you with, Faith?"

Because he couldn't stand not knowing. Not that it was any of his business, but Kay had led him to believe Faith had gone to lunch with a man. The man she'd been seeing prior to their weekend? A man she hadn't slept with up to that point, but what about now? Was she spreading those lush thighs and…? No, he wouldn't let his mind go there.

But, hell, if fire didn't burn in the pit of his stomach at the thought of another man touching her…

Regarding him with narrowed eyes, she unnecessarily adjusted her glasses. "Not that it's any of your business, but I had lunch with Sharon."

Sharon?

"What did she want?" Then it hit him. "She talked to you about Steve."

Faith nodded, a loose strand of her hair caressing her face as she did so. "About him cheating on her, yes."

Women. Steve loved Sharon with all his heart, was devastated at her reaction to his confession, yet Sharon now refused to speak to her new husband.

"It was a long time ago during a time when they had broken up. She needs to quit acting like a spoiled child and go home to her husband."

"Excuse me?" Faith's brow arched upward. "During

her *honeymoon*, she found out the man she loves cheated on her. I think she's entitled to be emotional right now."

"Sharon's being more than a little emotional. She's threatening to file for divorce," he said, knowing his cousin was acting rashly, rather than with logic. Steve loved her.

Faith just nodded and the way she didn't quite meet his eyes said she knew more than she was letting on.

"Don't tell me you encouraged her to continue with this nonsense?" When she didn't answer, Vale let out an exasperated sigh. "How dare you give her advice on marriage, or anything else? You know nothing of what our life is like. The media will be all over her and Steve. Everything either of them has ever done will be plastered in the gossip rags."

Faith placed her fingertip against the bridge of her glasses, thrust them up her pert nose. "It's not my place or yours to decide what's best for Sharon."

"She needs to stop this nonsense before she destroys her marriage. She needs to see reason."

Faith's eyes narrowed. "Reason being to take back a man who cheated on her?"

He placed both palms down on the deep-burgundy, high-back chair across from her desk, dug his fingers into the soft leather. "Don't pretend to be an expert in things you know nothing about."

"I know what she told me. Her husband cheated on her, destroyed her trust in him, and she wants a divorce."

"She acts as if he slept around after they were married. He didn't. They'd broken up at the time of his indiscretion."

Faith's mouth dropped open, then her eyes narrowed. "Isn't that just like a man, to focus on a technicality? If he loved her, whether or not they were having an off time shouldn't have mattered. According to Sharon, they broke up quite frequently, but always got back together. She never slept with anyone else and feels he shouldn't have either."

Gritting his teeth, Vale squeezed the top of the chair. Was Faith purposely trying to antagonize him? Because of what had happened between them? "Steve didn't deserve her abandoning him in Rio during their honeymoon."

Faith's brow quirked. "Perhaps he should have thought about that prior to telling her during their *honeymoon* that he'd had sex with another woman, but no worries because she didn't mean anything to him and he and Sharon had broken up at the time so it didn't really count."

Vale wouldn't argue that Steve's timing had been lacking, but the man had thought he was doing the right thing, had wanted to clear his conscience, because he truly did love Sharon.

"I know my cousin. She's confused." He met Faith's gaze. "Don't you have enough problems with your own family's marital issues? Stay out of mine."

She sucked in air loudly, looked at him with shattered eyes, making him wish he could take back his words. But he couldn't and maybe he didn't even really want to.

Regardless, he'd had enough.

Faith stared at Vale's retreating back. Had he really just ordered her to stay out of his family's marital issues? Hadn't he been the one to drag her into his family's marital issues to begin with by insisting she be his "date" for his cousin's wedding to save him from his family's matchmaking?

Weeks of frustration at the change in their relationship,

at his cold shoulder, rose to the surface, blowing her top like a champagne cork. Her anger spewed out in messy, foamy white bursts.

"Don't you order me around like you own me and then walk out of my office all sanctimonious and holier than thou," she retaliated, jumping up from her desk to chase after him.

Surprised by her outburst and probably more so by her gripping of his jacket and tugging him round to face her, Vale's gaze cut into her. She rushed on before he could stop her.

"If Sharon wants me as her friend, I'll see her any time she wants and there's nothing you can do about it."

"We're talking about *my* cousin," he reminded her, angry pink stains flushing his cheeks.

"Which doesn't mean you own her. Sharon is a grown woman and, yes, she may be confused right now, but that doesn't mean she needs some *man* telling her what she should and shouldn't be doing right now."

"Some man?" he growled. "Oh, you were just waiting to get that dig in, weren't you? This just reinforces all your hang-ups about relationships and marriage, doesn't it?"

"Marriage is an outdated sentiment. Disposable in to-day's society, just promises made that are only meant to be kept until the man grows bored and moves on. I want no part of it." Faith stood on tiptoe, nose to nose with him, hating that even in anger her body had taken notice of his proximity, of his spicy aftershave, of the sexuality radiating from his every pore.

"Obviously," he sneered. "But Sharon doesn't share that sentiment as she chose to marry Steve. Keep yourself and your jaded views away from my family."

Did he have any idea that she wanted to pound her fists

against his chest? Did he have any idea she'd cried over the loss of his friendship? Of all the precious moments they'd spent together? Of course not. Because if she wasn't willing to have sex with him, he obviously didn't want anything more to do with her.

"No, you, you *man*!" She wasn't sure if she was denying his request to stay away from his family or if she spat the word out in protest of him not caring at how they'd ruined their relationship, a relationship she'd treasured.

"This isn't up for debate." Angry sparks flew from his eyes and she was glad.

Anger meant she was eliciting some type of emotion from him. She wanted emotion, wanted a reaction from him. For weeks she'd been getting nothing but him ignoring her.

"You're right. It's not. You have no right to tell me what I can and cannot do," she insisted, earning herself a gritted-teeth growl from a man known for his cool composure.

Good. At this point she wanted a knock-down, drag-out fight. Arguing with him felt so much better than walking around on the eggshells she'd been treading since the morning after they'd come back from Cape May.

"Sure I do," he said arrogantly. "You work for me."

"Just because I work for you, it does not give you the right to say who I can and can't be friends with." Her chin rose another few notches.

"Then you'll be doing it elsewhere because as long as you work for me, you'll do what I say. Got it?"

Faith's stomach knotted, what was left of her heart shattered into dust, and pain like she'd never felt erupted deep within her, battling with her anger for pole position.

"Fine," she spat at him, clinging to her anger in the hope of abating her pain. "Consider this my official resignation. I quit. Effective immediately."

CHAPTER TEN

AT FAITH'S threat, Vale's blood instantaneously froze to hard chunks of ice. Coldness seeped into his extremities, leaving him numb and spent.

"You can't quit," he told her, wanting to take her into his arms and shake her, but he didn't need to. Her entire body was already shaking, whether from anger or frustration or what he didn't know.

She crossed her arms over her chest, jutted her chin up at him, and gave him the most seething look he'd ever seen cross her face. "I just did."

"We have a contract," he reminded her, battling the frost claiming his insides, not liking the panic in his chest, knowing he couldn't let her quit. "One that says you work for me."

"Fine, take me to court," she said flippantly, not backing down from her position. "I'm sure any judge will release me under the circumstances."

"What circumstances?"

She rolled her eyes. "Oh, don't give me that. You know exactly what circumstances I'm referring to."

"Our sleeping together?"

She smiled, as pretty as you please. "What else?"

"You're being ridiculous, Faith. You can't quit because we slept together."

"No, you're the one who's ridiculous, Vale." His name came out a sarcastic slur. "Sleeping with you has apparently destroyed my career. Was I that bad in the sack?"

That bad? Shouldn't he be the one asking that question? He'd wanted to continue sleeping with her. She'd been the one to say no. "That's enough, Faith."

"No, it's not enough. Do you want to know what's enough? Me putting up with you ignoring me after what we shared. Me crying night after night, trying to figure out what I did wrong that weekend when the truth is I didn't do anything wrong. You did, you pompous jerk!"

He winced. He'd known she was hurting, that he'd hurt her by backing away from their friendship, but when he wanted her so badly, how could he spend time with her and not end up seducing her? She needed to realize that they were worth pursuing and not because he'd charmed his way between her delectable thighs.

His pride had come into play as well. He'd wanted her to admit she'd been wrong to push him away, that he'd been right to say he wanted to continue beyond their weekend together. Had he pushed her away for ever instead?

"I'm sorry if I hurt you."

"I don't want your pity or your apologies."

"What is it you want, Faith? I told you I still wanted you, that I wanted to explore what was happening between us. You were the one to say no. What would you have me do to make things right between us?"

She studied him for several seconds, then lowered her arms to her sides in a defeated gesture. "There's nothing you can do, Vale. It's too late."

He realized that now, realized that the moment he'd kissed her it had been too late to salvage their professional relationship.

Maybe he'd handled her rejection of him all wrong.

But he hadn't been thinking clearly, still wasn't thinking clearly.

Faith was leaving him.

No, not him, she was leaving the clinic.

Hell, same difference. Either way, she would no longer be a part of his life.

If she refused to acknowledge that they'd had a chance for something special to develop between them, then maybe her leaving was for the best.

Maybe that was the only way for either of them to forget the weekend in Cape May.

"You win, Faith," he said in a low voice. "You're an excellent neurologist and the clinic will be taking a hard hit to lose you. Still, you can leave if that's what you want, but you know I don't want you to go. Not personally and not professionally."

He didn't want her to go. He wanted her to stay, to say they could pick up where they'd left off. But they'd just end up back at this same point. Why delay the inevitable? Faith didn't want the same things he did.

"What you want is irrelevant to me, Vale. Totally irrelevant."

Had she still been screaming at him, he might have put her words down to emotional stress. But Faith wasn't screaming. She spoke with a calmness that chilled him. Almost as if she'd read his thoughts and was answering, assuring him that she didn't want him beyond the physical—and for once that wasn't enough.

"You don't mean that."

Surprise filled her eyes, and when she met his gaze, she shone with confidence. "Actually, I do. Goodbye, Vale. I'll send for my things."

"Faith." He grabbed her shoulder, refusing to let her pass, cursing himself for not being strong enough to let her go without one last desperate appeal for her to stay. "Don't go like this."

"Is there a better way for me to go? Some way you'd prefer? Maybe if I came into your office and told you I'd accepted an offer from another clinic so you wouldn't have to feel guilty over our liaison? Would that make you feel better? Would that free you from your guilt?"

He winced. Was that what the twinge in his chest was? Guilt? Guilt that he'd taken her virginity? Guilt that he couldn't look at her without wanting to strip her naked?

She was right. He did feel guilty. Guilt he clung to, because if what he was feeling wasn't guilt, then he'd have to find another label. Guilt was so much easier to deal with than the alternative.

"Do you have another offer, Faith? Is that what this is really about?"

First raking her gaze over him with cool disregard and a touch of disappointment, she nodded. "Yes, Vale, that's exactly what this is about. I'm leaving you for another clinic."

Blindly, chin high, shoulders straight, heart breaking, Faith made her way through the hallway leading away from her office, away from Vale. She kept her composure until the ladies' restroom door swung shut behind her.

Then sobs hit her in full force.

She shook. She ached. She sank against the inside of a stall and cried till her eyes throbbed.

What was wrong with her? She'd cried more in the past three weeks than she had her entire life. No man was worth this. Hadn't she watched her mother shed useless tears? Had she learned nothing at all from years of witnessing her mother's mistakes? From having lived through her father leaving?

"Faith?" a female voice asked from outside the stall. "Are you okay? What am I saying? Of course, you aren't okay. Can I come in? That is, well, maybe you could just come out of the stall instead?"

"Sharon?" Faith swiped at her eyes beneath her glasses, wishing she hadn't put on make-up that morning as she likely had raccoon eyes. "What are you doing here?"

"I heard your fight with Vale," the woman admitted, compassion filling her voice.

Great. Faith didn't need Sharon feeling sorry for her.

"I didn't mean to eavesdrop," she continued. "I thought of some things I'd forgotten to mention at lunch so I came back. I was outside your door, heard my name, and did exactly what I shouldn't have done. Eavesdropped."

Faith took a deep breath, hating that she hiccupped, hating that when she opened the stall door there was no way could she hide how pitifully she'd been crying. "I'm sorry you had to hear my argument with Vale."

"Why? You were wonderful."

Faith blinked, sure she'd misheard. She opened the stall to stare in shock through the tear-induced fog of her glasses at Vale's cousin. "I was?"

"Absolutely," Sharon replied. Reaching for a tissue and Faith's glasses, she took it upon herself to blot away Faith's tears. "I've never heard anyone put Vale in his place that way. Never. Even most of the family are a little scared of him." Sharon stepped back, surveyed her clean-up job of Faith's face, and smiled. "You and I are going to be great friends."

Faith's head was spinning. "But—"

"No buts." Sharon opened her purse, dug around until she pulled out a zippered pouch. Removing liquid concealer, she squirted a pearl-size drop on her fingertip. "Look up," she ordered, dabbing beneath Faith's eyes, then smoothing out the make-up to her satisfaction. "Any woman who can stand up to my cousin and leave him speechless has my complete admiration."

The reality of what she'd done sank in. "Oh, God, I just quit my job."

"But you said you were going to a different clinic," Sharon pointed out, confusion marring her flawless complexion as she handed Faith a new tube of lipstick. "That's my favorite color, by the way. I always carry extras, just in case I lose one."

Vale's cousin carried extra tubes of the same shade of lipstick? Taking the lipstick, she read the label. Pouty Pink Passion.

"I lied," she admitted, peeling the plastic seal away and opening the tube to stare at the color. Not bad.

"Oh," Sharon said, her mouth forming a perfect circle and creases lining her forehead. "But you're still a brain doctor, right?"

Smoothing the lipstick onto her lips, rubbing her lips together to smooth out the cream, Faith nodded. "Yes, I'm still a neurologist. Just an unemployed one."

So why wasn't she freaking out? Why was she standing next to a bathroom stall, putting on make-up while chatting with Sharon Wakefield Woodard as if they were discussing the weather?

"Great!" Sharon clapped her hands in glee. "You'll work for yourself, start your own clinic, and be my doctor. Goodness knows, I need my head examined for getting married."

Faith's Pouty Passion Pink–covered lower lip dropped open. "I can't start my own clinic."

"Why not?" Sharon asked, so matter-of-factly that Faith stopped and asked herself the same question.

Why did she have to work for someone else? Let them

decide her fate? Sure, prestige came with working for a clinic of Wakefield and Fishe's caliber, but prestige could be earned.

Then reality sank in again. "I appreciate your enthusiasm, but I don't have the money to start a clinic and get it off the ground."

"Hello…" Sharon rolled her eyes. "Yes, you do. I'm loaded and Vale is always telling me I need to make good investments, to find something to do with my life." She giggled with excitement. "I could work for you. Be your silent partner, even! This is the perfect solution for us both, Faith."

Stunned by Sharon's generosity and by her good humor when they were talking about Faith leaving her cousin's clinic, she shook her head. "I appreciate your offer, but I can't do that."

"Why not?"

"It wouldn't be ethical for me to accept money from my former employer's family."

"Ethics schmethics. We're talking about your future here and I'm offering you a way to really get under Vale's skin. The correct response is, 'Yes, ma'am, Miss Wakefield.'" Sharon held up her hand. "Don't even remind me that my legal last name is Woodard, because I want no part of Steve right now."

Faith stared at the crazy woman standing in the opening of the stall. "I don't want to get under Vale's skin."

"Yes," Vale's cousin assured her, looking way too confident for a woman who had yo-yoed during their lunch between bawling her eyes out and professing that she wanted to castrate her soon-to-be ex-husband. "You do. Every woman wants to get under the skin of the man she loves." She gave a knowing smile. "Why else do you think I'm making Steve pay for his sins?"

Not quite believing her ears, Faith ventured a guess. "To get under Steve's skin?"

"Darned right." Sharon put her manicured hand on her hip and straightened her shoulders with determination. "He'll think twice before he ever cheats again."

Faith hadn't believed Vale when he'd commented on his family being crazy, had only believed they were the lovable, generous souls she'd met in Cape May. Now she knew he'd been on to something. Sharon was certifiable. Perhaps she herself was too, because a slow smile spread across her face and her future suddenly didn't look nearly so bleak.

Two weeks had passed since Faith had walked out of Vale's office. She wouldn't talk to him. Not that Vale blamed her, but the entire situation grew more and more ridiculous. How had he ended up on Steve's side rather than his cousin's in an argument that shouldn't have been happening in the first place?

Sharon wouldn't return his calls. Faith wouldn't return his calls.

He rapped his knuckles against her apartment door yet again. Apparently, she wouldn't answer the door at her apartment either.

Unfortunately an angry little lady had opened her apartment door and threatened to call the police if he didn't leave.

"I need to talk to Faith," he explained, frustrated that he'd been the one pushed away, he'd been the one left behind, yet here he was at her apartment door and yet again she was ignoring him.

When a tiny dog launched past the woman and attached itself to his ankle, Vale was the one yelping in frustration and pain. The dog might be small but his teeth were sharp and sank into Vale's flesh with unerring ease.

"Don't hurt him," the woman squealed, coming after the beast Vale was trying to shake free without permanently mangling his leg in the process.

"Don't hurt him?" Vale snorted, dancing around in effort to dislodge the dog. "What about me? This mutt is vicious."

"Yoda, get back here," the older woman called to the dog Vale had managed to free from his flesh but which was still latched on to his pants with tenacious determination.

Then what the woman had said sank in as surely as the dog's teeth had.

"Yoda?" He glanced behind her. Sure enough. Apartment 907. The angry lady was Faith's dog-sitter. "This is Faith's dog."

Vale smiled a devilish smile, knowing he wouldn't have to worry about whether or not Faith took his calls or answered the door. She'd be calling him before the day ended.

Bending down, he scooped the dog into his arms, prepared for the pain that was sure to come in doing so. He wasn't disappointed.

Sometimes getting what you wanted was a pain in the kisser. Or, as in this case, a pain in the arm.

He turned to the dog-sitter who scowled at him and was telling Yoda to "get him".

"Tell Faith I have her dog. If she wants Yoda back, she knows where to find him."

Faith blinked at her neighbor. "He did what?"

When Mrs. Beasley had burst into the tiny office space she'd rented, face red, chest puffing, eyes wild, Faith had feared for the elderly woman's life.

"That handsome devil who you went away with, the one you've been moping around over, he dognapped Yoda!" Mrs. Beasley panted, her wrinkled hands fluttering against her heaving chest. "Call the police, now, so they can catch the scoundrel."

"Sit down, Mrs. Beasley." Sharon came over to the older woman, handed her a glass of water, and motioned to the empty chair she'd placed behind the exhausted woman. "You're going to have a stroke if you don't calm down."

"I'm not going to have a stroke," the woman denied, her face flushed with excitement. "We have to do something. That awful man has stolen Faith's dog."

"Hmm, he always did want a dog, but taking yours is a bit much, even for a Wakefield," Sharon mused from beside Faith, both of them eyeing Mrs. Beasley with concern.

The poor woman really had been frantic when she'd burst into Faith's new office a couple of blocks over from their apartment complex.

"Do you think we should call for an ambulance? You're looking a little winded, Mrs. B."

"An ambulance?" Mrs. Beasley stared at her as if she was daft. "We need the SWAT team, not a defibrillator."

"It's okay," Faith assured her neighbor, taking her pulse and respirations. Tachypneic and tachycardic. She patted her neighbor's shaky hand, motioned for Sharon to get her a blood-pressure cuff and stethoscope. "Vale won't hurt Yoda."

At least, Faith didn't think he would.

"He might," Mrs. Beasley cried. "Yoda could tell he was a rascally fellow and didn't like him one bit. Even if he was dashing."

Wasn't it just like Vale to have caught Mrs. Beasley's eye even while the woman had been threatening to have him thrown into jail?

"What did Yoda do?" Faith took her blood pressure. Slightly elevated at 140/90, but not too bad considering how upset the woman was.

"Attacked him."

Mouth agape, Faith asked, "Yoda attacked Vale?"

Mrs. Beasley nodded proudly. "Probably brought blood with the way he was attached to his leg. That'll teach him to keep banging on your door and disturbing the peace."

Vale had been banging on her apartment door?

Faith bit the inside of her lip.

Maybe she should have answered one of his zillion calls to her cellphone, but she hadn't. She'd erased his messages without listening to them. Talking to him would accomplish nothing. Not at this point. Maybe when time had passed and she was stronger, when he didn't make her dream of things she knew better than to dream about. But not yet because her dreams were filled with him.

"That's why Vale dognapped Yoda?" She tried to wrap her brain around how Vale had gone from beating on her apartment door to stealing her dog. "Because Yoda attacked him?"

"I've no idea why the scoundrel took Yoda." Mrs. Beasley shuddered at what she obviously considered a harrowing experience. "He didn't ask for a ransom, just said if you wanted your dog back, you knew where to find him."

Faith fell back into a chair, her hand going to her temple.

Yoda dognapped by her former boss.

If she wanted her baby back, she had to go to him.

She had a good mind to do as Mrs. Beasley suggested and call the police and have Vale arrested. Watching his arrogant face plastered across the nine o'clock news would please her to no end. The great Dr. Vale Wakefield, talented neurosurgeon and playboy heir to a real estate empire, arrested for stealing a *helpless* dog. Oh, the press would have a field day.

But instead of picking up her phone, she glanced at a giggling Sharon.

"This really isn't funny, you know," she advised the woman who was quickly becoming a dear friend. "Your cousin has my dog."

"You have to give him points for creativity. Dognapping Yoda was quite ingenious in assuring you'd stop avoiding him." Sharon smiled smugly. "We Wakefields are known for our resourcefulness when it comes to getting what we want."

"You could go and get Yoda for me," Faith suggested, knowing Sharon's answer even before the woman said a word. Despite not being willing to budge an inch where Steve was concerned, Sharon seemed quite positive Faith should give Vale a chance to prove that he really had wanted to continue their relationship, that he'd wanted more than just a weekend fling with her, that she really was different from all the women he'd known.

But why give him a chance to prove that when doing so would only lead to pain down the road? Horrible pain because he wouldn't stick around and then where would she be?

"No way." Sharon shook her head. "Yoda is your dog. You know he has no taste and gnaws at my shoes. If you want the mangy mutt back, you'll have to go and get him. Personally, I say good riddance."

But the amused gleam in Sharon's eyes told she was teasing. Mostly. Yoda had yet to be completely forgiven for destroying an Italian shoe he'd mistaken for an expensive chew toy.

Vale wanted to talk to her. They'd talk. But she didn't

have anything different to tell him from what she'd said two weeks ago. Not really.

Of course there were all the things she hadn't said that last day. Like how much she missed the time they'd spent together. How much she missed consulting with him, laughing with him, just being with him. How much she missed how it had felt to lie in his arms and breathe in his masculine scent.

No, she hadn't told him any of those things and being away from the office for two weeks hadn't helped matters, had perhaps made things worse.

She missed Vale. Horribly. With all her heart.

Wherein lay the problem.

The truth was that Vale had stolen much more than her dog.

And as much as she'd like to think staying away from him would help prevent her from hurting, she wasn't so sure anything could help her from the devastation of being without Vale. Which made her no better than her mother. Destined to move through life searching for an elusive feeling she'd known once and desperately strove to find again.

"Fine," she told the two women anxiously waiting to hear her plans. "I'll go and get my dog."

CHAPTER ELEVEN

FAITH hadn't been inside Wakefield and Fishe since the day she'd quit her dream job. Marcus Fishe had come to her, tried to get her to tell him what had happened, had probably already figured out the truth.

In the end, Vale's partner said he hated to lose her, that the clinic would provide a generous severance package, see to it all her patients were taken care of with minimal disruption, and that he understood her need to move on. He hadn't really, though. No one in the neurology profession would.

Wakefield and Fishe was *the* place to work.

Faith greeted the Wakefield Tower night security guard, who smiled and had obviously been told to expect her as he waved her in, no questions asked even though he had to know she no longer worked in the building.

Vale was here. Waiting on her. Forcing her to talk to him.

What was left to say? She'd already said more than she probably should have on the day she'd lost her temper and quit.

Apparently, he hadn't said all he'd wanted to say. To get her dog back, she'd listen to whatever he needed to get off his chest.

But, really, what was the point? He should be grateful

she'd walked away rather than stick around mooning over him, because she'd had enough of him ignoring her just because she'd said no to continuing their affair.

When she stepped onto the fifty-sixth floor, her breath caught as she took in the scope of Wakefield and Fishe's reception area. She'd loved working here, loved working with Vale.

But that was in the past, and this wasn't a time for recriminations. She'd moved beyond that, was putting the pieces of her life back together, with Sharon's friendship and silent financial partnership in planning for her own neurology clinic.

She didn't need a man in her life.

The office was unusually quiet for only a little after 8:00 p.m. Had Vale sent everyone home at a decent hour for once?

Part of her wanted to go to her office, to see what had happened to the room she'd happily occupied for a year and a half of her life. The best year and a half of her life? But she wasn't here for reminiscing either. She was here for her dog. Nothing else.

Forcing one high-heeled foot in front of the other (Sharon had insisted she deck herself out), she made a beeline for Vale's office and didn't bother knocking. He knew she was there. The security guard would have alerted him the moment she stepped into the elevator.

He sat at his desk, pretending to read a document. She knew he was pretending, didn't know why he bothered.

He looked wonderful, a sight for sore eyes. Why did just seeing him undo what little progress she'd made over the past two weeks on putting him behind her?

Who was she kidding? She hadn't made any progress on getting over Vale. Perhaps she never would.

His gaze lifted to hers, studied her with his intense blue eyes. "You came."

Had he for one moment thought she wouldn't?

"You have my dog. I want him back." She used a tone of voice she hoped warned she wasn't to be messed with.

His gaze flickered to his desk, lingered a moment on nothing in particular, before meeting hers again. "Sit down, Faith."

Why was he torturing them this way? She'd stepped out of the picture and planned to stay out of the picture. He should be thanking his lucky stars she hadn't made a stink about the Cape May weekend.

Yet he didn't look as if he felt lucky.

He looked as if he was nervous. Which was insane. Vale didn't scare easily, if at all.

Yet, he did look nervous. From the way his gaze darted around to the way he fidgeted with the papers on his desk.

What was she doing? Looking for excuses for Vale's behavior? There were no excuses for how they'd ruined their relationship.

"This isn't a social visit, Vale. Give me my dog."

He stood up, towering above her and making her believe she'd imagined whatever vulnerability she'd thought she'd seen in him. He wasn't vulnerable. He was a Wakefield. One who didn't care who he hurt, just so long as he got what he wanted.

And for whatever reason, he'd thought he wanted to continue their affair and she'd thwarted his plans. That had to be what this was about.

"Not until you listen to me."

Faith plopped down in the chair in front of his desk, crossing her legs and staring at him as if he were a bug under a microscope. "Fine." She attempted to sound bored.

"Get to talking because I've a lot of things to do. Places to go, people to see, you know the routine."

Vale raked his gaze over Faith. She was wearing make-up, no glasses, and was dressed in feminine clothes that accented the body he craved. Her hair was down, brushing over her shoulders, teasing him with its multifaceted golden colors, teasing him with memories of his fingers clenched in the soft strands when he'd made love to her.

He'd never seen anyone more beautiful.

But, truthfully, what she was wearing didn't matter. Just that she was there.

"I've missed you."

"Having trouble finding someone else to handle your calls?" she snipped, picking an invisible speck off her short skirt.

Had she purposely worn the skirt to distract him with those long legs of hers? Had she known he'd take one look and start remembering what having those legs wrapped around his waist felt like?

He moved around his desk, sat on the corner, staring at her. "You didn't quit because of fielding calls on mutual patients."

She didn't answer, just examined her fingernails. When she looked up, their gazes met.

Enough was enough. If they were going to get anywhere one of them had to take a leap into uncharted waters. He'd never considered himself to be a coward, but he'd prefer her to go first, to admit that she missed him, missed not only their previous relationship but also the closeness they'd developed during Sharon's wedding weekend.

Not that he expected her to. Not after what he'd done.

He'd hurt her with his high-handedness.

As much as he hated it, he'd have to grovel if he wanted her forgiveness.

"I'm sorry for what happened the day you quit."

Her gaze snapped to his, but otherwise she just sat, long legs crossed, not saying a word. But her fingernails curled into her palms. She wasn't as immune to what he was saying as she acted.

"I was wrong to ask you to stay away from Sharon. I wasn't thinking clearly and hadn't been for a few weeks."

"Agreed." Again, she went for bored, but those fingers remained dug into her palms. "Can I go now?"

"No, you can't go." He stood up, unable to remain perched on the edge of the desk. "I don't want you to ever go, Faith. I want you back."

She jumped to her feet, her heels putting her at mere inches beneath his eye level. "You can't have me back."

Her eyes glittered almost violently. Her hands had fisted at her sides. Her chin had lifted in the most stubborn of tilts. He'd never wanted her more.

"I refuse to accept that as your final answer. I will have you back, Faith. One way or another, you will be mine again."

"My final answer?" Her mouth dropped open and she shook her head at him. "This isn't some game where you get to toy with me until I change my mind. I'm not coming back to the clinic. Or any clinic. I'm opening my own practice."

The pride in her voice raised his admiration for her. Faith was a survivor, a woman who could make her own way in the world. No surprise there. He'd always recognized that she was a rare jewel. Had instantly recognized that he wanted her on his side. He just hadn't meant to come to depend upon her quite so much. To the point that he truly had wanted her at his side on each and every patient consult. At his side all the time.

"If you won't come back to me, I'll come to you, Faith."

"What?" she asked, clearly confused. No wonder. He himself certainly wouldn't have understood fifteen seconds before.

"Hire me," he urged, knowing exactly what he had to do, what he was willing to do to have Faith back in his life. "I have excellent references, am willing to work cheap, and haven't lost my clinical skills." He hesitated, took a strand of her hair between his fingers, wanting to take hold of so much more. "Actually, the only thing I've lost that's ever mattered to me is you."

"Is that the problem, Vale? I walked out on you?" She pulled free of his touch, just as he'd known she would. "Let me remind you of how things really went down. You pushed me so far away I had no choice but to walk. For three weeks you ignored that I even existed, treating me like I didn't exist. Maybe I'd been spoiled by you including me in so many of your cases, but to suddenly be cut out for no reason other than that I refused to continue to have sex with you was wrong."

She was right, but how could he explain the way he'd felt when he'd looked into her eyes in the lighthouse and known the weekend wasn't nearly enough time with her? The way he'd felt when she'd told him she didn't want to continue their relationship?

"I couldn't be near you without wanting you, Faith."

She shoved against his chest, her hands sending shock waves through him. "You were around me for months and months without wanting me. You just want what you think you can't have," she continued, practically in his face. "Typical man."

"Don't fool yourself into believing that I can't have you if I wanted you, Faith," he warned, pride kicking in. "We both know that if I touched you right now you'd go up in flames."

"You're wrong." But she was lying. "You're a player who couldn't hold on to his new toy quite as long as he'd have liked. We both know if we'd pursued this you would have grown bored before long."

Vale shifted his jaw, reminding himself not to lose his temper, wondering why she was the only person able to push him beyond the point of reason. "I never made you promises or told you I was some great catch, but I was sincere when I told you I wanted us to continue what we'd started."

"Your point is?" She quirked her brow at him, obviously having already lost her temper. "Shall I remind you that I left? That I understood you never made me any promises?"

"I don't need reminding, Faith. I know you left me." For two weeks he'd been able to think of little else. Faith had left him. He missed her. He wanted her back. Whatever the cost. "Shall I remind you that I'm the one fighting to have you back in my life?"

She stared blankly at him.

"I'm serious about the job, Faith. Sharon did tell me your plans, so perhaps you no longer want to work here." He shrugged. "If you won't come back to Wakefield and Fishe, I'll come to work for you."

She studied him with suspicious green eyes. "Why would you want to do that?"

"Have you not listened to anything I've said? I miss you. I want you in my life. If not as my lover, then as my friend, my co-worker. Whatever you're willing to give me, I'll take."

She closed her eyes, swallowed. "Why are you doing this to me, Vale? I was here for eighteen months and you never noticed me. Why now, when I'm moving on, putting the pieces of my life together in a way I believe I can be happy about? Just leave me alone, please. I don't want to be hurt by you and we both know we'd never work out in the long run."

With her eyes squeezed shut, she looked so vulnerable. Part of him wanted to just step away, to let her be. But the truth was he *had* noticed her. Maybe he hadn't realized just how much he'd noticed her, how much he'd come to expect to spend his days with her, but he had noticed her.

Maybe he hadn't been willing to admit just how much he'd expected her to be a part of his life because then he would have had to examine why that was so.

The thought of losing her though had him examining all kinds of things he'd prefer not to.

"I can't leave you alone, Faith," he answered honestly, causing her eyes to flutter open.

"Why not?"

"Because I'm not me when you're not here."

Her gaze lifted to his. "Explain."

If only he could. "Nothing works the same when you're not with me. I don't work the same. It's like I get up on the wrong side of the bed and my days go downhill from there."

Her forehead wrinkled. "What are you saying? That I'm your lucky mojo or something?"

He shook his head. "It isn't that."

"Then what is it?" she demanded, losing patience with him again. "Tell me why I'm here, Vale. Why you dognapped my defenseless dog."

Defenseless, his hind end.

"I need you here, Faith. I need you with me."

"I thought you were willing to come to work for my clinic," she countered.

"Is that an offer?"

"No." But he saw the wall she'd built around her crack, knew he was starting to get through to her, and that made him all the more determined to lay everything on the line, to make her see reason.

"I think about you all the time," he admitted, chipping away at the crack, wanting to completely tear down the wall she'd built around herself. "When I wake up, when I go to sleep, all in between. I think about you."

She took a step back, bumping against his desk. "Guilt does strange things to a person's conscience."

"It's not guilt I feel for you, Faith."

As if she couldn't stand, she sat on the edge of his desk. "What do you feel?"

"This." He took her hand into his and kissed each fingertip. "This is what I feel, Faith."

She trembled. "That's just sex."

He shook his head. "I can get sex from anyone, Faith. I don't need sex, but I do need you. *You.*"

Her lip disappeared between her teeth. "You need me?"

"As much as the air I breathe. Quit shutting me out of your life."

She winced, pulled her hand free from his and slid her fingers beneath her thigh protectively. "This makes no sense, Vale. I was here every day, wanting us to go back to the way we were before we went to Cape May, and you shut me out. It was you who pushed me away. You can't go changing your mind."

"Why not?" he asked, cupping her face. "Why can't I admit I made a miscalculation and pushed away the best thing that's ever happened to me?"

"Because…because…" Her eyes closed again. "You just can't."

"People make mistakes, Faith. I thought if I stayed away you'd realize we were worth giving a chance. I thought you'd miss me and come to me. You didn't, and the longer you stayed away the more frustrated I got. I took that frustration out on you. Forgive me."

Moisture welled in her eyes, but she held fast, shaking her head. "I can't."

"Why not?"

"Because you'll hurt me again, and I don't think I could bear it when you did."

"Give me a chance to prove I won't."

She shook her head. "There's nothing you can do because I know you'll hurt me. You're you and I'm me and even under the best of circumstances couples don't last. We don't stand a chance."

He sighed. "I never meant to hurt you. You must know that. You shut me out too, Faith. I was offering you something I'd never offered any woman, was wanting things with you I'd never wanted before. You weren't the only one hurting. You're not being rational."

She crossed her arms across her chest, glared at him. "Nowhere is there a law written that says I have to be rational."

"Fine, then be irrational and marry me."

Faith's eyes bugged out of her head.

His probably did too.

Where had his proposal come from? He hadn't intended to ask Faith to marry him. He wanted her back in his life, but marriage? That was extreme.

But even as he thought it, if marrying Faith meant having her back in his life, proving to her he wanted her in his life long-term, he'd walk down the aisle. He enjoyed her company. She was smart, beautiful, and he craved her body.

"No."

He gritted his teeth, staring at her in disbelief. "No?"

"No, I won't marry you. You know how I feel about marriage. Do I need to spell it out for you?"

"Apparently," he said dryly.

"I don't need you or any man in my life."

Enough was enough. He'd tired of the games, of the going back and forth. "We both know you're in love with me, Faith. Quit clinging to your hang-ups about marriage because of your father leaving, because of your mother's multiple weddings."

Her eyes narrowed and her mouth dropped open in disbelief. "I've never told you that I loved you."

"Haven't you?" He called her bluff.

"I'd definitely recall if I'd said 'I love you' to any man. I haven't. Ever."

He leaned in, placed his hands to either side of her on his desk, trapping her beneath his gaze. "You don't love me?"

Not meeting his eyes, she swallowed. "I—I…well…"

"Well, what?" He wasn't going to let her off the hook. Not until she answered him. "It's a yes or no question. Either you do or you don't."

She took a deep breath. "The point isn't whether or not I love you."

"Then you do love me?" His pulse hammered at his throat, beating him into a dizzy head spin as he waited for her to answer. Why was hearing her say the words so important?

"Quit twisting my words."

"Quit being stubborn, and admit you've missed me as much as I've missed you."

"Fine, I've missed you, but that changes nothing."

Vale smiled. Finally he was making progress, was stepping behind that wall. "And you've thought about me?"

"I've thought about you." Her chin lifted. "Occasionally."

"In the mornings?" he pressed. "In the evenings? In the shower?"

"Vale, this is crazy," she scolded, frowning, twisting free of where he had her pinned on his desk. She walked across his office, standing beside the long mahogany work table they'd spent many a night sitting at with data files spread out around them. "I'm pleading the Fifth."

"Those who plead the Fifth are always guilty, Faith." He stood, moved to just behind her, tempted to touch, but waited for a sign she'd welcome him.

"That's not true," she denied, her gaze narrowed.

"Sure it is."

"Then answer me this—why do you want to marry me?"

"I'm not pleading the Fifth, if that's what you're expecting."

"But you aren't answering, are you?" she challenged, looking so sure of herself Vale had to slide his hands into his pocket to keep from taking her into his arms and kissing her stubborn mouth.

"I want to marry you so I can hold you in my arms every single night."

Her eyes widened.

"I want to marry you so I can wake up and see you first thing every single morning."

Her lips parted.

"I want to marry you so I can push up your skirt and make love to you any time I want, starting right now on the table you're leaning against."

"Oh." She straightened from the table.

"I want to marry you so I can kiss away your tears and take you with me to family functions so you can protect me from my crazy family."

Her fingers clenched and unclenched at her sides.

"But mostly, Faith, I want to marry you so I don't ever have to be without you again. I want you to be mine."

CHAPTER TWELVE

FAITH stood stock still, uncertain what to say or do.

Vale wanted to marry her?

What rabbit hole had she fallen into and bumped her head? Then the obvious reason for his pursuit hit her.

Why hadn't she realized? She should have already told him, should have realized that was why he'd kept calling.

"I'm not pregnant if you're concerned that something resulted from our weekend."

Surprise filled his eyes. "I didn't think you were, Faith, but we can rectify that if you'd like to be."

This time Faith was the one filled with surprise. Was he kidding?

"Quit saying things like that!" Didn't he realize that his words were like a searing iron to her heart? Words that a deeply buried part of her wanted to believe yet couldn't.

"Why?"

"Because you don't mean them."

His face clouded. "You don't think I'd strip you naked and make love to you right here, right now, on the table behind you in the hope of making you pregnant?"

Had someone drugged him? Or maybe he'd fallen into a rabbit hole and hit his head. Because, one way or another, one of them was out of their head.

"I've repeatedly told you I'm sorry, Faith. Is it so impossible to forgive me? To trust me?"

"Yes!"

"Why?"

"Because if I forgive you, if I trust you, then I have no reason to stay away from you." Her eyes widened and her hand popped over her mouth simultaneously at her admission.

"Would that be so bad?" he asked gently, taking her fingers into his and pulling her hand away from her mouth.

She closed her eyes. "Yes."

"Why?"

"Quit asking me why!"

"Then I'll ask you to love me, Faith, because I want your love every day for the rest of our lives."

She blinked. "Since when?"

"Since you walked out on me and took my heart with you."

Her face squished into contorted confusion. "What are you saying?"

He smiled down at her. "What I've been trying to say since you walked into this room."

Faith's heart tapped a wild beat in her chest. Could it be true? Could he be telling her what she thought he was telling her? Could this really be happening? Did she want this to be happening?

And if it was, could she take a chance on Vale? Could she believe he could really love her? Could really want to spend his life with her and wouldn't leave her? Oh, God, what if he left?

But what if he didn't ever leave?

What if he really did love her and wanted to be with her for ever? Wouldn't that be worth any risk?

"Tell me," she whispered, staring into his eyes and

seeing everything she couldn't quite believe reflected in the way he was looking at her.

"I love you, Faith." He cupped her face, brushing his thumb along her jaw line. "With all my heart and all my soul and all that I am, I love you, and I want to spend the rest of my life giving my love to you. Open up and let me."

She hadn't dreamed it was possible. Hadn't even contemplated what he was saying as a realistic possibility.

But Vale didn't hide his emotions, didn't attempt to mask them. He let his feelings for her shine in his eyes and she basked in the glory, letting his love thaw the wall she'd protected her heart behind since the day her father had walked out, since the first time she'd watched her mother walk down the aisle.

"This is crazy," Vale muttered, and took her in his arms before she could say anything. "If you won't let me tell you, if you won't believe my words, I'm going to show you."

With an offer like that on the table, Faith held her tongue. But when his lips covered hers, she kissed him back with the desperation of a woman who'd thought she'd forever lost the man she loved. With the joy of a woman who'd found him again.

Loved. Oh, God. She loved Vale.

With all her heart and all her being. Which left her so vulnerable. But if he was just as vulnerable to her, if he was there to look out for her vulnerable heart and vice versa, everything would be okay, right?

Oh! She couldn't think about that right now. Not when Vale's hands were everywhere. Cupping her face, tangled in her hair, beneath her blouse.

She didn't stop him when he made haste of ridding her of her clothes. Didn't stop him when he laid her back naked on the table while he shed his suit in record speed.

She certainly didn't stop him when he spread her legs and thrust inside her. She clung to his shoulders, clung to his body, loving him with all her heart and all her body.

Deeper and deeper he surged inside her, taking her back to that magical place she'd called Cape May but which had really been in his arms. Taking her back to explosive ecstasy.

Her thighs spasmed in sweet, hot throbs, pulsing in rhythm with her heartbeat. With his heartbeat.

Their heartbeat.

"I love you," she mouthed on the peak of her orgasm, feeling his body tighten against hers, feeling him lose his control and explode deep inside her.

Body slick with sweat, he rested his forehead against hers and stared into her eyes. "You'll marry me?"

She bit the inside of her lower lip. "Marriage scares me."

"I won't settle for less, Faith. I want the world to know you're mine."

"And that you're mine?"

"I am yours, Faith. Completely and irrevocably. I'll never leave you. Trust me."

Heart slamming against her ribcage, she wrapped her arms around his neck, holding him close. "It's not as if I really have a choice, is it? Now that you've made up your mind you want to marry me, you won't stop till I say yes."

"We Wakefields always get what we want."

She smiled up at him, awe still filling her at the magic this man had brought into her life. "You do realize that if we marry, I'll be a Wakefield, too?"

He looked at her with pure unadulterated love reflecting in his eyes. "And what is it you want, Faith? Because I'll give you anything within my power."

"You."

"You have me. Always and for ever."

They dressed slowly—so slowly they ended up undressed again rather than clothed.

This time Vale made love to her more slowly, gently, staring into her eyes with each thrust of his body into hers. Deeper and deeper until he was so tangled with her she didn't know where she ended and he began.

Her breaths came in ragged pants. Her heart beat thudded in arrhythmic bursts. Her soul merged with his.

When he came, she cried out his name, cradling him in her body, stunned by what they'd shared.

Stunned by how loved she felt.

Stunned by how much she trusted him.

Stunned by the fact they'd made love twice without protection.

"Vale?"

"Hmm?"

"I do love you and I will marry you, but I'm not ready for a baby."

He rose up on his elbow, staring down at her. "No? I'm in no rush to start a family. The idea of having you to myself for a while appeals." He waggled his brows knowingly. "But when you're ready to start trying for a baby, I'll be an eager participant." His lips quirked into a half-smile. "What are you ready for, Faith?"

"You did offer me my job back," she reminded him, sitting up and reaching for her clothes.

He watched her replace her bra, fastening the hooks between her breasts. "I also offered to come to work for you."

"I doubt starting a new business and getting married at the same time would be a wise decision." She pulled her blouse over her head, straightening the material at her waist, and looked around the table for her panties. Looking way too sexy, he held up her panties like a prized trophy. Faith rolled her eyes and snatched her silky underwear from him. "I loved working here with you, our research and the progress we're making on Parkinson's."

He sat up, pulled on his boxer briefs and slacks. Not bothering with his shirt, he leaned against the table. She tucked her blouse into her skirt. He stood silent a few minutes, then shifted his gaze to her.

"If starting your own clinic is what you want, we'll make it happen, do our research there." He sucked in a deep breath, met her gaze. "I don't want us being together to stand in the way of your dreams. Not ever."

Straightening from slipping her shoes back onto her feet so he wouldn't tower over her, she turned to him. Vale was a top-notch neurosurgeon, used to having his way, leading the pack. Was he seriously saying he'd help her build a neurology practice of her own?

"You'd really come work for me if I wanted my own clinic?"

He nodded. "In a heartbeat."

She stared at him in wonder, seeing the sincerity shining in his eyes. "I believe you would."

One corner of his mouth lifted and he gave a low laugh. "Haven't you figured out the truth yet, Faith? I'd move the world if that's what it took to make you happy, to make you mine for ever."

"No moving the world necessary." Pressing her palms to his bare chest, she smiled up at him, happier than she could recall ever being. "But I would like my dog back."

He grinned. "About that…"

Faith narrowed her gaze, giving him a playful glare. "What have you done to my poor Yoda?"

He held up his arm, displaying the tiny teeth marks. "Your poor Yoda is anything but poor. We need to work on his people skills."

Faith rubbed her finger over the red spots. "He was just trying to defend my honor."

"We need to sit down and have a talk with him, let him know that in the future that's my job."

"Where is Yoda?"

"At Sharon's."

"Sharon's?" Faith shook her head in wry amusement. Her friend had sure played it cool that evening. Faith had never suspected a thing. "She was in on this? Agreed to watch Yoda?"

He shook his head. "Nope, but I shut the little Cujo into her bedroom along with water, food, and newspaper. I figure he should be okay there for a few hours until she comes home and finds him."

Uh-oh. Faith grimaced. "You didn't happen to notice if her closet door was shut, did you?"

Looking confused, Vale shrugged. "I didn't notice. Why?"

Faith started laughing. "You are going to be in so much trouble when she discovers Yoda. Sharon isn't Yoda's biggest fan."

"See…" he grinned "…another example of needing to work on your dog's people skills."

"Maybe it's just Wakefields he takes issue with."

"That may present a problem in the near future, then."

She smiled up at him, loving the way he looked at her, at the warmth in his eyes. "Why's that?"

He lifted her chin, kissed her. "Because just as soon as it can be arranged you're going to be my wife, making you a Wakefield, too."

EPILOGUE

THE sun was shining on the first day of August. A gentle breeze blew in off the Atlantic and butterflies fluttered around the grounds of the Cape May lighthouse.

When Vale had first suggested having their wedding at the lighthouse, she'd thought he was teasing. When she'd realized he wasn't, she'd agreed that the lighthouse was the perfect place to start the rest of their lives.

Unlike his cousin's wedding, they'd opted for small, and had somehow managed to keep their upcoming nuptials out of the press.

Faith had invited her mother and stepfather, a beaming Mrs. Beasley, and a couple of friends from med school and work. Vale had his mother, Sharon, Angela, their parents, and Marcus Fishe, who served as his best man. Sharon stood next to Faith as her matron of honor.

Vale had also invited Steve, but mostly so the handsome footballer's presence could get under Sharon's skin.

All Wakefields apparently enjoyed getting under people's skins and based on how the former beauty queen kept stealing glances at her estranged husband her skin was crawling.

Vale had wanted to marry at the top of the lighthouse, but had conceded that Faith would have problems with the one hundred and ninety-nine steps in her wedding gown.

He'd offered to carry her, but thoughts of him being too tired for their wedding night had Faith convincing him that standing just behind the lighthouse on the grassy fenced lawn would be perfect, and a lot less windy for their photos.

Faith had struggled with asking stepfather number six to walk her down the aisle and had ended up deciding to walk alone. Her mother had seemed to understand. Vale, however, had wanted to track down her real father, to help her put to rest her abandonment issues. She'd assured him that he'd already done that by loving her. She didn't need anything more to have her happily-ever-after.

When the wedding march began to play, Faith walked to the man she loved with all her heart. The stubborn man who had so much pride and arrogance, but also the capacity to love her fully, completely, and without holding anything back.

The man who gave her so much. The whole world.

He was her whole world.

She handed her simple bouquet of wildflowers to Sharon, then turned to face the man she'd spend the rest of her life loving and being loved by.

The only other member of the wedding party was a tiny cream-colored poodle with a tiny black bowtie collar.

Yoda followed Faith down the aisle, sat at her feet, and quirked his head in silence at the vows being exchanged.

"I do," Faith promised, not able to keep the tears of joy from her eyes as she slid the ring onto the third finger of Vale's left hand.

When he took her hand in his, stared deeply into her eyes, his love shining as brightly as the sun above them, happy bubbles danced in her belly.

"I do," he promised, placing the golden band symbolizing that promise on Faith's finger. "For ever and always, I do."

Her insides melted and her knees wobbled.

"You may now kiss your bride," the minister told Vale.

His hands caressed her neck, holding her as if she were a fragile flower. "I love you, Mrs. Wakefield."

Then he kissed her, sealing his promise for all time.

Faith returned his kiss, knowing deep in her heart that, although there would be times of troubled waters just as there were in any relationship, their love would light the course safely back to each other.

WHEN ONE NIGHT
ISN'T ENOUGH

BY
WENDY S. MARCUS

MILLS
BOON

First published in Great Britain 2011
by Mills & Boon, an imprint of Harlequin (UK) Limited,
Eton House, 18-24 Paradise Road, Richmond, Surrey TW9 1SR

© Wendy S. Marcus 2011

ISBN: 978 0 263 88592 7

Harlequin (UK) policy is to use papers that are natural, renewable and recyclable products and made from wood grown in sustainable forests. The logging and manufacturing process conform to the legal environmental regulations of the country of origin.

Printed and bound in Spain
by Blackprint CPI, Barcelona

Dear Reader

Thank you so much for picking up this copy of my debut Mills & Boon® Medical™ Romance.

I've heard it said, "Men marry women like their mothers, and women marry men like their fathers." Is it true? I have no idea. But my mother-in-law was a nurse, like me, and my husband is an accountant, like my father.

What if your father was an insincere flirt, a womanizer, the absolute last type of man you'd choose to share your life with? Yet you're drawn to someone just like him, a man who visits your dreams and your nightmares, a man you crave with an intensity impossible to ignore. What then?

In this first book set in the fictional Madrin Memorial Hospital in upstate New York, meet Nurse Allison "Ali" Forshay who faces that exact situation. Haunted by memories of her childhood, Ali is adamant about not repeating the mistakes of her mother. Unfortunately, Dr. Jared Padget is damn hard to resist.

Sometimes life doesn't follow the plan. As long as you remain open to the possibility, happily ever after is still within reach.

I hope you enjoy Ali and Jared's story. Look for Ali's best friend and colleague Victoria's story, coming soon.

I love to hear from readers. Please visit me at www.WendySMarcus.com.

Wishing you all good things!

Wendy S. Marcus

This book is dedicated to my mom and dad, who taught me to always work hard and do my best. I wish they were here to see the result. And to my sister Dale, for loving me, encouraging me, and never letting me give up. I love you.

Special thanks go out to:

My editor, Flo Nicoll, who worked almost as hard as I did to get this book published. I couldn't have done it without your guidance, your patience, and your expertise.

My agent, Michelle Grajkowski. With you on my team I feel anything is possible.

My critique partner, Joanne Stewart, who wouldn't let me skimp on emotion.

My neighbour, Nancy B., who was the first person to ever read and critique my work.

All my writing buddies who cheer my accomplishments, commiserate over my disappointments, and motivate me to get back to work—especially Susan Wilson, Amy Strnad, Regina Richards, Jennifer Probst and Abbi Cantrell.

And last, but certainly not least in my heart, my husband and children, who have supported this endeavour from the start and have never once complained about eating takeout. They make every day worth living. I am truly blessed.

CHAPTER ONE

FLOAT nurse Allison Forshay glanced at the clock on the institutional white wall of the staff lounge in the emergency room, wishing she could accelerate time with the snap of her fingers. Then the eight hours and six minutes that remained of Dr. Jared Padget's last shift would vanish in seconds.

Along with him.

Hallelujah!

The chorus of sopranos belting out a private concert in her head came to an abrupt halt when the door opened and chatter from the busy outside hallway overpowered her glee.

Ali cringed, keeping her eyes on the patient chart open on the round table in front of her, struggling to maintain focus on her documentation for little Molly Dawkins, her first patient of the night. The three-year-old, blond-haired, blue-eyed terror had tried to bite the triage nurse and kicked at Ali when she'd attempted to expose the girl's infected big toe. Then Dr. Padget had arrived, complimented the pink polish on Molly's tiny toenails, the delicate gold bracelets on her ankle and wrist, and the princess tattoo on her hand. In less than three minutes he'd charmed that little girl right out of her sandal, confirming Ali's suspicions. Women of all ages were susceptible to the man's charisma.

If there was a vaccine to protect against it, Ali would have opted for a double dose.

The subtle change in the air gave him away, some type of electrostatic attraction that caused the tiny hairs on her arms to rise and lean in his direction, her heart rate to accelerate and her breath to hitch whenever he found her alone.

His blue scrub-covered legs and red rubber clogs entered her peripheral vision. He pulled out the chair beside her and sat down, brushing his arm against hers. No doubt on purpose, the rat.

"You've been avoiding me," Dr. Jared Padget said.

"You're hardly worth the effort it would take to avoid you." Although, in truth, she was.

"I'm leaving on Monday."

Yes! Finally! His arrival three months ago had thrown her life into a state of flux. Now, his temporary assignment over, his departure meant she could finally settle back into a normal routine free from his constant badgering at work and "coincidental" encounters on her days off. With a flippant wave of her hand she said, "Here. Gone. Alive. Dead. Makes no difference to me."

"Come on, Ali Kitten." He snatched her pen. "You know you're going to miss me."

"About as much as I'd miss a painful hemorrhoid," she said, glaring at him from the corners of her eyes. "And you know I don't like it when you call me that."

"Yeah," he said with a playful twinkle in his peridot-green eyes and that sexy smile, complete with bilateral dimples that tormented her in her sleep. He leaned back in his chair and clasped his long fingers, and her pen, behind his head. "That's what makes it so much fun."

Ali grabbed at her pen, making sure to mess up his neatly styled dark hair. He raised his hand over his head and back out of reach, his expression daring her to come closer.

She didn't.

He chucked the pen onto the table.

"I hear a bunch of you are going out tonight to celebrate my departure," he said, making no mention of the fact he hadn't been invited.

She shrugged, tamping down the other, less joyful, reason for the night out. "It's as good as any other excuse for the girls to get together. And it's easier and less fuss than burning you in effigy."

He moved forward, rested his elbows on the table and leaned in close. "Was that supposed to hurt my feelings, Kitten?" His voice, soft and deep, vibrated through her.

Four hours into a busy twelve-hour night shift, and he had the nerve to still smell fresh from the shower. A picture of him naked, water sluicing down his tall, firm body, slick with suds, forced its way into her mind. It took immense self-control not to pound her fists against her head to get rid of it.

"What's going on in that pretty little head, I wonder?" he teased, staring at her face as if trying to see behind what she hoped was a disinterested expression.

Heaven help her if he could. For months she'd fought this attraction. First she couldn't act on it. Now she wouldn't.

Distance was the only thing that worked so she gathered her charts and stood.

Jared rose to stand directly in front of her, so close she noticed a tiny freckle on the skin exposed by the V-neck of his scrub top, a minuscule droplet of chocolate she wanted to lick clean. He smelled so good, his scent an intoxicant that impaired rational thought.

She stared straight ahead at his clavicle, wouldn't meet

his eyes for fear the way he affected her would show. "Please, move."

"I think you don't want me to move, you like me right here."

"Now you can read minds?" She took a step back. Distance. What she wanted was distance between them. Preferably a continent, but the opposite side of New York State, the site of his next temporary assignment, would have to do.

"Yes, I can." He tilted his face in front of hers. "And you are thinking some very naughty thoughts, Nurse Forshay."

"Only if you consider me beating you with the bell of my stethoscope naughty. Now get out of my way." She pushed his arm. "I've got to get back to work, and so do you."

He turned serious for a change. "Are you ever going to forgive me?"

"To forgive you I would have to care about you." She looked up and locked eyes with him. "And I don't. Not one bit."

"You could if you'd try."

It was the same old argument. "Why on earth would I want to? From day one of your assignment here, an assignment that your friend, my *boyfriend,* recommended you for, might I add, you've been hell-bent on coming between us."

"Not at first." Jared held up his index finger. "Not until I realized neither one of you were happy."

More like until he'd decided she wasn't good enough for his friend. "I was happy." Maybe comfortable was a better word. "And so was Michael. Our relationship was just fine until you showed up." Wasn't it? She'd worked so hard to be the type of woman she thought Michael wanted.

"You didn't love him," Jared pointed out.

No, she hadn't. But Dr. Michael Shefford had been perfect for her. Stable. Dependable. Predictable. And in his quiet, unassuming way, he'd treated her well. Maybe she could have fallen in love with him if she'd had more time. *Right, Ali,* she chided herself. A year wasn't long enough?

"How I felt about Michael is irrelevant." She slammed her files onto the table and turned from him. "You took him out, got him drunk and sent him home with Wanda from Pediatrics. You knew she had a thing for him."

"I didn't force him into the car, Ali. I didn't strip off his clothes and push him into her bed, either."

Heck, there was a visual she could have done without. "And you most certainly didn't try to stop him. What kind of friend are you?"

Not hers, that's for sure. She could have had a nice, stable life with Michael, who, until Jared had come to town, never stayed up past eleven unless he was working, never went out drinking with the boys and never showed an interest in any woman but her. She'd have done her best to make him happy, to have the quiet, anonymous life she'd dreamed of since childhood.

"Over the past month we have beat this to death." With an uncharacteristic disregard for his appearance, Jared ran his fingers through his hair. "If I thought Michael was making a terrible mistake, by all means I would have stopped him. But he and Wanda are good together."

A point Michael had made four weeks ago, during what was supposed to be his apology for cheating. The one thing Ali would not forgive. Usually sedate, Michael hadn't been able to tamp down his new-romance exuberance as he'd extolled all the attributes that made Wanda perfect for him, inadvertently identifying all the areas he'd found Ali lacking. No breakup remorse there.

"They're happy together," Jared said.

Yeah. The only one not happy was *her*.

"Michael was a great study partner in medical school," Jared went on. "He's a good friend. But he's the most boring person I have ever met. He's plain old vanilla ice cream, and you're chocolate fudge ripple with rainbow sprinkles. He's high-fiber cereal and skim milk for breakfast. You're blueberry pancakes with warm maple syrup. You lost your spark when he came around. He's so dull, he tarnished your shine. Are you so desperate to get married you'd settle for a lackluster, routine, boring life?"

"I am not desperate to get married." Holy cow. She'd actually stomped her foot. Well, she wasn't desperate. Really. But after all her unstable mother had put her through, bringing a lineup of losers into their home, dozens and dozens of destined-for-failure relationships, new-romance euphoria followed by bitter breakup histrionics that enticed nosy neighbors out to gawk and brought the police around several times a year; a stable life, free from drama, with one trustworthy, committed man, held great appeal. "And my life is none of your concern."

"Over time he would have made you miserable. In return you would have made his life a living hell. I've seen it happen. Hell, I've lived it."

"The only one around here who's making me miserable is you, Dr. Padget."

"You need a real man, Ali. Someone as passionate as you are, not Mr. missionary position, lights off, once a week on Wednesday night Shefford."

Ali gasped, couldn't believe Michael had shared that with his friend.

"Let me show you what it's like to be with a real man," he said with the cocky confidence that made him so appealing. He lowered his voice, adding, "And you will never again settle for mediocre."

God help her, she wanted to take him up on his offer. Every cell in her nervous system tingled with frenetic energy at the thought of spending the night in his strong arms, allowing his experienced fingers full rein over her body. Damn him! She refused to belittle herself for one night of pleasure, to allow him to assuage his lust with her, when any woman would do. "That hey-baby-I-want-to-fill-your-cannoli-with-my-cream personality get you a lot of dates?"

Jared laughed.

Ali plowed on. "If you ruined my relationship with Michael so you could have a crack at me, you've wasted your time. Because as wrong as you think Michael was for me, no man is more wrong for me than you." A man like her philandering father. A flirt. A schmooze. A woo-a-woman-into-bed-using-any-means-necessary man.

The door to the lounge opened, ending their private conversation. Tani, the E.R.'s unit secretary, popped her head in, her jet-black hair an interesting configuration of twirls and curls, in staunch contrast to her pale complexion. "Ambulance on the way. Forty-seven-year-old male, three hundred plus pounds, full cardiac arrest, CPR in progress, paramedics unable to intubate. ETA—four minutes."

Jared transformed back into a dedicated professional in an instant. "Clear—"

"I'll clear out Trauma Room One," Ali finished for him.

"I'll need—"

"ET tubes, assorted sizes on the tray by the head of Bed One, two pediatric, just in case, IV primed and the crash cart open and ready."

"Call—"

"Respiratory Therapy and Radiology to let them know what's coming." Ali scooped up her charts and headed for the door. "I'm on it." Their differences aside, they made a great team at work.

Forty minutes later, Jared stood on the stoop in front of the E.R., arms crossed over his ribs, staring out into the dark parking lot, down the tree-lined hill to the distant lights on Main Street. The crisp November air cleared his head, the quiet calmed him. Slowly, his tension began to ease.

"You were supposed to save him!" an irate male teenager yelled, disrupting Jared's solitude. "It's your job to save people!"

Jared turned to his left. The fifteen-year-old son of the man he'd pronounced dead five minutes earlier stomped toward him. Baggy pants, long hair and pierced eyebrow aside, the kid looked ready to commit murder.

Jared pushed off the pillar he'd been leaning against, thankful the blame game would be played outside rather than in the crowded E.R. corridor. Through the electronic glass doors he saw Ali with the boy's distraught mother under one arm and his hysterical little sister under the other, trying to calm them.

"I'm sorry," Jared said.

"You're sorry?" the boy screamed, his voice cracking, tears streaming down his enraged face. "What good does that do me? My dad is dead because *you*..." he stopped in front of Jared and poked him in the chest with his index finger "...didn't do your job."

Jared took a deep breath, channeling calm, understanding it was easier to blame the doctor, knowing that pointing out the obvious—his patient had been at least one hundred and fifty pounds overweight, smoked two packs of cigarettes per day and led a sedentary lifestyle—wouldn't negate the fact that a forty-seven-year-old husband and father was dead.

And, despite his best efforts, Jared had been unable to resuscitate him.

"Sometimes," Jared said, looking down into watery brown eyes, working hard to keep his voice calm so his own anger and frustration didn't show, "no matter how hard we try, things don't turn out the way we want them to." Put those words to a nifty jingle, and they could be the theme song to Jared's life. "I did everything within my power to save your dad."

As if someone had stuck him with a pin, the tough teen deflated against him. "I don't want him to be dead. What am I going to do without him?"

Jared grabbed the boy in a tight hug, holding him upright, which took a good amount of strength. "I've been where you are," Jared said, agonizing over what the kid would go through in the next few days, weeks and months. "You're going to get through this." But it wouldn't be easy, and he'd never forget this day.

"He yelled at me to turn off my music," the boy said in between sobs. "I didn't listen. If only I had, maybe I would have heard him call for me. Maybe he'd be alive right now."

Jared remembered the "if only" scenarios that had run through his head when, at the same age, he'd been alone to deal with his own father's heart attack. If only his mom hadn't gone to the store to buy antacids, leaving him in charge of his sick father. If only he hadn't listened when his dad had told him not to dial 911, the delay the reason the ambulance had arrived too late to save him. If only he'd taken the CPR elective offered the first quarter of his sophomore year of high school. If only he'd run next door to see if Mrs. Alvarez, a nurse, was home, instead of staying by his dad's side, holding his hand, watching him take his last breath.

"Your dad was not a healthy man," Jared said, patting the boy's back. "He suffered a massive heart attack. There's nothing you or I or anyone could have done to save him."

"What do I do now?" the boy asked in a small voice.

Jared placed both hands on the kid's shoulders and took a step back so he could look him in the eye. "You go back into the E.R. You pick up your little sister and reassure her you're still here, and you'll look after her just as well as your dad would have. You kiss your mom on the cheek and tell her you love her, and you're there for her, and you'll do whatever you can to help her." Jared shook the kid to make sure he had his full attention. "Don't just say the words. Mean them. Live them. And no matter what happens, do not let your mother push you away." If only Jared hadn't, maybe things wouldn't have fallen apart.

Maybe he'd have been able to honor his father's final plea: *"Take care of your mother."*

"There you are." Ali walked over to them. He hadn't heard the electronic doors open. How long had she been standing there? How much had she heard? "Are you Jimmy?" she asked the boy, who nodded. "Your mother's looking for you."

Jimmy turned away from Ali, inhaled a shaky breath and wiped his eyes.

"I'm so sorry about your dad," Ali said, placing a caring hand on Jimmy's shoulder.

"Me, too," he replied, and, with a composed look that earned Jared's respect he took a deep breath, straightened his spine and walked into the E.R.

Jared turned back to the parking lot, needing a few minutes to regain his own composure, remembering the ride home from the hospital, his mother's anger, her harsh accusations and the years of being treated as if he didn't exist that followed.

To quell the painful memories trying to escape the remote part of his brain where he'd locked them, Jared contemplated his favorite topic of recent weeks. Nurse Ali Forshay.

He remembered their first interaction, before he had known she was his friend's girl, in the close confines of the clean utility room. He'd brushed against her, reaching for a roll of tape, and they'd both gone still, shared a stunned did-you-feel-what-I-just-felt look. More than a tingle, he'd been jolted by an awareness, a powerful attraction that'd had him on the verge of taking her into his arms and kissing her, a women whose name he hadn't even known.

Soulmate? Maybe.

His type of woman? If he allowed himself to have a type, she'd be it.

Pretty. Smart. Funny.

A great nurse with an unparalleled bedside manner.

If he were free to shack up for a while, she'd be at the top of his I-want-her-in-my-bed list. But he wasn't free, mentally or legally.

"You okay?" Ali asked, coming to stand beside him.

"Just peachy. How about you?"

"You were great with Jimmy. I'm sorry you lost your dad so young."

He couldn't look at her. "It's why I became a physician, so no kid would have to deal with what I went through. I'm doing a great job of it, huh?"

"You're not God." She set her hand on his forearm, sending a flare of soothing warmth throughout his body. He craved her touch with a ferocity that excited him as much as it unnerved him.

"You coded Jimmy's dad twelve minutes longer than

any other physician here would have," she said. "You did your best."

He tilted his head down and to his left, and their eyes met, held. Hers conveyed genuine concern, empathy. He'd seen it dozens if not hundreds of times over the months they had worked together, directed at her patients, never at him. Yet, instead of using the moment as an opportunity for a sincere conversation between them, he chose to ignore the unwanted, long-suppressed feelings starting to stir deep in his damaged soul for a chance to play, to forget.

"Careful, Kitten," he said in an exaggerated whisper, taking care to make sure there was no one around to hear his term of endearment that delighted him as much as it aggravated her. "I might get the impression you're starting to like me." His mood lifted. "That as hard as you're trying not to, you can't help yourself."

"Nah." She looked down at her watch. "The hospital pays me to be kind and compassionate. Lucky for you I'm still on the clock."

"Good." He leaned in close to her ear. "Maybe we can go someplace private and you can give me a little more of your commm…passion."

She pinched him.

Good for her. The girl had spunk. "Ouch." He rubbed his upper arm. "Where'd the kindness go?"

She looked up at him, her light blue eyes narrowed.

"I'm on the verge of breaking down." He wiped at his dry lashes. "I think I feel some tears coming."

She turned and walked back toward the E.R. without giving him a second glance. And she looked just as fine from the back as she did from the front, her lavender scrub pants hugging her perfectly shaped rear, her long brown hair up in a loose knot and sensible little gold hoop earrings curving under her kissable earlobes.

"Don't women like it when a man shows his emotions?" he called after her.

She stopped. "Lust is not an emotion, Dr. P.," she answered over her shoulder.

"It sure is. Come over to my place after work and we'll do a Google search. Whoever's right gets to choose what we do next. You wanna know what I'll pick?"

Ali hit the button beside the electronic doors.

As they started to open he called out, "Time's running out, Ali."

She hesitated before walking back into the E.R.

Jared waited a minute, trying to contain his smile. He knew she wouldn't bite, but provoking her was so much fun. No one entertained him like Ali. For the first time in the two years he'd worked as an agency physician, traveling from hospital to hospital throughout New York State, Jared might actually miss someone when an assignment ended. A sure-fire sign it was past time for him to move on.

Relationships, loving someone, getting married, weakened people, made them dependent and vulnerable. His father's death had crushed his mother's spirit, left her brokenhearted, angry and unable to find joy. His wife's deceit, desertion and the resulting legal problems that had him fighting to stay out of jail had almost done the same to him.

No. He preferred to go it alone. No attachments, no expectations, no one for him to disappoint and no one to disappoint him.

Ali took the patient chart her coworker held out to her. "I'm heading down for break," the other nurse said. "I put a D&D in Exam Room One."

A drunk and disorderly isolated in a private room at the

far end of the inverted T-shaped hallway. "Thanks," Ali said with mock appreciation.

"His friends are helping him change into a gown."

Super-de-duper. A bunch of rabble-rousers to egg him on. She glanced at her watch. Four-twenty-two in the morning on the night shift that would not end. Opening the folder, she reviewed the Reason for Visit: patient injured at strip club. Attacked by bouncer during lap dance. Pain in left eye, left cheek, jaw, abdomen and right ribs.

Ali listened outside the door before knocking. All was quiet until a male voice called out, "Come in."

"My name is Allison," she said as she pushed the wedge under the door to keep it open. "I'll be your nurse." Before entering, she evaluated the room's four occupants—three visitors with their dress pants and button-down shirts disheveled, two of whom were slumped in chairs, one leaning with his back to the wall. They looked tired. Sedate.

Good. She placed the patient chart on the counter by the sink and walked toward the dark-haired man sitting with his bare legs hanging over the side of the stretcher, his head hanging low, both arms braced at his hips, not quite holding him steady. "Can you tell me how much you've had to drink tonight?"

She placed her hand on his wrist to take his pulse and began her assessment. AOB—alcohol on breath.

He looked up. "Enough to make you the most beautiful woman in the world."

"Gee, thanks." Left eye swollen, partially closed, mild bruising, dried blood in the outer corner. Left cheek swollen and red. Dried blood noted to the left nostril.

He blinked as if trying to clear his vision. "Ali?" He lowered his eyes to her name badge. "Well, hot damn." He turned to his friends, swayed and latched on to the bedrail for support. "Looks like my chances of getting lucky are on the rise, my friends."

Hell. A guy she knew from high school. His face battered, she hadn't recognized him. "Your pulse is fine." She snapped the plastic covering over the thermometer probe. "Hold this under your tongue."

"There are other things I'd rather do with my tongue." He stuck said body part out and flicked it rapidly from side to side. His friends snickered.

"And as soon as you leave the E.R., you can do them all," Ali replied. "But right now I need you to lift it and hold this thermometer under it."

He smiled and slid the probe between his closed lips. Slowly.

Ali took a moment to return to the chart to document his pulse rate and learn his name. Robert Braylor. Oh, no. Bobby "B.B." Braylor.

A beep sounded. Bobby's sojourn into silence ended. "Ali here is my favorite backseat cowgirl," he said. "She likes a hard ride. Isn't that right, Cream Cheese?"

Cream Cheese. Bobby's high school nickname for her. Because her thighs were so easily spreadable. As a stupid teenage girl she'd found it amusing. As an adult she recognized it for what it was, a shameful and humiliating moniker for a girl so desperate for affection and love she'd tried to find them in the arms of boys who'd doled them out in ten-minute increments. Usually while half dressed, in the backseat of a car, in the woods, or, if she was lucky, in a bed when no grown-ups were around. Good for sex and nothing more.

Ali considered walking out of the room, letting someone else deal with Bobby. But no. She was a trained professional, skilled at handling every type of patient. So she ignored his rude comments and proceeded with her evaluation. The sooner she finished the quicker she could leave, without shirking her duties.

Removing the blood-pressure cuff from the metal basket on the back wall, she fastened it to Bobby's upper arm. "After I take your blood pressure I'll get Dr. Padget. He'll probably want some X-rays."

Ali tightened the cuff around Bobby's arm, ignoring a twinge of dread at the thought of Bobby meeting Jared, the two of them discussing her, Bobby reinforcing Jared's opinion of her. Instead she listened through her stethoscope, focusing on the beats while she watched the mercury in the sphygmomanometer drop. One eighteen over seventy-four. Ali removed the cuff and placed it back in the basket.

In the few seconds it took to reach over the head of the bed, Bobby stood, grabbed her by the waist and ground himself against her butt. "I've got another pressure that needs tending before you go."

Ali swung her upper body around. They were alone—the visitors had left, closing the door to the room behind them. "Stop it, Bobby."

"Come on, Ali." He ran a hand up her belly to her chest and squeezed her breast. Hard. "For old times' sake."

"No." She tried to pull away, did not want this. She was a different person now, didn't sleep around anymore.

He turned her to face him, pushed her back into the wall, forced his body against hers, making it difficult to expand her chest to take a breath. He jammed his erection between her legs. She tried to move. Couldn't. Alcohol had not affected his strength one bit. When had he gotten so tall? Aggravation turned to fear.

"I know I was one of your favorites," he said.

Because ten years ago he'd had a car, a fake ID and a never-ending supply of money for beer and cigarettes. For a wayward fifteen-year-old girl looking to escape her life, he had been the perfect date.

"I need you so bad," he said, moving one of his hands to the back of her head, crushing her mouth to his so hard she tasted blood. His other hand fumbled with the drawstring of her scrub pants.

"Get your hands off of me," Ali yelled. She tried to twist away, to lift her knee. Neither worked. So she bit his lip. When he jerked back his head she screamed, "Help! Dr. P. Anyone. Help!" She prayed someone would hear her.

"Quiet, Ali." He clamped his hand over her mouth. "You know you want it. You always wanted it."

CHAPTER TWO

JARED was on the computer behind the front desk of the E.R., checking a patient's lab results, when Ali cried out for help. Without hesitation, he closed down the confidential screen, jumped to his feet, his chair rolling into the file cabinet behind him with a loud bang and ran in the direction of her scream.

The door to Exam Room One, where Ali had gone to admit a new patient, was closed. Jared slammed it open. A tall man, the back of his hospital gown flapping open, exposing his red and blue plaid boxer shorts, had Ali pinned to the wall, one arm clamped around her waist, holding her, while his hips jabbed in her direction and a hand behind her head crushing her lips to his while she fought to turn her head and push away.

"Get your hands off my nurse," Jared said, keeping his voice deadly calm, trying not to escalate the situation.

"Easy, Doc," the assaulter said with a minimal slur. "Ali and I go way back. We were just getting reacquainted."

Ali struggled in his hold. "We were not. Let go of me, Bobby."

"I'd listen to the lady," Jared said, walking into the room, one careful step at a time, letting the door close behind him. "Or you're going to find yourself flat on your back on that stretcher, in four-point restraints, with a garbage bag full of ice on your groin." He walked up next to Bobby, close enough to smell the booze on his breath and see the lust in his bloodshot eyes. "Here in the emergency room, that's the only treatment we offer for swollen genitalia."

"Come on. Give me a break," Bobby said, still holding on to Ali. "I'm getting married in a few hours."

"Lucky girl to score a winner like you," Jared said, hoping the patient would come after him, provide justification for him to fight.

It worked. Sort of. The patient turned to Jared, must have loosened his hold because Ali broke free, stumbled toward him, into his waiting arms. Eyes locked with the sexual predator, he held her and murmured, "You're okay."

She nodded against his chest and inhaled a shaky breath.

The second she moved to step away from him, Jared released her, not wanting her to feel at all restricted. And as if she hadn't just been attacked, she gave him her report. "Twenty-five-year-old intoxicated male involved in an altercation with a bouncer at a strip club. Suffering from facial trauma, abdominal and rib pain. Vital signs within normal limits, documented in his chart."

"I'll take it from here, Ali. Go take a break." Jared didn't want any witnesses when he "helped" his patient onto the stretcher.

"I'm fine," Ali said. But her voice trembled.

Jared wanted to take her back into his arms, to hold her, comfort her, let her know she was safe, that he wouldn't let anyone hurt her. But he needed to deal with the deviate first. "Can you climb on to the stretcher alone, or do you require my assistance?" Jared asked, more than willing to "assist."

In what was probably his first good decision of the early morning hours, the man climbed on to the stretcher.

Jared walked over to Ali, keeping the man in his sight. "Your lip is bleeding," he whispered, lifting her chin to get a better look, hating that a remnant from her altercation marred her beautiful face. "Go clean it. You don't know where his foul mouth has been."

With a surprised look, Ali reached up to touch her swollen lower lip.

"I'm guessing in your condition..." he looked at the man's tented hospital gown "...you'll have a hard time giving me a urine specimen, which means I'm going to have to insert a catheter into your bladder to obtain a urine toxicology screen."

Nah. He winked at Ali. Let the idiot sweat for a few minutes.

"Like hell you will," Bobby said. "Where are my clothes? I'm getting out of here."

"You're not going anywhere," Jared said, channeling composure. "Not until the police get here. You see, I have zero tolerance for men who mistreat women."

"Let's not make this into a big deal," Ali said.

"I've treated too many sexual assault victims to let his behavior slide."

"Sexual-assault victim?" Bobby piped up. "Are you nuts? It's only Ali. She was playing hard to get. No harm."

"He's right, Dr. P." Ali looked defiant, but he'd seen the flash of hurt at Bobby's cruel words, the glitter of tears in her eyes as she turned to leave. "It's only me. No harm."

"You..." Jared pointed to the drunk "...stay put. Do not leave that stretcher." Then he followed Ali. "Ali, wait." Halfway to the staff lounge she stopped, but didn't turn to look at him.

When he caught up to her she said, "We knew each other in high school. Leave it alone, it's over."

"You need to teach that man a lesson. He needs to know the way he treated you is not okay."

"What I need," she said wearily, "is to clean my lip, shake this off and get back to work. And what Bobby needs is to be examined, treated and discharged so he can go get married."

Like Jared would let him off that easy. "You don't want to stand up for yourself, fine. I'll do it for you. I'm calling the police."

Fire blazed in her eyes. Good. With all of her negative energy directed at him, she wouldn't focus on how vulnerable she'd been, on how that punk had disrespected and degraded her.

"Tomorrow you'll be gone, Dr. Padget. I, on the other hand, live in this town. If you call the police, I'll be stuck dealing with the fallout, the questions, the rumors and people dredging up Bobby's role in a past I'm not all that proud of."

"Your past has nothing to do with what happened tonight. A man tried to force you…" His voice cracked. He couldn't say the words, wouldn't consider what might have happened if he hadn't heard her scream. "If you don't want to press charges, fine. But I can't overlook this. I have to report the incident. I'm sorry."

"Yes, you are." She looked up at him, not a tear to be found in her angry blue eyes. "A sorry excuse for a man I thought wanted to be my friend." And she stormed down the hall into the lounge.

He'd made her mad. Nothing new there. But deep down it bothered him. He didn't want her to hate him, didn't want to leave on bad terms. Huh. Never bothered him before. Why did she matter when no one else did?

* * *

"No. More. Tequila," Ali insisted that evening when their waitress walked over with her second, no, third tray of the Sunday night special: Watermelon Margaritas. "I have a nice buzz going. Next stop sloppy drunk."

"Says the woman who rarely orders anything stronger than seltzer with lime. What's going on with you?" asked Victoria, Ali's best friend since eleventh grade and the head nurse on 5E. Short dark hair and makeup flawless, her taste in clothes impeccable, she looked more ready for dinner at the country club than a night out with the girls.

The waitress set each of the four drinks she carried on the table then cleared off the empty glasses.

"Come on, Ali," her friend Polly, a fellow E.R. nurse, slurred. "We're shelebrating."

"Soon you're going to be puking if you don't slow down," said Roxie, a nurse from 5E, a medical surgical floor, as she wiped up the spillage when Polly wobbled her glass on the way up to her mouth. Roxie was tan, tall and thin to Polly's pale, short and chubby. Roxie was loud and outgoing to Polly's quiet and shy. Roxie was the bad girl to Polly's good girl. The two couldn't be more opposite, yet they'd been best friends since Ali, who floated between the two units, had introduced them last year.

"We didn't order these," Victoria said, always the pragmatic one.

"Maybe we did and we don't remember," Roxie rationalized. "I say we drink 'em."

"They're from him." The waitress pointed to a man at the far side of the bar.

O'Halloran's Tavern, a favorite hangout for Madrin Memorial Hospital personnel, served delicious food and trendy drinks in a casual atmosphere that offered something for everyone. Small groups of onlookers crowded around both pool tables in the back, where a mini-tournament was in progress. A few guys she recognized from work guzzled beers while throwing darts in the corner, thankfully in the opposite direction from where Ali and her friends sat listening to the jukebox. A football game played on a large television screen beside the bar.

From their spot along the side wall, all four women scanned the bar, glasses raised in homage to their mysterious benefactor.

Dr. Jared Padget. Who, with a cunning grin, raised his beer mug in their direction.

Ali almost broke the stem of her glass in two. He picked a bad night to make his final move. She sipped her cocktail as she watched him, doing nothing to hide her blatant perusal. His black leather jacket gave him an air of bad-boy toughness that attracted her even more than the tight-fitting scrub pants he wore at work.

The hairs on her arms lifted, her body softened, remembered how it felt to be wrapped in his arms, to feel the solid wall of his chest against hers.

As the ten-year anniversary of her mother's death, the other reason for girls' night out fast approached, she could barely control the tumultuous feelings churning inside her. Prior to her second drink, she'd actually considered a screaming run through the streets to release the building pressure.

Sadness that her self-absorbed mother had been so consumed by trying to find a man she could love as much as Ali's father, she had spent little time tending to the unplanned result of their dysfunctional union. It hurt that she had never been able to earn her mother's love, and now it was too late.

Anger at her playboy father for getting her mother pregnant and, despite claiming he'd loved her, refusing to marry her. Rage that he flitted in and out of their lives when it had suited him, giving her mother false hope that each time he'd returned he'd been there to stay.

Thanks to Dr. P.'s arrival she added lust, frustration and disappointment to the unstable concoction. Lust for his body, frustration she couldn't knock that cocky grin from his face and disappointment, in herself, for wanting him even though he was the worst sort of man.

She felt on edge, needed an outlet, a way to vent.

"Ignore him," Victoria said.

"And he brought you these." The waitress returned to their table and placed a white bakery box in the center.

Roxie pulled open the top. "Cannolis! I love cannolis!" She picked one up and took a bite of a chocolate dipped end.

I want to fill your cannoli...

Damn him. Ali gulped down the rest of her drink in an attempt to stop the smoldering desire she'd been battling for weeks from engulfing her in flames.

"Try one. They're delicious." Roxie passed around the box.

Ali locked eyes on Jared. He gave her a wicked smile, ran his fingers through the condensation accumulated on his mug and brought the tips to his lips. His full, sexy, perfectly puckered lips.

And Ali lost it. An uncontrollable lust like she hadn't felt in years surged inside her. He'd pushed and pushed, pursued her with a relentless focus, wore her down until she craved the release he offered. She hated him for it. Hated herself for not being strong enough to resist him.

"I know that look." Victoria leaned close to her ear. "Don't do this, Ali. You're going to hate yourself in the morning."

"She's right, Ali," Polly said. "Don't let him get to you.

Tomorrow he'll be gone and you'll never think of him again."

Wrong. He'd invaded her thoughts and dreams. She needed to exorcize him from her brain and knew only one way to do it. Take sex between them from abstract to reality. Take control, take what she wanted and be done with him.

She called out to the bartender. "A parting shot. Tequila for my friends." She narrowed her eyes and pointed to Dr. Padget, whose surprised expression indicated he sensed a change in the dynamic between them. "And him." Ali turned and smiled at the irony. A parting shot. That's what she was about to give him.

The waitress delivered their shots.

Ali tossed hers back, swallowing it in one gulp, not wasting time with salt or lemon. She slammed her empty glass on the table and stood. "I'll see you all tomorrow. There's something I need to do."

"Ali, please," Victoria said.

She forced a fake smile. "Don't worry about me, Vic. I always come out on top." Again she smiled at the irony, because on top was where she planned to be in a few short minutes.

Her body throbbed, part tension, part arousal, as she started to cross the bar. Posture erect, shoulders back, she feigned a confidence she didn't feel. With each click of her heels on the hardwood floor, each step closer to her destination, Ali's nervousness doubled. She'd never propositioned a man before. In her youth, they'd always come looking for her. Palms sweaty, she stuck them, one at a time, into her jacket pockets to wipe them off.

About ten feet away from him, she hesitated, considered ordering a drink from the bar instead of continuing. Was Victoria right? Would she hate herself in the morning?

She glanced in his direction. Their eyes met. Locked. She drew power from his stare, gave in to the pull of attraction between them, taking the final steps toward him without a second thought.

Ali slid in next to his stool, making sure her breasts rubbed against his arm as she did, and dropped a cannoli on the bar in front of him. A few crumbs scattered. It would have been more impressive to drop the entire box, but Roxie had refused to relinquish it. "This is about sex, right?" she asked, maybe a little louder than she should have. "Okay. Let's go."

Jared didn't move, actually looked a touch shocked by her boldness.

Good!

"Come on, Doc. Time's running out. You said so yourself. You want to have sex or not?"

Someone tapped Ali on the shoulder. A deep male voice behind her said, "If he doesn't, I do."

"Thanks for the offer," Ali answered, without looking at who spoke, refusing to be mortified despite a full-body heated flush of embarrassment. "But I've got my sights set on this one." The first man in years to rattle her self-control, to make her want to say yes to anything. Everything. She leaned in close and said, "Come now or don't come at all." Pun intended. She swallowed a laugh. "This one-time offer is about to expire."

For a few seconds, after the front door closed behind her, she thought he hadn't followed. Her bravado wavered. Maybe he wasn't interested in her after all. Maybe it had all been an act, a game. When the door opened again, she glanced back and smiled. After making sure he saw her, she darted down the alley to the small parking lot behind the bar.

"You are in no condition to drive," he yelled from behind her.

No. She wasn't. But adrenaline pumped through her system, making her feel capable of anything. It felt so good. She sidestepped the shadow of a garbage can and pushed off the brick wall on her right to avoid crashing into it. "Come on, Dr. P. There's something I want to show you." A good time. She giggled to herself, running past the cars into the dark, down the grassy incline to the bench tucked in behind a bunch of trees. Moonlight guided her way. Her limbs feeling loose and floppy, how she didn't trip and fall was a mystery.

Out of breath, she plopped onto the old wooden bench, lost herself in the moonlight swirling on the slow moving river while she waited.

"Ali," Jared said as he burst through the trees, his shadowed form looming above her. "Let me take you home. It's late. It's cold."

If it was cold, she didn't feel it. "Sit," she said.

He hesitated but did.

"This is where I bring the guys I pick up at the bar." Actually, it's where she and her gramps liked to feed the ducks. Gramps, who'd taken her in when her father hadn't, who'd nurtured and encouraged her, taught her about respect, for herself and others. Gramps, the person she loved most in this world, his heart attack the reason she'd returned to town after college. Gramps who would be so disappointed if he knew what she was about to do.

Ali pushed Gramps from her mind.

She needed this. Had to have it. Now.

In a quick move she'd perfected long ago, Ali lifted her skirt to her hips and straddled Jared's lap, the sensitive skin of her inner thighs brushing his jeans, effectively pinning him in place. Of course he could move if he wanted to, but in her experience no man wanted to escape their present position. "You were right about me, Dr. Padget," she said, whispering in his ear, forcing her breath out hot and steamy as she rocked her hips, moving rhythmically over the denim covering his growing erection. "I'm a tramp who doesn't deserve a good man."

He stiffened beneath her. "Ali, I never said that."

She ignored his statement. He may not have said the words, but his actions had implied them. "If you're cold, I'll warm you up." She kissed down the side of his neck. "I'm real hot inside." She opened the sides of her jacket and rubbed her body against his. "You want to feel me on the inside, Doc?"

"Call me Jared." He reached under her skirt, beneath her panties, and gripped the bare skin of her butt with his large hands, pushing her down while lifting his hips, grinding his erection where she needed him most. God, it felt good.

He rocked against her again and again. She reveled in his strength, the intensity of his desire. In his masculine scent, the feel of his firm body beneath her, around her.

"Please, Ali. Call me by my name."

Nope. Too personal. She sucked on his neck, tasting a mixture of salt and soap. The thing about controlling a situation was not to get too personal. "Not in a truck or in the muck or for a buck." She giggled.

"You're drunk."

Buzzed—definitely. Giddy—oh, yeah. She was on the verge of acting out a fantasy. But drunk? No. "How did you expect I'd be after a girls' night out? Isn't that why you came looking for me?" She reached between them to unbutton his jeans, lowered his zipper and released him, took his hard length into her hand. Even though her back blocked the moonlight, making it too dark to see, he looked down, tried to watch.

She cupped her hand around his thick, hard shaft and began a leisurely slide along his hot, silky skin. "Didn't you figure you'd have more luck getting some skin-on-skin action after I'd had a few drinks?"

He let out a frustrated breath. "I can't do this." He palmed her ribs like he planned to lift her off of him. Didn't make any attempt to remove her hands, she noticed. "Let me take you home."

So she would have to live with the memory of them together in her bed? Absolutely not. Right here. Right now. Or not at all. "Don't worry about me." Her knees resting on the bench at either side of his hips, she lifted up, slid her panties to the side, and lowered onto his impressive length. They were not leaving this bench until she got what she came for. "We experienced girls can get off anywhere."

He sucked in a deep breath.

Slowly Ali sank down, moved up a bit then down, again and again, as her body stretched to make room for him, until she took him all. Aaaahhhh. *Exactly* what she needed.

Jared sat perfectly still, his head back, moonlight illuminating his handsome face, a face she wouldn't mind waking up to, morning after morning, year after year, if he were anyone else. His eyes closed, his features relaxed, there was no sign of the dimples that seemed to wink at her every time he smiled. His hands dropped to her waist, held her loosely.

Physically, he was everything that attracted her in the opposite sex. Tall. Firm. A commanding presence. And he filled her like no man had before, touched something so deep, so unexpected and thrilling she didn't want to move for fear she'd never feel such a perfect union again. Like he'd been made for her and her alone. Sublime.

She'd waited her entire life to feel this connection with a man. Why did she have to find it with him?

She started to move.

He groaned. "This is so wrong. You're Michael's…"

Suddenly he'd developed a conscience? "Not anymore." Thanks to him. "Right now I'm yours. Now show me what you've got."

With a growl he did just that, holding her tight, plunging into her like a man who had gone too long without intimate contact. "I knew you'd feel this good." One hand found her breast, teased her nipple. A flare of arousal exploded inside her, her jaw went tingly, her eyes fluttered closed.

His words echoed in her thoughts. *I knew you'd feel this good.* Pleasure. The letters floated through her brain, the sensation traveled to every part of her body. Jared Padget, a strong, confident, uninhibited man; a caring, competent doctor who made her body sing like a soloist belting out a sustained high C.

She flopped onto his chest, matched each of his thrusts, moved her hips harder, faster, driving painful memories of her mother's suicide from her brain, seeking release, sweet oblivion. Salvation.

"I've dreamed about this. About us," Jared said between panting breaths, his hands roaming the bare skin of her back.

Me, too.

"It's so much better than I ever imagined."

Oh, yeah.

"You're so beautiful."

So are you.

"But I have to stop."

What? Ali sat up. "Oh, no, you don't," she insisted,

leaning back to place her hands on his knees, swiveling her hips, driving him into her. "You have tormented me for weeks, teased me, flirted with me. We are not stopping. Not yet." She was so close.

"I don't have a condom."

Usually those words would have ground the action to a halt. Ali didn't take chances. Yet here she was, already at risk, so intent on keeping Jared close, on taking the sexual and emotional release she so desperately needed, she hadn't even considered birth control. The higher her blood alcohol concentration climbed, the lower her capacity for rational decision-making plunged into the abyss of irrationality.

"I don't care." She arched her back, took him deep, then relaxed. "You said you're a real man. Don't real men have control?" Arch. Relax.

He expelled a huge breath as if trying to muster some of that "real man" control.

She leaned forward, rubbed her lips over his. "Please," she whispered then kissed him, thrust her tongue into the warm confines of his mouth.

He turned his head. "Ali, I'm… We shouldn't…" He tried to push her away.

"No," Ali cried out, throwing both arms around his neck, holding him tight. "Don't leave me," she begged, willing to do anything to keep him there, to not be alone. She squeezed her inner muscles, trying to hold him inside her. "Stay with me," she whispered in his ear, slowly tipping her pelvis forward then back. "Love me. Make me forget."

Jared moaned in surrender and began to move beneath her, gradually increased his pace until he rocked into her with a power that matched her own.

Ali's head started to spin, scattering her thoughts as

effectively as a centrifuge. All but one. Perfection. The ultimate satisfaction was within reach. "Do. Not. Stop."

"I won't, Ali. I want to make you feel so good." His hand slipped between her legs.

"I do. Oh…" With a few flicks of his talented fingers a surge of ecstasy flooded her system. It was different, intense, freeing. It wiped her mind clear, and a blissful contentment spread through her. A dark, satiated calm engulfed her, until the chime of the big clock at the top of the town hall echoed through the thick haze of her mind.

Ali counted. Twelve.

Approximate time of death—midnight, November 23rd.

Her tequila-soaked defenses failed, allowing the memory of that fateful day to seep into cognition.

Sophomore year of high school.

Ali's mother and her married high-school principal caught doing the nasty on his desk, the act broadcast on the wall-sized movie screen in the auditorium during a full school assembly. In surround sound.

Girls looked at her with more disdain than usual that day. The boys kept their distance. Even her teachers turned away rather than look her in the eye.

Storming into the house after school, Ali had one purpose—to find her mother and make her feel as bad as she was feeling. How much was a fifteen-year-old girl expected to take? This time her mom had gone too far.

Ali pounded up the stairs, down the hallways, craving confrontation, in desperate need of an outlet for the anger and frustration raging inside her. She found her mom in the last place she looked, on the back porch. She must have heard Ali calling out, slamming doors, yet she hadn't moved from her sprawl on the cushioned wicker couch.

She just stared off into the backyard, seeming oblivious to Ali's arrival.

"Mom," Ali yelled.

With awkward, sluggish movements, her mom repositioned herself, slowly turning toward Ali, getting tangled in the multicolored afghan covering her. An empty wine bottle slid off her lap, crashed onto the wood decking and rolled under the coffee table. In hindsight, Ali should have taken pity on her mom, drunk in the afternoon, her eyes droopy, her face devoid of makeup and emotion, her hair an unwashed, blond, scraggly mess in need of a dye touch-up.

But Ali's anger had overtaken rational thought, her adolescent angst-ridden brain focused solely on her pain and anger, and how her mother's actions had caused both. "You have ruined my life," she screamed at her mother. "I hate you."

Ali had been poised for battle. She'd needed it.

But her mother seemed unaffected by her outburst. Calm as could be, she said, "Right back atcha, kiddo."

Ali stood immobile, her urge to fight replaced by a cold, empty feeling.

"If I had to do it all again," her mother went on, staring off into the distance, her slurred speech doing nothing to conceal the malice in her tone, "I would have given you up instead of giving up my dreams to keep you."

Her mother's last words to the daughter she'd blamed for every bad thing that had happened in her life, the daughter she had never wanted or loved.

Jared's lungs were heaving, his skin tingling, his mind clogged by post-orgasmic fluff, following the best, albeit the only, sexual encounter he'd allowed himself in years, as he fought to make sense of what he'd just done.

He'd had sex with Ali. Without removing a single piece of clothing. Without a condom. He felt sick. He'd pulled out just in case she wasn't on birth control but still… He'd driven into her like an animal. On a park bench, for God's sake. According to Bobby, who had refused to shut up about his history with Ali, Jared had treated her no better than the jerks from her high school.

He felt like the lowest form of life, a maggot living on a rotting corpse at the bottom of a filthy dumpster.

Jared thought about Bobby and couldn't help but wonder how often Ali had to fend off the unwanted sexual advances of men she'd known as a teenager. If last night had been the first time one of them had used force? If the reason she'd been willing to settle for a man like Michael was for the protection being married might offer?

Something balled up at the back of his throat, making it difficult to swallow.

Bobby had taken pleasure in sharing his high-school nickname for Ali. And in explaining why. But Jared didn't care about her past. Ten years ago he'd been a different person, too. Present-day Ali, the smart, sassy, thoughtful woman, the kind, compassionate, skilled practitioner, was all that mattered. And she deserved so much more than the man he'd become. Jaded. Distrustful. Unwilling to love.

"I'm sorry," he whispered into her hair.

She didn't respond.

Back before he'd gotten married, before Typhoon Cici had blown through, nearly destroying his life, when Jared had dated, he'd enjoyed making women feel special. Flowers. Candy. Dinner at fancy restaurants. He'd complimented their outfits and hair, acted the perfect gentleman, waited for them to invite him in. He'd never, ever, had unprotected sex in the middle of the woods. Never, ever felt guilty after a sexual encounter. Until now.

And yet he couldn't bring himself to regret one minute of it.

Ali lay slumped against his chest, her head wedged in the nook between his neck and shoulder, the only indication she was alive the puffs of warm air on his skin when she exhaled. She'd fallen asleep. He appreciated the quiet disturbed only by the movement of water from the stream, the rustle of dried leaves, an occasional car pulling into or out of the bar parking lot.

He had no desire to talk, or move. So he sat, with her still straddling his lap, in no hurry to leave, enjoying the feel of her in his arms, which he tightened around her, slipping his hands under the bottom of her sweater to warm them. They fit together like two distinct halves purposely manufactured to become one seamless whole, a feeling he wouldn't soon forget.

What a mess. He hadn't intended to take things this far, hence the lack of condoms. He never should have shown up at the bar where he'd known Ali and her friends would be.

But he'd been at odds with himself. After a few hours of sleep, he'd packed his life into his rolling duffel then prowled around his apartment with nothing to do but think. Of Ali, and how he wanted to see her one last time. A smiling Ali, not the angry one who'd scowled at him when the police officer had shown up at the E.R. Or the one who, when her shift ended, had left the hospital without so much as a glance in his direction.

Break them up before Michael proposed. That had been the plan. One glimpse of the fire in Ali's eyes the first time they'd touched, of her temper when she'd joined a young mother's fight against Child Protective Services, and Jared had known she'd never achieve Stepford wife status, no matter how hard she tried. Yet, in Michael's presence, she'd transformed herself into the soft-spoken, malleable woman Michael wanted in a bride.

The ultimate deception, a relationship based on pretense.

Having suffered through one, Jared had every intention of sparing his friend the heartache, and legal problems, he'd experienced.

Jared's plan:

Stage One: flirt. Reveal what he sensed was Ali's true nature. Evoke her passion, a passion Michael wasn't man enough to satisfy. A passion she'd tamped down with rigid control. Until tonight.

Stage Two: tease, taunt and prod. Point out Michael's shortcomings. Joke about them. Give Ali a chance to vent her frustration with Michael's routine tendencies, to realize what a mistake it would be to marry him. Instead she had praised and defended Michael, never saying an unkind word. Deep down, Jared longed for the day a woman spoke with such conviction in support of him.

When Ali had proved too strong to manipulate, Jared had implemented Stage Three, turning his energy to Michael. A few carefully chosen words, a "chance" encounter at a bar with a woman Michael thought highly of, and the deed was done with remarkable ease. It turned out Michael had harbored a growing concern about Ali's malleable nature when she'd tried to change up their bedroom routine.

Now Michael, one of the few friends who'd stood by him during the DEA investigation, was genuinely happy with his equally boring new girlfriend. While Ali, a woman he barely knew, a woman who had tried to con his friend, was anything but happy. It shouldn't have mattered, but it did.

So he had amended the plan, adding a Stage Four: make Ali forget about Michael by turning her focus onto *him*.

Who'd have known he'd enjoy her so much? Their banter over the past month the most fun he'd had in years.

Since the day he'd said, "I do."

Jared stretched out his legs. His feet were cold. He reached down to touch Ali's bare thighs. He couldn't believe she wasn't shivering. He shifted her weight. "Come on, honey. It's time to go."

She didn't budge.

"Ali." He kissed the top of her head, her soft hair tickling his chin.

Nothing.

He took her by the shoulders and pushed her off his chest. Her head hung down between them. Great. Now what the heck was he supposed to do?

CHAPTER THREE

Five weeks later

THE storm dubbed The New Year's Eve Nor'easter raging outside had no effect on the festivities or attendance at the Madrin Memorial Hospital New Year's Eve Gala.

"No champagne?" Victoria yelled to be heard over the dance music blaring from the DJ's speakers immediately to the left of their table.

Ali shook her head. Not that she was ever a big drinker, but she hadn't touched a drop of alcohol since her park-bench encounter with Dr. Padget. Didn't trust herself. Waking up in her bed with no clear memory of how she'd gotten there, or what she'd done after straddling his lap down by the river, was an effective motivator for maintaining sobriety.

"You're missing out on some primo bubbly," Roxie called out, chugging down the contents of Ali's flute after the waiter topped it off.

"Who's driving you home?" Ali asked Roxie, who scanned the crowd.

"I haven't decided," Roxie answered with a mischievous smile and a wink.

Polly slapped Roxie's arm. "You are so bad." She leaned

in close to Ali. "We came together. I'll be driving Roxie home."

Ali scanned the dance floor packed with her smiling coworkers and wanted to shoot off a champagne cork or two into the crowd. No. Just because she was in an awful mood it didn't mean she begrudged her friends a good time. But having no one to kiss when the ball dropped, and watching everyone who did, was not on her agenda for the night. Excuses that would get her home before midnight started to take form.

Stomachache? A possibility. Menstrual cramps? She wished. Itchy rash? Headache?

Back when they'd been dating, she and Michael had talked about getting engaged prior to the New Year. Michael made good on the plan, proposing to Wanda on Christmas Eve in front of the Christmas tree on the pediatrics floor. It'd been the talk of the hospital. Ali could have done with a bout of sudden-onset hearing loss.

No such luck.

So she smiled and told everyone she wished the sickeningly happy couple well. In private she researched how to make voodoo dolls. Three of them. And stockpiled enough pins to start her own clothing line.

The DJ took a break, blessing them with some quiet background music, and Lyle Crenshaw, the catering manager on staff at the hospital, took the opportunity to approach their table.

Three years ago, after a major expansion and renovation to upgrade facilities, hospital management had left space in the rear of the building for class and conference rooms and a large party room for hosting fundraisers, staff appreciation luncheons and the occasional hospital celebration. While the outside of the building screamed hospital, the inside could have been the lobby of any four-star hotel. The transformation from abandoned medical services departments to premier catering hall was so significant; people in the community had expressed an interest in holding their weddings, communion parties and the occasional Bat Mitzvah at the hospital, creating an unanticipated stream of income and making Lyle Crenshaw a bit of a hero in town.

"Hello, there, ladies," Lyle said with his trademark southern drawl. "I'd like to invite ya'll on a tour of my office later this evening. I've brought some Southwestern charm to the Northeast, and I'm eager to show it off."

"Do you want us all at once?" Roxie asked with a twinkle in her eye, her voice taking on a seductive tone. "Or one at a time?"

"Well, I'll take you any way you want, sugar." Lyle smiled, well aware of Roxie's antics after her behavior at last week's new IV pump in-service held in the large conference room.

Roxie batted her eyelashes and smiled back.

"Is that who I think it is?" Polly asked, pointing at the main entrance to the ballroom.

Ali turned to see Jared Padget decked out in a tux, looking too handsome to be a real flesh-and-blood man, and her heart skipped a beat. A few beats actually, allowing the blood to drain from her head. At the same time her lungs ceased to function, and she held on to the table to keep from falling to the floor.

Shame and embarrassment did not begin to cover her feelings at that moment. She'd accosted him in a bar, forced herself on him, and proceeded to pass out immediately following the finale. And the signs he'd been in her bed had not boded well for her going right to sleep upon returning home. Despite the lack of blood flow to the upper reaches of her body, her face felt on fire.

While she regretted her choices that night five weeks ago, her gramps had taught her there's nothing you could do about your past so focus on your future. Ali had put their interlude behind her, didn't allow herself to think about it, or him. And had no desire to revisit either.

Voilà! The perfect reason to blow this party, before the horns and noisemakers. "I'm out of here," Ali said to Victoria as she stood, stooping a bit, trying to blend in with the people milling around the dance floor.

Victoria knew what had happened between Ali and Dr. Padget. At least the parts Ali remembered. "We'll head him off," Victoria said, sending Polly one way and Roxie the other.

Ali ducked behind the DJ, watched her friends make their way through the crowd. Roxie reached him first, grabbed at her throat, pretending to choke, and collapsed to the floor at his feet. Ali smiled at the scene, Dr. Padget dropping to his knees to render first aid, a crowd gathering, Victoria and Polly off to the side, laughing. As if sensing her watching, Victoria motioned for Ali to get moving. Which she did, heading for the rear hallway, planning to loop around, pick up her coat and boots at the coat check and hop into one of the designated driver cars, coordinated by the hospital, lined up outside.

No sooner had she entered the brightly lit hallway of closed doors than she saw an entwined Michael and Wanda leaning up against the wall of her planned escape route. While she no longer had feelings for Michael, and had conquered her anger at Wanda, she preferred to avoid seeing the two of them together. Or alone for that matter. So she turned, only to see Jared walking in her direction. The hairs on her arms rose and leaned in his direction. Ali scanned the hallway, looking for an alternate route. When she saw none, she tried the doorknob for the main conference room on her right, ecstatic to find it unlocked, and slipped inside before he spotted her.

In the safety of darkness, Ali leaned against the closed door, allowed her breathing to slow and her eyes to adjust to the shadowed interior.

A few minutes and she'd peek outside. If she skipped the coat check she could duck out the rear exit and be home in five minutes.

The doorknob at her right hip turned with a click. Had Dr. P. found her so quickly? And if not him, how would she explain standing alone in the dark in an empty conference room?

"Michael," she heard him say just outside the door. "Have you seen Allison?"

She froze.

"Hey, Jared," Michael answered. "I heard you were coming back."

What had he heard? And why hadn't she heard?

"Four weeks this time," Jared said.

Joining the traveling nurse corps was looking better and better.

"Have you seen Allison?" he asked again.

Ali didn't wait to hear the answer. Instead she took off in a rapid tiptoe, as quietly as she could, into the black, cave-like conditions at the far end of the rectangular room. Feeling along the wall, she found the rear door that led to Lyle's office, and slipped inside just as the door to the conference room opened.

Ali didn't want to risk making any noise so she rested the door against the frame rather than pulling it closed.

Aside from knowing where it was, Ali had never been inside Lyle's office before. It was darker than the conference room. There didn't appear to be any windows, just a thin strip of light at the base of the door on the far side of the room. She stood perfectly still, willing her eyes to adjust, wishing she hadn't left the protection of her friends and cursing the impractical trendy stilettos that pinched her toes.

"I don't see anything but darkness," Allison heard Wanda say, her deceptively sweet voice too close for comfort.

Allison didn't know which was worse, looking like she was stalking Michael and Wanda or being found by Dr. Padget. She took a step back, preparing to duck behind the door if necessary, and bumped into what felt like a tall filing cabinet. Apparently Lyle was not as conscientious as he appeared because the file drawer he'd failed to secure in place, the one her right hip connected with, shifted the few centimeters necessary to click closed, the top corner snagging a section of Ali's skirt in the process.

"Does Lyle really have an award-winning cactus in his office?" Wanda asked. "Or did you plan to get me alone so you could have your wicked way with me?" Wanda giggled.

Wicked way? Yuck!

And a cactus was the little bit of Southwestern charm Lyle had invited them to his office to see? Exactly when would his tours begin?

Ali tugged at the drawer to find it locked in place. She yanked on the beaded mesh of her ridiculously expensive dress. It didn't budge.

Tears threatened.

Tonight was supposed to be her night to shine, to show her coworkers partying down the hall that she'd put Dr. Michael Shefford behind her. That she'd moved on. And she'd planned to look damn good doing it. Only nothing had gone as planned.

First, Victoria's brother, who had agreed to pose as her enamored out-of-state date, had fractured his fibula in a skiing accident and hadn't been able to travel to New York. As a result, Allison was dateless, on New Year's Eve, at the same party as her ex and his fiancée.

And now this, attached to a filing cabinet, in the dark, like a pagan sacrifice to the god of stupidity.

She twisted a lock of hair around her finger until the roots pulled at her scalp.

There has to be a way out of this, Ali thought. Calm down and think of it.

"I heard people talking about that cactus," Wanda said. "I want to see it."

Don't you dare bring her back here, Michael. In a panic Allison tried to twist free. With a distinctive *rrriiippp,* she gained some room to move, but not her freedom.

"I'll show you something much more impressive than that puny cactus," Michael said in the Humphrey Bogart voice he'd imitated so many times throughout their relationship. Hearing him use it with Wanda caused the surf and turf in Ali's stomach to churn. Unwilling to sacrifice her favorite designer heels, she swallowed back the urge to vomit.

"Here, on the conference room table?" While Wanda sounded surprised, Ali couldn't be more shocked. This was totally out of character. Michael didn't have an adventurous bone in his body, at least while he'd dated her.

Wanda giggled again. "Oh, Mikey," she said a moment later, her words ending in a moan.

Just great. Here she stood caught like a fish on a hook, forced to listen to the man she'd planned to marry make love to the woman he'd chosen over her. To make the situation all the more nauseating, Wanda was a moaner. The only bright spot was that Michael made love like Speedy Gonzalez on stimulants. The torture would be over quickly.

Not quick enough to suit Ali, however, who spent the minutes of their lovemaking continuing her futile efforts to escape the filing cabinet's clutches. By the time the conference room door closed behind the lovebirds, not only was Allison still stuck but she'd managed to twist and turn to the point that the lower portion of her dress was now bunched up around her hips.

The conference room door opened again.

She held her breath.

It closed.

Her body tense, she listened, waited for someone to walk in and find her, braced herself for the questions, the laughter. Her heart rate shot up. But she heard nothing. No footsteps. No voices.

She sighed with relief, but still had to free herself. Now. Before someone stumbled upon her. Freedom was all that mattered.

Then it happened, like it usually did whenever her desperate need to escape a situation overrode her capacity for rational thought: she did something that would inevitably make the situation worse.

In a fit of desperation, she yanked and tugged and pulled with all her might, until the side seam of her dress split open, a portion of her skirt still stuck.

"No," she cried out in frustration. A week's salary, fifty hours of bedpans, IVs, catheters, dressing changes, medications and back-breaking patient transfers destroyed as efficiently as if she'd used scissors to hack her paycheck into hundreds of tiny, unidentifiable pieces.

"Ali?"

Ali recognized Jared's voice instantly. She froze, near tears. *Please, please, please, not him, not now.*

The rear door to Lyle Crenshaw's office creaked open. Bright light blazed from the overhead fixtures. Allison squinted in response, trying to hold the side of her dress closed with one hand, splaying her other hand in front of her hips, seriously regretting her choice of panties, knowing the translucent pale pink thong she wore left her lower body, for the most part, totally exposed.

His shiny black dress shoes came into focus first. As she lifted her head, her eyes traveled over the black pants covering his long legs, the black tuxedo jacket, perfectly fitted over his broad shoulders, the satiny black bow tie tucked beneath his snow-white shirt collar, finally meeting the peridot-green eyes of Dr. Jared Padget. As good as he looked in a pair of hospital scrubs, strutting around the emergency room, nothing could compare to the man decked out in a tux. His dark brown hair was cut shorter than the last time she'd seen him. He looked smart, astute. He looked hot.

Don't think like that! Jared was a womanizer, a toxic pollutant contaminating the dating pool. *No. Don't think of him as Jared. He's Dr. Padget. A colleague. That's all. He is not your friend.*

"What are you doing here?" she asked, hoping if she ignored the absurdity of her situation maybe he would, too.

"Looking for you," he replied innocently. "As if you didn't know."

"You have some nerve showing up uninvited." Unannounced. Unwanted.

"I think you're pretty lucky it's me who showed up and not someone else." His eyes scanned up the length of her legs to her bare hips, leaving a trail of warmth. They paused at her breasts, his heated gaze as effective as a caress, making her nipples harden. They traveled to the spot where her dress connected to the filing cabinet. He had the nerve to smile. "What the heck did you do to yourself?"

Ali looked around for something to throw at him. Never a bowling ball around when you needed one.

"Dare I ask what led to your current predicament?"

She'd been trying to avoid *him!* "Not if you want to walk out of here with all your body parts intact."

He laughed. "You're awfully feisty for someone in obvious need of assistance."

A good point. She let out a deep breath. "Sorry. It's been a rough night." And she had an ominous feeling it would get worse before it was over.

He stood there looking at her, his eyes slightly squinted.

"When you're done staring, do you think you could find a pair of scissors on that desk and cut me loose?" She tugged to show him she was, in fact, stuck.

He continued to study her, tilted his head and ran his fingers over his chin.

"Hello?" Ali waved her hands in front of him. "In need of a little assistance here."

He snapped back to life. "I think I like you right where you are."

He interrupted Ali's protest, holding up a hand to stop her from talking. "Just for a few minutes. I have a proposition."

"You have got to be kidding me. Your prospects are so slim you'd stoop to propositioning a woman in dire circumstances?" Unable to slap his face after what he'd said insulted her.

He chuckled. "Your circumstances are hardly dire. Are you uncomfortable?"

No, she wasn't. But… "Yes. Terribly uncomfortable. Release me this instant."

He scrutinized her face. "You're an awful liar," he said.

"Two minutes. I have a few things I'd like to say, and I'd rather not have to chase you around while I do."

Ali looked at her watch and made like she'd activated a stopwatch feature, even though she didn't have one. "Okay. Go."

"I think we got off to a bad start."

"Ya think?" Her voice came out laced with sarcasm.

"I'm not going to apologize. Whether you realize it or not, I did the right thing."

"According to you." As a result of his actions, Ali was once again alone, with no prospects for the future of contentment she'd hoped to have with Michael.

"I'd like for us to start over."

"Ah." Ali nodded. "I get it. No luck getting laid over in Buffalo? You figure I took pity on you once, maybe I will again?"

Jared looked like she'd slapped him. "Once?"

Too late she remembered finding evidence he'd shared her bed the night before he'd left town. "I mean twice." Shoot. Her "twice" came out more question than statement.

"You don't remember?"

Ali thought about refusing to answer on the grounds she might incriminate herself.

"Three times, Ali." He held up three fingers to emphasize his point. "After the bench by the river, when I tucked you into your bed, you dragged me in there with you." He folded down his ring finger with the index finger on his other hand.

He was big and strong. If he'd wanted to fight her off he could have. Fight her off. How humiliating.

"After the second time, I tried to leave again. You begged me for more." He folded down his middle finger.

If a giant sinkhole were to form beneath her, it would be perfectly okay.

"And the third time..." He folded down the last finger standing. "Let's just say I will never again call you Kitten."

Her face felt like she'd fallen asleep in the midday sun on a tropical island beach. Maybe the erotic dreams that plagued her sleep were actually snippets of memory. Wait a minute. Ali felt sick. Three times? They'd had sex without a condom three times. Because she hadn't found any wrappers at her condo—she'd checked. Everywhere. If the filing cabinet hadn't been holding her up, she'd have collapsed down to the floor.

Someone jiggled the front doorknob to the office. Ali spun her head in that direction. It sounded like a group of people stood just outside in the hallway. In his southern drawl Lyle called out, "Hold on there, darlin'. I've got the key right here." The ticking time bomb counting down the seconds to disaster echoed in Ali's ears.

CHAPTER FOUR

JARED glanced at the door, then back at Allison, who stiff-ened, her eyes wide, a look of absolute horror on her other-wise beautiful face. "That sounds like Lyle Crenshaw," she said.

The key slid into the lock.

"If he finds me like this I will never forgive you."

Because he hadn't freed her the minute he'd found her. Selfish ass, so concerned with keeping Ali in one place so she couldn't run from him, he'd never considered the ramifications of his actions.

The light switch beside them was closest, so Jared dove in that direction, plunging the room into darkness. He'd planned to run for the door to the hallway next, prepared to throw his body against it to push everyone back before they had a chance to look inside, but the blackness slowed him down, disoriented him.

Jared figured he could make it to the entryway in four, maybe five giant steps, assuming he didn't collide with anything on the way. He tried to map out the office from memory. The desk. The guest chairs. The huge cactus in the left corner. And what if the door swung open before he reached it? Ali would be left exposed, literally, way too much of her creamy smooth skin on display for all to see. That was the last thing he wanted.

The door pushed open. Light from the hallway flooded the far end of the room.

Lyle Crenshaw babbled about his cactus. "I had this giant Fishhook Barrel Cactus species *Ferocactus wislizenii* hauled up here from Arizona. It's over six feet tall and weighs several hundred pounds."

"Too late," Jared whispered, moving in front of Ali, positioning his back to the door so his larger frame would block her from view. Please let this work, he prayed as he slid close until her full breasts flattened against his chest, until his hips met hers. He opened the sides of his tux jacket and she ducked inside. God he'd missed the feel of her. For five long, lonely weeks she'd invaded his thoughts. At work. At home. In bed, alone in the darkness was by far the worst, the memory of their night together taunting him, the illusion of her far from satisfying.

The overhead lights came back on.

He pulled her close.

"What the…?" Lyle asked in a shocked voice.

"Give us a minute, will you?" Jared faked a cocky calm.

"Hey, I recognize that shoe," a man that sounded like an outraged Michael said. "Allison, is that you? What do you think you're doing, Jared?"

Assorted voices spilled in from the hallway.

"What's going on?"

"Who's in there?"

"Why isn't anyone moving?"

A man called out, "Dr. Padget from the E.R. is doing Ali Forshay in Crenshaw's office."

Ali's forehead banged against his chest.

"Put down that cell phone, you jerk," a woman said.

"Get out," Jared yelled, fiercer and louder than he'd meant to. It took all the willpower he could muster to keep from storming the doorway and beating every last one of them until their eyes and mouths were swollen shut, and they had no memory of what they'd just heard. But Ali clung to him, her hands gripping the lapels of his jacket.

Lyle sounded enraged when he said, "You've got five minutes." He slammed the door shut behind him.

Jared didn't move. Neither did Ali.

He tried to lighten the mood. "You know, we could…" He swiveled his hips, knowing she wouldn't agree, half hoping she would.

"No, we can't." She flattened her hands on his chest and tried to push him away. "What on earth compelled you to do that?"

He stepped back. "I was trying to block you with my body so no one would see you. I was being gallant, sacrificing myself to protect you. How was I supposed to know someone would recognize your shoe?" What a mess.

"Michael," she almost growled. "He couldn't remember my birthday or the combination to my locker at work, but he remembered my one pair of outrageous heels."

"Those are some sexy shoes," Jared agreed. The stiletto heels had to be at least three inches high, with one thin strip of plum-colored leather at the base of her toes and thin, matching straps crisscrossing from her heel midway up her bare calf. She had long, smooth, slender legs that were the topic of many of his dreams, and splendid curves partially wrapped in a short, once form-fitting, plum-and-lavender-colored dress.

A deep purple chopstick held her light brown hair in a seductive knot. He fought the urge to yank it and watch the waves fall loosely around her shoulders. "Have I told you how beautiful you look tonight?"

"I can already hear the gossip," Ali said, ignoring his

compliment. *"'Did you hear about Ali Forshay? Sex in Lyle Crenshaw's office. She's just like her mother.'"*

Who'd been caught having sex with Ali's high school principal in his office. "Would you rather have been found half dressed all alone in the dark? Because I've got to tell you, either way you were destined to be the topic of conversation."

"Thank you for your insightful observation." It was obvious from her deadpan tone she was not amused. "If you'd unhooked me as soon as you found me, this never would have happened."

"I'm sorry," he said, meaning it more than any apology he'd ever uttered. "I didn't think…"

"No. You didn't." Ali twisted around and yanked her dress so hard the filing cabinet wobbled.

He steadied it then swatted her hands away. "Let me do that."

"Now you're ready to help me?"

He set to work trying to do just that, once again praying, this time, that he hadn't ruined his chances for a four-week reconciliation.

"Why did you come back to Madrin Falls anyway?" she asked.

"I wanted to see you." Talk to you, cheer you, banish the memory of your anguish from my brain. Okay. So he wasn't a total altruist. He also wanted to hold her, kiss her and make her scream with pleasure. Again. And again and again. "I thought it'd be nice to ring in the New Year together."

"You said you make it a point not to work at the same hospital twice in one year."

To avoid the snare of ongoing relationships, of expectations he never seemed to meet, no matter how hard he tried, and disappointment in himself and others as a result. Yet here he was, unable to decline Madrin Memorial's offer of another temporary assignment, unable to pass up a chance to spend more time with Ali. "It's a good thing I happened to be here, don't you think?"

"I'm not one hundred percent sure I wouldn't have done better on my own," she muttered.

"I'm going to have to cut you free," he said, walking over to Lyle's desk to look for something sharp.

He'd thought of her nonstop since leaving Madrin Falls. The dichotomy of the Ali he knew from work, the tough yet sweet, sarcastic yet caring nurse. And the Ali he'd seen his last night in town, the woman tormented by her past who'd begged him to not leave her, to love her, to make her forget.

So he'd spent the night with her, listened as she'd spoken of her mother and father, her lonely childhood. He'd mumbled comforting words and dried her eyes as she'd cried. He'd given her his body when she'd needed it, until they had both been too exhausted to move. It had been then, lying in Ali's bed in the dark with her cuddled next to him, that he'd realized she'd caused a huge crack to form in the concrete barrier he'd erected around his heart, seeped inside and settled there. Her sorrow, her pain and desperation, caused an uncomfortable ache in the once numb muscle. An ache that hadn't gone away.

Her hospital offering him another temporary assignment had been serendipity. It gave him a reason to return to Madrin Falls, to check on her, be close to her, with an end date four weeks away. Twenty-eight days and nights to have his fill, to get her out of his system, so he could return to his nomadic life unencumbered by feelings for her. And this time when he left, he would not come back.

Finding the scissors, he held them up and walked back toward her.

"You can't show up and expect to pick up where we left off," she said.

"I didn't come back just for sex." He told the truth. Their connection was so much more than physical. He knew firsthand the burden of being tormented by your past. "Although I won't turn it down if you offer."

"Us together…" she moved her hand back and forth between them "…was a one-time thing."

"A three-time thing," he reminded her, remembering every sweet detail. "We were good together, Ali." So very good. "It's a shame you can't remember."

"I remember enough."

"Do you dream about us like I do?" He moved in close, inhaled her alluring scent, purposely brushing the soft skin of her bare hip with his hand as he reached for the bottom edge of her dress. "Do you wonder if our night together was an anomaly, if it will be as spectacular the next time?" He stared down at her.

She turned her head away, avoiding eye contact.

With two snips, Jared sliced through the fabric of her dress with mixed emotions. While glad she was free, now he'd have to move away from her, when what he really wanted to do was pull her into his arms and hold her, like he'd dreamed, night after night.

"Thank you."

He watched Ali try to hold the sides of her ruined dress together, while she glanced nervously at the door. The urge to help her, care for her and protect her surged within him.

He shrugged out of his tux jacket and placed it over her shoulders. "Here. Wear this."

She looked up, her eyes so big and blue he wanted to dive in and swim around. "Thank you, Dr. P."

"Dr. P.? After everything we've been through together, you won't call me by my name?"

Her lips curved into a hint of a grin. "Nope."

It amazed him how many people "just happened" to be standing in the hallway leading from Lyle Crenshaw's office back to the lobby. Men, some colleagues he recognized from the hospital, others Jared had never seen before, smiled and nodded in approval at what they thought he'd done. Some had the nerve to give him a thumbs-up.

Allison walked with her head high, looking straight ahead as if no one else existed. To an observer it would have seemed like she was unaffected by the incident. Only he could feel the slight trembling in the ice-cold hand she had clamped around his upper arm with a grip he would have expected from a person twice her size.

They were almost to the doors at the main entrance when the countdown began. Allison stopped short. "Five! Four! Three! Two! One! Happy New Year!" The crowd cheered in the distance. Paper horns sounded and noisemakers buzzed. The DJ played "Auld Lang Syne." The two of them stood alone in the lobby, away from the celebration. Allison looked up at him; vulnerable, her spirit depleted. A tear trickled down her left cheek. He wiped it away with his thumb.

"My new year is off to a terrible start," she said sadly.

"That's funny," he replied, lifting her chin with his bent knuckle, lowering his lips to meet hers. "I was just thinking my new year is off to a great start."

She tried to say something. He silenced her with a kiss.

Monday morning was business as usual in the E.R., as long as Ali ignored the speculation generated by her and Jared's New Year's Eve encounter.

"You and Dr. Padget, huh?"

"Does he taste as yummy as he looks?"

"Boxers or briefs?"

And the nausea.

Psychosomatic gastrointestinal distress. That's all. Her mind freaking out her digestive tract. She was not pregnant. Absolutely refused to be pregnant. Sometimes her period came late. Especially after working rotating shifts, and she'd recently finished three weeks of them. Occasionally—well, maybe not occasionally, but at least once before—she'd skipped a period. No big deal.

No need to panic. If she missed her next period, then she'd panic, but not before.

She took a sip from the bottle of ginger ale she'd stashed behind the high counter of the nursing station.

A child's scream sliced through the drone of daily activity.

Since she had only one patient under the age of twenty, she ran to Exam Room Three, Bed One. Four-year-old Tina Patel. High fever. Lethargy. Bilateral ear pain.

The curtain drawn around the stretcher, she heard Dr. Padget's frustrated voice, which was unusual. He loved kids, and they loved him. "Come on, Tina. One quick look and we're done."

"Knock, knock," Ali said, before pushing the curtain aside to see the little black-haired girl on her side facing away from Jared, pressed up against the side rail, trying to get as far away from him as possible. Her hands covered both ears, tears streamed down her cheeks. "Pick her up, Mom," Ali said to Tina's mom, who, with a look of relief, scooped up her daughter and cuddled her close.

"We have two ambulances on the way," Jared said, closing his eyes and pinching the bridge of his nose. "I'm trying to move out a few non-urgents before they get here."

Ali motioned to the visitor's chair by the stretcher. "Sit down, Mom." She wiped the crying girl's eyes with a tissue and reached into the pocket of her scrub jacket for one of the special lollipops she'd put there when her shift began.

"Sit her across your lap like this." Ali helped position Tina so she sat sideways on her mother's lap, her shoulder to her mom's belly, one ear to Mom's chest. Ali squatted down in front of the child and held up the hard candy cartoon character, willing to stoop to bribery to expedite the exam. "Do you know who this is?"

Tina gave a small smile and nodded.

Ali handed her the pop. "I need you to hold real still while Dr. P. looks into your ears." The girl stiffened. "If you want him to stop, all you have to do is lift up the stick and he will. Let's give it a try, okay?"

The girl nodded.

"Get to work, Dr. P." They shared a smile.

Jared kneeled on the floor at mom's feet, tugged on the girl's ear and lifted the otoscope.

Tina raised the pop, as Ali and Jared knew she would. He stopped.

"Excellent. Now, hold one hand on her head like this," Ali told Mom. "And one around her shoulders, like this." She positioned the woman's hands where she needed them to hold Tina still. "Let's try again."

The second time Tina let him touch the otoscope to the opening of her ear canal before raising the pop. He stopped.

"Third time's the charm," Ali said, the signal for make this one count. "If you let Dr. P. look inside your ear, you can keep the pop," Ali said. "And no giggling if it tickles."

"Hold her tight," Ali mouthed to the mother as Jared

pulled the helix up and back to straighten the ear canal, inserted the scope and finished the exam. With Ali's help Mom shifted Tina on her lap and he quickly performed the same routine on the other ear.

"Just as we thought," he said. "Bilateral ear infections. Does she have any allergies?"

"No," the mom said.

"I'll give you a prescription for antibiotics." He wrote it out and handed it to Ali. "Give her acetaminophen according to package instructions, for pain or fever. Follow up with your primary-care physician or come back to the hospital after she takes *all* the antibiotics."

An ambulance siren rang out.

"Ali will give you your discharge instructions," Jared went on. "Feel better, sweetie," he said to Tina, who shied away from him. "Thank you," he said to Ali, his heartfelt words echoing in his eyes, a look of sincere appreciation on his face.

Her heart fluttered.

He started to say something else.

She watched his lips, remembering their New Year's Eve kiss. Yearning for another one. Stop! She looked away.

He turned and left to meet the EMTs.

Ali shook off the warm, gooey feeling he caused. "Do you have children's medication for pain or fever at home?" Ali asked, because she never assumed all parents did.

Tina's mom looked down at her feet.

"I'll get you some samples."

In the hallway Ali watched Dr. Padget talking to an older couple, probably family members of the patient brought in by ambulance. He remained calm in a crisis, treated family members with respect and took the time to break down his explanations into easily understandable form. He gave them the truth, in a professional, tactful way, providing options, never giving false hope.

She respected that, admired him for it.

His confidence, the way he carried himself, combined with his good looks and caring attitude at work, made him innately sensual, and appealed to her like no man had before.

The queasy feeling that had started on Ali's drive into work that morning did not subside. And just before lunch, after she gave up the fight to keep down the half a bagel and cream cheese she'd eaten to settle her stomach, she exited the staff restroom into the lounge to find Jared waiting for her, arms crossed, one shoulder resting against the wall, a suspicious look on his face.

Feeling grungy from kneeling on the bathroom floor and her scrub top stained with Betadine solution from a suture tray mishap, he was the last person she wanted to see. "If you're here to bug me, turn right around and skedaddle. I'm not in the mood."

Her stomach sore, her throat raw and her mouth tasting foul, the last thing she wanted to see was Dr. Padget, all clean and neatly pressed. The last thing she wanted to smell was the noxious aroma wafting from the coffee cup in his hand.

"You feel okay?" Jared asked.

Did she look like she was feeling okay? "Mrs. Freer's abscess got to me, that's all." Ali pulled down a cup from the dispenser on the side of the watercooler, filled it and took a sip. Two face masks and a dab of mentholated ointment on the skin above her upper lip weren't enough to protect her from that putrid mess. What she'd needed was a scuba mask suctioned over her eyes and nose, and some type of self-contained breathing apparatus. "How could she wait so long before coming in for treatment?"

"It was a bad one."

Ali visualized the one-inch, circular, oozing sore on the patient's upper leg…and grabbed for a tissue, covered her mouth and retched.

"Sit," Jared said, taking the lid off the garbage pail and sliding it next to her.

Ali pulled out a chair and sat.

He placed her half-full bottle of ginger ale on the table in front of her. "Tani said you've been sipping this all morning and looked about to vomit several times before you ran into the lounge."

Traitor.

He handed her a few packs of saltine crackers from the closet above the sink.

"And you came to check on me. Aren't you the sweetest thing?" she mocked him. But it was sweet. Really. She took a sip of soda.

"She said you looked sick to your stomach a couple of times last week, too."

"Obviously Tani doesn't have enough to do if she's spending her days watching me." And being a tattletale. A quick reminder that Ali had covered for her so she could duck out of work fifteen minutes early last week should put that to a stop.

"When did the nausea start?" Jared asked, using his professional voice, not the teasing one he reserved for whenever they were alone together. A scowl marred his handsome face.

"What's wrong with you? You look sicker than I feel."

"Please tell me you're not pregnant."

His words—no, the way he'd said them, on a par with *please tell me the lump isn't cancerous*—hit her like an elbow strike to the chest. "I'm not pregnant," she responded, feeling close to tears, hoping what she'd said was true. "The rancid smell of infected flesh made me nauseous. It's no big deal." No. Big. Deal.

"You're on the Pill, right? I saw them in your medicine cabinet."

She had been on the Pill until Michael had tossed her aside for another woman. "What were you doing, poking around my medicine cabinet?"

"Looking for condoms. Jesus, Ali. You really don't remember?"

She shook her head. Bits and pieces here and there, nothing substantial after the bench by the river. "Why were you looking for condoms in my medicine cabinet?"

He looked ready to vomit himself. "Because I didn't have any, remember?"

Right. And she'd begged him for more sex. "What did you do when you didn't find any?" She didn't keep condoms at her condo, didn't need them. When she and Michael had begun dating seriously she'd started on birth control. They hadn't slept together until both had had blood tests declaring them free from STDs. Before that, no man under the age of sixty had ever been in her home.

"Since you're on the Pill, it didn't matter. Down by the river, when we first... I didn't wear one. You said you didn't care."

At the time she didn't. Now she most certainly did. "So you..."

He let out a breath and rubbed his hand over his regretful face. "Went ahead without one."

Good thing she was already sitting.

"What a mess." He ran his fingers through his hair, leaned back against the wall, and let out a breath. "I can't believe this. I saw the pills. I never would have done it otherwise."

Of course not, because she was good for sex and nothing more. Don't want to risk any long-term attachments with someone like Ali. "Calm down, Dr. P. I'm not pregnant. But thanks for letting me know how you feel about the subject."

"I'm sorry. It's just—"

"Don't worry," she cut him off. "I don't want to be pregnant with your spawn any more than you want someone like me to be the mother of your child."

"Stop it, Ali. That's not what I meant. You'd make a great mother. I see how good you are with the kids who come in. They love you. I spend my life on the road. I'm a drifter. The last thing I need is the hassle of having to worry about a baby."

Although she couldn't be certain, she'd bet a weeks' wages her father had once spewed something along those lines to her mother.

"No worries, Dr. P." Ali stood up, using the table for support, her legs a bit shaky. "No baby. No hassles." She straightened and walked to the door. "Don't give it another thought." Because she wouldn't. At least, not for another two weeks.

CHAPTER FIVE

WHAT was it with women? Jared wondered two days later. You do one thing to tick them off and they turn on you. First his mother, then his wife and now Ali.

Okay. To be fair, in Ali's case he'd done a few things: put the kibosh on her plans to marry Michael; made use of her lovely body when, even though she'd begged him to, he shouldn't have and hadn't handled concern over a feared pregnancy in a manner befitting a gentleman.

But still. He did not like the silent treatment, second only to withholding sex in a woman's manipulation-of-man arsenal.

Even worse, forced to interact with him at work, because she was and always would be a consummate professional, Ali called him *Doctor.* Not Dr. Padget. Not Dr. P. Just Doctor. A nondescript, completely impersonal term for any physician in a profession of thousands. Doctor.

"Yes, Doctor."

"No, Doctor."

"I'll get to it as soon as I can, Doctor."

"I put Mr. Smith's lab results on his chart, Doctor."

"If you'd move out of the way, Doctor, I'm happy to do that for you."

He would rather she came at him with a bat, yelled and screamed, let her anger loose, wreaked havoc. Instead she held it in, seethed, upped the tension between them. Not in a good way. At least if she blew up he'd get the chance to defend himself. To apologize. He'd acted like an irresponsible, low-class punk. He was the one who'd shown up at the bar unprepared, who, after seeing birth-control pills in her medicine cabinet, had made the assumption she was protected.

Yes. A baby right now would be a major inconvenience. But he was an educated, successful professional more than capable of supporting a child if it had come to that. So why his overreaction? Why lash out at Ali, when he was as much to blame as she?

Because, with time, he realized he didn't want his parental role reduced to his name on a check. He wanted to be a full-participation parent like his father, involved in his child's life, teaching him, encouraging him, loving him, every single day. And how could he do that when his job involved so much travel he'd be away more than he'd be home? When he wasn't married to his child's mother, couldn't marry her, didn't *want* to be married, not to anyone?

But these were his problems, not Ali's. At the very least, he owed her an apology.

So here he stood, on the cement step outside the Madrin Falls Senior Center, about to enter Wednesday-night bingo. The one activity Ali had refused to give up while dating Michael. Bingo with her gramps.

Jared pulled open the front door. Let the groveling begin.

"I'm looking for Allison Forshay," he asked the first senior he saw. "Do you know if she's here?"

The elderly man pointed to a crowd of people in the back of the room and said, "As soon as she's done we'll get started."

Done doing what? Jared wondered as he walked over to where the man directed him.

"Yes, I'm sure, Sally. One twenty-four over seventy-two is very good," he heard Ali say. "Let me write it down in your blood-pressure journal."

Jared walked around the table to see Ali, dressed in blue jeans and a soft purple sweater, removing a blood-pressure cuff from a white-haired woman's arm. "Come on, Les. You're next." The woman stood and the man behind her handed Ali a small notebook, rolled up the sleeve of his button-down shirt and sat.

Ali gave Les a warm, genuine I-care-about-you smile. Just once Jared would like to be on the receiving end of one.

Tonight was not to be the night. When she noticed him her eyes narrowed and her lips formed a grim line. If her eye sockets had had the ability to vaporize, he'd have been reduced to a puff of mist. "What are you doing here, Dr. Padget?"

At least he got a Padget with his Doctor, a step in the right direction. "I heard bingo at the senior center's where the town's most beautiful women can be found." A few women giggled, Ali not among them. "Since I'm here, is there anything I can do to help you? They're waiting for you to finish up before they start."

Ali looked torn, like she'd rather tighten the cuff in her hand around his neck than accept his offer. If there weren't so many witnesses, he had no doubt which one she'd choose. She glanced at her watch. Jared raised his eyes to the clock on the wall behind her. Six-forty. According to the sign out front, bingo started at seven.

"Who's waiting for help with their medications?" Ali turned and asked the group.

Two women and one man raised their hands.

"Step over here." Ali motioned to the half of the long table he stood behind. "This is Dr. Padget, a colleague of mine at the hospital. He'll be happy to help you." She turned to him. "Won't you, Dr. Padget?"

"Yes, I will, Nurse Forshay." He slipped out of his jacket and placed it on the back of a plastic chair, eager to do whatever it took to get on her good side.

For the next thirty minutes Jared answered medical questions, battled child-resistant caps and dispensed pills and capsules into the small plastic compartments of weekly medication organizers. At the same time, out of the corner of his eye, he managed to watch Ali, too. She knew each senior by name, greeted most of them with a hug, some were lucky recipients of a kiss on the cheek. Jared liked affectionate women, had enjoyed frequent touches, quick kisses and holding hands. Until Cici had soiled each sweet gesture by using them to con him into thinking she'd loved him. The woman was incapable of love.

He shook off the memory of his wife. She'd done enough damage, he wouldn't let her infringe on his time with Ali.

"On some days that woman takes seventeen pills. It's no wonder she can't keep them straight," Jared said to Ali, who sat next to him copying the side effects of one of the woman's new medications in large print on a full-sized sheet of paper.

"She lives alone and has no family in the area," Ali said, looking genuinely concerned. "I've been sorting her meds every Wednesday for years."

The reason Ali had refused to give up Wednesday night bingo. Dozens of people depended on her to be there. "Do you do this through the Health Department?"

"No. I do it because it needs to be done."

So her caring and compassion didn't shut off the minute

she left the hospital, as she'd implied. Deep down, he'd known that. Ali was the antithesis of Cici, which made her all the more appealing.

"Helping others is not without perks," Ali said with a half smile. "What'd she give you?"

Jared looked in the plastic grocery bag his last senior pushed into his hand when she'd thanked him. "An apple fast approaching rotten and a pack of chewing gum with one stick missing."

"I worry about Emma's finances." She sighed. "I signed her up for Meals on Wheels so at least I know she has one good meal a day, and I cook for her when I can."

She also delivered chicken soup to colleagues who were sick, and sometimes, when the weather was cold and gloomy, brought in a crockpot of delicious chili or a hearty soup for the E.R. staff.

Jared reached into his pocket. "I also got a business card for a free haircut at Bill's Barbershop."

"I'd think twice before using it." Ali rubbed the back of her neck while she tilted her head from side to side. "Bill's got a bit of palsy in his upper extremities, which is why he comes to me for help pouring his meds."

Jared promptly ripped the card down the middle.

She yawned and took a sip of ginger ale from the can beside her.

"You feeling okay? Your stomach still bothering you?" he asked.

"Don't look at me like that," she snapped.

Like what?

"I had dinner at the Chinese buffet restaurant, which I hate but Gramps loves, and the greasy food sat heavy in my stomach."

"Okay." He ducked his head and held up his hands to ward off her attack. "Just trying to make conversation."

She looked down at her arm and picked a white string off her sweater. "After your tirade on Monday I didn't want you thinking…"

That she was pregnant. "I'm sorry. I acted like a fool. I…" Overreacted. Am an ass. Deserve to be beaten.

Someone called out, "Bingo!" The crowd mumbled. The caller confirmed the numbers.

"Can we go somewhere?" Jared asked, desperate for a few minutes alone with her away from the hospital. "Maybe get a cup of coffee?" At the mention of coffee Ali brought her hand up to her mouth and swallowed hard. "How about hot chocolate? Or ginger ale?" He'd drink anything, go anywhere, to get her to agree.

She thought about his invitation, all too long if you asked him, before eyeing him askance and asking, "Why?"

"Because you're the reason I accepted another assignment at Madrin Memorial when I make it a policy to never return to the same hospital twice in one year. You don't answer my phone calls and I can't seem to find ten minutes to speak with you alone unless you're anchored in place. I'd like to take advantage of this brief window of harmony between us for a serious conversation. Who knows if I'll ever get another opportunity?"

After telling Gramps she was going to talk to Dr. P. in the meeting room down the hall, and instructing him to come find her if she wasn't back in ten minutes, Ali sat down in one of the fabric-upholstered chairs surrounding an oval table and looked at the man beside her.

In his red thermal shirt, the three top buttons left open, khaki pants and workboots, he looked casually comfortable, laid-back, an all-around nice-guy type, nothing like the confident professional from work or the dark and dangerous man from the bar. Tonight he'd been so nice to

Gramps and his friends, her friends, answering their questions freely, seeming happy to be among them. Michael had had no interest in accompanying her to bingo, a fact he'd made clear on numerous occasions while reminding her of the inherent risk of liability in offering medical services outside work.

Dr. Padget fit right in and didn't appear the least bit concerned.

"Before you start," Ali said, "I'd like to thank you for your help out there and apologize for my behavior the night before you left town. As you know, it was the anniversary of my mother's death and, while that's no excuse, I am not in the habit of accosting men in bars and forcing myself on them."

He turned to face her, his expression serious. "You didn't force me into doing anything I didn't want to do."

"Whew." Ali wiped pretend sweat from her forehead. "Good to know." She shifted in her seat and looked him in the eye. "Is there anything else I should apologize for before you get started?" She fought the urge to look away.

He smiled. "It took a few weeks for the scratch marks on my back to heal."

Ali dropped her head into her hands and groaned. She'd scarred the man.

He tugged on a finger. "I'm kidding."

She let out a breath. "Oh, thank God."

"Not about the scratch marks but that you need to apologize for them. I liked seeing them in the mirror. They made me think of you. I was kind of sad when they faded."

She waited for him to crack a joke, ask her to make new ones. He didn't. Instead he cleared his throat and reached into his back pocket. Taking out a piece of gum, he popped it into his mouth, something she'd seen him do dozens of times, right before a serious talk to deliver bad news to a patient's significant other and/or family.

Uh-oh.

"On the bench by the river and in the staff lounge at work on Monday, you made comments implying I think you don't deserve the love of a good man, and I wouldn't want someone like you to be the mother of my child," he said. "Ali, neither statement is true."

At least he'd had the decency to leave off her tramp reference. "Okay. Good." This was a little more personal than she'd like to get. "You feel better now that you got that off your chest?" She tried to stand. He stopped her with a hand to her arm.

"You gave me ten minutes. Now sit down and listen to what I have to say."

"Tsk. Tsk. Tsk." Ali looked down at the hand holding her. "Using your superior strength to try to intimidate me, Dr. P.? Shame on you." She didn't want to discuss this. She knew who she was, what she was, knew what he thought of her, didn't need to hear words of condemnation come out of his mouth.

"Please." He released her. "Sit down. I'm not finished."

The hint of begging in his tone prompted her to do as instructed.

"You are a caring person," he said. "You treat each one of your patients like family. You go out of your way to make them comfortable, to ease their fears. When you find the right man, someone who appreciates you for you so you don't feel you have to change for him, I have no doubt you're going to make the lucky guy a wonderful wife. You'll have a pack of happy, well-cared-for children, and your house will be the one where all the neighborhood kids congregate."

Tears filled her eyes. It's what she wanted more than anything. "Why are you being so nice to me?"

He handed her a tissue. "Would you believe I'm a nice guy?"

When he wanted something. She dabbed at the corner of each eye. "Is this a new tack to get me into bed? Because I've been there, done that, Dr. P. Shouldn't you be initiating a new chase, pursuing a new conquest? If you put forth a little effort, I'm sure you can find a female who'll actually welcome your advances." It was hard to get the words out because even though she didn't want him bothering her anymore, she hated the thought of seeing him with another woman.

"You're the one I want," he said simply, his voice calm, determined. He leaned in and took her hand between two of his. That simple touch energized her. A scene flashed in her mind. Jared's weight covering her, his hands, fingers entwined with hers, holding her arms over her head. Panting breaths. Moans. Ecstasy.

"You may not remember our night together, but I can't forget it. The feel of your beautiful body pressed to mine, your legs wrapped around my hips, urging me deeper…"

"Stop!" Though she'd never admit it, since his return she'd been remembering more and more details of their night together. The sound of his voice, his scent, his touch when he went out of his way to brush up against her triggered erotic flashes of memory at the most inopportune times. Like right now. She shifted in her seat and took back her hand.

"I'm nowhere near good enough for you," he said, moving even closer. "I can't give you the future you have your heart set on. But if you'll let me, I can give you the best twenty-four days of your life. We have great chemistry. We could have a blast together."

"For twenty-four days." Good for sex and nothing more. Ali's body cooled at the reminder. "And then what? You'll flick me to the curb like a used-up cigarette butt? Never to be thought of again?" Until he wanted more. Men always came back for more.

"And then I'll leave town and you can resume your search for the man of your dreams."

Right now he was the man occupying her dreams, interrupting her sleep and making her body ache with need. Unfortunately, he was also the man of her nightmares, a man who didn't value commitment, monogamy or love. A man like her father. A man to avoid. "Thanks, Dr. P., but I'll have to pass. I won't take the chance my Mr. Right will happen by while I'm—" she made air quotation marks "—'having a blast' with you."

Thank heavens Gramps chose that minute to knock. "Allison? You in there?"

"Yes, Gramps," she called out. "Be right there." She turned to Jared. "Night, Dr. P. Sorry you wasted your time coming out on this chilly evening."

"No time spent with you is ever wasted," he said. "I'm not giving up," he added as she walked toward the door.

An unwanted thrill zipped through her traitorous body. He was right. They had great chemistry. If she agreed to his proposition, for the next twenty-four days she could go loose-in-a-fudge-factory wild, indulging every one of her repressed sexual desires to the point of gluttony.

Tempting.

Except she wanted more. Devotion. Trust. Marriage. Stability. A chance for a happier life than her mother had had.

Jared watched her leave. Since his father's death, except for a brief few months of happiness before he'd learned his wife's true nature, Jared had lived a solitary life focused on work and school. He'd learned to enjoy his own company, liked reading and searching the internet when he had the time. Until Ali, he'd never longed for companionship, never felt lonely or wished he were somewhere else.

Missing her, craving her was slowly driving him out of his mind.

They weren't scheduled to work together the next day. At first Jared had been disappointed. Maybe it was a good thing. It'd give her time to think over his offer. And she was considering it. Jared stood and walked out into the hallway. He'd seen the indecision in Ali's eyes, the same helpless-to-stop-it lust he'd noticed in his own reflection after encounters with her.

He entered the community room to grab his jacket. Ali was nowhere in sight. He smiled. She had a talent for making herself scarce when she wanted to.

A layer of pristine white snow blanketed the parking lot. Big flakes drifted to the ground around him. Jared turned his face to the sky, welcoming the chilly wetness, enjoying the peace and quiet.

"Un-friggin-believable!" Ali's voice yelled out.

He looked around but didn't see her.

"Ali?"

"Perfect. This night keeps getting better and better."

He followed her words to a car parked beneath one of the huge lights at the far end of the lot. She wasn't there. He circled the car, looked over the edge of an embankment beside the car and found her, six feet down, on her back, lodged in a huge pile of snow. She didn't look hurt, was moving her arms and legs. Their important chat over, he decided to have a little fun. "Watcha doing?"

"Why, I'm sunbathing, Dr. P." She sounded totally frustrated and looked absolutely adorable. "Can't seem to pass up an opportunity to work on my tan." She squinted up at him, the wintry precipitation hitting her in the face.

"Care for some company?"

"Not especially." She struggled into a sitting position, snow caked in her hair, her legs now buried. He removed his jacket and threw it down to her because she wasn't wearing a coat of her own. "Put that over you. I'll be down in a minute to help you up."

"I don't need your coat."

"Neither do I," he answered as he took the first step down toward her, the snow coming up to his knees. "I prefer to sunbathe in the nude."

She mumbled something.

He smiled to himself, happy to have had the opportunity to plant that visual seed in her fertile mind. Although, to be honest, since his return his need had grown into more than simple sexual desire. He wanted to talk with her, laugh with her, spend every minute with her.

Halfway down Ali called out, "Wait. Stop. Look at your right boot."

Jared did. The light above reflected off a set of keys. He picked them up and shook them off. "Yours, I presume?" He dropped them into his pocket.

"Wow. You're really bright, Dr. P. Medical school must have been a breeze."

Jared smiled again. Too bad about her predicament but he was enjoying every second of her rescue. She lifted his spirits, made him want to laugh out loud, frolic even.

"Look out," she yelled at the exact moment his right foot slid out from under him. He flailed his arms to help regain his balance. His foot continued its slide, forcing his legs into a split that would have made a goalie in ice hockey proud.

Ali howled with laughter. He would not give her the

satisfaction of screaming out in pain. Instead he dropped forward and rolled, and rolled, until something stopped his motion. Ali. Next thing he knew he was facedown on top of her.

That shut her up.

"You okay?" He tried to lift his body but his arms sank into the loosely packed snow.

"I. Can't. Breathe." Her words came out muffled beneath his chest.

He lifted his head. "Good thing I'm trained in mouth-to-mouth resuscitation."

A handful of snow mashed into his right ear. "There's more where that came from." As if to make her point, another handful landed on the back of his neck. "Now get off me."

"Fine thing when a man risks life and limb—" and his reproductive organs being ripped in half "—to rescue a woman, and this is the thanks he gets." Jared wiped the snow from the side of his face and neck.

"Thank you. Now please get off me. I'm cold."

"I have some ideas on how to get you warmed up." He looked down at her and cocked an eyebrow.

"I'm thinking a hot shower and a warm bed."

Oh, yeah. "That'll work, too." He turned onto his side, moving carefully.

"Alone."

"Where's the fun in that?" He managed to stand, wiped the snow from his clothes, and held out his hand to Ali.

A huge tug and she was free. When she tried to put weight on her right foot she cried out, "Ouch. Shoot." And grabbed onto him for support.

"What is it? What hurts?"

"My ankle." She looked up the steep slope to the parking lot. "How am I going to…?"

"Don't worry. I'll get you out of here." Jared retrieved his coat and shook off the snow that had accumulated on it. He held it open for her. "Put this on." She did. Then he turned his back to her and bent his knees. "Jump on."

"I think I'd be safer if I crawled up."

He wouldn't allow her to risk doing more damage to her ankle. "Piggyback or fireman's lift. You have ten seconds to decide." Playtime was over. They were both chilled and he wanted to get a look at her injury.

"Don't think you can boss me around. I'll…"

He turned to her. "Fireman's lift it is." He reached for her waist.

"Wait. No." She grabbed for his hands. "Piggyback. I choose piggyback."

He pivoted around and helped her onto his back. In the process his shirt pulled from his pants. The cold, wet denim of her jeans chilled him further.

"Tyrant," she mumbled.

"Ingrate," he replied.

She crossed her arms loosely around his neck.

"Don't get any ideas." He leaned forward and started to climb. Ali clung to him, her strong thighs clamped above his hips.

"I'll try to control myself."

The climb was harder than it looked. Each step sank his foot into deep snow that shifted and crumbled under their combined weight. It seemed for every two steps up he slid one step down. "How did you wind up down there?" Jared asked, to keep from thinking about the fragrant smell of her hair, which hung down the side of his left cheek, and the feel of her breasts flattened against his back.

"Apparently there was a patch of ice behind my car. When I went to get the containers of stew I'd made, I slipped. My keys flew out of my hand. I thought I could reach them."

"And fell."

"Yup."

By the time Jared reached the parking lot his hands felt frozen, his pants were soaked and he was breathing hard. But he wasn't ready to part from Ali.

"Hey, you're passing my car."

"You can't drive anyway." Since it was her right ankle that was injured. "I'll take you home."

"You don't have to do that."

No. He didn't. But he wanted to. "It's no problem."

CHAPTER SIX

A WEEK ago, if someone had told Ali she'd spend her Tuesday night out on a date with Dr. Jared Padget, she would have laughed. Yet here she was, in the ritziest restaurant in the county, sitting catty-corner to him at a table for two. Brushing knees with him and inhaling his alluring eau de aphrodisiac cologne.

After Jared had driven her home from bingo last week, he'd carried her into her condo and gently removed her boot to examine her ankle. Then he'd got her set up on the couch with a pillow to elevate her foot, an ice pack and a mug of hot chocolate. When he'd got up to leave, she'd made the mistake of saying, "I don't know how to thank you."

To which he'd replied, "Have dinner with me." He'd been so sweet, so helpful. How could she say no?

Sure, she could have backed out at the last minute, she'd thought up some great excuses. But the sad truth was she hadn't wanted to cancel. Over the past few days she'd started to look forward to their date, to getting to know more about him. Like why did such a superb physician travel from hospital to hospital when, with his skills, he could easily land a job at any leading trauma center?

The restaurant had dream date potential. The lighting subdued, the piano player superb, small tables situated for optimum privacy. Huge windows and strategically placed outdoor lamps showed off the picturesque, snow-covered landscape. Jared wore a dark gray pinstripe suit with a purple shirt and matching checkered tie and looked like he'd just walked off a photo shoot for upscale menswear.

Edible from head to toe.

"I've wanted to come here since it opened," she said, trying to ease the uncomfortable silence that settled between them after they'd exhausted conversation about the menu. "There's a two-month wait for reservations."

He winked. "It's good to have connections." Aka the thirty-two-year-old male chef who'd sustained first- and second-degree burns on his hands and face from messing with the pilot light on the restaurant's commercial oven last week.

"You look beautiful tonight," he said, making shopping for a new dress, waiting an hour for a haircut and undergoing an unplanned midwinter wax job all worth it. He'd stood speechless in the doorway of her condo forty-five minutes earlier, staring at her with a look of complete rapture, while the beautiful bouquet of flowers he'd brought her had hung blooms down, from his hand.

Mission accomplished.

Presenting her best possible look made her feel confident and empowered. It fortified her defenses against him. Unfortunately he'd spent a bit of time putting together his best possible look, too, and the result had neutralized her confidence, weakened her power and whacked at her defenses with a giant-sized sledgehammer the second he'd slipped off his overcoat.

"Thanks. So do…" She shook her head and let out a small laugh. She'd almost called him beautiful. She was as nervous as a teen out on her first date. "Sorry."

"It's only dinner, Ali." He placed his hand on her forearm and her entire body, including the tiny hairs on her arms, which stood at full rigid attention since he'd picked her up, relaxed.

She could do this, smile, make small talk. She decided to start with a few neutral topics. "So, Dr. P., where's home?"

He swirled a piece of *focaccia* bread in olive oil. "Wherever I happen to be."

Ali's mouth watered at the *focaccia*'s fresh-baked aroma. On edge about their date, she'd been a bit queasy all day and didn't want to chance eating it. "I mean, where are you from? Originally."

"Rochester."

Now they were getting somewhere. "Does your mom still live there?"

He kept his eyes on the plate of oil, looked a bit stiff. "Yes."

"Do you have any brothers or sisters?" At this rate dinner would be over before she learned anything significant.

He lifted the bread to his mouth and took a bite, chewed, and swallowed, before answering. "No. Ali, there are so many things more interesting than me to talk about. You, for instance. How long have you been going into the senior center?"

"Nice try, Doc. But we're talking about you right now."

He leaned in and, with a flirty smile, said, "Only if you call me Jared."

She smiled back. If he meant to deter her, he had another think coming. "Okay. Jared. Tell me about your mom."

He let out a breath. "You want to know about my mom? Fine. I'll tell you. But first we dance."

Ali glanced at the empty dance floor, the dozens of people sitting at tables around the room, and suffered a wave of uneasiness at the thought of everyone watching her and Dr. Padget dancing together. What if someone from the hospital saw them? The gossip from New Year's Eve was just starting to quiet down.

He sat back in his chair, his arms crossed over his chest, his eyebrows raised in challenge. She wanted to smear butter all over the pleased look on his face. Blending into the background was more her style, not standing center stage, and he knew it.

But Ali would not let him win. "I'd love to dance, Jared." Arms resting on the table, she leaned in, as he'd done a moment earlier.

Without giving her a chance to reconsider, he stood and offered her his hand. She stared up at him. God, he was gorgeous.

Entranced, she rose, and with his hand at the small of her back allowed herself to be guided to the dance floor, where he promptly left her standing all alone while he went to whisper something to the pianist. Deserted and on display, with dozens of eyes watching her, Ali was seconds away from walking back to their table when he returned.

"I requested a song that makes me think of you every time I hear it." He took her into his arms and everyone in the room vanished, only the two of them existed. His left hand, mere centimeters above her butt, held her firmly against him. She inhaled the delicious scent of him and fought the urge to bury her face in his neck.

The notes from "Unforgettable" by Nat King Cole filled the room. Jared hugged her close. Ali reveled in his strength and the smooth sway of his hips as they moved to the music. He dipped his head, his mouth at her ear, his breath hot as he quietly serenaded her, singing in time with the melody from the piano.

Her heart swelled with affection. No man had ever sung

to her so sweetly, so meaningfully. No man had ever made a gesture so poignant, so romantic.

Was this the practiced seduction of an accomplished seducer of women, or did he mean the lovely words sung so tenderly for only her to hear? And did she want him to mean them? Yes. Yes she did.

When the song ended Ali asked, "You woo a lot of women this way?" With flawless dancing and inspired singing. A niggling voice of reason urged caution.

He pulled her close. "I'm hardly the womanizer you think me to be, Ali."

She wished it were true.

Jared was in heaven, holding Ali in his arms, their torsos pressed together through a second song. They danced like they'd been doing it for years, perfectly in sync. Her hair smelled like flowers in spring and he, like a bumblebee in search of her pollen, couldn't get enough.

At one point she'd gone tense, tried to pull away. "Please," he'd said, not ready to release her, not knowing if he'd ever have the chance to hold her again. "Not yet. One more song."

She'd studied him, must have seen his desperate need, and stepped back into his embrace. Jared lifted her arms and told her to clasp her fingers behind his neck. He rested his hands at the concave curve of her waist and pulled her close, wishing their time together didn't have to end.

But it did. She wanted marriage. And he couldn't marry her now even if he wanted to, which he didn't. When the song ended, Jared reluctantly released Ali and escorted her back to their table, where the waiter promptly served their entrées.

After eating a minuscule piece of her plain broiled

chicken breast Ali said, "I held up my part of the bargain, now it's your turn. Start talking."

"Bargain?" He put a forkful of veal marsala into his mouth. "I don't remember making any bargain."

She kicked him with her pointy-toed boot. "Tell me about your mother."

Jared took a sip of water and fought the urge to take out a stick of gum. Ali stared at him, waited for a response. Way to ruin a perfectly good dinner. He blotted his mouth with his cloth napkin. Ali already thought him the worst sort of man. After this, any chance he might have had with her would evaporate. *Poof.* Gone.

Maybe it was for the best. Her opinion of him would be solidified, and he could stop entertaining the possibility of anything more than a professional relationship between them.

"I haven't spoken with my mother in twelve years." Since he'd returned from his high-school graduation to find all of his belongings packed into boxes stacked outside their apartment door, which had sported a shiny new lock to which he had not been given a key.

Jared knew what came next. What kind of son doesn't talk to his mother for twelve years? What kind of son gives up his attempts to reconcile when he was the one responsible for the rift between them? What kind of son doesn't fulfill his father's dying wish? *Take care of your mother.*

But Ali simply asked, "Why?"

Jared's heart pinched. "Mom wasn't at all happy I waited to call 911 after my father started complaining of chest pain, thus allowing my dad to die in his recliner chair before the paramedics could arrive to save him."

"He told me he'd be okay in a few minutes. He said it was indigestion," Jared had said to his mother, trying to justify not making the call until after his father had lost

consciousness. He hadn't mentioned the fact that while all that was happening, his mom had been out at the store, buying the antacids her husband had requested.

"You stupid boy. Can't you tell the difference between indigestion and a heart attack?"

Years later Jared realized his mom had likely been as angry with herself as she'd been with him. Although at the time her anger at Jared had consumed her, and was the only emotion she'd let him see. Coping mechanism? It didn't much matter now.

"Jared, you were what, fourteen, fifteen years old? What kind of mother blames something like that on her child?" Ali asked.

She surprised him, choosing to question his mom's actions rather than his. "An angry one." Someone who had been jealous of the close relationship between her husband and his biological son who'd come as part of the package when she'd married. One who'd wanted a daughter of her own, but had got stuck with an adopted child she resented, unhappy when the man she loved devoted his time and attention to anyone but her.

"What did she expect you to do?"

"Let's see. I should have dialed 911 immediately and left my dad to run next door to get our neighbor, who was a nurse. Turns out she'd been home. Mom checked." But at the time, obeying his father, staying with him so he wouldn't be alone, had seemed like the right course of action.

"I'm so sorry, Jared." She placed her hand on his forearm. Not at all what Jared had expected. She studied his face, saw something that made her say, "You have to know his death was not your fault."

Yes. But on rare occasions, a small part of him still wondered...what if. What if he hadn't waited to call 911? What if his father had received prompt medical attention? Would he have survived? "Irrelevant. Mom needed someone to blame." He shrugged. "I was handy. It all worked out. She barely acknowledged me for a bunch of years." At a time when a guilt-ridden, grieving teenage boy had desperately needed the love and understanding of the only mother he'd ever known. He'd tried so hard to earn her forgiveness, taking on two after-school jobs, maintaining the house, the yard and then their apartment, shopping for food, making meals she'd refused to eat. *You will never be the wonderful man and husband your father was, so stop trying.* Many years later, it was with those hurtful words in mind that he'd proposed to his wife, determined to do better, to prove his mother wrong. Turned out she'd been right.

"It gave me plenty of time to work like a dog to get my grades up and earn money for college, apply for scholarships." To become a physician so no kid would have to go through what he'd gone through. How naïve he'd been.

"And after so many years you still haven't worked things out?" Ali asked, with a look of disbelief.

Jared shook his head. His sadness over his father's death and hurt at his mother's subsequent alienation had barely lessened with time. Chances were his mother's anger and resentment toward him hadn't either.

"The day my mom took her life, we'd had a terrible fight," Ali said, looking up at him with sad eyes. "I told her I hated her. Those were the last words she'd ever heard me say."

He didn't know how to respond so he put his hand over hers, which still rested on his arm.

"For years I've regretted not being able to apologize or tell her I loved her with all my heart. There was a time, if I could have bargained a few years off my life to get my mom a message up in heaven, I would have." She took his right hand between both of hers and looked up at him. "You have a chance to make things right with your mother, before it's too late. You have to do it, Jared. Don't wait."

From time to time he'd considered it, but doubted his mother would be interested. Did he want to give her an opportunity to reject him? Again?

"You'll at least think about it?" she asked, looking hopeful.

He didn't want to disappoint her. "I will." Maybe he could enclose a quick note in the next monthly check he mailed her, or at least put a return address on the envelope in case she wanted to contact him.

"It seems we've both overcome difficult childhoods to get where we are today," Ali said. "Something in common. Who knew?"

"Oh, we have lots in common," Jared said, ready for a change of subject. "We are both well-respected healthcare professionals, outside work we are both snazzy dressers, and…" he leaned in close for the last similarity "…we are both hot for each other."

She swatted his arm, laughing. He loved the sound.

Sharing bits of their past seemed to put Ali at ease. For the rest of the meal they chatted and teased. Jared couldn't remember ever enjoying a dinner date more. While they waited outside for the valet to retrieve his car, the temperature below freezing, she didn't balk when he pulled her close to warm her. Progress.

On the drive home he took a chance, removing her mitten and taking her hand in his, skin on skin, settling both on her thigh. "I had a nice time tonight."

She didn't pull away. "Me, too."

Later that night, in her bed, Ali tossed and turned, restless and unable to sleep. Each day she learned or noticed something new about Jared, started to like him a little bit more. Eighteen days. Whenever she thought about him leaving it was as if, in the background, a gigantic pendulum ticked away each second, reminding her time was running out.

The telephone rang.

She fumbled in the dark, trying to locate the receiver on her nightstand. Finding it, she glanced at the orange glow of the numbers on her alarm clock as she picked it up. It was almost midnight. Had something happened to her granddad? An emergency at the hospital? Her pulse sped up. "Hello?"

Jared's deep voice, smooth as a shot of blackberry brandy, soothing her, warming her from the inside out, said, "I called to say good night."

"We already said good night." An hour ago, her back pushed up against the outside of her front door, with a mind-altering kiss that'd had her on the verge of dragging him inside her condo.

"And," he rushed to add, "to see if you're thinking about me like I'm thinking of you?"

She was. "I might be."

"We never had dessert. I think I can rustle up half a box of chocolate-chip cookies. How about I bring them over?"

"I'm in bed, Jared."

"Perfect." He sounded like he was smiling. "Dessert in bed. I like it."

"I don't think so." Although, boy, did it sound tempting.

"You want to know what I'm doing right now?" he asked. The teasing, sexy tone of his voice gave her some idea.

"I'm naked, in a big bed, all alone, thinking of you,"

he said. "Wishing you were here." His voice dropped an octave. "Pretending my hand is your mouth, driving me wild."

The mouth in question watered. She swallowed. "You have got to be kidding me. Phone sex? That's why you called?" She pretended to be outraged but the idea had some appeal. Satisfying her urge for him without tender touches and caring words that put her heart at risk.

"I'd prefer real sex, but I'll take what I can get. Now, pretend your hand is mine. Tell me what I'm doing to you."

For weeks, while alone in her bed, she'd pretended her hands were his, roaming her body. Hearing his voice made the experience more real. Unable to stop herself, she wedged the phone between her ear and shoulder, and slid her hands up her flat abdomen. "You're cupping my breasts while your thumbs flick over my nipples." Her ultrasensitive nipples, sending a shockwave of arousal to every nerve ending in her body.

"Are they hard?" His voice roughened. "Your nipples."

"Yes." She moaned, pretending her hands were his, her hips rocking, searching for what wasn't there.

"Are you wet?"

"So wet." So aroused, so hot. She wanted so much more. "Oh, Jared. I wish you were here."

"Hold that thought," he said.

"Jared? Jared!" she yelled into the phone, talking to the dial tone. "Dammit!"

She paced the hallway from her bedroom to the kitchen, twirling a lock of hair around her finger over and over until it knotted. A frantic pounding broke the tense quiet in her condo. She jumped, waited, hoping he'd give up and go away. Like that might actually happen. When the knick-knacks on the shelf by her door began to rattle she knew it was only a matter of time before her neighbors began to peer outside.

The robe she'd put on was no protection from the blast of freezing-cold air that blew in when she yanked open the door. "Come in before—"

It turned out no invitation was necessary, because he pushed inside before she could finish, a man possessed, shrugging out of his jacket and kicking off his boots.

"How did you get here so fast?"

"I'm subletting in Building B. I ran over."

His heavy breathing didn't slow him down one bit. In two giant steps he had her in his arms.

"What, no cookies? You said you'd bring cookies." She tried to distract him.

Not going to happen. He buried his face against her neck. "God, what you do to me, Ali." He held her tight, kissing up to her ear. "I can't stop thinking about you, dreaming about you, wanting you."

"This is a terrible idea, Jared," she said, trying to push him away, hoping that saying it out loud, hearing the words coming from her own mouth, would counteract the enormous surge of lust overwhelming her good sense. She wasn't an eighteen-days-of-fun kind of girl anymore. Though, through the thick fog of arousal, she couldn't quite remember why.

"This is a wonderful idea." His lips met hers, hard and fast. "Better than pairing chocolate with peanut butter. We are so good together. I want you to remember this time." He kissed her again, slow, tender. "Everything."

He cupped her breast, his thumb sliding back and forth over her nipple, sending a potent charge of desire straight to her core, and Ali lost the will to object. His erection rubbed between her legs and all logical thought fled.

More. She wanted more, needed more. Ali couldn't

remember one reason why she should tell him to stop. All she could think of was getting naked, touching him, holding him, keeping him in her bed until she was too weak to move.

Jared almost shouted out in victory when Ali's small hands tugged up his shirt then pushed down the elastic waistband of the sweatpants he'd barely remembered to put on before running out of his rental. "Bedroom," he said against her lips, because it had been a chilling trip to her unit. He needed to be under a comforter, between the sheets, skin on skin. Now.

He no sooner got the word out than she wrapped her arms around his neck and lifted her legs, clamping them around his waist and locking her feet at his lower back. They were of one mind. Again he was off running, this time to her bed, where he planned to enact a couple of fantasies that had been plaguing him over the past few weeks. In his haste he took a turn too sharply and whacked her knee on the wall. "Sorry."

"Mmm." She was too busy sucking on his neck to answer. And that was okay with him.

"Mmm," she mumbled again, and moved lower. Her mouth felt so good on his skin, hot and wet, leaving a cooling trail of moisture in its path. She leaned down and sucked his nipple into her mouth and Jared's legs almost gave out.

Once inside her bedroom he loosened his hold on her butt, expecting her to slide down his body until her feet reached the floor. Only she didn't budge. She clung to him unassisted, her thighs squeezing his waist, her lips suctioned to his chest.

"Come on, baby." He worked to detach her. "We're here."

"I love your chest, firm and muscly, with just a sprinkling of hair." She brushed her fingertips up his ribs, across his nipples, looping down below his belly button. He shivered at the sensation. Goose bumps sprouted on his skin.

"I love yours, too." In the light from the hallway he spotted the bed and walked over to it. He bent over and released her. She flopped onto her back. He followed her down. "Now, where were we?"

"You were about to kiss my..." She struggled between them to untie her robe.

"Oh, yeah." He laughed. "Sit up." He helped her out of her robe and slid her nightshirt up over her head. "I want to do this right." To make it so good it wiped every other sexual encounter from her mind, so memorable she couldn't lie in her bed without thinking about it, without wanting him there with her.

Once he had her upper body completely naked he positioned himself where she wanted him, sucking in one taut nipple. The roughened texture met his tongue and her taste, the smoothness of her full breast in his palm, her moans of pleasure almost made him lose control. It had been too long. He'd missed her too much.

He released one nipple to move on to the other, shifting to lie beside her as he did. He slid his hand down her firm, flat belly to her hip, slipping a finger under the thin elastic of her panties to draw them down to her knees so she could kick them away. She squirmed, gripped his head, held him to her.

"Please," she said, her hips bucking. "I want more."

So did Jared. "And I'm going to give it to you." He jumped up, shucked his sweats, and, with his last shred of common sense took out the strip of condoms he'd stashed in his pocket, ripped one off and tossed the rest onto the night table beside her bed. He'd dodged the pregnancy bullet once. From now on he controlled protection.

Ali lay naked in the center of the bed, waiting for him, a thing of beauty, inside and out. As he approached, she bent her knees and dropped each to the side, opening for him. Jared took pause. Did she expect him to drop on top of her and go into rut? Like all the inexperienced, self-centered losers before him?

No. Tonight would be different, better.

He'd take his time, make it special. Teach her the difference between having sex and making love. Show her what it's like to be with a real man who treasured women and gave pleasure before taking his own.

He crawled onto the bed, settled his naked body on top of hers. His skin came alive on contact, felt charged. He whispered in her ear, "I've dreamed of this for weeks."

"Me, too." She squirmed beneath him, tried to align their hips.

He traced the inner rim of her ear with his tongue. She stilled. "I'm going to make you feel so good." He kissed down her jaw on his way to her lips. He started off soft, a simple meeting, a light pressure, a basic exploration. He lifted slightly. She parted her lips, exhaled, her breath a pheromone that instantly upped his attraction.

He dropped his lips to hers, plunged his tongue into her sweet mouth, savored her. Ali was not a docile lover. She gripped his head, held him to her, challenged him, tested his restraint.

Breathing heavily and painfully aroused, Jared needed to slow things down. He pulled away and, trailing little kisses down the side of her neck, slid his body lower on the bed.

"You're moving in the wrong direction, Doc." She tried to stop him.

"Last time you were in charge." He ran the bottom of his tongue down the valley between her breasts. "Tonight it's my turn."

"Just so you know, I like sex. I don't need a lot of fore-play."

"Well, I do."

"But I'm—"

"Do not make me leave this bed in search of duct tape." He sucked a nipple into his mouth. She arched her back and moaned. That's what he wanted to hear. He moved his lips along the smooth skin covering her ribs, kissed across her abdomen, licked around her belly button. Then he moved on to her arms and legs. He paid attention to each sound she made, each movement, each time she reached for him. He made a mental note of what she liked and where she liked it so he could return to those places again and again.

On his way up her inner thigh he ran his fingers through her curls. Moved lower.

"Wait." She tried to push his head away. "No one's ever…"

"Good." He wanted to be the first, the only.

"I don't think I'll…"

Jared blew cool air on her slick flesh, his mouth watering in greedy anticipation. "If you don't like it…" his tongue flickered across the focal point of her arousal "…I'll stop." He reached for a pillow. "Lift up."

She didn't respond verbally. Her body gave him the go-ahead when she lifted her hips and allowed him to slide the pillow underneath. He bent her legs, eased them apart and set in to feast. He lapped and swirled, dipped and flicked. He used his lips, his tongue, enjoying his actions almost as much as if she'd had her mouth on him.

Ali squirmed and moaned. "I can't take it." She tried to scoot away. "It's too much."

He gripped her hips, pulled her closer. "Come for me." He thrust two fingers inside her, worked them in and out while he continued his oral assault.

With a cry Ali came apart, with an orgasm that satisfied him as much as it excited him. As soon as the first wave ended, Jared went back for more. With a series of breathless gasps, Ali came again.

"No more," she said, her body falling limp.

Jared stopped.

"I never knew it could be like that," Ali said in between deep shaky breaths.

Jared removed the pillow and worked his way up her body. "That was only the beginning." He kissed her lips. "The next time will be even more intense." He'd see to it.

She brought her fingers up to his face, traced his lips. "I won't be able to look at your mouth without remembering."

He smiled. Good. He'd make sure to leave her a picture to keep by her bed.

"But what about you?" Ali asked, reaching between them to take his erection into her hand.

His hips jerked forward of their own accord and he lunged for the nightstand to retrieve a condom, ripping it open with his teeth and sheathing himself. He'd be lucky to last more than five minutes. Fighting the urge to plunge inside, he took it slow, rocking into her, inch by glorious inch. "You okay?" he asked, not wanting to hurt her.

"I'm better than okay. I need all of you." She swiveled her hips, lifted them and he slid all the way in. She felt so good, her wet heat surrounding him, the residual contractions from her orgasm rippling along his length. Her tightness embraced him, didn't want him to leave.

Jared withdrew, took his time, the friction unbelievable. If he didn't concentrate on something else this would be over embarrassingly quick. He rotated his hips as he thrust in deep, kept his movement controlled, changed his angle of entry, worked hard to find it.

Ali sucked in a breath. "What the heck was that?"

G-spot.

And he let himself go, careful to hit the right spot each time he drove inside.

Knees bent, feet flat on the bed she increased their pace, meeting every powerful thrust with one of her own. "Just like that. Don't stop."

Only death could stop him.

"Oh, Jared. You feel so good inside me."

Hearing her say his name, made his heart flip, made things so much more personal, special.

Fierce arousal and the feeling he was on the verge of something bigger than big had him matching her stroke for stroke, moving his hips faster than the heartbeat of a tachycardic patient.

Ali moaned, lifted her legs and dug her heels into his butt. "Oh, God," she said between panting breaths. She lifted her pelvis, forcing him deeper.

Thank, God, Jared thought. His movements choppy, lacking his usual finesse. He'd make it up to her, next time, and the time after that, and the time after that. Right now all he could think about was finding a release for the weeks of desire built up inside him, the pressure inside his groin unbearable.

He tried to hold on, to give her time to catch up.

She let out a deep moan, tightened around him, massaged him in the midst of her release and he gave up trying to fight it. He came like a firework shot into the sky, on fire, exploding into a spectacular display of vibrant colors, floating on the breeze, before his spent embers drifted slowly back to earth.

He lay collapsed on top of her, a panting, sweaty mess. He wanted to move, really he did, but in its euphoric state, his brain wouldn't process the command.

"That was…" he said, after regaining control of his facial muscles.

"Yeah," she responded on a contended sigh, stretching as he eased his weight from her. Then she curled onto her side.

"I'll be right back." He tucked the covers around her then walked to the bathroom.

"I'll be here," she said drowsily. "Waiting."

When he returned she was right where she'd said she'd be, in exactly the same position, fast asleep, her body completely relaxed, her respirations shallow.

He wanted nothing more than to climb in behind her, lose himself in the feel of her naked body cuddled close to his. But he felt on edge, unable to settle down. So he put on his sweatpants and went to the kitchen for a glass of water.

He'd shared some of his past with her tonight, prepared for her to get on him about neglecting his mother, not doing more for her. She hadn't. In fact, she'd taken his side, encouraged him to make things right with his mother before it was too late.

Why couldn't he have met Ali three years ago, when he'd still believed in happily ever after? Before another nurse, one with a well-hidden drug addiction, had manipulated him into marriage, lured him by pretending to be all he wanted, fooled him into thinking she loved him and couldn't live without him.

The day after their courthouse wedding, boy, did things change. His wife had morphed into a demanding, unhappy shrew. Nothing he did was good enough, and yet, like he had with his mother, Jared had tried so hard to please her.

He'd drawn the line at prescribing her narcotic pain medication for an alleged back condition she'd never mentioned prior to their nuptials.

He let out a bitter laugh. Ali thought him a womanizer. That couldn't be further from the truth. Not since his wife had maxed out his credit cards and emptied his bank accounts on her way out of town a mere eight weeks after their marriage, leaving him broke, betrayed and the subject of a Drug Enforcement Administration criminal investigation a little over two years ago.

If he could have scrounged up the money, he'd have set the divorce in motion right away. But paying an attorney for a divorce had been the last expenditure he could afford. Keeping himself out of jail and trying to hold on to his house had taken priority. A year later, his finances back in positive territory, the need for a divorce hadn't seemed all that urgent. He had no plans to remarry, to ever open himself up to the pain of having someone he loved turn on him again.

So he'd tucked his marriage certificate in his wallet, a shield to fend off ever pursuing a relationship with another woman. It had worked like a charm. Until Ali. She was the reason he'd finally contacted his attorney and instructed him to proceed with his divorce, using any means necessary, no matter the cost. Every day since he'd checked his post office box, hoping to find the documentation declaring the marriage he'd thought would be for life officially over. To date, it had not yet arrived.

Technically he was still married. A liar. An adulterer. The type of man Ali would run from. She deserved better. But, God help him, he hadn't been able to pass up this opportunity to be with her again. In his defense, he'd thought for sure thirty days was enough time to process an uncontested divorce. But nothing in his life ever went as planned. Now the guilt of not being honest with her ate at his insides. Maybe he should come clean, tell Ali the truth.

CHAPTER SEVEN

ON THURSDAY, Ali was eight hours into a twelve-hour shift on 5E when she received the call. A school bus versus school bus MVA—motor vehicle accident. Estimated seventy-six children and two adults injured. ETA thirteen minutes.

The nurse administrator instructed her to proceed to the E.R., stat.

A winter storm had moved in earlier than predicted. Madrin Memorial was the hospital closest to the crash site. With dangerous travel conditions no patients would be diverted. Ali gave report to Victoria, who would cover her patients until the next shift of nurses arrived.

Before leaving the floor, Ali made a call of her own.

"We need you, Gramps, and Mrs. Meyer. Two elementary school buses collided out on Clover Hill. Wear your hospital volunteer blazers and bring your ID badges. The E.R. is going to be a madhouse."

"We'll see you in ten." He hung up the phone.

Ali would have offered to send someone to get him, but, living three blocks from the hospital, she knew Gramps would have refused.

"All non-essential personnel report to the emergency room, stat," boomed over the hospital PA system. Ali ran for the stairs.

Hospital employees from every department, in a rainbow of scrub colors and uniforms, moved with purpose throughout the emergency room. Extra stretchers brought out of storage lined every spare inch of wall space along the main inverted T-shaped hallway. Staff from Housekeeping washed them down while men from Maintenance trailed behind them, tying on clean sheets. Wheelchairs, which never seemed to be around when you needed them, were collapsed and lined up three deep along the back corridor.

Security guards set up tables and barrier screens. Staff from Food Service assisted staff from Patient Registration by putting together and stacking new patient files. Men from Engineering hung premade signs directing ambulance staff and family members of the injured, signs that, for the most part, were ignored.

After receiving her assignment, Ali found Jared in Trauma Room One, Bed One, listening to the chest of an elderly man through his stethoscope. The patient looked up at her, sighed, and said, "I've died and gone to heaven."

Jared lifted his head and bent toward his patient's ear, his eyes fixed on Ali. "I feel the very same way every time I see her, too," he whispered loudly, making certain she heard.

He smiled but it didn't reach his eyes. Something wasn't right. She'd thought he might show up at bingo last night. He hadn't. Their last contact had been physical in nature, and when she'd woken up in the morning, he had gone. He'd snuck out, again.

"Is there anything I can help you with, Dr. Padget?" she asked.

"Why, yes, Nurse Forshay," he countered. "Mr. Conran fell at the nursing home and is having some left hip pain. Let's get a left hip X-ray."

"Right away, Doctor." She hesitated, stared at his luscious mouth, remembered.

He smiled, this one genuine. "Penny for your thoughts?"

Not for a million pennies. Her body in the midst of a heated flush, she turned and left the room, heard him laugh behind her. At the front desk she entered the radiology request into the computer.

"Do me a favor, Ali," Tani said. "Tell Dr. P. his attorney is holding on line three. He promises this is his last call. He says it's important."

Ali met Jared outside Trauma One and relayed the message. He stiffened, looked…guilty? Well, he should feel guilty about sneaking out the way he did.

The first ambulance siren rang out and Ali's attention turned to her patients. Her heart went out to the young children, especially three scared little girls who refused to be separated: a five-year-old in a right arm sling; a five-year-old in a left arm sling and a seven-year-old with her right leg immobilized, all snuggled close on a stretcher. The oldest held it together until Jared ordered X-rays all round and the one stable force in the group lost it. "I don't want an X-ray," she screamed, as if the word "X-ray" was synonymous with a blow to the head with a blunt object.

"Calm down, honey," Ali comforted the oldest of the girls, while her bedmates looked up at her like she was an alien preparing to suck their brains out of their ears. "An X-ray is a picture of your bones. Pictures aren't scary, are they?"

Then help, in the form of a spunky senior citizen wearing a red-wine-colored polyester pantsuit, arrived. "Pictures? Did I hear someone say pictures?" She patted her springy white curls. "I love having my picture taken!" Gramps's neighbor Mrs. Meyer, all five feet two inches of her, loved to mother little girls. Growing up, she'd helped Ali through quite a few difficult years. With her navy-blue volunteer blazer and photo ID proudly displayed on her chest pocket, she walked in like an army sergeant reporting for duty. "Where do you need me, Allison?"

"I think right here will be perfect. These little ladies are first-timers to the E.R. All three need X-rays. Would you please talk them through what happens during an X-ray, while I arrange for transport to Radiology? And if you would accompany them, I would greatly appreciate it."

Her three little patients well in hand, Ali went to look for Gramps. She found him in the lobby, working with a male medical technician arranging screens to give the children some privacy. He'd brought his stash of board games, which were stacked on a chair next to a box of old coloring books and crayons.

He saw her in the doorway and waved. "We've got everything under control." As if she'd had a doubt. He took his volunteer work at the hospital very seriously. And when children were involved, he gave two hundred percent.

When she returned to the E.R., a triage nurse called down the hall, "Ali, eight-year-old male in respiratory distress, possible asthma, ETA three minutes."

"Put him in Trauma One, Bed Two," she called back.

After calling a respiratory therapist to the E.R., she went in search of Jared, finding him in Exam Room Five with two of the older boys sitting next to each other on a stretcher, their legs dangling over the side. "Wow," Ali said looking at the reddish, purplish swollen eye each one wore with pride. "You two are going to have some cool shiners tomorrow."

"What'd I tell you?" Jared asked, playfully elbowing the boy closest to him. "Chicks dig bruises. Now, tomorrow when someone says, 'Oh, Tommy, oh, Bobby what happened?'" His voice slid from falsetto back to tenor when he added, "What are you going to say?"

Both boys puffed out their chests, smiled and said in unison, "You should see the other guy."

"My work here is done," Jared declared.

His joking lifted Ali's spirits. Things were back to normal. Maybe his distant behavior had something to do with the calls from his attorney. Maybe things between them were fine. "Jeez Louise," she said. "The macho vibe in this room is so strong I have the urge to challenge someone to arm wrestle."

Jared stepped forward, sliding the sleeve of his lab coat up over his left elbow and flexing his arm. "What do you say, boys? Think I can take her?"

They both smiled up at their new hero. "I bet you can pin her in ten seconds flat," the smaller of the two said.

"Ah, the naiveté of youth," Jared said to Ali, then turned his attention to the boys, who listened raptly. "When in the presence of a beautiful woman, you never want to rush. You need to take your time, draw out the pleasure of her company."

Ali heard the ambulance siren and put a stop to the fun. "Hold that thought, Romeo. That ambulance is for us. Pediatric respiratory distress. Possible asthma. Going into Trauma One, Bed Two. Respiratory Therapy is on the way. I'll finish up with these bruisers and meet you there."

Playful Dr. P. disappeared. "They're both free to go. No fractures. Give their parents the closed head injury instruction sheet."

She nodded.

After a respiratory treatment and the arrival of his mother, her asthma patient was breathing easier. Ali was walking between rooms when Gramps called her over to the door leading to the lobby. "One of my boys isn't looking well. He's holding his belly."

"I'll get Dr. Padget."

She found him in Exam Room Seven, involved in an intense discussion about how his patient's favorite cartoon heroine would have reacted to getting stitches in her hand. He was so good with children. He'd be a great father some day. "Knock, knock." She peered around the curtain. "Almost done?"

He tied off his last stitch. "Ta-dah. I think this was some of my best work."

His patient seemed to concur, holding up her hand for Ali to see. "Now I have stitches just like my brothers."

"You sure do," Ali said.

"And she didn't even cry."

Ali walked to the bedside. "I'll finish up here. Bacitracin dressing? You're needed in the lobby. Now. Grab a wheelchair on your way."

He snapped off his exam gloves and stopped at the sink to wash his hands. "Bacitracin dressing. Suture instruction sheet. She's ready for discharge."

Allison made fast work of the dressing, updated the chart and headed for the lobby. Halfway there Jared rushed through the door back into the E.R., pushing a pale, diaphoretic little black-haired boy, who sat hunched over in the wheelchair. "Possible internal injuries. I'm taking him straight for a CAT scan. Call them and tell them I'm on my way. Stat."

The call made, Ali walked into the lobby. Her gramps and a nurse's aide were looking after fifteen children, all sucking on lollipops. The man loved sugar and thought everyone else should, too. "I hope you made sure none of these children have diabetes."

"I checked with the nurse when each one was brought out."

"Everything okay out here?"

"Fine now, except this little imp keeps beating me at checkers." A little blond girl sat on the other side of a checkerboard, a big toothless smile on her face.

"Good call on the little boy." She gave him a quick hug.

"Thanks, Allison."

The next few hours flew by. Around dinnertime, Ali stood in the doorway to Trauma Two, waiting to ask if Jared wanted anything from the cafeteria. She watched him examine a construction worker who'd fallen from scaffolding, his movements purposeful, self-assured. He took charge, didn't second-guess himself. She loved those qualities in a man. At the same time he acknowledged his patients' fears at being in the E.R., didn't narrow his focus to symptoms only, like some physicians did, so intent on solving the mystery of a patient's condition they paid little attention to their emotional trauma.

He engaged his patients in conversation when they were stable enough to converse, got to know them, put them at ease. He had a calming way about him when he wanted to. Charming. He had all the qualities she valued in a man, in a mate, except one. The ability to commit to a lifetime with one woman.

"Caught ya," Victoria said, coming to stand beside her. "He is worth a second look, isn't he?"

Ali nodded.

"So what's going on between the two of you?"

Ali shrugged.

"Come. Take a quick break with me." She took Ali by the arm. "Tani," Victoria said. "Ali'll be in the lounge if you need her." She held up two fingers. "Two minutes. Promise."

The door to the lounge wasn't even halfway closed when Victoria said, "You like him. I can tell."

Busted. It'd crept up on her little by little each day. A smile. A joke. A caring word or gesture. But it had been their date, and the night that had followed that had pushed her feelings from plain old lust to liking. A smidge past liking, to be honest. "I've gotten to know a bit more about him this time around."

"The two of you make a great-looking couple."

"He is totally wrong for me, Vic." Ali threw up her hands and started to pace. She held up her index finger. "He is not at all interested in marriage."

"Very few men are at first," Victoria said. "It's up to you to bring him around."

Ali brought up a second finger. "He's leaving town in two weeks."

"Maybe if he had a reason to stay, he would." She made it sound so simple. "I hear a position in the E.R. may be opening up in March."

Ali had never considered the possibility of Jared staying in town. Excitement started to simmer inside her. If they had more time together, maybe like would turn to love, and days of fun would transform into a lifetime of happiness. Dare she hope?

No. She added a third finger. "He's just like my father."

Victoria laughed. "Where did you get that idea from? In all the time he's worked at this hospital, the only woman I've ever heard his name associated with is you."

How could that be? "Michael said—"

"Ali, you of all people should know that everyone

has a past. It's how you live your life in the present that matters."

Victoria was right. Ali had based her opinion of Jared on stories from Michael. His horn-dog antics toward her seemed to corroborate Michael's claim. Yet she couldn't recall any rumors about Jared sleeping around. And at Madrin Memorial, nothing remained secret for long.

I'm hardly the womanizer you think me to be.

"I'm an idiot," Ali said.

"Don't tell me. Tell him."

Ali hugged her friend. "Thanks, Vic."

"Where are you going?"

"To have a talk with Jared."

Ali couldn't find him anywhere in the E.R. According to Tani, "He ran down to the cafeteria to get some dinner."

"I'm going to run down, too," Ali said. "Page me if you need me."

A few minutes later Ali slammed a yogurt onto her orange cafeteria tray, lifted it and moved to the fresh fruit display, where she had a perfect view of the cozy couple. *Gak*. Dr. Padget could have dinner with whoever the hell he wanted. Jerk. The unnaturally big-boobed blond nurse she recognized from 4B leaned in. Jared met her halfway, to get a better view down the deep V of her floral scrub top, no doubt. The hussy placed her hand on his arm, said something, they both laughed. An intimate moment between lovers?

Ali seethed, picked up an orange, tested its weight and eyed the trajectory necessary to whack him between the eyes. Years of tossing a baseball around with her gramps made it easily doable.

Less than twenty-four hours after getting her into bed, he was flirting with another woman. He'd probably never stopped, probably had dates lined up for every night of the week and she had fallen into his Tuesday slot. She needed to spend more time listening to hospital gossip and less listening to Victoria. She was a fool to have considered, even for a few minutes, the possibility of something more than sex between them.

No longer hungry, she picked up her yogurt, grabbed a banana for later and tossed her tray on the stack. In line for the cashier, her eyes drifted back to his table. A perky brunette had entered the fray. Ignoring the blonde's I'm-about-to-rip-your-earrings-out glare, she chatted away, holding him enthralled.

"You squeeze that banana any tighter it's gonna be mush," the cashier said when Ali reached the front of the line.

"I like them that way." Ali smiled, paid and got the heck out of there.

Seconds from a clean getaway a hand closed around her arm. "Wait up."

Jared.

"Take a break for a few minutes. Come sit with me."

She pulled her arm out of his loose grip and turned to face him. "I'd rather suffer through a bikini wax."

He laughed. "There's a visual that will keep me smiling for the rest of my shift."

"How nice you find the thought of me in pain entertaining." Ali looked past him. "I see you've already moved on. So why are you here, bothering me?" She turned and exited the cafeteria.

He followed.

"Hey." He stopped her again. "For the record, Jilly and Tara sat with me."

"You remember their names. Good for you." She hated that she sounded snarky.

"Funny," he said, his voice turning flirty. "I never took you for the possessive type."

Ali gasped. She wasn't. Never had been before. "I most certainly am not possessive. I couldn't care less what you do and who you do it with, Doctor. Makes absolutely no difference to me."

"Doctor." He threw up his hands. "We're back to Doctor. If it doesn't matter, why are you all ticked off?"

Because he was supposed to be pursuing *her,* paying attention to *her.* She had sixteen days left. "I can't do this," Ali said. "Wipe that smile off your face."

"You're jealous," he said, sounding far too pleased with himself. "I like it."

"What I am is disgusted." That she'd allowed herself to fall for him. God help her, her eyes filled with tears.

"Whoa. Come over here." He guided her to an arrangement of potted plants off in the corner. "I didn't mean to upset you."

She wiped at a tear before it ran down her cheek. "I'm not upset. It's been a long day. I need to get back to work."

As if on cue, with two pings the hospital operator's voice came over the PA system. "Dr. Padget and Allison Forshay return to the emergency room. Stat. Dr. Padget and Allison Forshay to the Emergency Room. Stat."

His meal forgotten, Jared took off for the stairs, Ali followed behind. He held the door for her then took the steps two at a time. "After work, you and I need to talk."

Yeah. Good luck with that.

Jared watched Ali duck into the rear hallway. He followed. She looked tired. And a bit sad. Not in front of her patients or the staff, but when she thought no one was around to notice. Jared wanted to lift her into his arms and hold her while she rested. She'd probably whack him in the head if he so much as brushed up against her.

And who could blame her?

They'd spent a terrific night together, a ten out of ten in every category from start to finish. And yet the next morning, instead of sending her chocolates and flowers thanking her for the best night ever, he'd spent his time overanalyzing their time together. Had it really been as perfect as he'd recalled or had his memory skewed the details to make it appear so? Had he been out with the real Ali, or had she been playing a role meant to entice? Like she'd done with Michael. Like Cici.

She stood, her back and head resting against the wall, her eyes closed. They were alone. She reached up to wipe her eye. Damn it. He'd done that to her, when hurting her was the absolute last thing he'd wanted to do.

But she'd tossed his well-ordered life into chaos. A loner, he no longer liked being alone. He sought out every opportunity to be with Ali, to see her and talk to her. He took on extra shifts to work with her.

When they weren't together he wondered where she was, what she was doing and with whom. She held him in her power, affecting his every thought and action.

Like years ago when Cici had invaded his life, altered his sanity.

It had to stop. He needed to detach.

He walked around the corner. "Look, I'm sorry. But—"

"Don't be." Ali pushed off the wall. "You're you. You can't help it. And I'm me. I won't stand for it." She stepped around him. "It's over, Jared."

He hesitated, enjoying the sound of his name coming from her mouth, before processing what she'd said. "Wait."

It's over, as in she'd moved past the incident with Nurse 42 triple D, or over as in the two of them?

"The X-rays are back on the girls in Exam Six," she said without looking back. "They're eager to see their bones."

He followed her, his eyes focused on the hypnotic sway of her hips, the graceful movement of her perfect butt. He felt the tug of attraction. To heck with his idiotic issues, the physical part of their relationship was far from over.

Completely focused on her work, Ali walked straight to the light box and turned it on. She handed him the first of two sets of X-rays, reminding him which patient was which. Her organizational skills were unmatched. She smoothed the hair off one of the girls' foreheads, made a joke and they both laughed.

She'd make an amazing mother. After their dinner date, he'd experienced a twinge of disappointment that she wasn't pregnant with his child, had fallen asleep trying to visualize what a baby of theirs might look like, how a future with Allison might play out.

He'd awoken in a cold sweat after a horrific dream, a replay of a terrible fight he'd had with Cici, only it'd been Ali he fought with. It'd been Ali's face contorted in rage, scrunched into a look of utter disgust, Ali's mouth and voice spewing Cici's vicious words and threats.

Jared would not live like that again. Ever.

"Dr. Padget." Ali brought him back. "Anna asked you a question."

"Sorry." Jared turned his attention to the little girl now in Ali's lap.

The rest of the night passed quickly in a blur of patients, young and old. Through it all, Ali comforted concerned parents and relatives, calmed upset children and kept him organized and on task. Before Jared knew it, it was midnight. Today had been his day off, so he didn't start work

until he was called in at three in the afternoon. Ali, however, had been working seventeen hours straight and he
hadn't seen her sit down once.

When he exited his office after finishing his chart documentation, the E.R. was quiet. Most of the children had
been discharged home with minor injuries and instructions
to follow up with their private physicians. Sixteen had been
admitted.

"Is Ali still here?" he asked the unit secretary on
duty.

"Last I heard she was in the staff lounge, reviewing her
charts."

And that's where Jared found her, sitting alone at the
large round table, her head resting on an open patient chart,
fast asleep.

He watched Ali, her face completely relaxed, beautiful,
one he would never tire of. Her dark lashes, the natural
glow of her cheeks and the deep coloring of her full lips
didn't need cosmetic enhancement.

It'd been pure male stupidity run amok to attempt to use
another woman to purge Ali from his brain, even for a few
minutes.

"Ali." He gently shook her arm. She didn't move, lay
there conked out like a kid after a day at a theme park.
"Come on, honey." He shook her again. "Wake up. I'll
drive you home."

She opened one eye, gave him a warm, sleepy smile,
and his heart melted.

One more night. He needed one more night with Ali. In
the morning he'd tell her the truth.

CHAPTER EIGHT

ALI awoke slowly, keeping her eyes closed, trying to delay the process for as long as possible. She held on to the last vestiges of a deliciously erotic dream, the firm male body beneath her seeming so real, his chest rising and falling, his chest hair rough under her cheek, his heart beating a steady, rapid rhythm. She lay straddled on top of him, his heat permeating her body, his aroused flesh pressing just the right spot.

She rocked her hips, shamelessly using him, so close. On the verge, one more minute…

Her dream thrust up his pelvis, tightened his arms around her waist and said, "Now this is what I call a good morning."

Ali sucked in a breath and jerked up onto her arms. Strong hands anchored her lower body in place, maintaining their intimate contact, making it difficult to think. Bright sunshine assaulted her eyes when she forced her lids apart to see Jared, a sly smile on his handsome face.

"What are you doing in my bed?" she asked after a quick glance to assure herself she was, in fact, in her bedroom.

"Getting cold. Come back here." He inched his hands higher up her back, applying downward pressure.

"Stop it." She locked her forearms.

He moved against her, heightening her arousal, making

her want to slide along his length, up and down, again and again. Orgasm first. Questions second. Wrong. "Stop that, too."

"Killjoy."

"I'm mad at you."

"You fell asleep in the staff lounge." He ignored her statement. "You're welcome for driving you home."

"I must have really been out. I have no memory of you bringing me home." Or him crawling into bed with her. She looked down at her thin white tank, her nipples protruding, stretching the thin, worn fabric. "You undressed me?"

"I had my eyes closed the entire time."

His satisfied grin said otherwise. "Yeah, right."

"I couldn't leave you in your dirty scrubs, now, could I?"

Apparently that went for his scrubs as well. "I was wearing a bra."

"It looked uncomfortable." He reached up and cupped her breasts. "I thought it best not to confine these beauties."

She swatted his hands away. "I have a drawer full of pajamas."

"Didn't want to jostle you around too much—afraid I'd wake you."

How considerate. "Did I sleep through anything else?"

He let out a breath and shook his head. "Honey, you are hell on a man's ego."

Not again.

"Don't look so horrified. Nothing happened. I'm kidding." He laughed.

Not funny. She twisted his nipple. Hard.

"Ouch." He grabbed her hand. "I'm sorry. I'm sorry."

She reached out with her other hand and twisted his other nipple. Her arms no longer supporting her, Jared pulled her down and rolled on top of her, pinning her on her back, holding her hands on either side of her head.

"That was not funny," she said.

"I know. I shouldn't have teased." He tried to look repentant, didn't come close. "Let me make it up to you." He swiveled his hips, rested his elbows on the bed and ducked his head down by her ear. "I saved all the good stuff for when you're awake to enjoy it."

And it was so good. His hips wedged between her thighs, his hand caressing her breast, his erection rubbing, probing through her skimpy panties. She should be angry, shouldn't she? She'd caught him flirting with another woman. He'd slid into her bed without an invite. But as much as she hated to admit it, she enjoyed having him there. Especially when he... "I can't think straight when you do that." Waves of pleasure rippled from between her legs to every part of her body, becoming more intense, her need for him more urgent.

"Good. Don't think. Feel."

Feel. The weight of him pressing her back to the mattress, the damp trail of his tongue on the side of her neck, the humid heat of his breath on her ear, the contours of his muscled back and firm butt. She slipped her hands below the elastic of his boxer briefs and squeezed, urged him closer.

He stared into her eyes, mere inches separating them, his body straining to get inside her, his expression intense. He watched her. Her eyelids heavy, she fought to hold his gaze when what she really wanted to do was allow them to close, immerse herself in the pleasure of his touch, pull him down for a kiss and hold him tight. Love him for hours and hours.

"Ali, there's something I need to... I..." He hesitated, seemed to consider what to say next, looked conflicted.

Ali played fill in the blank. Want you. Need you. Can't live without you. She waited.

A noise distracted him. He turned his head to look toward her open bedroom door, disrupting what might have been a pivotal moment between them. "I think there's someone in your kitchen," he said.

Not now.

What? Someone in her kitchen? Who? "Shoot." She planted both hands on his chest and pushed as hard as she could. "Get off of me." She rolled out from under him. "Gramps, is that you?" she called down the hallway.

"Yup," he called back. "I brought you breakfast."

Used her as an excuse to go for donuts, no doubt. "Stay where you are. I'll be out in a minute." Twenty-five-years old and she felt fifteen, caught with a boy, again.

She grabbed her robe from the hook on the bathroom door and put it on, ran her palms over her hair. "Stay here," she whispered to Jared, pointing at the bed for emphasis. "I'll get rid of him."

As Ali walked down the hallway to the kitchen, she realized that trying to hide Jared's presence was useless. To the left, his big man-boots stood on the mat by the front door. To the right, his man-size black winter coat hung over the back of a kitchen chair. In case that wasn't enough to clue Gramps in, Jared's stethoscope, complete with a big white label identifying him as the owner, lay coiled on her kitchen table, right next to his photo hospital ID badge, his watch and a white bakery box.

Plan B. Ignore the obvious, maybe he will, too. "Morning, Gramps." She kissed his cheek.

He picked up Jared's ID badge. "Dr. Padget is here?"

Okay. Plan C. Except she didn't have a Plan C. "Shh. Keep your voice down."

"I like him, Allison. He seems like a good man, he's well-liked around the hospital."

His reaction took her by surprise. No look of disappointment? No telling her men didn't respect women who were easy to get into bed? No lecture warning her men engaged in premarital sex to avoid marriage, like he'd given her while she'd dated Michael?

The good man chose that moment to enter the kitchen. "Good morning, sir." Jared, fully dressed in the same blue scrubs he'd worn last night, his lab coat buttoned over the top, reached out to shake Gramps's hand. "You saved that boy's life. Nice work."

"He didn't look right." Gramps shrugged. "All I did was tell Allison. How'd he make out?"

"I checked before I left the hospital. He was admitted overnight for observation."

"I saw you on the local news at ten last night and again this morning. You're a regular celebrity," Gramps said.

"There was a press conference last night?" Ali asked. How had he been interviewed without her knowing?

"School bus accidents are big news. A bunch of reporters showed up at the hospital looking for a story. The chief of staff dragged me out there to give them one."

"Where was I?" she asked.

"Taking that nine-year-old boy with the concussion up to Pediatrics. It took all of five minutes. And this isn't what it looks like, sir."

"I thought I told you to call me Gramps."

"Okay. Gramps. I drove Ali home from the hospital last night. We were both exhausted. I sat down for a minute, and the next thing I knew it was morning."

Nice try. He'd passed her kitchen chairs and her couches to sit on her bed? Makes perfect sense. Not.

"You don't need to explain, son. What Allison does with her life is her business."

Huh? Since when?

"I'm just here to deliver breakfast," Gramps said as he reached into the box on the table, snatched out two vanilla frosted donuts and headed for the door. "I'll be on my way." He blew Ali an air kiss, and with a big grin said, "From now on I won't use my key unless it's an emergency," and escaped before she could grab back one of the donuts.

"I've got to head out, too," Jared said, picking up his stethoscope, ID and watch from the kitchen table, and stuffing them into his coat pocket. "I have to go in tonight." He kissed the top of her head. "May I come back after work?"

She smiled. "To pick up where we left off?"

He hesitated.

Ali looked up. Their eyes met, held. Fifteen days left. In two weeks he'd be gone from her life. Ali accepted that. Did she want to squander the time remaining, sleeping alone, holding out hope for a Mr. Right she might never find, who might not even exist? Or did she want to spend them wrapped in Jared's arms?

No contest.

"I'd like that," she said with a smile, feeling happy and excited about the days, and nights, to come. "But only if you agree while we're together, no other women."

"None," Jared said. "I promise."

Jared couldn't believe his luck. He slid out of his twelve-year-old Toyota Camry, sidestepped a slushy puddle and jogged toward his rental. After four days out sick with the stomach flu that had decimated hospital staffing, Dr. Reynolds arrived at the E.R. three and a half hours before his assigned shift to give Jared some much-needed time off.

He unlocked the apartment door, dropped his keys on the counter and his coat on the couch. If he rushed, he could be at Ali's by 5:15 p.m., sharing dinner with her by five-thirty and slipping into her bed to pick up where they'd left off that morning by six.

After major consideration, speckled with rationalization, Jared could find no benefit to sharing his marital status with Ali. No one in Madrin Falls knew about his marriage. Soon he would be gone. It seemed senseless to upset her.

He picked up the phone, ordered a pizza and jumped into the shower. Half an hour later, a bottle of Merlot in one hand, a steaming meatball and mushroom pizza in the other, Jared knocked on Ali's door.

Unfortunately, the look she gave him when she cracked open her door just wide enough to stick out her head wasn't the look of adoration and longing he'd hoped for.

"What are you doing here?" she asked, not inviting him in. "I wasn't expecting you until later tonight."

"I got off early." He held up the pizza and wine. "I thought I'd surprise you."

She didn't move.

"May I come in, please? It's freezing out here." Especially as his hair was still wet from his shower.

She looked over her shoulder at something inside her condo, then back at him. Was that guilt he saw in her expression? She hesitated before stepping back, opening the door just wide enough for him to follow the pizza box inside.

"I sort of have plans," she said. As if her kitchen table set for two, with a small bouquet of fresh flowers in a crystal vase in the center wasn't explanation enough. She had plans all right, and they didn't include him. Suddenly it hurt to breathe. Ali had plans to share that pretty little table with someone else. Disappointed didn't come close to describing how he felt at that moment. It must have showed on his face because she rushed to add, "Let me explain."

A knock at the door preempted what she was about to say and something inside Jared snapped. Ali was his. She'd been on his mind all day, and he was desperate to hold her, to feel her and taste her. The last thing he wanted to do was share her.

Ali glanced at the door but made no move to open it.

Jared placed the pizza box and wine on the kitchen counter, took a deep, calming breath and, praying for restraint, strode to the door. Even though physical violence was totally out of character for him, he visualized opening it, punching her date in the face and slamming it shut. Only Ali, being the caring person she was, would probably fawn all over the loser lying on her front porch, and *he* would be on the receiving end of Ali's caring concern and tender touches. Jared would likely get chastised and sent home, alone, which was absolutely not part of his plan for the evening.

Plastering his most intimidating look on his face, Jared whipped open the door to stare down the intruder trying to cut into his private time with Ali. Way down, it turned out, because the person before him couldn't be more than four feet tall. Even with her thinning white up-do teased and hairsprayed, adding at least another three inches to her stature, she didn't come up much past the middle of his ribcage. Her posture hunched, her skin wrinkled, she looked to be closing in on the century mark.

"This your new fella?" the woman asked as she banged him in the shin with her metal quad-cane and used his moment of shock and discomfort to limp past him. "He's got the manners of a baboon, making an old lady stand outside in the cold."

Her thick, rust-colored down coat zipped up to her nose, the hem an inch or two above her ankles, would likely keep her warm down to thirty below zero, he figured. But she was right. "Sorry. You caught me by surprise."

"Come in, Mrs. Tupper," Ali said, rushing to the woman's side to take the plastic grocery bag she carried and help her out of her coat. "My friend was just leaving."

Her friend? Was that all he was? A mere friend? For some reason the term irked him. Did all her "friends" have the same benefits he did? They'd better not. And why should he care? Because as long as he was in town, Ali was his.

"He doesn't have to leave on my account." She held out her hand. "Martha Tupper, Allison's next-door neighbor. Who might you be?"

Jared took her small cold hand into his. "Jared Padget. Ali and I work together at the hospital."

The woman stiffened, yanked back her hand and looked him up and down with equal parts distrust and distaste. "You a doctor?"

"I'm sorry, Mrs. Tupper," Ali intervened. "Yes, Jared is a doctor. But I didn't invite him here to see you. Lord knows, I'll never do that again. Not after last time." She turned to him. "Mrs. Tupper doesn't like doctors."

That explained Ali's initial apprehension about letting him in.

"A doctor killed my Melvin," Mrs. Tupper said. "And had the nerve to deny it."

"I'm very sorry for your loss, Mrs. Tupper," Jared said. "I didn't mean to intrude on your dinner plans. I'll be heading home now." He almost choked on the words as he said them. He didn't want to go to his empty rental with its smelly sofa and five-channel black-and-white television set.

Ali looked torn, like she didn't want him to leave but didn't know what else to do.

Mrs. Tupper looked back and forth between them. "Now, hold on. There's no need for you to rush off." She walked over to a chair. Jared slid it out from beneath the table, and she lowered herself into it. "I guess if you can keep your doctor mumbo jumbo to yourself, I can keep quiet about my opinion of some members of your profession," she said to Jared. "I haven't had dinner with a looker like you in ages."

Jared glanced at Ali, who smiled. "Consider my mumbo jumbo mute," he said.

"Dinner's ready whenever you are," Ali said.

Jared shrugged out of his coat so fast the sleeves turned inside out. "Smells good."

"Homemade beef barley soup and cranberry walnut wheat bread fresh out of the oven."

Jared's mouth watered. Ali's soup smelled delicious. It reminded him of delectable homemade meals his mother had prepared before his father had died, when they'd sat down at the table together every night, a loving family, joking and discussing their day. He'd hoped to recreate that tradition with his own family. Stupid him for ever thinking life would turn out the way he wanted it to.

Ali set an extra place at the table.

"Is there anything I can do to help?" Jared asked as he washed his hands, noticing how cute she looked in her red "Kiss the Cook" apron. He couldn't wait to kiss the cook.

"Nope. Just dig in and enjoy."

Jared did just that. For years he'd eaten alone in low-budget restaurants, crowded hospital cafeterias or at whatever rental he called home at the time. Sitting around the table with Allison and Martha, in Ali's cozy kitchen, eating homemade soup that tasted as good as it smelled, and engaging in friendly conversation, he felt like part of a family, included and accepted. He hadn't felt any of those things in a very long time.

Jared watched Ali. She tucked a wisp of hair behind her ear and smiled at Mrs. Tupper, her eyes warm and caring. She listened with interest to news of Mrs. Tupper's grandchildren and her plans for a new afghan. Mrs. Tupper, a woman who looked like she didn't smile often, beamed under Ali's attention. Most people did.

He'd judged her unfairly. Thanks to Cici, no woman was above suspicion. He'd thought her an opportunist, trying to manipulate his friend, a successful physician, into marriage for her own personal gain. Later he'd thought her a plaything, something to entertain him until he moved on. Until he'd learned her soul was as damaged as his. Until he'd taken the time to really see her, a woman desperate to be loved, a woman committed to helping others, not only while at work but in her personal life as well. A beautiful, sensual woman intent on making the world a better place for those around her. A woman he'd be proud to call his.

Only he couldn't, wouldn't. But the more time he spent with her, the more the idea of weekend trysts, maybe the occasional mini-vacation in a location where bikinis were mandatory attire, increased in appeal. Not a relationship, but an if-you-don't-have-anything-better-to-do-let's-get-together sort of thing. Until she found a man to marry.

The thought of Ali with another man left him cold. He tightened his grip on his spoon.

"How's your soup?" Ali asked, looking at him with concern.

"Delicious." He smiled and ate the last few spoonfuls.

She stood. "Would you like some more?"

Without waiting for his answer, she took his bowl to the stove and refilled it, like his mother used to do for his father each night at dinner. Mom had served Dad, not because he'd expected it but because she'd loved taking care of him.

When Ali placed the full bowl of soup and another piece of bread in front of him, Jared croaked a thank you past the sadness and loss balled in his throat.

After dinner, Ali insisted on walking her neighbor next door to carry a bag of leftovers. Jared prayed she wouldn't be gone long. He'd missed her every minute since he'd left her that morning, and couldn't wait to get her back into his arms, for as long as he could, as often as he could, until the time came for him to leave.

Ali returned from accompanying Mrs. Tupper next door to find Jared relaxed on the couch, sipping from a wine glass filled with what looked like the Merlot he'd brought earlier. He patted the cushion beside him. "Saved you a seat."

He looked so comfortable, like he belonged there. She could get used to coming home to him, having someone to talk to over dinner, to snuggle up against night after night.

But soon he'd be gone and she intended to make good use of the limited time they had left. She hid a yawn as she hung up her coat. Instead of sitting on the couch, she knelt at Jared's feet, inserted herself between his legs and rested her hands on his thighs. "It was nice of you to agree to take a look at Mrs. Tupper's heel ulcer."

He shrugged. "I'm a doctor, it's what I do."

It was so much more. He'd offered to visit Mrs. Tupper in her condo, without Ali having to cajole or entice to elicit his involvement, like she'd had to do with Michael.

"What happened the last time you sprang a doctor on her?" He covered her hands with his.

"Michael came on a little too strong." Too pompous. Too condescending. "He tried to scare her by telling her what could happen if she refused treatment. She developed chest pain and I spent the night with her in the E.R." Michael had not been happy she'd chosen to stay with Mrs. Tupper instead of going home with him. Putting thoughts of Michael to one side, she looked up at Jared, knew what he'd like. His muscles tensed under her wandering palms.

"It's all about gaining a patient's trust."

Jared's particular area of expertise. She placed her mouth over the growing bulge in the front of his nylon sport pants and forced out a hot, moist breath. He moaned and opened his legs wider.

"Did you have your heart set on picking up where we left off this morning?" Ali asked, lifting her head briefly before releasing another burst of heated air against his groin. "Because I thought it might be fun to mix things up a bit." She nuzzled his aroused flesh through the thin material.

He worked his fingers through her hair and held her head in place. "You know I like variety." He swiveled his hips. "Mix away."

She couldn't contain the next yawn, and eagle-eyed Jared noticed.

"Hey. You don't have to do that. Come up here," he said, lifting her onto the couch. "You're exhausted. You have bags under your eyes. You hardly ate your dinner."

Lately, in the evenings, she'd had no appetite. In the middle of the night, however, she more than made up for it. She leaned into his side, inhaled his familiar scent and allowed her heavy eyelids to close. "I'm sorry. I'm just so tired. Will you stay over anyway?" She wanted him to, so much, didn't want to miss one opportunity for them to be together. She yawned again. "I mean even if we don't… Maybe after a little nap."

"Honey. Stop." He pulled her onto his lap and kissed the top of her head. "Go to sleep. I'm happy to sit here and hold you."

"And I'm happy to sit here and be held." By him. More than he could ever know. "In case you change your mind, I put together a package for your lunch tomorrow. It's in the fridge with your name on it."

He wrapped his arm around her shoulders, drew her head to his chest and kissed her forehead. "Thank you," he said. "You can give it to me in the morning."

Seconds before drifting off to sleep Ali asked, "If a full-time position were to open up in the E.R., would you take it?"

He didn't answer right away, seemed to consider his words carefully. "No," he finally said, rubbing his hand up and down her arm as if to comfort her. "At the end of the month I'm leaving." He spoke softly. Then almost to himself he added, "Nothing and no one will keep me here."

After a few hours of sleep, and some pre-dawn sustenance, Ali "accidentally" woke Jared when she climbed back into bed, and they made slow, lazy love. He kissed her deeply, thoroughly. He whispered in her ear, telling her he loved her body, loved how she touched him, loved how she made him feel. She'd hoped he'd take it one step further and say he loved her. He didn't. And she realized how much she wanted him to.

In the morning Ali had barely closed the door behind Jared before she had to run to the bathroom to vomit. She could no longer ignore the signs. Breast tenderness. Weepiness. Exhaustion. Nausea and vomiting. And, if those indicators weren't blaring enough, as of that morning her second period in a row had failed to make an appearance.

After her shower, Ali drove to the small pharmacy out by the college to pick up a pregnancy test.

CHAPTER NINE

LATER that evening, Ali applied pressure on the brake pedal and eased her car onto the exit ramp for Madrin Falls. At the stop sign she took a moment to look over at the passenger seat. "Are you sure you're feeling okay, Gramps?"

"Just some indigestion," he said, fumbling to open a roll of antacids he'd taken out of his jacket pocket.

"I told you we shouldn't have gone for Italian food." She turned onto North Street.

"You said I could choose the restaurant, and Antonella's has the best tiramisu in five counties. A little heartburn is a small price to pay."

That might be so, but his color didn't look good, and he kept rubbing his hand over his sternum. "I'm taking you to the hospital for an EKG."

"Relax, Allison. I'm fine."

He was not fine and, whether he liked it or not, they were going to swing by the E.R. before heading home.

She'd just turned onto Main Street when Gramps cried out. "Ow, ow, ow, it hurts." Both hands clutched to his chest, his body went rigid, then limp.

"Gramps!" Ali yelled. She glanced over to see him slumped in his seat, his head lolled to the left. Her eyes watching the road, with her right hand she shook him. "Gramps!"

No response.

Should she stop to render first aid or plow on to the E.R. less than a mile away? "Gramps," she yelled, shook him again. This time he moaned.

Gas pedal met floor mat and the car took off. Ali made a screeching turn up the hilly drive to the hospital, honked at pedestrians too stupid to look where they were walking and skidded to a stop under the bright red "Emergency Room" sign. She slammed the car into park, and, heart pounding, jumped out and ran for help.

"Come on. Come on." Gramps could die in the time it took the freakin' electric doors to open. Once inside, Ali yelled out as loud as she could. "I need help. Now." She ran for the empty stretcher in Trauma Room One. "Dr. P., Polly. Where is everyone?"

Pushing the stretcher to the sliding doors Ali met up with Jared, who ran out of Exam Room Three, and Polly, who came from Trauma Room Two.

"It's Gramps." Nothing more needed to be said. Polly helped her navigate the stretcher. Jared ran out ahead of them. By the time Ali and Polly had the stretcher out to the curb, Jared stood holding Gramps in his arms.

"He's conscious," Jared said.

The second Jared laid Gramps on the stretcher Ali started to push.

"Wait," Polly called. "The side rails."

Ali knew better than to transport a patient without the side rails up. She locked the railing on her side of the stretcher into place while Polly did the same on the other side.

"Let's go. Let's go," Jared called out. On the way in Ali rattled off Gramps's past medical history, including a myocardial infarction five years ago and his current medications.

Another nurse on duty joined Jared, Polly and Ali in Trauma Room One. She whipped out her scissors, prepared to cut up the front of Gramps's shirt. "Wait. That's his favorite shirt," Ali said, fumbling to undo the buttons.

"You shouldn't be in here," the nurse, not one of Ali's favorite people at the moment, said.

The shirt unbuttoned, Ali struggled to take it off. Polly tried to help, twisting Gramps's arm into what looked like an uncomfortable position. "Careful. You're going to hurt him," Ali said.

"We need to get him hooked up to the monitor," Polly said. "Think like a nurse or Teresa's right. You shouldn't be in here."

The shirt finally off, Polly attached the chest leads, Teresa hooked up the oxygen and Ali primed the IV tubing. That done, she grabbed the basket of IV supplies and prepared to insert the peripheral intravenous cannula. She straightened the arm and tied the rubber tourniquet above his elbow. She exposed the antecubital fossa and palpated for the vein. Once she identified the insertion site, she opened the prep pad and cleansed the area. She operated on autopilot. Had done this thousands of times.

Bevel up, she positioned the needle and prepared to puncture the skin. Gramps's skin. Her eyes filled with tears. She wiped them away. Lowered the cannula. Her hands shook. A tear dripped onto the surface she'd just disinfected.

"Outside," Jared said. His tone authoritative.

She didn't move, knew she was hindering their care but couldn't get her legs to walk. Gramps's color looked gray. Not good. The cardiac monitor beat out an irregular rhythm, far slower than normal. He lay motionless on the table, except for the shallow rise and fall of his chest.

A strong arm came around her shoulders and led her to

the door. "We'll take good care of him, Ali," Jared said. "Wait in the lounge."

"Line's in," Polly said. "IV infusing."

"Waiting for medication orders, Dr. P.," the other nurse said.

Ali pulled away and ran for the stretcher unable to bear the thought this might be the last time she'd see him alive. "I have to tell him where I'll be." She leaned in close to Gramps's ear, crying in earnest. "I'll be right outside, Gramps. Polly's here. And Dr. P. They'll take good care of you." She kissed his cool, clammy cheek. "I love you. Don't you leave me. I need you so much. Especially now." How could she possibly raise a baby on her own without Gramps's help?

His lips moved. At first no sound came out. He tried again. "Quit…your…carrying on," he struggled to whisper. "Love…you, too."

She clung to his chest, didn't want to leave.

"Come on, Ali," Jared said, his hands on her shoulders, gently urging her to stand.

She didn't want to wait all alone in the staff lounge away from what was happening. Instead she paced outside Trauma Room One, in case Gramps needed her, in case there was anything she could do to help. The door opened. As if Polly knew Ali would be there, she handed out vials of Gramps's blood to take to the lab. Ali ran like world peace hinged on how fast she got there. A few minutes after she got back, the nurse assisting Polly came out. She picked up a chart for another patient and walked toward Exam Room Two. "What's going on in there?" Ali asked.

"Dr. P. said he'll be out to talk to you in a few minutes."

Huh. The next time she asked Ali to cover a shift for her—*fugetaboutit.*

Ali paced some more.

The third time the door opened, Jared walked out. And—oh, my God—he popped a piece of gum into his mouth. Ali's last thread of control snapped. "What happened? What the hell happened?" She peeked through the partially opened door to see Polly pulling a blanket up to the head of the stretcher. Had Gramps died? Was Polly covering the body? She tried to push past Jared.

He held her tight. "Let's go to the lounge."

Rule number one about delivering bad news: Do it in private.

Panic surged inside her. Ali's vision blurred, her heartbeat pounded in her ears. "I am not going anywhere." Her body went frigid, started to shake. She struggled to take in enough air. "Somebody had better tell me what's going on or I'm going to make a scene the likes of which you will never forget."

"Calm down, Ali. Gramps is stable for now. He's resting comfortably."

Ali went limp with relief, thought she might faint.

Jared caught her, held her. "Hey. Are you okay?"

No. She wasn't. Her world revolved around Gramps. She loved him more than anything, couldn't imagine life without him.

"Come." Jared coaxed her toward the lounge. "You need to sit down."

She tried to turn. "I need to see Gramps."

Jared tightened his hold. "You need to get yourself together before you go in there. I don't want him upset."

He was right.

Inside the staff lounge Ali sat at the table, feeling shaky and unsettled, while Jared filled a paper cup with water from the cooler. Her hands trembling, water dribbled down her chin when she took a sip. Jared grabbed a napkin and blotted the wetness like a parent would do for a child. Yet he didn't want children. She fought to keep from crying, looking down at her lap when she said, "Thank you."

"Dr. Ansari is on duty in the cath lab," he said, back to business. "He has one more patient for angioplasty. He agreed to stay late to add Gramps to today's schedule."

Ali's eyes filled with tears. "Thank you for arranging that."

"He's doing it for you, Ali. A professional courtesy. Gramps will stay down in the E.R. so I can monitor him until they're ready."

Tears overflowed her lids, streaming down her cheeks. "Thank you, Jared. I don't know what I would have done if…"

"Shh." He sat down beside her, took her hand in his. "Gramps is asking for you. You can't go in there looking a mess." He handed her some tissues. So sweet. So caring. So temporary. She cried some more.

"I know." She sniffled and blotted her eyes. "Please tell him I'll be in in a few minutes."

"I will."

Two hours later, Ali sat alone in the cardiac cath lab waiting room, watching the seconds click past on the wall clock. Three minutes after seven. Dr. Ansari had planned to be done by seven.

The hallway deserted, as it was after hours, there was no one to talk to. No one to bother with questions, to keep her mind from thinking the worst.

She stood and walked to the window, looked out into the darkness, watched snowflakes lazily drift into lit areas of the tiered parking lot below. It was the type of night she and Gramps loved to turn off all the lights in the house, push the sofa over to the bay window in the family room and watch the snow pile up on the street. And snowplows. There was something about clearing snow, piling it into mounds, they couldn't get enough of.

"Oh-oh. Here comes another one," Gramps would say. Then they'd identify shapes in the snow banks piled under the streetlights. Gramps loved the snow. Never complained about shoveling it. Would he ever make another snow angel? Feel an icy flake melt on his tongue?

Just when she'd thought her tear ducts swollen shut from overuse, more tears formed in her eyes. Toughen up. Being weepy and unstable would not help Gramps. Seven-ten. She twisted a section of hair until it knotted and pulled at her scalp. Counted the people walking on the sidewalk. Seven. An ambulance raced up the hilly drive, its lights twirling.

Someone walked into the waiting room. Ali spun around so fast she lost her balance and had to grab on to the window ledge.

Jared, still in his scrubs, hurried forward, reached out to steady her. "Whoa. I didn't mean to startle you."

"Sorry. I'm waiting for Dr. Ansari. He was supposed to be done at seven."

Jared glanced at the clock. Seven-fourteen. "Some procedures take longer than others."

She knew that. Patients suffered reactions to medications, unexpected complications, cardiac arrest, death.

"I know that look," he said. "Stop it. Don't think the worst. No news…"

"Don't you dare say no news is good news. No news could also mean the doctor is putting off giving you the bad news."

"You're a piece of work." He shook his head. "Here." He handed her a strawberry yogurt, a plastic spoon and a banana. "I thought you might be hungry." He took a bottle of water from his back pocket and held it out to her with his other hand.

Instead of taking them, she walked between his outstretched arms and didn't stop until her cheek settled against his chest. With Jared she didn't have to pretend to be strong, didn't have to worry about saying the right thing, about acting or looking a certain way. He'd seen her at her worst, and it hadn't scared him off. "Thank you for coming."

He hugged her tight. "You're here. Where else would I be?"

Such sweet words. She started to cry. Again. "I don't know what I'll do if he doesn't make it. He's my only family." The only person who loved her. A sob escaped her. "If he dies I'll be all alone."

Ali couldn't stop the outpouring of emotion that followed. Steady rivers of tears ran down her cheeks, her nose dripped and her lungs drew in air via gasping breaths. For Gramps, who might die. For Jared, who would soon leave. For the baby she was carrying. For herself, left to deal with it all on her own.

Jared stood with his arms wrapped tightly around her, supporting her, while his hand stroked her hair and down her back. At one point he guided them to a small coffee table so he could hand her some tissues. He didn't offer empty words of comfort, didn't tell her everything would be okay. She needed to cry and he let her, remaining strong for her, taking care of her while she did.

For the second time in two months Ali broke down in his arms, turned to him for solace. It felt good to be needed. Never before had he wanted to say the right thing, do the right thing, more than he did right now. He would not fail her.

"Let it all out, honey." He guided them to a chair, pulled her onto his lap and held her close to his heart. "I'm here for you. I'll take care of you. Whatever you need."

"I need you." She wrapped her arms around him.

He kissed her temple. "You've got me."

It sounded like she laughed. He sat back and looked down at her. Sure enough, he noted a hint of a smile on her drippy-wet face.

"When did you become such a nice guy?" she asked.

On the night a special young woman bared her soul to him, trusted him enough to share her pain, reached out to him and asked him to love her, to make her forget. He could have used this moment as an opportunity to create a bond between them, to share his growing feelings for her. But that would make it even more difficult to leave. So he decided to lighten the mood. "You seem to be under the mistaken impression I'm not a nice person. I'll have you know I'm the epitome of nice. Google search 'nice guys' and you will find a link to me."

Her smile widened a fraction. "What about humble?"

"Nah. Not so much."

He unscrewed the top on the bottle of water he'd brought and handed it to her.

She took a sip. "Thanks."

He went to work trying to detangle one of the knots she'd twisted into her hair, a testament to her nerves. "I thought for sure the waiting room would be crowded with people here to keep you company," he said.

She looked away. "I didn't want to bother anyone. Polly had a date, I told her not to cancel. I'll call Mrs. Meyer after Gramps is settled."

That's Ali. Always thinking of everyone but herself. "If I'd known, I would have tried to get off work early."

"I don't expect you to... I mean it's not like we're..."

Ali stopped in mid-sentence and jumped up when Dr. Ansari entered the waiting room. Jared rose to stand beside her. She leaned against him, reached for his hand and threaded her fingers between his, like it was the most natural thing to do. He squeezed her hand, offering his support, his strength.

"Everything went as expected, Allison," Dr. Ansari said. He started to explain the procedure and Ali interrupted.

"So he's okay? Where is he? Can I see him?"

"He's on his way to CCU for the night. I'll be in to evaluate him first thing in the morning."

"Thank you, Dr. Ansari." Ali threw her arms around the other doctor. "Thank you so much." She turned to Jared. "I'm going up to CCU. I'll talk to you tomorrow." She quickly kissed his cheek. "Thank you," she said, her words heartfelt, her eyes conveying the depth of her appreciation.

Jared wanted to go with her to make sure Gramps's transfer went smoothly. Instead he spent a few minutes talking to Dr. Ansari, physician to physician, getting the details of the procedure, the outcome, prognosis and treatment plan, which Ali would want to know once the panicked granddaughter in her relaxed and allowed the knowledgeable nurse to take back control. Then he headed up to CCU.

He spoke with Gramps's nurse, handed her a card with his cell phone number. "Please call me if either one of them needs anything. No matter what time it is."

The nurse smiled. "Sure thing, Dr. Padget."

Jared arranged for a colleague to cover for him on Sunday so he'd be available for Ali. Unable to sleep, he returned to the hospital at six-thirty in the morning. When he found no one at the nurses' station, he popped his head into Gramps's room.

Behind the curtain he heard, "Allison Elizabeth Forshay, you are most certainly not going to give me a bed bath. I will bathe myself."

Gramps sounded surprisingly strong, and agitated, which was not good. Jared knocked on the partially closed door. "Can I come in?"

Ali pulled back the curtain. Her hair a mess of tangles and twisty knots, her clothes disheveled, her color pale. She looked frustrated and exhausted and confused. "Don't you work today?"

"I took the day off in case you needed me." Her expression softened, until Gramps called out from behind her.

"You've gotta save me, Doc."

Jared looked past Ali. Gramps sat up in his hospital bed, sounded like his usual self. "Ali's trying to finish me off. I didn't get a moment's peace all night, and I've got company coming."

"I'm trying to get him ready for his company but he's refusing to cooperate," Ali snapped.

An older woman dressed in the hospital's navy-blue volunteer blazer hurried into the room. He recognized her as Gramps's neighbor who had helped out in the emergency room after the school bus accidents.

As if on cue, Gramps flopped back onto the bed. He coughed. His facial muscles drooped. When he spoke his voice came out raspy and sounded weak. "Mrs. Meyer. Thank goodness you're here."

What the heck happened? The man had gone from feisty to feeble in mere seconds. Jared glanced up at Gramps's cardiac monitor to see if he'd had some sort of arrhythmic episode, expected to hear an alarm any second. He reached for the stethoscope usually hanging around his neck, forgetting he was not on duty.

Ali looked ready to pound on Gramps's chest and begin CPR.

"I was just telling Ali." Gramps struggled to get the words out. "I don't feel comfortable with her helping me with my bath. But I'm too weak to do it myself."

Why, that conniving faker.

Ali's jaw dropped.

"Then I got here just in time." Mrs. Meyer slipped out of her blazer, setting it, her jacket and her pocketbook on the chair by the window. She pushed the sleeves of her sweater up to her elbows and approached the bed. "You go on home, honey," Mrs. Meyer said, giving Ali a kiss on the cheek on her way. "I'll take it from here."

Ali didn't look at all ready to leave or transfer care duties to Mrs. Meyer. In fact, she looked ready to do battle.

"Go on, Allison," Gramps prompted, lifting his head, sounding a bit stronger, albeit briefly. "I'm sure Mrs. Meyer will take good care of me." He gave the older woman the smile of a man on the make.

"You know I will, you old coot." Mrs. Meyer giggled.

Ali watched the exchange like she'd walked in on them having sex.

"Come on, Ali," Jared said, walking over to where she stood, threading his arm through hers, intending to drag her to the door if need be.

She leaned over and gave Gramps a quick kiss on the cheek and, surprise, surprise, followed Jared willingly.

"Bye, sweetie," Gramps said weakly. "No need to come back later. You'll stay, won't you, Mrs. Meyer?" Cough. Cough.

"Of course I will, you sweet man, for as long as you need me."

Outside in the hallway Ali asked, "What the heck just happened?"

Jared smiled. "I think Gramps has got a girlfriend."

"Mrs. Meyer? They've been friends for years. They're like brother and sister."

"Not anymore. Come." He tugged on her arm. "I'll take you to breakfast."

She walked beside him but seemed in her own world. "I'm the one who takes care of Gramps," she said almost to herself. "I pour his meds and go with him to the doctor and stay over when he's sick. I straighten the house, cook for him and keep him company."

"Apparently Mrs. Meyer gives him a different sort of company."

Her eyes went wide. "Eww. Do not go there."

As they turned into another corridor Ali looked up at him, her eyes sad. "He doesn't need me anymore."

But I do, Jared thought. It took him completely by surprise. Shocked him to the point he stopped short.

Ali kept walking, too caught up in her own thoughts to notice.

Jared watched her, the sway of her hips so seductive yet she had no clue. He liked to look at her, enjoyed time spent with her. He lusted after her. But no. He didn't need her. Jared Padget refused to need anyone. And in two weeks, when it was time for him to leave, he would. And, just to be sure, he'd signed and mailed out the contract for his next assignment early. There was no getting out of it.

CHAPTER TEN

ALI sat at her kitchen table, fiddling with the box that contained her pregnancy test result, waiting for Jared. After breakfast at the diner, Ali had come home for a shower and a nap. Jared had offered to come over with lunch and a DVD around one.

It'd seemed like a good idea at the time.

Until she decided, even though waiting for him to leave and dropping the pregnancy bomb via telephone would be much easier, she owed it to Jared to be honest, to not keep it a secret now that she knew for sure.

He knocked. Seven minutes early. A surge of nervousness made her heart jump and her chest tighten.

After a deep breath, she slid the box back into the pharmacy bag, rolled the top and tossed it into the cabinet under the sink. If he didn't believe her, she'd take it out and show him the indisputable proof.

She opened the door. Jared handed her a beautiful bouquet of peach-colored roses. "You shouldn't have." In a few minutes he'd know why.

He leaned in to give her a kiss, which landed on her cheek when she quickly turned her head.

"What's wrong?" he asked.

She couldn't bring herself to kiss him, knowing what was to come, feeling certain their conversation would not end well, that today their relationship would change forever, and not in a good way. The thought made her insides feel hollow. "We need to talk."

"Can we talk while we eat? I'm starved." He took off his coat and hung it in the closet. She resisted the urge to tell him he might want to hold on to it.

Ali eyed the bag of deli sandwiches he'd set on the table. Even if she drank copious amounts of water to keep food from lodging in her dry throat, her stomach was clenched so tight, nothing could get in.

"It'll only take a minute." She returned to her chair, felt light-headed. Now that he stood a few feet away, telling him no longer seemed like such a good idea. Focus. A responsible mother acted in the best interests of her child, starting with informing the daddy-to-be. What he chose to do with the information was up to him.

"You've been twisting your hair." He reached above her right ear.

She found the knot, and started to detangle it, happy to have something to do with her hands.

"That bad, huh? Okay. Get it off your chest, and then we'll eat."

"Sit. Over there." She pointed to the seat opposite hers, the one with a clear path to the door.

He sat.

"There's no easy way to put this so I'm just going to say it." She clasped her hands tightly in her lap.

He nodded, his eyes fixed on her.

"I'm pregnant."

He looked at her like she'd spoken in another language and he was having trouble translating her words into comprehensible form. After about a minute he stiffened. "You told me you weren't pregnant."

He'd started out calm. Maybe this wouldn't be as bad as she thought.

"Damn it, Ali." He speared his fingers through his hair. "How the hell did this happen?"

Was he kidding? How did he think it happened? The sperm. The egg.

He jumped up and started to pace. "After that first night I wore a condom every single time."

She didn't expect him to be happy about the news, but a tiny, unrealistic part of her she hadn't known existed until that very minute had hoped for a miracle, and now felt good and pissed she didn't get one. "Yes. I know how diligent you are about your condoms."

"Don't make me out to be the bad guy here." He pointed at her in accusation. "You're the one who climbed on top of me down by the river without protection."

"You know I wasn't thinking clearly that night."

"Oh, I bet you knew exactly what you were doing." He jammed both hands in the front pockets of his jeans as if trying to keep from throwing something.

She sucked in a breath. "What's that supposed to mean?"

"That you women are all alike, that's what." A vein she'd never noticed before bulged in his forehead. "You manipulate men to get what you want. You did it with Michael, and now you're trying to do it with me."

His words seared a burning path right through her. "I don't want anything from you." Ali did not like being looked down on so she stood, too. "I am perfectly capable of raising this baby on my own."

His eyes narrowed and he stared her down. "If you got yourself pregnant to drag me down the aisle, you've made a gross miscalculation," he said slowly. Although she knew he would never hurt her physically, if she weren't so angry herself, she might have backed away from him.

"Newsflash, genius, a woman cannot get herself pregnant. You had sex with me without a condom, right here, in my bed. Twice. How is that my fault?"

"I thought you were on the Pill," he yelled, loud enough for Mrs. Tupper to hear.

"Well, I wasn't," she yelled back, even louder.

He lowered his voice. "You said it was okay, that you trusted me."

"If I made any gross miscalculation, it was that. You took advantage of me the night you left town and you know it. I'd had too much to drink, I was an emotional wreck and you saw your chance to have me and took it."

That shut him up. He actually had the decency to look guilty. "It wasn't like that, Ali," he said quietly. "You needed me. I gave you what you wanted, what you begged me for."

"Whatever." She dismissed him with a wave of her hand. "I've said what I had to say." Ali walked to the closet to get his coat.

"Wait. We need to talk about this."

"There's nothing to talk about. I'm pregnant and you're leaving."

"Stop." He held up both hands. "Give me a minute to catch up. You've known about the baby for a while. I'm still dealing with the shock."

"Only since yesterday," she said in a calmer tone. It was important he understood she hadn't kept the truth from him. "I would have told you as soon as I found out but Gramps had his heart attack. I didn't lie, Jared. I honestly didn't think I was pregnant back when you asked me. My period gets screwy when I do rotating shifts and I'd come off three weeks of them when you came back."

"I want to do the right thing, Ali. I'm here for you." He sounded calmer now, too. "I'll help out. I'll pay your medical expenses."

Tears filled her eyes, overflowed down her cheeks. "That's a great offer. Thanks."

"Then why are you crying?"

She ran a knuckle under each eye. "Because I cry at everything lately, haven't you noticed?"

"Come on, honey. Tell me."

He took a step toward her, like he planned to take her into his arms. She held up a hand to stop him.

"In all the years I've dreamed about telling the man I love I was pregnant with his child," she said with a sniffle, "never once did he reply, 'I'll help out. I'll pay your medical expenses.'"

Jared stared at her.

Crap. She'd been fighting it for days, had tried to convince herself she hadn't fallen in love with him. And in the heat of an argument the words flew out of her mouth before her brain could censor them.

"I lo—"

"Don't you dare say you love me." Ali walked to the closet and yanked his coat so hard the hanger flew onto the couch. "It's an insult to say the words when you don't mean them just because you think I want to hear them. I don't. Not from you." *Liar.* She did want to hear the words, but only if he meant them.

"I have excellent benefits." She wiped her eyes with the back of her hand. "I don't need your money. I have great friends, and I'm sure Gramps and Mrs. Meyer will be tickled to babysit. The only thing I'd like you to do is leave. Town. For good."

"We can work something out."

"You don't get it. I don't want to work things out with

you. I want to get married. I want lots of children, a dog and a house. It was a mistake to spend time with you when you didn't want those same things." She held his coat out to him.

"I want you. I want our baby. I'll even agree to a house and a dog. I just don't want to get married."

"Well, I do." She took a stand, unwilling to settle for less.

"Damn it, Ali, I'm not even out of my last marriage and you're trying to push me into another one."

His words sucked all the air from the room, hung between them, an impenetrable barrier.

Married.

Jared had a wife somewhere, maybe children, too. A perfect little family. She was the other woman. Good for sex, nothing more. A stabbing pain speared her heart. She leaned against the closet door in shock, tried desperately to draw air into her lungs.

He wiped his hand over his face, reached into his back pocket and took out a piece of gum. If there was a God, Jared would choke on it.

She stared at him, a carbon copy of the man her father had been at the age of thirty. Handsome. Accomplished. Likable. A lying, cheating, heartbreaking scoundrel.

An adulterer who had no respect for the sanctity of marriage.

"Let me explain," he said, as if trying to calm a frantic patient.

"You're married?"

"Technically, yes. But—"

She held his jacket tight to her chest. "There is no technically about it. Either you are or you aren't."

"If you'd let me speak—"

"Get out." She threw his jacket at him. It landed on the floor by his feet.

"Ali, please."

"Get. Out."

"Not until—"

"Fine." She stomped down the hall to her bathroom, on the verge of throwing up. "Stay as long as you'd like." And she slammed the door behind her. With shaky hands she fumbled to lock both doors then leaned up against the cold, tiled wall and slid down to the floor. Jared, married. She dropped her head into her hands, felt tears fill her eyes. She'd fallen in love with a married man.

He didn't come after her, didn't call through the door, didn't make any attempt to continue their conversation.

Instead glass shattered.

A door slammed.

He was gone.

Jared picked up his jacket from the floor, meant to throw it over the back of the chair, overshot, and took out the glass vase filled with roses he'd brought for Ali. Water spilled onto the table, soaked into the bag containing their uneaten lunch and trickled onto Ali's hardwood floor. He yanked up the bag, inadvertently clearing the path for the vase to roll, unimpeded, off the side of the table.

He walked to the closet, threw his jacket inside and slammed the door. Now things were a mess literally and figuratively. He opened the cabinet under her kitchen sink, looking for paper towels and found a pharmacy bag. The top had uncurled, revealing a hot pink box.

A pregnancy test. He lifted the bag to the counter, opened it and removed the box. Shook it. The test stick rattled inside. A receipt fluttered out. He glanced at it. She'd made the purchase yesterday. Ali had told the truth, she'd confirmed her pregnancy some time in the past twenty-four hours.

Curiosity got the better of him. He opened the box, poured its contents onto the bag, stared at the result window. Two pink lines.

"I'm not a liar," Ali said from behind him.

So focused on the validation of his fatherhood, Jared jumped at the sound of her voice.

Ali picked up the test stick, box and bag and threw them into the garbage. "And if you feel like smashing things, very mature by the way, please do it at your place, not mine."

"It was an accident." Not that he expected her to believe him. Credibility was not one of his strong points at the moment.

She walked into the kitchen, wearing a pair of knit slippers.

"Stop. There's glass on the floor," he warned.

She didn't listen. Without another word she opened a roll of paper towels, got down on her hands and knees, and began to sop up the water. He worked around her, picking up the larger pieces of glass.

The roses lay scattered, wet and crumpled on the floor. "Do you want me to try to salvage the flowers?"

"No."

Of course not. Because they were from him and she planned to get rid of him from her life. Well, she'd better think again. He had no idea how he would go about it, but he planned to play an active role in his child's life. And Ali's.

Her stomach grumbled.

"I saved the sandwiches. Go eat," he said. "I'll finish up."

As if he hadn't spoken, she continued to wipe the floor

with much more vigor than the job required. "Where does she live?"

"Who?"

"Your wife, Jared." She looked at him like he was an idiot. "Where does your wife live?"

"I don't know. She left me over two years ago and I haven't seen or heard from her since."

Ali's stomach growled again.

"How about I answer all of your questions over lunch?"

She moved on to drying the chairs. "Do you have any children?" She kept her eyes averted.

Jared let out a breath. This was the way she wanted to do it? Fine. He stepped back and leaned against the fridge. "No. The only child I have is the one you're carrying." Despite everything, he felt a growing elation at the thought of being a father.

"How long were you together?"

"After two months of dating, we had a courthouse wedding. Unbeknownst to me, Cici, that's her name, had a whopper of a drug problem." That she'd hidden remarkably well during their brief courtship.

"Once she found out I wouldn't prescribe my new wife the narcotics she craved and I didn't have the endless supply of cash she thought I did, she made my life a living hell for the two months it took her to max out my credit cards and plan her next move. One day, while I was at work, she packed up the car I'd bought her as a wedding present, cleaned out my entertainment center and my bank accounts and left town." Swinging by her drug dealer to pay her debt and almost ruining Jared's life in the process.

"Did you love her?"

He wanted to yell, *Hell, no.* But to be honest, "At the time I thought I did." Now he knew what he'd felt for Cici was a mere pittance of affection compared to the depth of his feelings for Ali. A day with Ali was a good day, even if twelve or more of those hours took place at work. Time apart felt empty, wasted and lonely.

"Do you still have feelings for her?" Ali asked, so quietly he almost didn't hear her.

Contempt. Anger. "You mean do I still love her? No." He'd love for her to spend time in jail as punishment for her crimes. But, no, he didn't love her.

"Then why didn't you divorce her?"

The million-dollar question. "Lots of reasons, none of which matter anymore. After I left Madrin Falls, I instructed my attorney to do whatever he could to expedite my divorce. I hired a private investigator, who found Cici." In a town an hour and a half north of Madrin Falls, of all places. "She's giving me some trouble—" worried that if she signs the divorce papers the DEA will find her "—but my attorney assures me in a few weeks I'll be a free man."

"I'm happy for you."

For us. "Me, too."

"Now the next woman you take to bed won't have to suffer the pain of finding out you're a liar, the way I did."

Bull's-eye. A direct hit to the gut. He deserved it. "I'm sorry. I should have told you, but in my head and my heart my marriage has been over for years."

"Yet you're still legally married."

"Yes. I have a certificate that says I'm married." Not until today had he realized how worthless it was. "A lot of good it did me. It didn't make my wife love me. It didn't stop her from lying to me, stealing from me or leaving me. A relationship between a man and a woman needs to be based on more than a couple of 'I dos' and a piece of paper."

"I agree. There needs to be honesty and trust. Without them we have nothing. You should have told me, Jared. You should have trusted me enough to explain the situation and given me the chance to make an informed decision."

"I know. But that night at the bar, everything happened so fast. The thought of leaving without kissing you, without touching you felt like I'd be making the biggest mistake of my life. I'm sorry, Ali. So sorry. But I'm not the only one who wasn't completely honest. You should have trusted me enough to tell me there was a chance you might be pregnant."

"After you flipped out on me?" She plopped onto one of the dry chairs, looked down at her feet. "You're right. I'm sorry, too."

He brought the sandwiches and drinks over to the table and sat down beside her, nudged her with his shoulder. "We're quite a pair." He pushed her plain turkey on whole wheat, no mayo toward her. "What do we do now?"

She unwrapped it. "There's nothing to do." She took a bite. "You've made it clear you're leaving. If I remember correctly, your exact words were 'At the end of the month I'm leaving. Nothing and no one will keep me here.'" She lifted her eyes from her sandwich and looked directly at him. "I'll take good care of our baby. I'll be the best mom I can be. You don't have to worry."

"I know." He wasn't worried, had absolutely no doubt she'd be a wonderful mother. But he wanted the chance to be a wonderful father, to be an important part of his child's life. To be there to change diapers, kiss boo-boos and read bedtime stories; to experience the first tooth, first steps and first haircut.

After a few bites of her lunch Ali stood. "I'm kind of tired."

For the first time he noticed how pale and drained she looked. "Are you feeling all right?"

"Just tired." She yawned. "I think I'll go back to bed for a while."

Jared would have given anything to join her, to hold her and reassure her. "I'm going to try—"

"Don't. I don't want empty promises like my dad gave my mom. 'I'm going to try to do better... I'm going to try to come around more often... I'm going to try to send a check for Ali's braces.'"

"You're not alone in this," he said.

"I know." Posture straight, head high, she gave him a dispassionate look. "I trust and can count on Gramps and Mrs. Meyer, Victoria, Roxie and Polly to be there for me. Goodbye, Jared. And if I don't see you before you leave, have a safe trip."

He watched her walk away.

In the two weeks he had left, he'd make it a point to see her, as often as possible. And much sooner than even he expected, because when he returned to his rental he realized his keys were no longer in his jacket pocket. They must have fallen out somewhere in Ali's condo.

He knocked on her door a good long while with no response from inside. She couldn't possibly have fallen asleep in the short time it had taken him to travel from her condo to his and back. He recalled how pale she'd looked and started to pound. "Open this door, Ali," he yelled.

By the time she acknowledged him his knuckles and the side of his fist throbbed.

"Leave me alone," she called through the door.

"I need my keys. They're not in my pocket. They must have fallen out."

She didn't respond. About a minute later the door opened

just enough for her to slide out her arm. His keys rested in her upturned palm.

Not good enough. He needed to see her, make sure she was okay. "What took you so long to answer the door?" He pushed on it.

She blocked his entry. "Go away."

Her voice cracked, sounded funny, like her nose was stuffed.

"You'd better step away from the door," he threatened, fully prepared to knock it off the hinges if necessary. "I'm coming in." When his push met no resistance, he stumbled forward into her kitchen.

"Next time I won't open the door at all," she said, standing defiant in her purple flannel pants and lavender tee, her eyes puffy and rimmed in red, her eyelashes clumped together with tears, the tip of her nose pink.

So she wasn't as unaffected by her pregnancy and, hopefully his leaving as she'd appeared. And while she had an excellent support system in town, she probably hadn't revealed her condition to anyone yet. "You look like you could use a hug."

She turned away, brought her handful of tissues to her nose, but didn't move.

"I don't know what the future will hold." He walked to her. "But I'm here now." He opened his arms. And almost wept with relief when she turned into them. He stood there, holding her while she cried, caressing her back, afraid the slightest movement in any direction would sever the closeness between them and he'd never get it back.

Ali showed her strong persona to the world. But with him she let down her defenses, shared her vulnerable side. She felt so good in his arms, so right in his life. How could he ever have considered leaving her?

After a while she sagged against him.

"Come on." He released one of his arms and shifted so the other landed on her shoulder. "You need to lie down." He guided her toward her bedroom.

From under the covers she asked, "Would you stay for a…?" He didn't wait for her to finish before he lay down on top of the comforter, cuddled in behind her and draped his arm across her belly. He held his family in his arms, and never wanted to let them go.

"Few minutes?" she said on a relaxing breath.

For the rest of their lives. Because that's what a man did when he loved a woman. He took care of her, gave her what she needed, within the law, of course.

And he did love Ali. She was his first thought in the morning and his last at night. She filled his drab life with color and cured the numbness that had taken hold deep inside him. She awakened his emotions, and although he didn't always like all the things she made him feel, she'd brought him back to life, gave him hope for the future. But only if she and their baby were a willing part of it.

For that to happen he'd need to find a job close by and a place for them to live.

CHAPTER ELEVEN

On Monday morning Ali stopped by the grocery store to pick up some healthy food to stock in Gramps's fridge and pantry. Then she went to his house to clean out the junk food and put fresh sheets on his bed in preparation for his return home that afternoon. But when she arrived at the hospital to pick him up she learned he'd accepted Mrs. Meyer's invitation to recuperate at her house. After Gramps's show in the CCU, Ali anticipated a long convalescence.

On Wednesday, Ali worked her second shift in a row on 5E. Around lunchtime, she hung up the phone at the nurses' station and turned to Nora—the unit secretary. "Transport is backed up. Radiology can take Mr. Clemmons if I bring him right now. While I'm down there I'm going to run to the cafeteria to pick up some lunch. All my patients have eaten except for 504B, who's down at PT. His tray is in his room. I'm expecting a post-op. If the recovery room calls, tell them I'll be back in fifteen minutes."

Nora nodded. "I'll call Roxie if any of your patients buzz."

Ali pushed a wheelchair into Mr. Clemmons's room. The frail, elderly man sat in the same chair where she'd set him up for lunch. "It's time for your chest X-ray, Mr. Clemmons."

She helped him up and to the bathroom. While he was

in there, she took his red and navy plaid robe out of his closet and handed it in through the door. "You'd better put this on. It gets cold down there."

"Thank you, Allison."

He shuffled out of the bathroom and Ali waited while he settled himself into the wheelchair. She placed a light blanket over his legs then combed his hair. "I don't know why you bother," he said. "I'm old and I'm dying of lung cancer. Who cares what I look like?"

"I care, Mr. Clemmons. Your wife and children care." She pushed the wheelchair out of his room and down the hall toward the elevators. "Your doctor was pleased with the outcome of your surgery. She says she may discharge you home tomorrow. And if you don't shave that over-growth of whiskers hiding your smile before the end of my shift tonight, I'm going to shave them for you."

"I'll think about it." He tried to sound gruff, but he was a sweet old man.

"While you're considering it, you may want to swing by the nurses' station and talk to Nora at the desk. She keeps a picture of the last man I tried to shave in her drawer. It isn't pretty."

She saw his smile in the metallic reflection of the elevator door.

After parking Mr. Clemmons in the Radiology waiting area and handing his chart to the receptionist, Ali headed for the cafeteria.

Déjà vu.

While in line for the cashier, a yogurt in one hand a banana in the other, Ali spied Jared sitting at a table in the far corner. A nurse she didn't recognize carried her lunch tray in his direction.

Look away.

Not likely.

With morbid curiosity she watched, surprised to see Jared shake his head when the nurse reached to pull out the chair across from him. After a brief conversation she walked to a different table. As she sat, she whispered furiously to the six women huddled around her.

Unfazed, Jared went back to reading his magazine.

Ali's heart lifted. It shouldn't matter that he'd turned the woman away, but it did. She shouldn't still want him, but she did. *I don't know how the future will turn out. But I'm here now.*

She paid the cashier and found herself walking toward his table. She hadn't seen him since he'd held her in his arms, for what seemed like hours. They'd barely spoken during that time. "Hi," she said when she reached him.

His eyes lit up. "How are you?"

Sad. Lonely. Confused. Scared about the future. "Better." She forced a smile. "Are you turning away all company?"

"Never yours." He leaned toward her and lowered his voice. "But in the interest of full disclosure, I told that nurse I'd rather she not sit with me because I'm involved with someone who's extremely jealous and I didn't want to have to deal with the fallout. If you share my table she, and all the women she's chattering to, will assume it's you."

Ali pulled out a chair and sat. "In a few months, when I'm big and fat, they'll be talking about us anyway." She didn't plan to broadcast her child's paternity, but she wouldn't keep it a secret either.

He rested his elbows on the table and leaned forward. "You won't be fat. You'll be rounded and I anticipate even more beautiful than you are right now."

Sweet-talker. "I'll have stretch marks, swollen ankles and a puffy face. My back will ache, my boobs will balloon until they look ready to pop and I'll probably complain nonstop. Be glad you won't be here to witness the transformation."

She'd meant to keep things light, to show him she was fine with him leaving. But hurt flashed in his eyes.

"I'm trying to—"

"Please don't," Ali interrupted him. "I don't want you trying to do anything as far as I'm concerned. I want a clean break. It's the only way I can do this. Shoot." She glanced at her watch. "I have to go." She stood. "I have a patient waiting in Radiology."

Jared stood. "I'll walk you."

"No."

Ali turned and hurried to the stairwell. As she climbed the steps she recalled the infrequent, awkward visits with her father, a man she barely knew. *"You remember Daddy. Go give him a kiss. No, you can't go to Sara's house. Daddy's coming to visit. And you'd better be on your best behavior."*

Missed birthdays. Broken promises. Hurt feelings. Ali would not allow her child to suffer the same fate. And she refused to turn out like her mother, pining for a man who didn't love her. Jared needed to leave. It was best for her and her baby.

On Friday afternoon Jared wondered how a day could go from a perfect ten to a minus five all in the course of a few hours. Sitting in the chair behind his desk, he took a few minutes to revisit the high and low points so far:

8:00 a.m.   Retrieved a message from his attorney. Cici had signed the divorce papers.

9:00 a.m.   Attended a meeting with the medical director. Asked to be considered as a permanent replacement for Dr. Rosen when he vacated his full-time E.R. position in March.

9:03 a.m.   Came clean about his brush with the DEA.

9:15 a.m.   Almost collapsed when the medical director told him he already knew about the charges, and had spoken with the DEA prior to Jared starting work at the hospital.

9:45 a.m.   Rushed to fill out an employment application in Human Resources.

10:30 a.m. Called a real estate agent to inquire about a house he'd seen on the internet. Scheduled an appointment for a walk-through after work.

11:00 a.m. Took a few minutes to bask in happiness.

Local job: looking good.

Local house: working on it.

Ali: still talking to him.

It was a start.

11:45 a.m. Noticed first disillusioned/distrusting look from a coworker.

1:00 p.m.   Learned that news he'd been the subject of a DEA investigation was now circulating around the hospital. And by the way some of the staff eyed him with suspicion, it appeared nobody had mentioned the case had been dropped and the DEA hadn't had enough evidence to formally charge him. That he was innocent, damn it!

It was Community General all over again—staff judging him on hearsay, not interested in learning the truth. It rankled that people were so quick to think him capable of breaking the law, of consorting with a low-life drug dealer.

Someone knocked on his door. Tani called out, "Medical director on line two."

Probably calling to give Jared the bad news. *In light of the damaging rumors upsetting the staff, we feel hiring you would be too disruptive to the working environment of the E.R.*

"Tell him I'll call him back."

For the next two hours Jared immersed himself in work, ignored the stares, the whispered comments and sudden silence when he entered a room. Every E.R. bed was filled with patients ranging from an infected fingernail to a traumatic amputation of an arm. No sooner did he discharge one patient, the stretcher was wiped down, the sheets changed and another was brought in. The hustle kept his mind occupied.

Sometime around three o'clock, Tani said, "The medical director called again and lunch is in your office."

"I don't have time to eat right now." He handed Tani a file. "Exam Room Three, Bed Two needs an X-ray of the left distal radius."

"Make time," Tani said, taking the file. "I'll call this into Radiology."

"I have to…"

When he tried to walk away, Tani reached out and grabbed his arm. "Ali's been waiting for over an hour."

Ali? The bottom dropped out of his world. He'd been so wrapped up in himself and his work, he'd completely forgotten about Ali. Stupid. His heart slammed against his ribs. Had she heard? Of course she had. Was she here to tell him off for not being honest with her? Again? Would she stand by him or leave him to fend for himself like his mother and Cici had? Would she believe he had been wrongly accused or look at him with disdain like other members of the staff? Would she use this to try to push him out of her life for good?

The acid in his stomach churned.

Walking the short distance to his office, Jared felt like a man on trial for murder about to enter the courtroom to hear the verdict.

She sat in the chair opposite his desk, wearing a pair of tight-fitting dark blue jeans, black boots and a red pullover sweater. She was so intent on looking out the window into the parking lot, she jumped when he opened the door.

He stood in the doorway, not sure if it was safe to go in any farther.

Her face showed no emotion. "Tani said you haven't eaten. I brought you lunch." She held out a deli wrapped sandwich and a bottle of water.

Food was good. Thoughtful. He relaxed a little, took a few steps and allowed the door to close behind him. "Thanks."

"Are there any other secrets you're holding on to? Because it's pretty obvious they're all going to come out eventually, and I'd just as soon get everything out in the open now rather than later."

Was that sarcasm in her voice? He could handle sarcasm. "This is the last one."

She stood, her blue eyes filled with caring and concern, not disappointment and disbelief. He let out the breath he'd been holding.

"You look like you could use a hug." She walked to him, and wrapped her arms tightly around his waist, pressing her cheek to his chest.

Jared hugged her back like his life depended on her closeness. Maybe it did.

He didn't know how long they stood there, locked in an embrace, in complete silence, unconcerned with the noises outside his office door. But it was long enough to rejuvenate him, to make him confident he would get through this, and cautiously optimistic Ali would stand by him while he did.

All too soon she unclasped her hands from behind his back, and he forced himself to let her go. "Tell me the basics," she said, resuming her seated position. At the same time, she unwrapped a deli sandwich that rested on his desk and handed him half. "I know you're busy. Eat while you talk."

He sat in the chair next to her. "A little over two years…" Something clogged in his throat, he tried to clear it. Ali unscrewed the cap on a bottle of water and handed it to him.

"Thank you." He took a sip. "Two years ago I was investigated by the DEA's Office of Diversion Control, the unit that deals with criminal activity of physicians and pharmacy personnel."

"I'm sure there's a logical explanation," Ali said. "Eat." She pointed to his lunch.

Jared's spirits soared. She didn't think the worst of him. He took a bite of his sandwich.

"When you're ready, start from the beginning."

Someone knocked on the door. Tani's voice came through. "Sorry, Dr. P. Ambulance on the way in. Sixty-two-year-old female. Cross-country skiing accident. Right leg, rib and facial injuries. ETA eleven minutes. And the medical director called again. He says it's urgent."

"Okay," Jared answered.

"Just hit the highlights," Ali said.

"Someone stole one of my Official New York State prescription pads. I didn't realize it was gone until the police showed up at my job to tell me it had turned up in the pocket of a drug dealer known for peddling prescription narcotics, complete with my signature and DEA number on fifteen blank prescription sheets."

"They couldn't tell the signatures were forged?"

Jared felt like smiling. "Are you sure they were forged?" he asked her.

"Of course they were forged. You would never sign blank prescriptions and give them to a drug dealer." She hesitated before adding, "Unless you had a very good reason."

Her belief in his innocence made him want to shout out with joy. "I'm almost positive it was Cici, but she disappeared before the investigation. That didn't stop the DEA from trying to build a case against me." And come close to charging him with prescription fraud after the drug dealer, a man he'd never met, picked him out of a line-up and after a search of his home turned up one prescription narcotic tablet on the floor of the bedroom closet he'd briefly shared with Cici, and another under the refrigerator.

In the end, whether due to his actual innocence or his high-priced attorney, Jared wasn't sure which, the DEA had dropped the case.

"The investigation was all over the news." The headlines were still vivid in his memory: 'Community General Physician Suspected of Link to Local Drug Ring.' 'E.R. Physician's Prescription Pad Found in Possession of Drug Dealer.' 'Local Physician under Investigation for Prescription Fraud.' "It didn't matter that I was never formally charged, or that the DEA dropped the investigation for lack of evidence. My colleagues made their own judgments, formed their own conclusions and found me guilty."

"Is that why you work for a physician staffing agency rather than directly for a hospital?"

He nodded. "The agency gets the assignments and handles credentialing issues. I don't have to deal with disclosing the details of the investigation." Or experience the humiliation of not being hired because of it.

"Until now," Ali said.

"Until you," he responded, looking deep into her eyes. Never before had remaining in one place mattered so much.

Someone knocked on the door. "ETA five minutes. And please call the medical director," Tani said.

Ali stood. "Go back to work and don't worry. I'll handle this."

"Handle what?"

"I've seen the damage gossip can cause. I watched my mother withdraw into the house so she wouldn't have to face it. I will never again allow rumor and innuendo hurt someone I care about. You're an excellent physician and don't deserve what is being said about you."

"So you care about me?" Jared wanted to jump on top of his desk and dance. Instead he took a step toward her.

She gave a shy smile. "Yeah. And you don't make it easy."

"Thank you." He pulled her into his arms. "For coming in today, for believing in me, for still caring about me, for everything."

"Go." She stepped back. When he turned to leave she added, "And make time to come back and finish the other half of your sandwich."

Ali's concern for him eating, her coming by to support him and her offer to help stave off the gossip gave him hope that things between them would be okay. "May I come by later?"

Before she could answer there was another knock at the door. This time the medical director's voice came through. "Open up, Dr. Padget."

The hope of a moment ago turned into a bitter taste at the back of Jared's mouth. He didn't want to do this. Not here. Not now. But he opened his office door. What else could he do? The medical director stood there, wearing wrinkled blue scrubs and black dress shoes.

"You should get going," Jared said to Ali, not wanting her to witness his humiliation.

"Don't run out on my account, Allison," the medical director said.

"Hi, Dr. Kleinman." Ali greeted him with one of her brilliant smiles.

"This isn't a good time, Dr. Kleinman. I have a—"

"I know. An ambulance on the way. I've been trying to call you. It has my sister-in-law in it. My wife's all in a dither. Told her I'd come down and see what I could do. But I'm just here for show." He winked at Ali. "To keep the peace."

"Well, I'll let you get back to work, Dr. Padget." Ali picked up her coat and purse. "Nice seeing you again, Dr. Kleinman," she added as she left the office.

"That the reason you want to stick around?" the older man asked.

Jared held up his crossed fingers.

Dr. Kleinman nodded in approval. "She's a good girl. I golf with her granddad."

That was all fine and good, but Jared needed to know the status of his new job. "Sir, about the rumors. I—"

"Don't give them another thought. They'll blow over. My assistant is in Human Resources as we speak. She'll find out who's responsible."

"So I'm still under consideration?" Jared could barely breathe.

"You're my first choice. I have two more interviews already scheduled for Monday morning. Call me late afternoon."

CHAPTER TWELVE

"It feels kind of decadent going to the movies on a Tuesday afternoon," Ali said to Jared as they waited in line for popcorn. "How did you manage to get the day off?"

"Money may have changed hands. I'm not at liberty to divulge the details."

She smiled, glad she'd let him convince her to go out for a day of fun. "A day to remember," he'd said. First lunch at O'Halloran's, where they'd shared the über-delicious nacho platter she'd been craving, followed by a walk to the arcade where she'd whomped him at air hockey, Pac-Man and Galaga—she'd spent a lot of time in that arcade growing up—and then a romantic movie.

"You are one busy lady. Today was the only day I could pin you down."

Because Monday she'd worked on 5E, Wednesday was early dinner and bingo with Gramps, and Thursday and Friday she was scheduled to work back-to-back twelve-hour shifts on 5E. On Saturday he'd be gone.

When the clerk came to take their order he turned to Ali. "Do you want artery-clogging butter?"

She nodded. "And a box of those." She pointed to her favorite candy-coated chocolates.

"Good for you. Go all out."

"There's something about sitting in a movie theatre that makes it okay to indulge."

He looked ready to say something, maybe about indulging more than her tastebuds. But he remained quiet. Good. After finding out about his marriage, Ali wouldn't entertain anything more than a platonic relationship between them.

Yet in the darkness, as they watched the story on the big screen unfold, when he took her hand into his, she didn't pull away. And when he put his arm around her, she leaned in close to rest her head on his shoulder, loving the feel of him, the scent of him. She was going to miss him.

"That wasn't at all what I expected," Jared said with disgust, tossing their empty popcorn bag into the trash can by the exit.

"Didn't you know what the movie was about?"

"No. I heard Polly mention you wanted to see it. The main character's a soldier. I pictured action scenes, fighting, blood and guts."

"There was some of that." There was also the angst of young lovers separated by circumstance, the man who didn't return when he was supposed to, the woman who married another. "But it was a romance." That had affected Jared. She'd seen him wipe at his eyes twice.

"It was sentimental crap. Let's get out of here." Jared took her by the hand. "It's time to go talk to Gramps."

Way to ruin a perfect day. "About that." She pulled him to a stop in front of the hardware store next to the theatre. "I decided I'd rather hold off and tell him in a few weeks." Or maybe later on, by cell phone, in between pushes. Holding his great-grandbaby would lessen the sting of disappointment when he learned his granddaughter had wound up unwed and pregnant like her mother before her.

"Come on." Jared dragged her toward the parking lot.

"I told you, I'm not leaving without accompanying you to tell your gramps. I own up to my responsibilities."

Great. She'd plummeted from an object of lust to a responsibility.

How low would she sink in Gramps's eyes?

She remembered one time, several times actually, when he'd caught her with a boy and yelled, "You are going to wind up just like your mother." The way he'd said it, winding up like her mother was the worst possible thing that could happen to her. "What if he...?"

Jared stopped, turned to face her and placed his cold hands on her cheeks so she couldn't look away. "Your gramps loves you. Regardless of how he reacts to the news, I'm confident that won't change."

"After Mom had me, they barely spoke." Growing up, she remembered seeing Gramps only a handful of times, each visit filled with tension.

"You don't know what went on between them." He took her hand and began to walk. "Let's get this over with so you can stop worrying."

In the short two-minute drive to Gramps's house, Ali dropped her knit hat to the floor and managed to twist two knots in her hair. Jared untangled them, hating to see her so nervous. "It's going to be fine," he said, believing it in his heart.

When Gramps opened the front door to greet them, Ali burst into tears. Thank goodness Mrs. Meyer was also there. "May we speak in private, sir?" Jared asked Gramps, who darted a concerned glance to the older woman.

"Come into the kitchen, Allison," Mrs. Meyer said, helping her remove her coat. "Whatever it is, it can't be as bad as you seem to think it is."

"Oh, yes...it can," Ali mumbled in between choppy

breaths as she followed Mrs. Meyer down the hallway leading to the kitchen in the back of the house.

"Sit," Gramps said, motioning to the out-of-style beige floral sofas in the living room.

"How are you feeling, sir?"

"Stop with the sir and tell me what's wrong with my granddaughter." Gramps shifted in his seat and threw a worried glance toward the kitchen.

Not wanting to drag this out Jared told him. "She's pregnant."

Gramps clutched at his chest and let out a breath. "That all?"

"She's a little emotional." Major understatement. "And she thinks you're going to be disappointed that she's wound up in the same situation as her mother. She mentioned you were estranged from your daughter and I think Ali fears the same thing will happen between you and her."

Gramps started to stand. "Of all the..."

"If I can have a moment of your time before you go in there, I'd appreciate it."

He sat back down. "Make it quick. I'm guessing you're the father."

"I am, sir. And I want to assure you I will take care of Ali and the baby."

Gramps grimaced. "Her father fed me the same line of bull."

"I love her, sir, more than I ever thought possible. She doesn't know it yet but I'll be starting at Madrin Memorial full time in March. And if she likes it, I'm planning to buy us a house on the next street over. I'm going to surprise her with both when we leave here."

"So you're looking to buy a house?" Gramps asked, looking contemplative. "Come by later tonight, after you take

Allison home, so we can talk more about it." He pushed up from the couch. "Now, let's see to my granddaughter."

In the kitchen Ali sat cuddled in Mrs. Meyer's arms.

"Allison Elizabeth Forshay, you come over here this instant."

Ali moved slowly, as if dreading what was about to happen. She rose to stand in front of Gramps and made Jared proud when she looked her grandfather in the eye.

"You are the bright light in my life, Ali." He reached up to cup her cheek. Ali leaned into his touch. "I love you, have always loved you, will always love you. And there is nothing you could ever do to change that. The problems I had with your mother had nothing to do with you, and how I feel for you has nothing to do with her."

Ali flung her arms around him. "I love you so much."

"Mrs. Meyer," Gramps said over Ali's shoulder. "Our girl's going to give us a great-grandbaby, and she didn't think we'd be happy about it."

Mrs. Meyer scooted out of her chair, tears in her eyes and pulled Ali into a hug. "That's wonderful news, dear."

"Our girl?" Jared asked.

"Mrs. Meyer's been like a grandmother to Ali for years."

"Like a mother," Ali clarified.

"Any woman would be blessed to have you for a daughter," Mrs. Meyer said to Ali. "Knowing you, watching you change and mature into the woman you are today has enriched my life."

Ali had enriched Jared's life too, made him want to be a better person, a better man.

"This calls for a celebration." Gramps reached into a cabinet and took out a box of cream-filled snack cakes.

"You can't eat those," Ali said, drying her eyes with a napkin. "They have absolutely no nutritional value."

"That's why I serve them with milk," Gramps replied, and they all laughed.

After saying their good-byes Ali and Jared stood out on Gramps's front porch. She looked up at him. "Thank you. For convincing me to tell Gramps today and for coming with me." And there it was: the brilliant I-care-about-you smile he'd waited months to see directed at him.

He knew in that instant that one would never be enough to last him a lifetime, as he'd originally thought. Because in that quiet moment, in her straight white teeth, her curving lips and sincere blue eyes, he'd found serenity.

He smiled back at the woman he loved. "Now it's time for my surprises." He was so excited, felt so high on life he would have skipped to the car, if there had been a way to do it without looking like a total dweeb in the process. He couldn't wait to share his news, to see her joy when she found out he was staying in town for her, and their baby.

A few minutes later Ali stood in absolute shock, the only indication she hadn't frozen stiff the white swirling mist of her warm breath hitting the frigid air as she stared at Jared's surprise. A house, a block over from where Gramps lived, a huge white two-story house, with black shutters, a white picket fence and a "For Sale" sign sticking out from the snow in the front yard. Window boxes held dehydrated remnants of summer flowers, now brown and straw-like, but Ali could picture colorful blooms brightening the bland facade.

Jared came up behind her and put a hand on each shoulder. "What do you think?" he asked.

"About what?"

"This house. Isn't it perfect? If you like it, I can call my real estate agent to give us a tour of the inside."

He had a real estate agent? She turned to look at him.

"You're buying a house?" He may as well have told her he was considering a sex change operation. "Why are you buying a house? In Madrin Falls?" A huge house that could easily accommodate a family of five. And a couple of pets. And probably a live-in relative or two.

"Because of you. Because you're here."

"It's so big."

"Four bedrooms, two and a half baths, and a finished basement," he said with pride, as if he'd pounded the nails himself.

"Four bedrooms?"

"Ali." He put his arm around her and lifted her chin so she had to look up at him. "We're having a baby, and I don't want to stop at just one. We're going to need someplace to put them."

"But you're leaving." In four days. Did he plan to set her up in his house so he had an open invitation to swing by whenever the mood suited him?

"True. I couldn't get out of my next assignment. But it's my last one. I took a full time job at Madrin Memorial. In the E.R. I start March nineteenth." He looked so happy, so proud of himself.

Ali looked for a place to sit down. Not finding anything suitable, she leaned on the fence railing, willing her legs to stay strong. Jared was staying in town, where she'd have to see him, work with him, day in and day out. What if he wanted to share custody, to take her child from her every few days?

"This one's my favorite. But if you don't like it there are three others we can take a look at."

"Why does it matter what I think?"

"Because I want the woman I plan to live with to love the house as much as I do."

Ali stumbled, gripped the wood she'd been leaning on like she'd fall to her death if she let go.

"What's wrong?" he asked, reaching out to steady her. "You said you wanted children, a dog and a house. I'm working in reverse order."

"And a husband." She took a step away from him. "I have no intention of living with you just because we're having a baby. Nothing's changed between us. You don't love me. You don't want to marry me. And I have no intention of tying my life to a man who thinks I tried to manipulate him by getting pregnant, a man who lied to me, had sex with me without telling me he was married to another woman. A man who's still married."

"I told you I'm sorry," he said. "And I expect my divorce to be finalized in a few weeks."

"Oh, goodie. And you being sorry is supposed to make it all better? Make me move in with you, become dependent on you? Make me risk the utter devastation of you moving on to someone else when you get bored, because you are a traveling man, after all, and you don't want to get married so there'd be nothing to make you stay?" Ali's heart pounded in her chest, circulating anger throughout her body.

"How many times do I have to tell you?" Jared yelled. "A marriage certificate won't make your spouse stick around. Grow up, Ali. This is the real world. There are no guarantees. I'm offering to try, to work with you, partner with you so we can raise our child together."

A marriage certificate won't make your spouse stick around. Ali's anger dissipated, all hope whooshed out of her. As a child she'd convinced herself life would be different if her parents had gotten married. Better. Instead of searching for love in the arms of men too numerous to count, Mom would have been with her one true love.

And Dad would have stayed in one place, lived with them. They could have been a real family, eaten meals together, gone on vacations. Maybe she would have gotten the baby brother or sister she'd longed for.

As an adult she had realized not all marriages were successful, but with the right person and hard work she could make her marriage last—she could have the type of life she'd always dreamed of. Couldn't she? Did Jared think she wasn't enough to make a man happy, to make him want to stay with her long term? "Please take me home."

"I can't believe this." Jared turned away from her, took a few steps then swung back. "I'm offering to change my life for you, to get a new job and buy a house. To live with you, take care of you and our baby, and that's not enough?"

"My dad bought my mom a house," Ali said quietly. "He promised to take care of us, and he didn't."

"Give me a break." Jared threw up his arms. "I am not your father, and you are not your mother. Just like you're not the girl you were ten years ago. You're stronger. You are a smart, independent, professional woman, more than capable of taking care of yourself and our baby. But you don't have to do it alone. I want to be right there with you, no matter what life throws at us, in good times and in bad. I love you, Ali."

As much as she'd longed to hear those words spoken from his mouth, she didn't believe them, not now, not when his sole purpose in saying them was to persuade her to live with him. "You don't love me. Maybe you love the idea of finally settling down after years on the road, of having a child, a family, but you don't love me."

"How can you say that? Of course I love you." He reached for her. She dodged his hands.

"A few weeks ago you were leaving as soon as your assignment at Madrin Memorial ended and you had no plans to return. You find out I'm pregnant and, boom, you love me, and you're buying a house for us to live in." It was too much, too soon.

"Come," Jared said. "Your lips are turning blue. Let's talk in the car."

Because her toes were numb, Ali followed without argument.

Once inside, the heat blasting through the vents, Jared turned to her. "I've made a lot of mistakes in my life. But the one thing I'm sure is no mistake is my love for you."

"You can't possibly—"

"Just hear me out." He silenced her with a finger to her lips. "I honestly think I was half in love with you before I left. The five weeks we were apart were the loneliest I've ever experienced, and I've spent a lot of time alone."

He took both her mitten-covered hands in his bare ones and stared into her eyes. "I love that when we work together you keep tabs on me to make sure I've eaten, and how you treat each one of your patients like family. I love how you volunteer at the senior center and cook batches of soups and stews for people unable to cook for themselves."

He reached up to tuck a wisp of hair behind her ear. "I love how you twist your hair when you're nervous, how you believed in me when you heard the rumors about the DEA investigation and how you came into work early, stayed late, and stopped in on your days off to champion my cause. How in the course of three days, because of your tireless efforts, I went from hospital pariah to paragon of emergency medicine."

It wasn't as big a deal as he was making it out to be.

"I love how you feel in my arms, how you respond to my touch and how your face takes on an expression of pure rapture when we make love. When we're apart I ache to be with you. There is no doubt in my mind that what I feel for you is the truest, deepest form of love possible."

Maybe in his mind. "Yet you were able to look me in the eye, day after day, and lie to me. That's how you treat someone you love? How can I believe anything that comes out of your mouth?"

"So that's it." Jared jammed his car into drive. "No second chances." He pushed down on the gas pedal. The wheels spun out before gaining traction. "No possibility you could ever forgive me."

She was trying, had put their issues aside so they could spend one last day together. But she hadn't forgotten or forgiven, the wound from his deceit too raw, her emotions a jumbled mess. Rather than answer him, she looked out the side window at the houses speeding by.

Before she knew it, they'd reached her condo. Jared didn't bother looking for a parking spot. He simply stopped and, staring straight ahead, waited for her to get out.

"I'm sorry," she said as she slid from the car.

She turned to say more but he snapped, "Me, too," and sped off before she'd even closed the door.

At a quarter after ten on Saturday morning, Ali sat at her kitchen table staring at the clock on her microwave through blurry, tear-filled eyes. According to Polly, Jared had planned to leave by nine that morning. He'd gone without anymore words between them. Not even goodbye.

Ali knew he would leave, believed it was best for her and her baby. So why did it feel like someone had cracked open her sternum, separated her ribs and exposed her heart to the harsh winter weather raging outside?

CHAPTER THIRTEEN

"You did what?" Ali's equilibrium went momentarily off-kilter. She grabbed onto the dresser beside her. No way had she heard him correctly.

"I sold the house," Gramps said. "Hand me that box."

Ali closed her eyes and inhaled deeply. The day could not end soon enough. First Jared leaving and now this. Gramps had sold the house she loved, the house that held countless happy memories, without a single mention of his intention until it was too late. "To who? Why? Where are you going to live?"

"To someone who offered to buy it. Put these in my suitcase." He handed her a stack of well-worn flannel shirts. "Because I'm tired of living alone when I'd much rather be next door spending my time with Mrs. Meyer, which is where I will be living as of tonight."

"With Mrs. Meyer? You're moving in with Mrs. Meyer? After all these years? What's going on? What aren't you telling me? Are you sick?"

"I'm fine, Allison. Calm down."

"I will not calm down. Why the rush? Why all of a sudden are you selling the house?"

"Because someone showed an interest and accepted my price. I had the opportunity to sell and I took it, and I couldn't be happier." He ducked back into his closet.

Ali looked around Gramps's cluttered bedroom. "What are you going to do with all your stuff?"

"I sold the house contents and all. As is. You can take whatever you want, of course. Everything else I'll leave for the buyer to sort through."

Piles of "collectable" sports memorabilia. Grandma's Hummel collection. Great-grandma's antique china set. Boxes and closets filled with photographs and personal items. In the possession of a stranger. Ali resisted the urge to feel his forehead to check for fever. Acute delirium was the only thing that made sense. "When is this person moving in?"

"Middle to end of March." He emerged from the closet, holding two handfuls of hangers with pants hanging from them. "Before I forget, run into the kitchen and get me your grandma's favorite pie server, the one with the roses on the handle, and my 'Number One Grandpa' mug. Oh, and that oversized bowl you made me in ceramics class. I like to eat my cereal out of that in the morning."

"That's all you're taking from the kitchen?"

He snapped his fingers. "Right. How could I forget? There are two boxes of oatmeal cream pies on top of the fridge."

"I will not pack up your snack cakes."

"Oh, for heaven's sake. The oatmeal keeps me regular."

Later that evening, with Gramps ensconced next door, Ali stood alone in what had been his living room, staring at what had been his favorite chair, mourning the upcoming loss of his beloved home, unable to imagine someone else living there.

She climbed the stairs, remembered how she used to skip the creaky third step whenever she'd tried to sneak in or out. Didn't matter. Somehow Gramps had always known. She walked into the pink tile bathroom with foil rose decorated wallpaper, and pictured herself on her knees, bathing her squirming toddler in the pink tub.

One more thing to add to her growing to-do list. Look for a new place to live. A one-bedroom condo with a tiny bathroom, no tub, would never work for a mother with a baby.

Ali walked into her old room, where she still slept several times a month, and climbed into bed, too drained to change her clothes. Life as she knew it was changing. Ali didn't like change.

Jared did. He would never have been happy living in this town. He'd be forever on the lookout for new surroundings and new faces. Things didn't change much in Madrin Falls.

She cuddled under the covers and wondered what he was doing, where he was living, whether he'd be working days or nights. She wondered what he'd say if she called him to apologize, to admit the baby, his marriage, Gramps's heart attack and changing relationship with Mrs. Meyer had overwhelmed her. Add confusion over her feelings for him, uncertainty about her future, and his surprises, and she'd lost all perspective, toppled over the edge of reasonable.

In time she would deal with it all. She needed time.

Would he take her call?

Probably not. She hadn't taken his after he'd snuck away without a good-bye in November.

She'd pushed him away one too many times. He'd given up on her, on them.

Ali felt completely depleted, her body weighted down, too tired to even cry. All she wanted to do was sleep.

* * *

On Sunday morning she began cleaning and sorting through Gramps's bedroom, prepared to go through every item in the house to be sure they wouldn't leave behind anything of importance.

On Monday she returned home, her car filled with stuff she couldn't part with. After numerous trips from her parking space to her condo, Ali swung by her mailbox. Between her cell phone bill and a junk mailer she found a letter from Jared. There was no return address, but she recognized his handwriting instantly.

She stared at the envelope as if his blue ink script held a clue to the message inside. Should she read it? Or figure he was gone and leave it at that?

Back in her condo, Ali sat at her kitchen table, the envelope in front of her. She'd felt something the shape of a credit card inside, or maybe a library card or the keycard to a hotel room. It spiked her interest. Maybe he'd forgotten to return his hospital ID badge and his letter was nothing more than a request for her to do it.

Slowly, Ali opened the envelope. Carefully, she eased out the handwritten note. In the process of unfolding, a credit card with Jared's name on it fell to the table.

Dear Ali,

Staying away from you these past few days, and leaving while so much turmoil remains between us, is the most difficult thing I've ever done. We have important decisions to make, but we owe it to each other, and our child, to not make them in haste, out of anger and hurt, or based on tainted ideas formed by past relationships.

We need time to deal with all that's happened, to consider our options calmly and rationally. I propose we do this during the six weeks I'm away. I think it best we have no contact until we're both thinking clearly. I don't want to risk either of us saying or doing something that may irreparably damage our chance for a future together.

In my rush to do the right thing, I failed to consider your feelings or the fact I'm still legally married and had no right to talk about us living together until that situation has been rectified. I made a plan, put it into action and expected you to be as thrilled about it as I was. I've given you no reason to trust me yet I lashed out when you didn't believe words I'd spoken from the heart. I'm sorry. All I can say is I will spend every day for the rest of my life striving to do better, to deserve you, to earn your trust. Because you're right, without it, we have nothing.

Know this, Ali, you're it for me. I want, no, I need you in my life. I love you, and I pray you can find your way back to loving me.

I will think of you often. And just so you know for sure, I'm going to call your cell phone every night as close to ten o'clock as possible (barring any life-threatening medical emergencies). Don't pick up. Just know that out of the thousands of times I'll be thinking about you throughout my days and nights, at that particular moment in time, you're on my mind.

I've enclosed one of my credit cards. (One with your name on it should arrive in a few days.) Please use it, if you need it, for anything that can't wait until my return. And I will return. And no matter what happens between us, I will be there to give you as much help as you'll allow, and to play an active role in our child's life.

See you soon.

All my love always,

Jared

Ali sat back, picked up the plastic card and flipped it over in her fingers. For a man whose wife had wreaked havoc with his credit then disappeared, it was a huge display of trust. That night, when her cell phone rang at exactly ten o'clock, Ali wanted to answer, to tell Jared how much she appreciated his letter and his faith in her.

As per his request, she didn't.

She did, however, answer the phone four weeks later, when his call came two hours and twelve minutes late and he hadn't responded to her three messages.

At the first ring she grabbed it from the pillow beside her and whipped it open. "Hello."

"I was worried I'd wake you," he said.

"As if I could go to sleep thinking something may have happened to you." Her body melted with relief at the sound of his tired voice.

"Hey. You're not supposed to answer the phone when I call."

"Are you okay?"

"I'm fine. Busy. Three gunshot wounds and an attempted suicide." Someone spoke in the background. "Give me a minute," Jared responded.

"I won't keep you."

He lowered his voice. "I miss you."

"I miss you, too." So much. She wanted to tell him she loved him and, despite all that had happened, she'd never stopped. That she might be willing to give cohabitation a try if he agreed to certain ground rules. That maybe the future didn't need to be all planned out, and they could start the journey into parenthood together, take one day at a time and see where the winding, bumpy trip took them.

"I've got to go," he said. "I'll see you soon."

If only she could bring herself to believe him.

* * *

At four in the morning, bleary-eyed and on the verge of falling asleep at the wheel, Jared steered his car into the driveway of his new house. A pile of plowed snow reflected in his headlights. The front walk had been shoveled. Nice surprises, as he hadn't told anyone when he'd be arriving.

Not talking to Ali, except for one brief conversation, not knowing what she was thinking or planning, had almost driven him completely insane. He'd considered every possible scenario, good and bad. Living apart, juggling custody. Living together, his personal choice. What if she insisted on separate bedrooms? What if she opted for a custody battle? What if she'd used his time away to leave town and he never saw her again?

Trust. He trusted Ali. She would never do that.

Jared popped an antacid into his mouth from the roll that had been his constant companion of late and hoped, once again, that he hadn't made the biggest mistake of his life by leaving.

Exhausted, he grabbed his small duffel from the rear seat and got out of the car. When he came to the garden gnome by the front steps, he reached around the back and opened the secret compartment, as instructed, to retrieve the key.

Worried he'd have to wait for the furnace to heat up, Jared said a silent thank you to whoever had forgotten to lower the thermostat. Then he headed upstairs, plopped face down onto the bed in the master bedroom, and went to sleep.

He had no idea what time it was when he awoke, but bright sunlight burned through his eyelids. His first purchase would be blackout curtains. He inhaled the aroma of French toast. Couldn't be. He inhaled again. Definitely French toast, with lots of cinnamon, the way he liked it.

Ali.

Jared jumped out of bed and took off down the stairs to the kitchen.

She stood at the stove, wearing a pair of flannel sleep pants and a clingy light pink tank that outlined her bigger-than-he-remembered-them breasts and the slight swell of her belly. Music played from a small radio on the counter. Ali moved her hips in time to the beat. A thing of beauty. The love of his life. His future.

He leaned against the door frame, content to watch.

She looked down at her arm, rubbed at the tiny hairs, then turned to him with a look of surprise. "You came back."

"I told you I would." Earning Ali's trust would take time. "I will never lie to you again. Ever."

She moved the pan off the burner, reached for the knob to turn it off and looked back at him. "So when I'm big and fat and ask you, 'Do these pants make my butt look big?' you'll tell me the truth?"

He nodded. "As long as you understand that when I look at you all I see is beautiful."

She gave him a small smile. "I missed you, so much."

"I missed you, too." He opened his arms and she lunged into them, held on to him as tightly as he held on to her. This was where he belonged. Jared had finally found home

"You feel like you've lost weight," she said.

"Because, when work got crazy, I didn't have you to remind me to eat." He kissed the top of her head.

"I never stopped," she said into his shoulder.

"What?"

"In your letter. You wrote you hoped I could find my way back to loving you. But I never stopped."

He pulled back.

She looked up at him with watery eyes.

"You mean…?"

"I love you, Jared." She took his hand and placed it on her belly. "We love you. And we need you in our lives, too."

His heart pounding with pure joy, Jared pulled Ali back into his arms. "You've got me." Day and night, every minute he could manage, from here on out. Jared held her close, perfectly happy to remain that way until he collapsed from exhaustion.

But in all too short a time Ali said, "Hey. How'd you get in here?"

"Gramps gave me the go-ahead to move in anytime. He told me where to find the key. What are you doing here?" Obviously not cooking him a welcome-home breakfast.

"Since I've been spending most of my time here, cleaning and sorting, I've been sleeping over. Wait a minute." She pulled out of his embrace. "Move in? You bought Gramps's house? *You're* the new owner?"

"He didn't tell you?" Based on her look of absolute shock, Jared didn't wait for an answer. "Hold on. I have something to show you. Do not move." He took the stairs two at a time, rummaged through his duffel until he found the papers he sought, and hurried back to the kitchen. He handed her the deed to the house.

"It's in both our names." She looked up. Stunned. "How? Why?"

"Gramps's attorney handled the sale so you'll have to address how with him. Come and sit down." He guided her to one of the four olive-green chairs surrounding his kitchen table, and she sat. He settled in next to her and shifted to face her. "As for why…" He took her hand in his. "When I suggested we live together, it was never my intention to make you feel like a guest in my home, to make you feel dependent on me or indebted to me. I want us to be equal partners."

She squeezed his hand. "Thank you."

"When I mentioned I was looking to buy a house, Gramps suggested this one. He said you loved it."

"I do."

"Which is why I bought it. Whether I live here, or you live here, or we both live here together, which is my personal preference, by the way—" his heart lifted when she smiled "—you will always be half owner. The house can't be sold without your consent, and you have just as much right to live here as I do."

"But I didn't pay my share."

"You don't have to. It's my gift to you." She looked on the verge of arguing.

"Jared, I—"

"Before you go on," he interrupted her. "Here." He handed her the other legal document in his hand. "My divorce is final. You have your reasons for not wanting to live together. I understand." But he planned to do his best to resolve each one. Starting with, "You can cross me being married off your list."

"I was going to say I don't know how to thank you. Purchasing Gramps's house and putting it in both our names means so much." She wiped at the corner of her eye. "I used to dream of raising my children in a house like this one. It's perfect. And you've made it possible. Thank you."

The house was old, in need of updating and a new roof. It was far from perfect. But if Ali was happy, he was happy. "You're welcome."

"Oh." She stood up. "I have something for you, too." She left the room and returned with two credit cards. "I didn't use either of them."

"I know." And as much as he loved and trusted her, he'd suffered a bit of trepidation when he'd received his bill.

"While I appreciate the offer, it's not necessary for you to give me access to your credit. If we live together, I'll expect to keep our finances separate."

"Anything you want." As long as he didn't have to spend one more night without her.

"Anything?" She stood and climbed on to his lap, the apex of her thighs flush with his growing erection. "You may want to think twice about that." She reached for the bottom hem of his shirt and pulled it up over his head. He lifted his arms to assist her.

"You see," she continued, swirling her knuckles over his nipples, "when I hit the three-month mark of my pregnancy my nausea vanished, but another problem cropped up." She rocked her hips and, after so many weeks apart, Jared almost cried out from the pleasure. She lowered her mouth to his ear and whispered, "I fear it may make me a bit demanding."

How had he managed to get so lucky? "I love you, Ali. And I'm fully prepared to take the bad with the good." He lifted her tank over her head and eased her forward until her bare breasts met his chest. Magnificent. "Feel free to demand away, whenever, wherever and however you like."

"You are a good man, Jared Padget." She reached for the button of his jeans.

And he proceeded to show her just how good.

EPILOGUE

Five months later

"YOU'RE having contractions, aren't you?" Jared asked his wife of four hours and thirty-five minutes.

She adjusted a strap on her voluminous tangerine—don't dare call it orange—sundress. "Braxton-Hicks. Nothing to worry about," Ali muttered out of the left side of her mouth and continued to greet their guests. "Welcome to our home, Mrs. Tupper. I'm so happy you could make it."

"Wouldn't have missed it, Allison." Ali's old neighbor turned to Jared. "You should see the bozo who moved into her condo, full of tattoos and earrings. I think he's running drugs."

"You look fabulous, Mrs. Tupper," Ali commented. "I haven't seen you without a cane in years."

"Your man worked some voodoo magic and my sore's all gone."

"And not a moment too soon." Jared arched his back and rubbed his belly. "I think I put on ten pounds from all the cake you fed me each time I came to visit."

"Food's on the back patio," Ali said.

"I hope there's dancing," Mrs. Tupper said, and walked off.

"You're having one right now. I can tell." Lips pursed,

she forced out a breath, both hands rubbed at her low back. She looked like she wanted to pinch him. Hard. He stepped out of reach and clicked the timer on his watch. "That's ten minutes apart."

Contraction over, she said, "Do not ruin my wedding day, Jared. It's my party and I intend to enjoy it. Gramps, Mrs. Meyer and our friends from the senior center have been preparing and decorating for days." She put her hand on his arm. "Don't make me take away that watch. I will tell you when I'm in labor. Now, go mingle."

"I am not leaving your side, Mrs. Padget." He threaded her arm through his. "If we're going to mingle, we'll do it together."

She let out a huff. He didn't care. He loved this woman and the baby she carried, his baby, and no way would he stray more than five feet away from her when she was having contractions.

"The house looks fantabulous and so do you," Roxie said, coming over in a flourish to give Ali a kiss on the cheek. She handed a big pink box to Jared, placed her palms on each side of Ali's rotund belly and rubbed in small circular motions. "Is Roxie going to find the man of her dreams at this shindig? One kick for yes, two for no." She closed her eyes and waited. "Nothing. The kid's unreliable. Typical male."

Roxie turned to Jared. "You are one lucky guy, Dr. P. Screw it up and I'll geld you. Don't you forget it."

"You won't let me," he replied with a big smile.

"Damn straight. Where's the booze?" Roxie walked off in search of the bar.

The doorbell rang. "Would you get that?" Ali asked. "I'll put this present on the table." She hurried off, looking rather eager to be rid of him.

Jared opened the door, prepared to welcome the next

guests to their small gathering, to see his mother standing on the porch. He felt like he'd taken an uppercut to the gut. His mother looked like she'd aged twenty years since the last time he'd seen her, her posture hunched, making her appear shorter than her usual five feet five inches, and frail. Her hair, now more gray than black, was cut short. Her eyes, once warm, now looked at him with apprehension.

"What are you doing here, Mom?" Jared asked, careful to keep his voice even.

"Your wife invited me."

Over her shoulder Jared saw an older man with thinning hair watching them from his car.

Ali walked up beside him. "Aren't you going to invite your mom into our home?" Bending forward so her belly didn't get in the way, she leaned out to give his mother a hug. "Welcome to our home, Mrs. Padget. We're so glad you could come."

We are? Jared wondered. Maybe if he'd had a little advance warning he could have mustered gladness. Right now he couldn't get past shock.

"Come in. Come in."

Once his mother walked inside, the man drove off.

Jared watched his wife walk his mother into the kitchen and introduce her to Mrs. Meyer like they were old friends.

The doorbell rang again. Jared braced himself for whatever might be on the other side before opening the door. "Whew. It's only you."

"That's some greeting," Victoria said, giving him a kiss on the cheek. "Don't take her for granted or you'll be sorry."

"Yes. I know. Sweet little Polly already warned me. Roxie threatened my manhood. Any more problems with the leg?" A few months back Victoria had taken a nasty fall in the stairwell at work.

"I can predict when a storm's coming but other than that I'm back to normal."

"Where's Kyle?" The new man in Victoria's life.

"At the hospital. He'll stop by later."

Jared looked down at Victoria's son. "Hey, Jake." He held up his hand for the eight-year-old redhead to slap.

"Is your baby here yet?" Jake asked.

"Soon, big guy," Jared answered. "I think Ali's in labor," he said to Victoria. "Help me keep an eye on her, will you?"

"Sure thing." Victoria and Jake walked into the party.

Not seeing Ali in the house, Jared walked into the back-yard in search of her. Gramps had a bunch of kids' games set up over in Mrs. Meyer's adjoining yard.

"Their parents are not going to be happy they're playing with water guns," his mom said, walking up beside him.

"I'm sure they all have several changes of clothes. Gramps is well-known in this town," Jared said. "How're you doing, Mom?"

"The arthritis gives me some trouble. Today's a good day."

"I'm glad."

"Well, I'd better get back into the kitchen. I offered to help plate some sandwiches. I just wanted to give you this." She held out a lavender envelope.

"Mom, you didn't have to…"

"When your daddy died I got lost in a dark place. It took a while for me to find my way back. I'm sorry, Jared. You were a good boy. You deserved better."

"It's okay, Mom."

"It's not. But maybe this will help. For the past few years I've had a man in my life. He lives with me. He's not your daddy, but he treats me good. I've saved as much as I could of the money you sent me. I want you to have it." She pushed the envelope into his hand.

"That money's for you."

"I'm doing fine, Jared. Spend it on your family. If I need you, now I know where to reach you. Go help your wife."

Jared looked in the direction his mother's gnarled finger pointed. "What the…?" Ali was carrying a huge glass platter filled with fruit. Jared ran to the patio.

"I am going to tie you to a chair," he threatened, taking the platter from her.

"Let me help." His mother moved some serving dishes around to make room on the table.

Something splashed at his feet.

"Uh-oh," Ali said. "I think my waters broke."

"You think?"

Victoria walked over to them. "Either that or she popped."

"I don't want to miss my party," Ali grumbled.

"We are going to the hospital. We'll invite everyone back after the baby's born." One at a time.

"You'd better slip out quietly," Victoria suggested, "or you'll have an entourage of people accompanying you."

Exactly what he did not want.

"I'll clean up this mess," Victoria offered.

Ali moaned through another contraction.

"Call us when we can converge at the hospital," Victoria said. "I'll make sure things go smoothly here."

"And I'll help," his mother said.

"What about Gramps?" Ali asked.

"He's having so much fun, let him stay." So Jared and Ali could share the birth of their first child in private.

"Would you tell Gramps we left for the hospital and

I'll call him when the baby's born?" Ali asked her new mother-in-law.

"He's the one wearing the balloon hat, the red bandana over his mouth, carrying the purple and yellow water blaster," Jared said before wrapping his arm around his wife and helping her around the side of the house to the driveway.

"Wait," she said as he shifted the car into reverse. "I forgot the picture I'm using for my focal point. It's on the shelf above the TV. And my suitcase."

"I'll find you a focal point at the hospital. I'll bring your suitcase later. We have to go." He put his arm behind the seat, turned to look over his shoulder and prepared to back out.

Ali opened her door. "I want the focal point I've been practicing with."

"Don't you dare get out of this car, Allison Padget." He threw the car into park, jumped out, ran like a man being chased by wolves, entered the house calmly, grabbed the picture from the shelf above the TV without even looking at it and ran from the house.

"What's so special about this picture that I had to risk you giving birth in the car to get it?" Jared handed it to Ali then rammed the car into reverse again.

"Look at it." Ali held it up for him.

Shouldn't the woman be screaming in pain or something? He sure felt like screaming. Didn't pregnant women about to give birth *want* to get to the hospital?

"Look at it." She moved it in front of his face.

It was a close-up picture of him and Gramps on the front porch, holding her sonogram picture between them. "My three favorite men," she said, just as a monster of a contraction must have hit, because she transformed before his eyes. "Now, get me to the hospital, and do not stop for anything."

"Yes, dear," Jared said, and did just that.

Sweet baby James, named for Jared's dad, was born one hour and seventeen minutes later.

are proud to present

June 2011
Ordinary Girl in a Tiara
by Jessica Hart
from Mills & Boon® Riva™

Caro Cartwright's had enough of romance – she's after a quiet life. Until an old school friend begs her to stage a gossip-worthy royal diversion! Reluctantly, Caro prepares to masquerade as a European prince's latest squeeze…

Available 3rd June 2011

July 2011
Lady Drusilla's Road to Ruin
by Christine Merrill
from Mills & Boon® Historical

Considered a spinster, Lady Drusilla Rudney has only one role in life: to chaperon her sister. So when her flighty sibling elopes, Dru employs the help of a fellow travelling companion, ex-army captain John Hendricks, who looks harmless enough…

Available 1st July 2011

Tell us what you think!

millsandboon.co.uk/community
facebook.com/romancehq
twitter.com/millsandboonuk

Medical Romance™

THE PLAYBOY OF HARLEY STREET
by Anne Fraser

Travelling the world for an exclusive Harley Street practice sounds great to physio Katie—until she discovers she'll be working (closely) with delectable doctor Fabio Lineham, with his playboy reputation in tow! Katie's determined to be the only girl *not* to fall for him…

DOCTOR ON THE RED CARPET
by Anne Fraser

Hollywood stuntman Kendrick has 'heartbreaker' written all over his roguish features—a distraction Dr Elizabeth Morgan convinces herself she *doesn't* need! Soon Elizabeth falls under the stuntman's spell—but Kendrick's whirlwind flings never end in *for ever*. Do they?

JUST ONE LAST NIGHT…
by Amy Andrews

Brent Cartwright, Grace's new boss, is the ex who has always held more of her heart than she'd *ever* want him to know. As impossible as he was to forget, Brent is now even harder to resist! Dare she dream of one last night with him…?

SUDDENLY SINGLE SOPHIE
by Leonie Knight

Suddenly single, miles from home and starting a new job, socialite Dr Sophie Carmichael is determined to show her boss Dr Will Brent she's not what she seems! Will isn't convinced Sophie will last, but before long he's willing her to prove him wrong!

On sale from 1st July 2011
Don't miss out!

0611/03a

Intense passion and glamour from our bestselling stars of international romance

Available 20th May 2011

Available 17th June 2011

Available 15th July 2011

Available 19th August 2011

2 FREE BOOKS
AND A SURPRISE GIFT

We would like to take this opportunity to thank you for reading this Mills & Boon® book by offering you the chance to take TWO more specially selected books from the Medical™ series absolutely FREE! We're also making this offer to introduce you to the benefits of the Mills & Boon® Book Club™—

- **FREE home delivery**
- **FREE gifts and competitions**
- **FREE monthly Newsletter**
- **Exclusive Mills & Boon Book Club offers**
- **Books available before they're in the shops**

Accepting these FREE books and gift places you under no obligation to buy, you may cancel at any time, even after receiving your free books. Simply complete your details below and return the entire page to the address below. You don't even need a stamp!

YES Please send me 2 free Medical books and a surprise gift. I understand that unless you hear from me, I will receive 5 superb new stories every month including two 2-in-1 books priced at £5.30 each and a single book priced at £3.30, postage and packing free. I am under no obligation to purchase any books and may cancel my subscription at any time. The free books and gift will be mine to keep in any case.

Ms/Mrs/Miss/Mr ———————— Initials ————————

Surname ————————————————————————
Address ————————————————————————

———————————————— Postcode ————————
E-mail ————————————————————————

Send this whole page to: Mills & Boon Book Club, Free Book Offer, FREEPOST NAT 10298, Richmond, TW9 1BR